Swamp Outlaw

Henry Berry Lowery
and his Civil War Gang

*****

The Lumbee Saga

David Ball

authorHOUSE®

AuthorHouse™
1663 Liberty Drive
Bloomington, IN 47403
www.authorhouse.com
Phone: 833-262-8899

Published by AuthorHouse 01/21/2021

ISBN: 978-1-6655-1201-5 (sc)
ISBN: 978-1-6655-1200-8 (e)

Print information available on the last page.

For Jimmy Lowry, the descendant who inspired it.

For Susan Chapek and Leslie Banner,
the guides who encouraged it.

For Katharine Margaret Wilson, the
strength who gave it heart.

Swamp Outlaw

Henry Berry Lowery & his Civil War Gang

*****

The Lumbee Saga

by David Ball

What might have been the Discoverer
Has become the Buccaneer
The Poet has become the Outlaw
For these be the days of vengeance.

ONE

1872. NORTH CAROLINA.

Swamp

The South had lost the War and was losing its soul. Uniformed Rebels who'd fought honorably in light of day now burned crosses and wore tattered sheets in the dark. In armed packs they dragged the helpless Negro or Indian from bed and stopped his hurried prayers with noose or buckshot. In Robeson county, the Ku Klux Klan did not see the vengeance it was stirring up: Henry Berry Lowery and his Swamp Outlaws, who ruthlessly protected themselves and the county's Indians and Negroes. Lowery was beyond society's control. "We kill anyone who hunts us, from Sheriff on down. If we must die, we'll die game."

Some northern outsiders hoped that Lowery, if they could control him, might prove a figurehead and guide. Instead of crippling a remote southern county, he might lead the nation's colored races. To explore this possibility and to get the Outlaw's full story, my employer, the New York Herald, sent me from New York on the 26th day of 1872 bound for the Robeson swamps.

En route I met with Virginia's Governor Walker. He rumbled, "Henry Berry Lowery? My Militia left yesterday with a hundred men to hunt the fellow." He smiled. "Lowery must be a good deal of a character."

I took the train south to Wilmington, North Carolina's largest town, where Lowery was on every front page. The conservative papers called his outlaws the Black Ku Klux. Radicals retorted by damning the White Ku Klux, who flogged and hanged thousands of peaceful Blacks but fled from Lowery's six young outlaws-in-arms. The Wilmington Star called the Robeson County people cowards for not clearing Lowery out. The Robeson paper threw back the charge but threw nothing at Lowery. Both sides blamed North Carolina's government.

Six desperadoes had mastered a commonwealth.

The people in Wilmington did not encourage my mission. "A dangerous game, stranger. Better you than me." With a stream of words and tobacco-spittle, one described the Lowery gang's murder of an earlier visitor, concluding, "And he was smarter than you look."

The Wilmington train agent sold me a ticket to Moss Neck and said, "You're a dead man." Everyone said the Lowerys were devils who would murder any White man.

From Wilmington I wrote to Henry Berry Lowery, offering myself into his hands in return for an interview. Next morning on the train the conductor told me of a braggart named Marsden who had announced his intention to travel that same line and kill Lowery on sight. When Lowery showed up on board, Marsden crawled between two ladies and hid under their seat.

The Rutherford Railway crosses Carolina's pine woods. White trunks, stripped and cut for sap, stand like tombstones. Swamps too wide to walk in a week divide the woods. Creeks and drain canals alternate with deserted rice fields, bogs, ruins of turpentine distilleries, the stubble of old plantations, a few weather-blackened shacks, and here and there a saw mill or pile of timber. In five hours and 80 miles we came to the Robeson County seat of Lumberton on the Lumber River. The town is built of bare planks discolored with weather stains. The streets are sand. About nine hundred Scottish Whites live there. These once proud slaveholders now looked with pinched faces at the Negro voting alongside them.

Lumberton's Court House is brick. In its crude upstairs courtroom, floor covered with sawdust, a magistrate carried on the comedy of justice. Informed he was being observed by a New York journalist, he adopted a professional attitude. "Make proclamation!" he cried to a sheriff. When the sheriff did not seem to understand him, the magistrate strode to an open window and roared down to the people waiting outside: "Neil McNeil! Campbell McGregor! Duckery Duncan! Come into court as you are this day commanded, or your security will be forfeit to the State!"

This kind of noise along with "O Yea! O Yea!" went on all day. The magistrate sat high up like a great overgrown tot, saying foolish things of no consequence and that if he ever saw Lowery he would kill him.

In front of the Court House, Whites and Negroes gather at the old public well. Mostly poor, dressed in home-made array and stiff felt hats. A lawyer says to a White man, “When your name is called, stand up, say ‘guilty,’ and pay your money.” The White man says he can’t remember all that.

Here also were the Scuffletown Indian mulattos, that strange race, oppressed for generations. They received no more justice in court than did Negroes, so violating them was no offense.

Around the corner stood an old red cart the Lowery gang once used to steal both of Lumberton’s safes, one from a store, the other from the Court House itself. Local Whites had hoped the outlaws would use the money to leave the county—cheap riddance, at least in the minds of those to whom the money had not belonged.

Beyond Lumberton lies Scuffletown, an Indian settlement with no streets or public buildings. Scuffletown lines both sides of the railroad for four miles. It is within the great Carolina swamp district, and before the War was the largest free Negro settlement in the United States. Its location is explained by the soil’s poverty and its endless streams and swamps, making the land cheap.

After the rains, Scuffletown is entirely flooded. Treacherous paths connect its rare rises of solid ground. In summer, luxurious undergrowth covers the swamps and all else, and a man can’t see his own step-length. In winter the streams flow full and the swamps rise. In the swamps grow gallberry tree, sweet and black gum, poplar, hickory, post and poison oak, cypress, and every kind of pine, all with impenetrable vines stretching between. Briars and brambles, not our garden dwarf variety but overgrown and barbed, tear the skin and dismally infect the traveler. Quicksand hides beneath a pretty carpet of green, looking for all the world like firm ground. These traps adjoin dwellings, with no separation from the primal swamp.

In a Lumberton tavern I met several leading citizens. One saw my reporter's notepad and could not stop talking. As the evening went on, his whiskey bolstered his narrative powers. Accustomed to southern tobacco, he eagerly accepted a sample of my Connecticut variety, of which I carried a journalist's supply.

Speaking in that slow southern pace that could have won the War by killing jittery Yankees with impatience, he began factually: "Henry Berry Lowery is a common mix of Indian, mulatto and White blood. He has spent 26 years on this earth, stands five feet nine inches, and weighs 150 pounds. He has straight black hair and dark thin-whiskered goatee. His face slopes cheekbone to chin, like our graceful southern physiognomy, but his eyes are different – grayish hazel, at times light blue, but black in anger. His face and expression are refined – notably so considering his mixed race, lack of education, and long career of lawlessness. His skin is whitish-yellow and copper, the Indian tint predominating. His voice is pleasant though he is not talkative.

"Even the relatives of the White men he killed admit he is the handsomest Indian they ever saw. His body is straight in shoulders and limbs. His feet are pointed and with arching instep, so he can wear a shapely boot. He has (a?) good chest, long bones, and good proportions.

In his dress he is negligent but not insulting: woolen blouse and trousers, and black, stiff hat."

My informant sipped whiskey for punctuation. "A belt around his waist holds five six-barreled revolvers, long shooters. A sling supports a Henry rifle of sixteen cartridges. So many weapons, more than 80 pounds, would be preposterous except for his circumstances: he is outlawed by the State, has no base of supplies, and needs enough arms and ammunition to fight a large body of men in pursuit. He also carries a long knife and a flask of whiskey.

"In full equipment he can run like a deer, swim, stand weeks of exposure in the swamps, walk all night when necessary, and never sleep."

This drunken biographer held out a new tobacco paper for me to fill, forgetting the cigarette in his other hand. He leaned close, and quietly spoke his conclusion: "Confronting an enemy, Lowery wears a fiendish smile, revealing a nature that is savage, predatory, and *fond of blood*."

He lowered his head to the table and slept. A listener, Parson McCay, added in brogue that three gentle things were acknowledged about Henry Berry: he never committed offense to females, never burned anything down, and never harmed a cart or work animal. I asked the Parson, "But how can this savage, with a handful of illiterate youth, master a society so recently at war and full of accomplished soldiers?"

The Parson answered, "Lowery is one of those natural spirits that arise from time to time in a primitive community, with no advantages but what nature gave him. He defies White society by his own superiority. He has passions but no weaknesses."

The only weakness Lowery was ever accused of was licentiousness, as are most men of note sooner or later. True or not, he did use women for protection. Once, when a White militia had surrounded his outlaws, a bevy of Scuffletown's prettiest native beauties appeared. The White soldiers dropped their rifles and showed that hostility of the races can be overcome.

Parson McCay told me of Lowery's wife, Rhody. One night in the street Henry Berry told a White hunter who had made advances towards her, "You are taking advantage of my circumstances and absence to be familiar with my family. Pack up and go from this county." The man lost no time in doing as requested, for Lowery was known to carry out every warning.

Parson McCay told me about an assault on the outlaws that would have succeeded but for the reliability of Henry Berry's threats. One morning the Militia arrested the outlaws' wives and sisters, including his wife, Rhody. Henry Berry sent word saying, "You have jailed my wife for no crime except she is my wife; that ain't her fault and you can't make it so. Let them go or I, Henry Berry in person, will take your White women to the swamp and they won't choose to go back when I let them." Rhody and the others were set free because no White husband or son doubted Henry Berry's threat or prediction.

As I was leaving the tavern, Proprietor Lear called me back, filled my cup, and gave me an article from the Wilmington Star:

GOVERNOR CALDWELL AND OUTLAW LOWERY

That Lowery and his little band of cutthroats defy the law and civilization, outraging and murdering with impunity, goes to show the sort of government we have, unwilling to protect us from the highway robber and the midnight assassin. Governor Caldwell is lukewarm and careless in this matter. While innocent blood cries to heaven for vengeance, Caldwell lifts not a finger against these assassins and ignores the suffering of his people.

Free citizens with souls in their bodies cannot shut their eyes to these violations of law, peace, and order. We must feel pity and shame at the spectacle of Indians outraging the law with fiendish abandon, endangering the industrial interests of a whole section and filling the public mind with terror.

Upon Governor Caldwell rests the blame. Would he do as little if this band were White Ku Klux? Oh, what a calling out of militia then! What calling for Federal forces, what crying of "Evil!"

We charge it upon Governor Caldwell that he would long ago have stopped the Outlaws if they had been conservative Whites instead of Radical Blacks. He is forever damned in the estimation of all good and peaceable citizens.

TWO

I LEFT THE TAVERN and strolled Lumberton, a primitive community considered the height of civilization by its lumpish White inhabitants. I understood how these complacent farmers could have entangled themselves in their War as they did, believing themselves bound for glory. Only the southern heat or having been waited upon by generations of slaves can explain them.

Out of the empty midnight streets a tiny old colored woman limped towards me through the gloom. She stopped and spoke but my Northern ear could not understand. She repeated: "Marz', be yaw de gemmen rou heah for Marz Henry?" (Was I the gentlemen looking for Master Henry?)

"Yes, ma'am, I am the one."

"Dey say he daid." Same vowel-sound in every word, but clear enough: They say he's dead. "Dey say he whang his own self." She lowered her voice. "But ain't so. Ain't daid."

Jaw muscles slacken in hundred-degree summers. A speaker's meaning conveys not by articulation but by melodic tone. Her consonants were frail and her vowels of few varieties. "Dey say he daid, but he ain't."

Understanding her was like connecting with a creature from a far world. This timeworn Black had never heard of New York, and I would regard a moment in her home as a visit to a planet. Yet in this mud avenue on the back step of the world, we communicated. "Ain't daid, but out killin' where killin' need done."

"Should I avoid him?" I asked.

"Suh?"

"Should I stay away from him?"

"Henry Lowry don't murder no one but that murder us. He just payin' back for killin' of his old father, his brothers, and his cousins. His old ma say, 'My boys ain't doin' right but I can't help it. I can only pray. They weren't brought up for all this kind of misery.'"

She tugged on my lapel. "Oh, Marz, this use to be dreadful hard country for nigas. See my teef?" She curled back her lip and showed the empty gum, ragged, only a tooth at each side. "My Marz knock them all out. I worked for him with all my might but he was having Black women and his wife was goin' to leave him, so he say me, 'Aunt Phoeb, you got to tessify my wife had Black mens.' But I'd have died first. So he whup me and beat a stick on my mouth, and Marz, all my teef droop on de ground." She opened her mouth wider. I am not scholar enough to describe its foul condition. "This a hard country. Henry just payin' back. Better days for de brack people now. He the king of this country!"

Like me, she wanted to tell the Outlaw's story. Was he not striking Western civilization on the nose? "Else we all perished by now." The old crone melted into the gloom. She had talked of Henry Berry with a glow in her yellowed eye as if she were newly free and babbling of Lincoln. I will not forget those blank, mutilated gums.

Next day I reboarded the train for Shoe Heel in the heart of the pine forest, from where I could send my message to Lowery. At first, I found no willing messenger. The reported killing of Boss Strong, the youngest of the gang and Henry Berry's best friend, had enraged the outlaws, making it a bad time to visit. But a young mulatto seemed unworried and for a few cents promised to deliver my letter.

In Shoe Heel, I met and interviewed James McQueen (or Donohue) of Richmond County, N.C., who said he was the one who had killed the notorious Boss Strong. McQueen was a shambling, dark-complexioned Scot whose weak eyes had the trick of dropping away as soon as he was looked at.

Next morning I left for Eureka, where an old Negro asked who I was looking for. I told him I wanted to go to Patrick Lowery's, Henry Berry's oldest brother. He pointed the way and added, "I'se scared of strangers most to death, but you ain't got no gun. Good God, this is powerful bad country; the Ku Kluk come with their shootin' and whippin' and hangin', and I'se scared to death."

I found the home of Patrick Lowery. He was in his carpenter shop, for though a preacher he was not above honest labor. Like many preachers he also served as an auctioneer, calling a tobacco sale one day and railing against Satan's weed the next. He thought my chances of seeing "Harry" Berry very slim, since the Outlaw Chief was now reported dead. Patrick had an unexpected opinion on his brother: "My brother Harry had reason for anger—same as all of us—when they killed our father. But Harry's gone bad, and I pray God has taken him from this world." He directed me through the swamp to the home of old Mrs. Allen Lowery, called Mary Cuombo, mother of Patrick and Henry Berry Lowery. For a fee he gave me a horse and hurried instruction in riding the thing. He said nothing of how to get along with it, nor told it how to get along with me. Referring to the swamp, Patrick warned, "If you fall in, move slow, no matter what," but did not say why. After a dinner of onion corn bread, cold bacon, and coffee, I started out. My heart sank as I lost sight of the railroad behind me and plunged closer to the swamps, the lurking place of the outlaws.

Though already far from my New York home, only when I entered the swamps did I feel truly removed. I swelled with that sense of worth a man feels when he suffers hardship and danger for larger purposes. I rode with grim determination alongside a canal losing itself uncertainly into a dusky smoked mirror of a lake reflecting the towering trees, festooned vines, and hanging moss. The swamp surrounded me like nothing I had ever seen—yet so affrontingly familiar that I was filled with dread. In my sleeping dreams I had seen this broad expanse of black water with its dim circling shores and its dark leaden waves disappearing silently among reeds and rushes. The canopy of cypress and juniper rise without a branch for a hundred feet, standing thick with living arches of foliage and moss, threatening to drop some venomous reptile upon the traveler below. Who has not dreamed of dying in such a spot?

I easily kept Patrick Lowery's horse to the road, for the beast was no more curious than I to learn what lurked on either side. In some miles we came to the "Back Swamp," where for hundreds of yards the black flow sluggishly crossed the road. Twice Patrick Lowery's horse reared, the second time slinging me into the opaque waters. Recalling Patrick Lowery's warning, I moved slowly, despite something against my leg. Patrick Lowery's horse waited 20 feet away, safe and dry. In my inching progress, this tiny slice of the swamp became the whole universe.

A dark bird circled, wings unmoving against the hard sky, hungry for me to fail. Each step without attack from beneath the surface was a gift from Heaven. No thought of Henry Berry or anything else entered my mind. This ability of the mind to focus is one of God's uncanny wonders, to whom I gave thanks when I finally reached the horse. Those who enter the swamp and remain have to be religious or superstitious.

The dark bird disappeared as I remounted. "Another day," I called. From the empty sky, a caw confirmed.

In another mile I passed the cabin of outlaw Andrew Strong where McQueen had shot his brother, Boss, the week before. From the door watched two silent women. As I later learned, Andrew Strong himself was watching from a thicket, rifles ready.

Another stretch of water, mud, and sand, and I came to the house of Henry Berry Lowery. At my approach a child ran inside, but the place seemed otherwise deserted. A patch was plowed and planted. By the outside chimney stood a barrel for washtub or lye-pot. Unexpectedly, I saw a woman under the tree that shaded the house, remarkable in that she had been there all along but I had not seen her. Her hair lay against her yellow dress like a dark shadow, though not so dark as her eyes. We exchanged no word, no nod, no expression. I fixed my eyes ahead and passed on. The Outlaw's wife stood motionless.

A quarter of a mile farther I reached my destination, the home of old Mrs. Allen Lowery, Henry Berry's mother. She welcomed me to stay as long as I pleased if I could put up with their rough hospitality. She had a large house, weather-boarded, with four good-sized rooms, a kitchen attached, and a wide porch. It was on seventy-five acres and had numerous outbuildings.

One son, Sinclear, superintended the farm. He was a dark mulatto Indian. He did not know whether Henry Berry was alive or dead. He said, "I will be glad if he's dead, for he is a bad man and has done a heap of harm." He spat tobacco but not offensively. He told me they had not been on friendly terms since Henry Berry's marriage to Rhody Strong. The marriage was to be held here at his mother's house, and Sinclear, fearing an attack by the Militia, objected to the location. They had been on poor terms ever since.

When I returned to the house I was presented to Rhody, who was standing in the firelight of the kitchen. She had followed me over at a distance. Her face was oval, light, with the large mournful eyes I had seen as I passed her cabin, long lashes, well-shaped mouth with even teeth, rounded chin, nose slightly retrouseé, and a profusion of straight, jet black hair. She had small hands and feet, was of medium height with a well-developed figure, and 21 years old. Her voice was low and sweet.

I must mention that she smoked a pipe, rubbed snuff, and was never one to refuse a chaw. I told Rhody the purpose of my visit. She said she did not know if Henry Berry was alive. Later I walked back with her to the family dwelling of the notorious outlaw.

Her cabin was like those of the poorer Indians—one story high, logs three to eight inches apart, spaces between covered by boards. The two doors opposite each other were secured by modern bolts and buttons, and on the third side was a great hearth lined and floored with clay. The cabin had a plank floor rather than the common clay dirt. It had a trap to a tunnel sixty yards long directly into the swamp, through which the Outlaw Chief had escaped several times when surprised by pursuers. The construction of this cabin was better than most, since Henry Berry was, as his father had been, a carpenter by trade. His father's skill had been well known, his works standing even today all through the region. The cabin demonstrated that Henry Berry had inherited his father's ability.

The cabin doors had been shot through many times but refilled with care and skill equal to the initial construction.

Opposite the fireplace stood the bed, over which stretched poles for hanging clothes. There were two windows for light, and a table, three chairs, and stools.

Over the fireplace hung pictures from the illustrated papers, including one of Geronimo, the Apache warrior.

Rhody's children—Sally Ann, six; Henry Delaney, three; and the infant Neelyann—were all of bright color, strong, active, and healthy, the boy particularly astute. Rhody said he resembled his father. Sally Ann would someday resemble her mother, and the baby Neelyann resembled a potato.

I spent an hour with Rhody before returning to Mary Cuombo's for the night. Next morning Mary Cuombo took me behind her house, where her husband, Allen, and her son William were buried. She told me the beginning of the story for which I had come.

Newspapermen are bystanders who record without being affected. In the Civil War, while photographers wept in the aftermath of battle, we reporters wrote in calm remove. But the broken voice of old Mary Cuombo engulfed me, dragging me into the heart of the affair as if into the swirling, snake-infested swamp. As if I were hearing a tale about myself. Her report was not the most terrible I ever heard; I did, after all, report the scaffolding collapse at Staten Island, going to press with the count of dozens of dead children not half done. By comparison, Mary Cuombo's tale of two quiet swamp-side graves was not so fearful. But her soft voice and tears made me think these graves were lying in wait. Overhead, leaves shivered as if expecting some future storm. A chilly breeze seeped like an omen from the fogs and murks of the swamp. I wanted to turn and run from her voice, but I was surrounded by swamp pits and quagmires. I felt something from far in the swamp peer at my back without comprehension—but with intent, as if the story I had come to get was waiting to get me.

As Mary Cuombo spoke, the day's last light drifted out of the clearing. The swamp stretched beyond, timeless as a cathedral. Here and there a grim cypress lifted its head above water and opened its moss-covered arms to great black-winged buzzards that circled. Nameless voices, weird sounds that fill a southern forest at twilight, cried their sinister welcome into the settling gloom. "But the miry places and the marshes thereof, they shall not be healed. And this shall be the border, whereby ye shall inherit the land."

Later we dined in Mary Cuombo's house. Rhody had returned to prepare the meal: cured ham with honey syrup, baked vegetable-bread, and tasty greens with spiced beet. "Do you like it there?" asked Mary Cuombo.

"Ma'am?"

"What, sir, is New York like?"

"The buildings," I said, "have many stories."

"Sir?"

"We have buildings of many stories."

"About?"

"Ma'am?"

"Rhody," she said, "shout that man's ear for me."

"She wants you to tell her the stories," Rhody said.

"What stories?" I asked.

Mary Cuombo, looking at me as if to make sure I did not escape, said, "From those buildings, sir."

Rhody nodded agreement, though I could not tell with what. Sometimes the gap between races cannot be crossed. "Your New York buildings got stories," said Rhody.

"Yes ma'am, they do."

"My house got stories too," said Mary Cuombo.

"One," I said. As she started to object, I realized what she meant. "Ah! Story! No, I mean floor!"

"Floor?" said Mary Cuombo, as if I had demeaned her house.

"Floors," I said, "not stories, but floors. Up in New York . . ."

"Down in New York."

Would she next speak Zulu? "'Down' in New York?" I said.

Individuals with Indian blood rarely cast sideways glances but Mary Cuombo now did. "Yes, down in New York!" She could not bring herself to alter her orientation of the world, not even for the sake of hospitality. It was for me to yield. I did, agreeing New York was down. We sat silently. Soon the evening brought a razor of moon and we went outside, where Mary Cuombo spoke of Henry Berry as a child. When she had told me of his youth I said, "And now?"

"And now," Rhody said, "it is the end of this day so tomorrow can come, and then you see for yourself."

"See what?" I asked.

"Henry Berry Lowery," she spoke as if a sacred name, as if pronouncing it were a spell: "HENRY . . . BERRY . . . LOWERY." The swamp hushed. "If he ain't dead," she concluded, and then it was quiet.

The owl broke the silence by welcoming the night with demon laughter. The moonlight fell like chinks on a ruin, silvering the trees and speckling the ground with? mist.

Rhody left for home. Mary Cuombo took me in and opened a mat near the hearth's glow. My head touched down and I was asleep in the house that had raised up Henry Berry Lowery.

THREE

I WOKE BEFORE SUNRISE and returned alone to the graves, hearing old Mrs. Lowery's story in my mind. In the dark I imagined I could hear Captain McGreggor calling for a spade as his men dragged off her husband and her son. I wept for their deaths as if for my own family's. (If the immediately preceding personal reference reaches the reader, then it must be that my Editor is dead and in Heaven where I hope he has found less meddlesome employment. A journalist often inserts phrases, thoughts, sometimes entire paragraphs as fodder for his editors to cut, distracting them from removing crucial passages. My own hawk-penned, icy-eyed Editor is never so misled, so if personal references survive in this text, he has not. Wherever you are, old eradicator, scratch away.)

When the sun came up I went to Rhody's and tapped softly. The door opened so sharply that I expected to see Henry Berry in full pistol. But my doorman was Henry Delaney. This miniature of his father looked up at me, then shut the door in my face. I boldly re-opened and entered. He shut it behind, plunging the interior into gloom.

Rhody stirred in bed. I stuttered my willingness, nay

eagerness, to withdraw and come back later. But turning to go, I came face to face with two full-grown fellows – armed. I confess to nervousness, but this was no time to allow weakness of heart to undermine my mission, and in any case they were blocking my way out. "This my brother," said Rhody from behind me, "and that's Henry Berry's brother." My impression was one of heavy woolens, heavy weaponry, muscle, and forcefulness. I extended my trembling hand to one and said, "My name is—"

"We know," he said, leaving my hand aloft.

Rhody told me his name, Andrew Strong, and the other's, Steven Lowery. "The very men I have come to see," I said. Both asked why. I told them that the great newspaper of America was interested in Henry Berry Lowery and his accomplices. I had come to hear from their own mouths why they had become outlaws. They replied that they were sorry but their leader was dead and unavailable for interview. But they would be happy to give me his story and theirs, for until now the papers had been telling nothing but damned lies.

A flare of new-stoked fuel flamed across the embers and illuminated Rhody listening in the bed. She was surrounded by mounds beneath the quilts, puzzling to me until one moved: they were her other two children, sleeping. Mention of the Outlaw Chief's death had not changed her face, not even her eyes. Her husband was alive. As a newspaperman I see what is revealed by eyes, and nothing in the shadowy cabin was clearer than her eyes. Looking in them was like looking down a well.

THE MEN I MET. Steve Lowery, called "Swarthy Indian Steve," looked like a New York ruffian. He was five feet ten inches, thick-set, well-muscled. He had a dark complexion, hollow eyes that gazed not quite head-on, black straight hair, and thin mustache and goatee. His glowering expression made him look like the robber and murderer he was said to be. He carried a Spencer rifle, two shotguns, and three six-barreled revolvers. Two United States cartridge boxes hung from his shoulders.

By contrast, Rhody's brother Andrew Strong was nearly white. The Strongs descended from a White man who came from Western Carolina and took up with one of the Lowery women. This made Rhody cousin with her husband.

Andrew was six feet tall and powerful, with a thin red beard, dark straight hair chopped short, and mild eyes that invited conversation. I had heard he was less intelligent than the rest of the gang, but that he knew how to appear meek and soft even while engaged in the worst treachery. It was said that honey dripped from his tongue into the wound he inflicted, and that he loved to see fear and pain. He was called the meanest of the band. None of this was what I would come to know.

His rifles, revolvers, and cartridge boxes weighed a hundred pounds. Weeks after I met him, he put them all on me and I could not stand.

Andrew said I could question them. I asked about the death of their leader. They said that the dead-or-alive bounty upon Henry Berry's head required secrecy lest a grave-robber take the body for the reward. "He's buried in a secret place and we're never saying where." I pointed out that the gang had reported Henry Berry's death twice before, and both times he was seen afterwards. Did they wish to comment on this?

They wished to step outside for a conference in the garden. Waiting, my glance fell on Rhody. Now and again one of the children stirred in sleep beneath the quilt. Rhody would place an assuring hand upon the lump that was a child's head, elbow or bottom. I was moved at seeing the maternal instinct no less strong in the Indian species than in my own.

As I became accustomed to the cabin's dim light, the eyes of Geronimo seemed to watch from his wall portrait.

The outlaws returned from the garden and responded to my request for comment by saying no, they did not wish to comment. I told them that this diminished their usefulness as a source of news. If they wanted me to report their tale, I said, they would first have to tell it to me.

They asked if I wanted to hear about the shooting of Boss Strong. I told them James McQueen (or Donohue) had given me his version, and I wondered if it was correct. I read them what he'd told me:

> Last Thursday night I reached the house of Andrew Strong at twelve o'clock. I fixed a good blind 150 yards off and watched all night and the next day. Seven P.M. Friday Andrew came from the woods looking in all directions, went in the house, came out and gave a low call, and then

> Boss come out of the woods. They were each armed with two rifles and two or three revolvers. At eight o'clock I slipped up to the house and looked through the cat hole in the door as they et supper. Some women were in there. Later Boss laid on the floor with his feet to the fire and the top of his head towards me, and played a mouth organ while the others sang. I pushed the muzzle of my Henry rifle into the cat hole until it was a foot from his bare head. I took aim by the light of the fire and shot. The women screamed and said "HE'S SHOT," "NO HE ISN'T," "YES HE IS." Boss's arms and legs moved as if he was trying to get up. Andrew Strong stayed in the shadow in the corner. He said to his wife, "Honey, go out and see what it is," and opened the other door and pushed her out. But then he said, "Come back, Honey, he was blowing on that mouth organ and it blew up and blowed his head off," and then he said, "My God! He's shot in the head; it come from the cat hole," and sent his wife out again and I slipped off. When I returned, the cat hole was shut up and the house was dark.

Steve and Andrew went out to hold another animated conversation in the garden, after which Steve told me: "We are keeping you till you put in the paper how we killed Donohue." This dismayed me because Donohue was not in fact killed, but having no choice I agreed to the arrangement. I would get to see life as not frequently viewed by civilized men. The outlaws told Rhody to keep me there, promised to meet me next morning at the "New Bridge" two miles away, and strode into the swamp. Then Rhody taught me how to rub snuff.

I saw and admired Rhody's tender care for her brood. She sang them a story tune, encouraging her eldest, Sally Ann, to insert a line now and again, and Henry Delaney a word or two. She sang of how Geronimo was offered gold to stop fighting for his people and forget his wife and three babies, to go live far off and rich. But Geronimo, instead of "running off where no one could hurt him," spat on the White man's offer and stayed to fight though he might die. "Oughtn't do no spit," observed Sally Ann, as Henry Delaney anointed baby Neelyann with a strand of drool.

"Stay to do what's to be done, and you can spit," said Rhody.

"Yes'm," said Henry Delaney.

On words: "miscegenation" is strange—not the act, but the word. Its prefix is misleading: *misce*, to mix. Not *mis*: error or a turn awry. Miscegenate means "to mix seed"; it carries no negative judgment. On the contrary, in mixture is strength. A bundle of varied woods is stronger than a solid piece of equal size. Thus our dark impulse to mix is powerful. All barriers fall away: race, family, civilization, morality, decency.

That night I slept in the Outlaw's bed, his children curled and pressed around me for warmth. Rhody slept in a hearthside chair. She woke at intervals to stoke the fire, its light giving her the flush of a half-waking dream, like a temptation from the Fiend. I thought of her eyes as I drowsed, inwardly violating the home of my absent host.

FOUR

NEXT MORNING I left for the "New Bridge." I followed the narrowing path into the swamp cypress and pines. Often Patrick Lowery's horse spied one thing or another he didn't like, but he continued on. The overgrown swamp behind was bald earth by comparison to what now lay around us. Soon a wretched, twisting creek came up on my right such as the outlaws had described. I rode up a low hill, wondering if I would ever come back down. The grove of hilltop trees opened to a flat of ragged green tumbling into an endless plain of mis-shapen trees, marsh, and brush surrounding a ramshackle bridge held together by habit, not upkeep.

The bridge spanned twenty feet over a twisting morass of sluggish water, inverted roots, moss and sludge, and ominous specimens of plant and animal waiting for the bridge to give way and deliver us. Patrick Lowery's horse shivered and stepped onto the bridge. At the same moment a figure on foot across the bridge stepped from the brush. His face was shaded by his full-brimmed hat. "STOP," he ordered, but the unexpected sight had already brought Patrick Lowery's horse to an utterly serious halt. The man drew back his hat revealing a young but cadaverous face. I needed no introduction to know Thom Lowery, reputed to be a thieving murderer. He had a long, straight, Caucasian nose, a good forehead, furtive eyes of bluish-gray, sloping but heavy jaws, scrubby black beard and straight hair. He was broad-shouldered and stood five feet nine inches. He said, "You the writing man?" A quiet voice, like a man who rarely spoke to strangers. He seemed shy and dangerous.

"Yes sir," I responded.

"I'm to say he's dead."

"Who?" I asked, though I knew.

"I'll tell who. I'll tell how. You'll write it." He waited. "Well?"

"Sir?"

"You ready?"

"I am," I answered.

"Got paper?"

"May I dismount?" I asked. My paper was in the saddle-bag behind.

"Wouldn't. Bridge ain't so sure now and then." The bridge, even as Thom Lowery spoke, shifted beneath the horse's weight. For me to get to the secure ground on the far side would eliminate the separation between Thom and myself, which Thom seemed unlikely to allow. Nor could I retreat the way I had come, because the bridge was too narrow for my horse to turn and I didn't know the science of making a horse go backwards, or even if it could. Thus, suspended on our swaying bridge over the abyss, I was to hear a tale of "THEE SAD DEATH OF THE OUTLAW HENRY BERRY LOWERY," as Thom announced.

I twisted behind me for my tablet, announcing distinctly, "I am getting a tablet of paper. I mention it so you will not think I am reaching for a weapon."

"You could have rifles in both hands and by the time you pulled the triggers you'd be knocked down, tied up, shot dead and drained Sunday clean, me alongside watching your balls go by."

"I believe you," I said.

"Don't care if you do."

Paper ready, I motioned him to begin.

"THEE ROTTEN DEATH O HARRY LORRY!" he said. His quiet voice abruptly turned to thunder. The chatter of surrounding creatures ceased and something scuttled away from beneath the bridge. He motioned me to write. I did. "Well?" he said. I read it aloud. A boy's smile erupted across his cadaverous face, his teeth a spectrum of variety. He spoke the title again, with an addendum: "THEE ROTTEN DEATH O HARRY LORRY, DEAR DEPARTED."

Seeing the way to this outlaw's heart, I read his words back, emphasizing the addition. Encouraged, he ornamented: "THEE ROTTEN DEATH O HARRY LORRY, MY POOR DEAR DEPARTED BROTHER."

I shook my head. He glowered and said, "Why not?"

"This is about Henry Berry, not you."

"Ain't I his brother or not?"

"You become famous by telling his story, not by your story with him in it."

"Says who?"

"I know these things. I'm a writer." He pondered as I contemplated the teaching of literature atop this viperous pool. He gave in and said, "THEE ROTTEN DEATH O HARRY LORRY," and added: "DECEASED!" I frowned. "Well he is," he said. "Deceased is exact accurate. No sense or use denying."

A literary dispute! I was suddenly at home here in this swamp of snakes and outlaws. For half an hour Thom and I negotiated title, agreeing only to resolve it later. The bridge undulated. Patrick Lowery's horse expressed its opinion in heavy breaths. Thom and I argued over whether I would transcribe or transliterate. I wanted to use his exact words. He wanted me to use proper English. I argued stirringly, citing precedent and contemporary practice, journalistic integrity, and the charm of his primitive speech. I pleaded to his sense of personal identity. He countered my elegant arguments by presenting a dark pistol and long rifle aimed so as to show me two holes black as eternity. Persuaded by this compelling proposition, one my Editor would use if he could, I wrote Thom's mulatto Indian speech into civilized expression, more's the loss:

> Four weeks ago, Mister Henry Berry Lowery, accompanied by his faithful comrade Mister Thomas Lowery, member of the acclaimed outlaw organization, was ranging the countryside in the vicinity of Moss Neck, North Carolina, while compatriots Steven Lowery, Shoe-Maker John, and Andrew and Boss Strong were anticipating rendezvous on the Lumber River. Within gunshot of the road, Henry Berry and Thomas discovered in the bushes a

> newly-made 'blind' (a means of concealment for ambush, constructed of intertwined branches of thick brush). It was unoccupied. Henry Berry concealed himself within while Thomas made his own blind across the road. Moments after they had placed themselves in their respective positions, a gun report was heard by Thomas from Henry Berry's place. Thomas, hearing neither any word from his chief nor an enemy's answering shot, cautiously approached. His dear brother Henry Berry lay upon his back, one barrel of his shotgun discharged, and his nose, brow, and whole front of his head blown off.

"Blowed," demanded Thom, despite his wish for civilized speech, deeming "blown" insufficient.

... whole front of his head blowed off. The broken ramrod showed Thomas's keen eye that Henry Berry had died while drawing a load from his gun. Thomas concealed the body within a thicket and notified his companions, who quickly buried their Leader where the eye of man will never find him, so that no robber of graves may reap fame or bounty. Thus perished he whose death marks the irrevertible dissolution of this formidable body of desperadoes. The money he was said to be in possession of is also lost. No member of the band, nor his wife, nor particularly his most-loved brother Thomas know the whereabouts of the treasure chest, which in any case would have contained little, it having been distributed to the poor and to churches.

Penniless and leaderless, the outlaw gang disbanded, nevermore to threaten even the Ku Klux.

> Thee End. As told by Thommy Lowery, brother to the famous Outlaw, and no less feared.

I read it aloud. Thom approved. "Everyone will read Harry's dead?" he asked. I nodded. "You believe it?"

"You told me. I wrote it. Harry is dead."

"Henry Berry," he warned.

"You said 'Harry'."

"You don't."

"Who can call him Harry?" I asked. I wanted to.

"Me."

"Who else?"

Thom walked away. I started to follow but without turning he waved me back and was gone. I waited. Patrick Lowery's horse pawed the bridgeway. His hoof rose and fell like a circus counting-horse. There was nothing to count, but scholar-like he did four.

Hearing a noise behind me, I turned. I saw nothing and looked back where Thom had disappeared. Across the bridge stood a man as still as if he'd been there an hour. "Got your letter," he said, showing it.

"Thomas said you're dead," I said, showing my tablet. The man nodded. Not a nod but a shift—the eyes, the faint expression. "You mustn't lie to a newspaperman!" I said.

"I'll tell Thommy," he replied. Manner casual, expression gentle, hands careless, as if idle and without intention. He turned to follow Thom. I started after but the Outlaw looked back. His gaze stopped Patrick Lowery's horse in mid stride, motionless with hoof raised, like a village square monument of a wounded warrior who survived. The Outlaw wanted me to follow on foot. I was sorry, for on horseback I had some protection from the swamp. Here there were spiders larger than shoes; here jaws await, here snakes are, all less able to reach me atop Patrick Lowery's horse.

But I dismounted and led the horse forward. Henry Berry motioned me to leave it. For all I knew it would be eaten by alligators, but I later learned that the gang would never allow such a thing. They might cheerfully steal a lamb chop off of a dinner table or yank the quilt from the bride-night couple, and on one occasion they hauled away an occupied outhouse. But they respected work animals and wagons.

Henry Berry led the way. What I had seen of the swamp so far was like a city park compared to this. If Hell were made of water rather than fire, it would be this place. The terrain was flat but some trick of light gave the feeling of constant descent.

The outside world had never understood the Militia's failure to find the outlaws. The swamp hideout was only a few miles from the world, yet no one from the world could find it. To me, accustomed to New York City's open boulevards, it had been unthinkable that any place could be wild enough to hide from so many pursuers. But this implausible place, where the sea's tentacles defiantly invaded the unyielding land, was God's vengeance upon the earth. The ooze and slime, alive with the crawlers of a dying man's nightmares, sat in hungry wait for whatever dared move. The terrain itself seemed in motion. One might blink and then see that what had been in front was now alongside, or gone, or that there were two. Or upside-down, I supposed.

The swamp was a secret society, outside the known laws of God, man, and nature. What was now a tree was then a creature, what was a peaceful brook was suddenly a pool of leathery skin thrashing its dinner. Everything was predatory. Such a place a hundred yards across would have driven off all but the most desperate, and this was miles across. Henry Berry was King of the Outlaws, but his greater achievement was to make these bogs of death his royal court, his secure castle.

We splashed through a pond and I emerged with clawed leeches on my clothes and one in my skin. I rapidly scratched away this curiously intimate connection of myself to this place.

Our way was indirect. The ground moved under us. The mire engulfed, surrounded, and overhung us. The word 'direction' had no meaning; 'path' was a fiction. The cypress, the bog mouth, the rivulet of ooze, the stinging beetle big enough to crush the hunting bird, all murmured, "You are doomed."

As we walked, I reflected that I had been the subject of a test. At Henry Berry's order, Thom had lied about the Outlaw Chief's death. Another desperado might have taken my arrival as a threat or annoyance, but Henry Berry had used it to find out if the fake story of his death was credible.

The last hour of our journey was an expedition

through hell. Finally we reached the infamous Devil's Den, the outlaws' hideout. The cabin was the usual Indian variety except for an ingenious chimney I am sworn not to describe—though I can divulge its purpose: to prevent any trace of revealing smoke. The precaution was unnecessary; even if the Herald printed a map and directions (which would have to employ such phrases as "turn left, possibly, at the cypress where the copperhead disappeared from view but not from striking range; then find the gap in the nearby brush but stay away for there is a swirling pit and who knows what lives in it?" and "here the ground moves"), no outsider could survive the trip unguided. Thus, the smokeless chimney was unnecessary. But by oath I cannot reveal the simple secret of its workings. The chimney's secret's safe with me, so city urchins must go on choking.

When I was a tot my father made us a tree house. Too young to climb, I had to be carried up and down. One day the older boys climbed down without me and ran off to other games, leaving me to "guard." Eventually I fell asleep, and they forgot me. That night I awoke shivering in a rainstorm. I stared into the darkness, thinking I could hear the tree-shaking Grizzly Bear searching Brooklyn's back lots for its supper.

The Devil's Den put me in mind of our tree house. Like lost children, these outlaws had their playhouse in the woods, the one place on earth where they could safely gather. The rest of the world had been confiscated from these fellows. Not even in his mother's home did Henry Berry dare unbuckle a gun-belt. Arms and vigilance chaperoned every move, constricted every breath. But the Devil's Den was their house of play where nothing real was allowed. If they had had a friendly pup, they would have tossed it a ball.

But their dogs were not friendly. They were solemn, on-duty curs, as wary in the swamp as the outlaws were carefree. But outside the swamp, where the outlaws became dark and wary, the dogs were on joyous holiday.

My first afternoon at the Devil's Den turned to night, the whole bright sky giving way to the onrush of darker forces. Afraid of the darkness around us, I scrutinized every outlaw glance and gesture, each word or silence. At the slaughterer's approach, do cattle worry, "Is he looking at me that way because I am next?"

The outlaws went to sleep with no more preparation than lying down. But I changed into my nightgown. Henry Berry stared. "Goodnight," I said. I wrapped myself fretfully into a rug of dried swamp moss, and slept. Though I dreamed of monsters, the night would bring things worse and realer.

FIVE

I AWOKE IN THE DARK. Outlaws snore louder than others. I had not shared a bedroom in years, yet now lay cramped among these notorious slumberers. The blackness was a wall. "Y'aright?" I heard from the tar-pitch blackness. I expressed my wellbeing and gratitude for his concern, and fell back to sleep.

Later I awoke again. To silence. No snoring. The swamp had completed its serenade and not yet started another. The silence and darkness were so pure that I thought the outlaws had killed me. Within the softness of my moss rug, and with the traveler's sensation of displacement upon first waking, I felt nothing of myself. It was as if existence was holding its breath, waiting. Slowly, I became aware of my bodily self—or rather, a particular part of my bodily self. Whatever had waked me was in my left ear: a mild bother, part tickle and part itch. I touched my ear. An object was in it. Hard, cool, marble-like exterior. But within, something different.

An outlaw joke? I had seen no humor here so far except, I hoped, when they told me what I had eaten at supper. Again I touched the thing in my ear and was sorry to discover it was a swamp roach, wedged tight and scrambling its horrid little legs against the inside of my ear trying to get out.

I suppose its dilemma in my ear was like my own dilemma within the swamp, but I didn't care. Holding my breath lest I scream and bring the thunder of pistols upon me, I made my way outside. The moon had turned the swamp into a platinum landscape of some fever vision. In the frigid light I pried at the creature, its frantic legs scraping and antennae rubbing, the sounds of the swamp boring into my brain.

Taste and shame prevent me explaining how I ended my dilemma. Suffice to say that I got rid of the swamp roach and we both lived. I wanted to go home. But I could not flee through the inescapable swamp, and back inside there might be roach cousins. I was three years old, ensnarled by witches no matter what I did, and in a considerable quantity of trouble.

I cupped my hands over my ears and forced myself to go in and lie down again on my swamp moss carpet. I rolled over, pulling my moss rug tightly around me against further terrors. I rolled again, wrapping and re-wrapping in the impenetrable stuff. It shrank around my form, as fine wool may do, walling out all things. Though I was as awake as if I had jumped off a cliff and was half-way down, I forced myself to sleep.

I beg the reader's pardon for reporting what follows:

Some hours later, not yet morning, I was awakened by the sensation of a hand—not my own—in such place as violates hospitality, decorum, and statute. Knowing no etiquette for the situation, I pretended sleep, hoping the hand would go away. I was significantly relieved when it began to move off. But as it moved, my embarrassment and shame disappeared with the abrupt comprehension—the most horrifying of my life—that the Uninvited was no hand, but had feet. Several. Lilliputian, cold, sharp, multi-toed feet.

Still afraid to cry out, I tried to leap to my own feet, but my moss-wrapping was a constricting tunnel of horror, preventing me from rising, rolling, or even moving my arms. I could only inch my hands towards the Uninvited. When I got a grip on it through my nightgown, it began to thrash, squeal, claw, and bite. My nightgown and my inability to free my arms kept me from flinging the snapper out. I turned it so its claws tore at the wool of my gown instead of my belly. It writhed and grew hot in my hands as if I some miniature Devil I was wrestling. I squeezed harder and harder until finally it gave way with a break, a sound like snapping a wine glass or popping a child's balloon. My hands were soaked with warm blood through the wool, and my belly was drenched.

I had uttered no sound. It was the sort of catastrophe one bears silently and alone. I unwrapped myself and rushed outside. The moon lit the broken, bloody aftermath, which my hand was shaking too much to release. I clenched my teeth, clawed the thing away with my other hand, and threw it high and far into the swamp. I feared it might return to life, sprout wings, and hover in the darkness, planning revenge. But something swooped and snared it from the black air.

"What was it?" said Henry Berry from shadow.

"Rat." I hoped he would disagree and suggest instead

pussycat, fluffer-bunny, or tomato. He did not. The night air chilled my bloodied hand and thickened the gown's wool against my belly lacerations. The Outlaw came to me. In the darkness and without weaponry, he seemed too small to command universal fear and respect. But his eyes caught the moonlight, giving me the sensation of communing with something from a far place, a span wider than the "New Bridge"—galaxies or millennia wide. "Show," he said of my wounds.

I had grown up in the city, where we did not run naked or display our private parts. So I declined.

Another man would have repeated his command but the Outlaw hoarded words like gold coins. His look carried the repetition. Ashamed in the merciless moonlight, I lifted my nightgown to show my wounds.

He suddenly had a bright object that I took for a knife. In man's oldest primal defensive move, I bent away in protection but he turned me back. It was no knife, but a cup whose inside surface was inlaid with a mosaic of mirror chips angled this way and that. Each facet caught the moonlight and reflected it back in a single beam the Outlaw directed at my wounds, a spot of daylight playing over my belly. Never had I been more closely examined even by New York physicians. Then he headed for the cabin. I started to lower my gown but the Outlaw shook a finger before going inside. I stood like a Boston Colony tableau, open to the wild swamp night and watching for any hunting owl that might swoop down at my vulnerable exposition.

The Outlaw returned with a dish of liquid. I aimed

the lighting cup at my injuries while he cleaned them. The elixir seared my open skin. Fire tortured my broken belly and the moonlight split my eyes like white suns. Yet the Outlaw continued as if he were a spa masseur and I the fat lady gurgling in bliss. I passed out. An evening later I awoke in the cabin—my lacerations scabbed over and without pain!

The Outlaw led me outside. The night was overcast with thick fog and drizzle. I could see nothing, so he guided me as we crossed the shifting, rough ground, and then sat me on a plank I could not see.

We were afloat. I heard a paddle in water and the grand ruckus of a thousand swamp things. I could not tell whether the shore was ten feet away or a thousand. Henry Berry's hand splashed into the water, dragged out something long and large that did not care to be out, and handed it to me.

It was angry, thick as a wrist, and as intent upon getting free to fang me as I was absorbed in holding on until Armageddon, if this were not it. Its length cracked against me, a bullwhip with its own will. "Why?" I shrieked.

"To scare you," said the Outlaw. It did. Swamp roach to swamp rat to swamp snake! What more?

Yet when the Outlaw finally took the serpent and let it go, I felt no anger towards the man, but affection, as if he were my best friend in all the world. I thanked him for rescuing me from the snake! The Outlaw had reduced me to his mercy and then filled me with gratitude and affection. I was now willing to do anything to please him. I was conquered.

I don't believe in shadow powers. But in this swamp darkness was the stuff of superstition and religion, miracle following miracle no more remarkably than duckling follows duck. A flame burst from the Outlaw's palm and blossomed into the gloom as if squeezed through a pinprick from Hades. I froze before the tiny ball of fire. Was this man Lucifer himself, whose very name means 'lit by fire'?

But the flame was from a tiny box: an ingenious arrangement of bottle, flint, and wick. Its light attracted as forbidding a variety of insects as might be found outside a picture-book. As a child I had such a picture-book. I chased screaming little girls with it, waving fearsome drawings of wiry legs, crusty jaws, serrated wings, eye clusters, stingers, and webs. Now those forgotten girls were revenged as the same images swarmed to life between myself and the Outlaw, as if he controlled all nature. "What do you want?" I cried.

He pointed a finger at me. A shiny-winged beetle landed on it, pursued by another. Henry Berry ignored them devouring each other on his finger. "To write your story?" I asked.

"My book," said the Outlaw.

"I don't know enough about you for a whole book." He said nothing. "You scarcely say three words in a row! Shreds don't make books. Books are vast, books are weighty, books are teeming." He flicked the cannibal beetles into the darkness. Something from the water snapped one; something flying snatched the other. I knew I was going to write his damned book.

We sat afloat until the drizzling dawn absorbed the

darkness. Low in the gray shell of sky, not thirty feet distant, the shore—if "shore" is what to call the soft, shifting mud bordering the waters—gradually came into view. Henry Berry pointed through the gloom at a cypress. A dim shape that had seemed a shadow or clump of lichen, moved. A hunting cat, and it had spotted something. "Always there," said Henry Berry.

"On that branch?"

"Everywhere." The cat suddenly dived without splash into the water, then broke back to the surface tugging to shore a screeching wet thing twice its size that put up a whacking fight, but the cat's jaws could crack a neck and did.

I turned away but Henry Berry turned me back. A splash of blood jeweled the morning vapors, arresting a vulture arcing above waiting its turn. The cat selected its grisly morsels in picky deliberation. I had thought that wild beasts gulped their food, but the cat dined gracefully, chew by savored chew. He might have been reading the Herald over his unrushed breakfast like a retired businessman, though with somewhat bloodier mouth and claws.

Filled, he haunched away. The vulture started down but something dark and faster snatched the leftovers into the underbrush. The vulture hovered with a cry, as did several smaller birds in order of ferocity. I assume they were succeeded by feeders of progressively lesser rank, down to worms and insects, maggots and fungi, and at last the invisible creatures, patient and inevitable. What treasure, the victim who until this fateful morning had had his own place in the treasure line. Nothing of him would go uneaten except for bones and a few teeth, and even those could have provided jewelry for some savage, or a Park Avenue lady. The most equalitarian must accept the feeding order. Something or someone must come before and some other after. All cannot dine at once. Justice is a creation as artificial as the Outlaw's smokeless chimney, light-cup, and flame-box, and resides outside the natural order. Otherwise the maggot would cry "justice" and eat the housewife's dinner. Henry Berry never pleaded for anything as unnatural as justice. He rested his case on the natural force of necessity.

Unaware of these matters but illustrating them, a Thing with Claw came over the side of our boat and fixed upon my trouser.

O world of pouncing variety! I stared at the Thing with Claw, which, with a row of eyes, was looking what to clamp next. Henry Berry motioned me to remove it. Did I refuse? Did I recoil in dread? No! I was a veteran of an ear roach, a belly rat, and a handful of serpent. So I grabbed the monster and yanked. It held on, jaws assailing my hand, and it looked in all directions at once. It was not going to release my trouser until it had something better. Henry Berry plucked a fish from the water and offered it to the clawed creature. It released my trousers to grab the fish's face, and the Outlaw plunged them both back into the drink.

SIX

BACK AT THE DEVIL'S DEN, Henry Berry said, "Write quick." Was it thus with the Medici? "Make haste with that ceiling!" I quickly set out to learn how a mother's quiet boy became the nation's worst desperado. He himself was little help because he didn't talk and his occasional songs contained no more history than a flower. But he encouraged me to ask anything of anyone, except Rhody.

"Except Rhody?" I countered. "That is the most ridiculous thing I have heard yet," though whether my disappointment was professional or personal I could not tell. "Every story is a love story," I explained, and said that not even the history of George Washington could be told without Martha.

"Who?" he asked.

"George Washington." He shrugged. I said, "People must understand you as a person, a father, a husband, not just a legend. I must talk to Rhody."

He gave in. I was pleased. I am not much affected by women, my profession leaving no time. Their paint and powder, their chatter and small thoughts are tiresome. But Rhody! That she smoked a pipe was reason enough, but she could spit a dozen times from one chaw.

I began to write about the swamp night. But squatting on a hill of dirt and hunching awkwardly over my tablet, I longed for my own desk in New York. I pictured it, dark and silent, a four-square bedrock on which to distill the jumble of life into clear prose. I missed its clean surfaces and defining corners, its hollows worn under a hundred years of elbows, and its cubbies of notes waiting to become the news of the day. A good desk is the opposite of swamp. I looked for a place better than my hill of dirt and saw only more hills of dirt. I put aside my tablet. From the cabin doorway Henry Berry watched.

I pushed by him into the cabin. No longer concerned with mere roaches or rats, I lay down to sleep. The outlaws tippy-toed about for my sake. Steve, at the fireplace warming a leather boot to re-shape it, was having a morning of sneezes. Several times he leaped to his feet and quickly tippy-toed outside to sneeze quietly into the swamp. I dozed, contemplating the courtesy of ferocious outlaws.

I awoke to an empty cabin. Outside, strings played a tune accompanied by sneezing. I tried to go out to listen but was barely awake and opened the wrong door. I found a small room, but it could have been the Federal Armory. Enough firearms lined the walls to supply a battalion. Silver, gray, and blue barrels, dark wood stocks and handles, the sharp smell of lubricant, glints of hard light on the polished metals, all carried the grave thrill of death. The walls held pistols and rifles four deep. In among the weaponry hung fiddles, a banjo, harps of various shapes, and an empty spot either for a rifle or the banjo I heard outside. Thus reminded, I turned to go out, but stopped at the sight of an unearthly white sheen. I took it at first for a shaft of light through a crack, but it was light gleaming off a pistol of silver and pearl. Captivated by its carvings and flowered etchings, I took it down. I had never held such a thing. It drew my arm to full extension and mesmerized my eye down its sights. It made me taller. This pistol would not miss. I sighted it through the closet door from object to object and it led itself, requiring nothing of me. It drew like magnetism to each thing I desired to aim at, skipping the space between. My heart slowed. My grip was loose, light. My finger curled easily into the etched guard and floated over the ebony trigger. My face reflected the cool strength I had seen upon Henry Berry's features. My eyes narrowed. The report exploded and I wondered who had shot, until I realized it was me. My random target had been an outlaw's boot on a low stool five feet away in the outer room. Shattered leather and wood shards flew in every direction. No foot would again wear this boot.

Like a child having broken his mother's mirror, I sat on the floor and daftly tried putting the scraps back together. I knew how these rustics loved their boots and wondered which killer had owned this one.

I heard a sneeze, and turned to see Steve Lowery, barefoot.

He was aiming two rifles and a pistol. I threw my hands over my head and sent flying the fragments of boot I had been clutching. He sneezed again. "Bless you," I said.

"There's every kind of critter in the swamp for practice, how come you hunt my boot?"

"I didn't mean it."

"You're lucky. If it was Thom's boot you'd be better off shooting your own self." He picked up a piece of the boot. "Daddy's," Steve said mournfully. "They killed him. And now this. What was you meaning to do?"

I had not meant to shoot his daddy's boot. I had not meant to shoot. I had not meant to be here. I had meant to be a journalist in the North where it is safe.

"Reload Harry's gun," he said, "and put it back exact, lest he show you how far off he can poke you a face hole with it."

"How?" I said.

"By shooting you where you stand."

"I mean how do I load the gun?"

It had not occurred to Steve that a full grown man could not load a pistol. "You ain't done it? You ain't done it but you shot my Daddy's boot?"

"I didn't mean . . ."

"I will show you." He gave me a pistol he said he'd taken from a drunk preacher. He taught me to load and then led me outside. "Set here. Look there. See something. Shoot."

"I don't want to kill anything."

"You won't," he said.

"I'm no Jesse James."

"Who?"

I sat. I looked. I saw nothing. He poked me. Fifty feet away a pretty raccoon was waffling along, unmindful that its poor life was in question. I did nothing. "You got to pull the trigger to make a gun shoot," Steve said. My gun seemed a sad thing, with such a creature its object. "What you waiting for? Old age of the 'coon?" I lifted the gun and hesitated. "Don't worry, you won't hit it." I aimed. "Good." Looking down the sights at my prey, I contemplated a dozen of its little steps. "Quit ole-lady settin!" I fired. The raccoon calmly ran, apparently gauging its danger by the width of my aim. "See? You won't hurt no critters." Steve gave me a box of bullets marked Tennessee Ordnance and went back to his banjo. I watched the swamp. A squirrel climbed a giant cypress. I fired and missed the tree. "Aim," called Stephen, sighting down his banjo at me as his fingers skittered the strings.

I skillfully saw another raccoon. I aimed, then put down the gun. "I'll set up rocks," I said.

"Shootin's to kill dinner or someone you don't like. Neither one sets still like a rock. Practice on what moves."

"I have no need to shoot my dinner or someone I don't like."

"You just got here." I put aside my soft city heart, but all my Tennessee bullets later I had endangered nothing but my foot. Steve instructed, "Breathe out when you shoot. Like the bullet's your breath." I followed his advice and came within a foot of hitting a bull frog. "Wok," it said and went away. Now I was getting somewhere. "You can even say 'bang'," Steve said, and though he might have been joking, I breathed out with my next shot, whispered "bang," and smashed a bunny's hind leg. The bunny squealed. I disgorged my digesting.

Steve yelled, "Shoot the poor Gawdam thing," but I could not.

"You said I wouldn't hurt any critters!"

Steve used my pistol to end the creature's distress. A cabin hound shuffled after the carcass. "How you Yankees won the War I can't figure," Steve said. We ate the bunny for lunch. That afternoon I shot enough food for two days. I was proud. The taste of bunny had made me a killer. "And if it were a human man?" asked Steve.

"I don't think so."

"One who done you wrong, who's trying to shoot you?" I shook my head. "You got to consider it. Unless you plan to stay here alone while we're off doing." I said hunting dinner was different from shooting people. "Not much," he said. He went inside.

I would not! The writer records and interprets, not shoots.

Steve came back out. From the door he shot a bird. "Fry nice," he said as it landed fifty yards off. The same hound stared as if the task were too great for so warm a day and so small a bird, but knowing his place in the universal order, and the bird's, he sullenly retrieved it.

Steve handed me his pistol, and did the peculiar thing of plugging its barrel with his finger. "I done this for Harry once." With no warning, he twisted my free arm behind me like a neighborhood bully. He still had his finger wedged into the gun barrel. "I'll break your arm unless you shoot." He tugged to make his point. I trounced his bare foot, and he lifted me off the ground. "First you shoot my daddy's boot and then you stomp my toe!" He yanked at my arm and I howled. I had only to pull the trigger to end it. He was right: how did we Yankees win? He yanked again and I discovered yes I could, for I pulled the trigger. Three times. He smiled and let go.

"I knew it was empty!" I shouted.

He smiled. "Go pick another gun and let's get with Harry and them."

In the gun room I looked once more at the silver and pearl beauty, left it hanging, and took a less elegant model. Two of them. I belted my guns on, fourteen shots ready to go, a two-gun desperado. I had shot and eaten a bunny and tried to shoot a man, at least his finger. I told Steve I felt dangerous and safe.

"Never feel safe," he said. "Men who get killed felt safe one second before." As to my feeling dangerous, he said, "A smart man knows he's no more dangerous than his own sad pecker flapping in the rain. Just don't tell nobody."

We departed. I soon lost track of the way. Every hundred yards the terrain forced us to double back within sight (but not accessibility) of where we had been. The swamp, like mountains, can't be crossed in a straight line.

Long after I thought I could go no farther, Steve led me into the maze of a briar thicket. Within was my old friend, Patrick Lowery's horse. It saw me, disdainfully smacked its lips, and turned its rump towards me. "I never seen a horse do that," said Steve. I mounted. It arched its spine to cause me discomfort. I pulled its ear and it stopped. We had communicated.

We proceeded to meet the gang. Patrick Lowery's

horse found a gait that jogged my brains and slapped my weapons against me, so I had to clutch both pistols to keep them from banging my chest raw. I tried to look fierce. Steven had the decency not to watch.

He did not ride. He ran alongside. The outlaws could run for hours even under the weight of full weaponry. They could cross the swamps faster on foot than on horseback.

Steve had taught me to shoot because, I thought, I was going to have to defend myself. Would I be chased by a posse? Would a bounty-hunter try to take me? Was I obliged to shoot back? I fantasized being a deadly aim, though any attacker smaller than a barn or more than ten feet away would be safe unless he offered to shoot himself. But in my fancy I shot off the ears and trigger fingers of distant, amazed snipers.

We started down a cleared ridge. Out of the setting sun appeared the silhouettes of dogs, then of four men. I reached for a pistol but Steve said, "Harry and them." We closed with the gang. Thom was the only one who laughed at the sight of me in arms. They had been distributing food, difficult because Henry Berry insisted they leave gifts without seeing the recipients (so as not to embarrass them) and without being seen by anyone else (so as not to endanger the recipients for consorting with the gang). "Harder to give than steal," said Thom.

Now after the day's charity would be new adventure. I was to be in an actual raid! "So keep your eyes open," said Thom. I wanted a thousand eyes to keep open for this unprecedented journalistic privilege. Henry Berry handed me a lump of gray clay wrapped in grease paper. I touched the clammy stuff and brought it to the tip of my tongue to eat. A correcting gesture from Henry Berry told me to smear it on my face. It was not so brown as a Negro nor so ruddy as an Indian, but it darkened me enough. With my face, hands and neck covered, I reached under my shirt to cover my chest. "We mostly don't undress in a raid," said Thom.

The gang moved off on foot in a silent rush of men and weapons. I rode Patrick Lowery's horse, who was not fooled by my disguise. My fellow outlaws, Henry Berry our leader, and I headed west, hats low over our eyes and—at least in my case—faces grim against what we were about to do, whatever it was. I was in this dreaded gang, we were afoot to break the law, and I felt no guilt. Had the coloring of my skin darkened my character? Does the moral sense adjust so quickly? We were doing no more than what the animals of the swamp did all the time. We were merely bringing the swamp's way to the world.

I cast a conspiratorial look at the gang. They were low-lidded and alert, but bodies relaxed as if without concern for anything in this world. Thom smiled as he ran, as did the silent night-black Negro who had not yet spoken in my presence. This was Shoe-Maker John, a gentle-faced man, though no one else could look so cold and murderous on a raid. He had woolly hair, large protuberances above the eyebrows, big jaws and cheekbones, and eyes of black that could take a stranger's measure in a single glance. When I'd first met him he had gazed at me like a Gypsy itemizing a chicken coop. I had stared back, having heard in Lumberton that he was dead.

We headed into the setting sun, bringing with us dusk from the swampland. A last ray of sun shrank to a bead of blood, then died out as we continued through the pines. The dogs trotted alongside like low shadows dancing out of the underworld. They had left their seriousness behind, the way I had left my innocence. They seemed bound for a garden party of bones and tree stumps. They romped as we came up out of the swamp, men and dogs dragging the darkness with us.

I was with Henry Berry, who had made the darkness his own. From out of his swamp we were going to battle not against flesh and blood, but against principalities, powers, rulers of another darkness: the outer world. I was being rushed towards adventures, powerless to stop myself. Would I murder? Would a new reporter be sent from New York to write of the outlaw journalist? Would my family see my picture with Patrick Lowery's horse rearing beneath me, pistols in my hands, my victims trampled beneath? Was this real enough for me to die?

Suddenly we stopped. From the dark a hand took my reins. A gunshot rang out beside me, its flare searing the scene onto my eye like a Matthew Brady photograph. The hand tugged my reins, jerking Patrick Lowery's horse away from where we had been. This photograph, not black and white but in sudden ruby hues and which I will remember forever, is of the outlaws leaning forward, listening, weapons raised. It is Steve yanking my reins as Henry Berry fires his long rifle into the darkness ahead. We're surrounded by the shapes of dark trees, the dogs at point like arrows, and the soft eyes and shiver of Patrick Lowery's horse.

Then from the distant dark comes a return shot and I understand why we moved. The gang volleys back at the shooter's flash. Even had the shooter known enough to move as he fired at us – and he had not – the gang's return fire came instantaneously.

Then came the screaming, a death cry that continued until his eternal night came down upon him. Thus! to the enemies of the gang, I thought, surprised at the intensity with which I thought it.

In the flare of Henry Berry's first shot, I saw that the outlaws had lost their unconcerned air. Every man alert, eyes wide, bodies low, balanced for aim, these virtuosi had practiced and mastered their measures. We moved through the dark to the dead sniper hanging upside-down by his boot, caught in the crotch of branch where he had climbed to fire at us. His blood drained down from several wounds. "Nobody missed," said Thom, counting holes.

"Me," said Shoe-Maker John, the first I had heard the Negro speak.

"How do you know?" asked Thom.

"I knows."

"Who is it?" I asked.

"Yankee bounty-man," said Steven, loathing in every syllable.

Henry Berry walked around the dead sniper, saying, "And the first born of the poor shall feed, and the needy shall lie down in safety: and I will kill thy root and slay thy remnant. The beast that ascendeth out of the bottomless pit shall make war against thee, and shall overcome thee, and kill thee. Amen."

"Amen," said Shoe-Maker John, hat removed.

"Quit that damn stuff, Harry!" yelled Steve, "It gives me the shivers, it would give a dead man the shivers." Henry Berry nodded as if that were the point. "Don't it give you the shivers?" Steve asked the gang, including me. Shoe-Maker John and I nodded, the former making clear that he liked the shivers. "Harry, one of these times you say them damn things," came Steve's voice, "and the ground will open and something bad will drag you down to screaming hell forever and ever."

"Amen," floated Henry Berry's voice high through the dark.

"Son of a bitch thinks he's a preacher," said Steve.

We left the corpse to birds, their great unseen wings flapping impatiently for us to be gone. The uneaten bones, I imagined, would enhance the reputation of the swamp as a bad place.

I felt less horror of the killing than I had for the rabbit. The rabbit, after all, had not shot at me. If the dead sniper had stayed North where he belonged, his heart's blood would not be draining over his face, turning the dirt below into slick violet mud.

We continued to our adventure. "Wrote it?" came Henry Berry's voice.

"Not in the dark," I said. "But I'll remember it." Though I did not yet know if I could write it. Once as a child I had been thrashed for some misdeed and ran to my room, slammed my door, and tried to write of the thrashing so intensely that it would forever end thrashings. But I only broke pen points.

I had a question: "How did you know he was there?"

Henry Berry had moved off. Another voice from the dark explained: swamp noises change with the presence of men, the kind of change depending upon the number, race, distance, and intention of the intruders. Careful listening can pinpoint an intruder within twenty yards. "Owls hunt by ear, and us too," said the voice. I started listening hard to the swamp. There was much to hear.

SEVEN

WE REACHED a town and moved through its back ways to a bank. I had assumed our raid would be on some farmer's barn, not a bank. I was not alone in my feeling.

"Can't rob no bank," said Shoe-Maker John. "White folks notice." Henry Berry did not listen.

Steve said, "Now Harry, now Harry, now Harry, lookit here, Harry, you got to consider, no need of show for the Writer, just steal him a couple chickens someplace, a goat, Jesus a field of goats but Harry, a bank again and they got to come after us, they take banks serious."

Henry Berry looked around as if to say, "Is someone talking?"

Steve continued, "They even got Jesse James on account of a bank."

"Who?" said Henry Berry.

"Harry, not a bank." Henry Berry looked into Steve's eyes. "Banks," said Steve less vehemently, "is protected personal by A. Lincoln in Washington."

"Who?"

"Mr. A. Lincoln!"

"Dead," said Henry Berry.

"Still a goatshit idea," said Steve.

Henry Berry smiled nose to nose with his big brother. "We do it," said Henry Berry. Steve's lower lip jutted stubbornly, but he nodded. "We doin' what?" demanded Henry Berry.

"Doin' your dawg Gawd damn goatshit bank and when we setting in jail we goin whop your stupid butt, you dumb dawg shit son of a bitch." Henry Berry put his arms around his brother, kissed his nose, and led us to a window. He unwrapped a package from under his shirt, opened a window, and met the rush of two fearsome dogs with the package's contents: red meat dripping as much blood as the dead sniper in the swamp. The dogs snapped and ate and did not bark. I eventually learned that these dogs had been bred by a mulatto family, one of several of Henry Berry's acquaintance that supplied guard dogs to farms, stores, banks, and anyone else who wanted protection. Henry Berry had thus been puppyhood friends with the county's most dangerous guard dogs. They regarded him an intruder no more than their own mothers – especially when he brought so tasty a slab of meat.

Soon we were inside the bank, and I was a criminal. Looking at the safe, Shoe-Maker John whispered, "Ain't goin to open its own self. Ain't goin to walk home with us on its own feets. What we doing here?"

"No safe," answered the Outlaw.

"Well what we doing?" said Thom, "The spittoon?"

"Why a spittoon?" said Andrew.

Steve tried a random combination on the safe, just in case.

Henry Berry lowered the blinds, lit a bronze oil lamp, and, watching me, placed the lamp one after the other on the three clerk's desks. The gang was baffled, but I understood. We weren't here for the safe. I sat at each desk, taking its measure and feel. My writer self had despaired of writing about the dead sniper in the woods, but now it returned, eager. These desks were a touch of home, like resting my head in mamma's lap at Christmas. One desk was oak, a second pine. The third I could not tell, but this dark brown beauty, its ripe grain steeped in the lamp's glow, lured me, calling for words to be written on it. Its corners were seamless, its drawers slid like water. Let's emancipate this worthy from the moneychangers.

Henry Berry sent Andrew to find a wagon and told me to choose whatever else I might require. I pointed to everything in sight: inks from India, nibs and a box of German Faber pencils, a seat cushion from someone's Aunt Annie Lou, blotting paper of three hues, and may I be forgiven but I enjoyed every minute. Shoe-Maker John gathered up my inventory while Steve tried more random combinations at the safe, like a boy flipping pennies hoping one might come down a dollar. "How much you think's in there?" Thom said.

"Enough to go all the ways to Toledo," said Shoe-Maker John.

"Where's that?" said Steve. He tried more combinations. I found stacks of beautiful cream paper, which I use even now. Is it fair that a bank affords such stuff while we poor writers suffer pulp stock by comparison?

"That picture?" I asked, looking at an etching of mountains. Henry Berry gestured me to get it myself. "Me?" He nodded. I set my jaw, breathed deeply, and stole it off the wall. Me!

Outside, Andrew tapped at the window. He was back with a grain store wagon drawn by a nasty horse disgruntled at being awake. We hoisted the desk out onto the wagon. Henry Berry watched, scratching the ears of the bank's ferocious dogs who were asleep with their heads in his lap.

Outside, the gang's dogs stood guard. If anyone came, they knew to nip and run, drawing him away and howling to warn the outlaws inside. The outlaws had trained three of the dogs to drool as if mad, which would send anyone running. The fourth dog learned this ruse from his fellows.

As we left, Thom looked at the safe. "Someday," he promised.

Conveying the desk through the swamp was a feat that matched the building of the pyramids.

Back at the Devil's Den I slept for an hour and dreamed of plunder. I dreamed of incarceration. I dreamed of mamma scolding me. I woke at sunrise and raced outside to my desk. I hung my etched mountains on a tree alongside. Henry Berry watched me write the whole day. As I worked, Thom and Shoe-Maker John built a roof over me. At nightfall I lit the bank's bronze lamp and worked until morning. Never in one revolution of the sun had I put so much to paper.

Within days I had written all I could without more interviews. I then met with Mary Cuombo, Rhody, a man named Groone, and others. Across the county I talked with Whites, Negroes, mulattos, Indians, poor Whites, even a Hebrew. My travels better acquainted me with Patrick Lowery's horse. To him I was one of the costs exacted from poor living creatures in return for their sunny days in this green pasture of life. My fondness grew for this sturdy, nut-brown, uncommunicative beast. He carried me trip after trip, waited while I listened to one and then another Robesonian, and then, barren of attitude, returned me to the margins of the swamp, from where we were guided by one of the gang back to the Devil's Den. I would then work at my desk beside my etched mountains. This was my place. I had business here. I was happy, assembling from a chaos of swamp and information the clean, true lines of the Outlaw's tale.

One night a storm came up, great black clouds flashing lightning over my pages like celestial exclamation. I found myself thinking in corresponding bursts, as if my brain was drawing electricity from the storm. I began to write about Rhody. I wrote a line or two, then listened to the storm, then wrote more of Rhody, and so on. Shoe-Maker John watched over my shoulder as he often did, not to see what I wrote (he could not read, except his name), but how much.

But I would not exploit the storm or the swamp for a literary symbol. A vine smothering a tree, or a reptile's nest in the mud, is just precisely what it is. It does not stand for something else. Symbols are literary fiddlefaw. I would not be a symbolizer even with so tempting a possibility as the swamp. The swamp is the swamp, a storm is a storm. Only people who know nothing about swamps and storms use them for symbols.

On evenings that the outlaws were not visiting their homes or off raiding, after I was finished writing for the day Henry Berry would get his fiddle from the armament room and the others would get their mouth harps and banjos. They would sing and play long into the night until they fell asleep one at a time, heaps of outlaw here and there, leaving Henry Berry singing slow and soft, drawing his bow across mellow strings. Even after I nodded off myself he sang on alone: silly songs, Christ songs, love songs, songs of pirates, mine disasters, railroad wrecks, fatal horse races, and card games, things he had never seen. Sometimes he plunked random notes while reciting disconnected, shuffled chunks of King James to the stars: "We will sing my songs to the stringed instruments all the days of our life," or "It is not the voice of them that shout for mastery, neither is it the voice of them that cry for being overcome: but the noise of them that sing do I hear." When Henry Berry touched his strings and I lay drifting in and out of slumber, his music seemed to come from heaven as surely as the words he spoke. Henry Berry Lowery, child of the South, Outlaw of Carolina, and if I were a fiddlefawing symbolizer, I would say symbol of a nation, for better or worse.

Henry Berry could not read, but had memorized the Bible like fiddle notes. And though he never spoke more than a few words of his own, on some drunken nights he talked the Bible's words for hours until he fell asleep, muttering of suns that riseth and silences that fall.

He would have been able to read if he had practiced what his mother taught him. Schooling was outlawed for Indians and Negroes, so Mary Cuombo taught herself to read by following hymnal words in church. As the leader spoke for the congregation to sing, she learned to associate his words with print. With hymns as accomplices, she broke North Carolina's enforcement of illiteracy the way her sons now broke other laws. But Henry Berry just memorized. Mary Cuombo narrated the Bible and he learned it by rote.

"Never once got in a fight," Mary Cuombo told me. "Turned cheek and left the others shamed for taunting. I never saw such a chile. He always wanted to do my work so I could go play. And he'd hurt nobody nor nothing. I seen him cry over little critters laying dead. That's how I know he never done them things they say. So be careful you, what you put in your book."

Henry Berry Lowery was born in 1847 in the single-room cabin of his father, Allen Lowery. Allen, part White, was 57. Mary Cuombo, part Portuguese and hence her name, was younger. They had ten surviving children, though five more had been birthed. Henry Berry was between youngest and oldest.

Robeson Whites despise the theory that these mulattos descend from Virginia's Lost English Colonists. The Whites reject the theory despite the European features of these Indians, lack of Indian custom or language, resistance to European disease, and even names (Henry Berry's and dozens of others), identical to the Lost Colonists. Present-day Scottish gentry wish that the Lost Colony had been considerate enough to die out in order to avoid the nasty question of miscegenation.

The first recorded Henry Berry was listed in the ship's manifest as a member of that lost Virginia Colony. His namesake and descendent, the Outlaw Henry Berry Lowery, looked like a London banker. White English blood flowed in the Outlaw's veins and he had an Elizabethan name. But Robeson's lowly Scots had escaped their English masters long ago and had no wish to see them resurrected in the person of primitive mulattos. A Scottish lady told me, "Anyone, even tree savages, may steal names as easily as they steal our silver."

White blood or not, the mulattos had long counted themselves Indians. Whites and Negroes also called them Indians, and so did North Carolina law, which at first classified Indians as free and denied them nothing. But by the Civil War, Indians had lost their rights to education, suffrage, and to bear arms. "We were demoted low as Nigras," said Mary Cuombo, "so we swatted Nigras down lower to get them out of our falling way."

When the Civil War started, North Carolina kept Indians out of the army, which was the strategic folly that lost the War. This stupidity was based on the law against Indians bearing arms. Had Indians fought for the Confederacy, the added manpower would have been a cut above the effectiveness of most who did serve. It would have swayed the War's outcome. And Henry

Berry, the gentle Bible-reciting child, would likely have died on one or another green-laced battlefield.

Instead, North Carolina's young Indians were conscripted to work alongside Negro slaves to build coastal forts without which the Confederacy could not survive. With construction at its pitch and the urgency growing, a Yellow Fever epidemic arose. Slaves and Indians died faster than they could be replaced. "If a man was a Nigra or Indian or any kind of thing, they sent him down to Wilmington and throwed him in the pits to build as much as he could before the Fever killed him," which took a week or two. Tar barrels burning on every corner stopped the stench of death, but not the dying. Yet the army superstitiously continued to burn tar, which had no effect but to attract swarms of mosquitoes.

Henry Berry saw it: at fourteen he went to see the world by hanging under a railway car, and climbed off without knowing where. Fumes billowing from pots filled the sweltering air with the stench of tar. On a far shoreline was a fort under construction, its Confederate flag dismal in the high smoke. The train unloaded young Indians, chained, who were struck by whips when they stumbled and herded into pits where others had been working all night. Some were forced to work chin high in seawater on the fort's breastplates. Others hauled heavy timbers and great barrows of earth up hills for twelve-hour shifts, all under the eye of armed masters.

As Henry Berry watched, a young Indian on the hill dropped, covered in blood though he had not been injured. A White officer ordered two other Indian boys to take him away. The sick boy's neck and head lolled as if unconnected to his trunk. Blood blanketed his face and chest and his mouth opened in an endless howl of pain, shock, and terror. The two boys who carried him displayed no emotion, as if they had been carrying others for hours and days. They pulled him a hundred yards and rolled him into a deep pit. One said something, perhaps a prayer, and both returned to work.

Henry Berry watched a dozen such interments. Then several workers were ordered to fill in the pit of the dying and dig another. One Indian boy, already sick, was among those forced to dig. When the task was done, he sank to his knees, bleeding like his predecessors, and cried. He fell back into the pit he had helped to dig. He yelled a few bits of unconnected prayer, then cried out for his mother. He flailed backwards, sand sliding out beneath as he tried to scramble back up. But the sand gave way and settled over him. Underneath, the boy struggled for a few moments, then stilled.

Henry Berry went home. To avoid conscription, he and the younger Lowery sons took to hiding in the swamps where no one had ever tried to live. They had played at its edges as children and could survive there now. Yet this laying out caused hardship on their family, who needed their work in the fields at home. But when they came home to take their chances, Mary Cuombo and Allen judged their youthful enthusiasm suicidal and sent them back into the swamps.

Steven, twenty-three, was the oldest to take swamp refuge. His older brothers Calvin, Sinclear, and Patrick (who owned my horse) were family men, unlikely to be conscripted. In the swamp, Steven was the official protector of young Thom and Henry Berry, a task he executed by his size and courage, not skilled leadership. In their second year of laying out Steven was guiding them through a deadly part of the swamp when he heard voices and signaled the boys to take cover. He told me, "I went on alone, though I didn't know if it was ghosts or Conscriptors or what. We only had one gun between us. It was Thom's turn to carry it, and as usual he forgot to bring it." The boys safely hidden, Steve crept closer and saw "Yankees in our swamp! They spot me where I hid and got twenty muskets up at me, bayonets and all. To save the young'uns I run right to the Yankees and throw up my hands and hollered, 'Confusion on the Confederation.' If I could've thought of the name of one Rebel general I'd have said, 'Death to him' but I couldn't. I wasn't scared till I seen they was mostly drunk." The Yankees had been fleeing and, hopelessly lost in the swamp, broke open a supply of stolen liquor. "Well, so they grab me and commence with questions.

"'How come I ain't off fighting the War?' they wanted to know. I said I was a poor boy hiding because I love the North. They said I sneaked up to chop off their heads for the reward. I ask 'What reward?' hoping Harry and Thom was in earshot. But the Yanks said, 'You are a dead man before you find out,' and they ask me who I was and what was I doing and where did I live? They talked weird, like you," Steve said, meaning me. "I could barely understand, and that made them ornery. Last they ask where's the nearest place somebody live. I said 'nobody lives noplace' in a right loud voice, hoping the boys would take them by surprise instead of letting me die of Yankees." Steve stopped talking, not wanting to tell me the next part of the tale, where he was tied helpless, reliant on his small brothers. Henry Berry nodded over at Thom, who had been whittling a big stick into a little stick, to continue.

"The Yankees finally went to sleep but for one little lookout," Thom began. "Stevie was tied pissy and scared, and I'm in a bush not knowing whether to go, stay, fly round a tree, or what to do. Then Harry whispers in my ear, 'Thommy Lorrie, soon as I get out there, make your duck noise.'

"'What for my duck noise?' I said."

"'Just do it,' Harry told me."

"'This is no time for fooling, Harry,' I said. 'They got Steve. Grow up.'

"'It's for seeing if they're sleeping deep.' Harry was more of a talker then."

"Well, in a minute Harry's amongst them, so I do what he told me and I goes 'QRKK QRKK QRKK.'" Thom did it well. As he Qrrk'd for me now, three far-spread replies came from the swamp. "Then I done it louder, 'QRKKK QRKKK QRKKK,' and I look again and there's no Harry, where he gone I don't know, so I keep on, 'QRKKKK QRKKKK QRKKKK,' and sure enough every Yank's sleeping sound. Pretty soon I didn't have to do it myself no more, because a load of ducks wakes up looking around to see which cousins was coming to visit. So I look for Harry. Couldn't see him. But I see by Stevie's face he seen him." Thom looked at sullen Steve to continue.

The secret to interviewing politicians, socialites, and criminals is to keep quiet; they'll talk to fill the silence. When Steve did not continue, I could have said, "And then what happened, Steven Lowery?" But I merely watched, pencil poised. And of course Steve finally spoke:

"It was hard to turn my head to see, but Harry was sneaking up on a sleeping Yank, just like we was playing soldier. Then, hello-what-you-know, Harry got that Yank's pistol and knives, and never woke him up. Then I didn't see Harry till right in my ear he whispers, 'Your hands is untied, why you still got them behind you?' He'd untied me so easy I never knowed it.

"'Let's go,' I said.

"'I want their guns and their food too,' Harry says. 'Take this pistol and get behind the one who's guarding, and poke his ear hole and tell him, "Quiet, or your head got two holes, one in and one out," say it just like I said it and no different, then guard him and the rest while I get the guns and all.'

"And that's what we done. Harry tied the foot of every sleeping Yank to their necks. Little Thommy, barely growed, is sitting in the bushes on their guns, and he says, 'Let's shoot them and get the reward.'

"Harry says, 'Can't shoot no varmints in their sleep.' And hell if he didn't just sit in the middle of 'em and start off to singing! Harry, sing what you sung." In a voice as dark as shade and sweet as dawn, he did:

Bring to me the light this day
Deliver me from night

The dark is passed once more away
And You are in my sight

Somewhere the sky is darkling still
Somewhere the fire burn
Stay with me, be it Thy will
For the night will soon return

Henry Berry's voice disarmed me. I said, "Surely such mild sound woke no Yankees."

"Did," started Steve, but he had to stop and clear his throat. "Woke 'em and they didn't know where they was, maybe died and in Heaven. Then they see what is what and reach for their guns. But their guns are gone so they get up to look and fall on their backasses because their feet's tied, and they blame each other till they see us pointing their guns at them, which gets their attention. 'What you doing in our swamp?' I said. 'Ain't no war in here. Who are you? And doing what? Where you live? And why ain't you off fighting the War?'"

"'Them's good questions,' Harry said."

"But they weren't talking, so I say, 'Let's feed them to whatever's out there that's hungry. Do I hear an alligator?'"

"'Two,' said young Henry Berry, already learning to say more in a syllable than the rest of the world in an hour.

"'Feed 'em the biggest Yankee first,' said Thom, looking at a fat one. 'Or the smallest, so the gators don't fill up on one bite.' The fattest and the skinniest looked at each other. But still no Yankee talked.

"'Feed 'em all at once except that old one,' said Henry Berry, 'He'll talk once there's no others to hear him shamed.' He turned to the Yankees. 'Tell us quick and leave them gators hungry.'"

"'Better to deliver us to alligators than send us back where we were,' said a Yank. The fat Yankee didn't agree.

"'Where was you and where you goin' and what you doing here?' Steve demanded. The fat Yankee explained they had been prisoners 80 miles away in South Carolina. When too many died in prison the survivors braved the guards, dogs, and infested swamps to escape, many dying in the attempt. Trying to get home, they had become lost in these swamps.

"'We mean you gentlemen no harm,' the fat Yankee said."

"'You was goin shoot my head off. Don't that harm a Yankee? Harms a Lorry,' said Steve."

"Their leader, a lieutenant from Maine named Owen Wright, said, 'We thought you were trying to capture us.'

"'And we done it,' said little Henry Berry.

"'You done it, Harry,' said young Thom, 'all by yourself you catched every Yankee in sight. No wonder they can't whup no dumb Rebel White boys, being caught by a squoke like you.'

"'We was sleeping!' said another Yankee in defense.

"'You sure was,' said Steve. 'Maybe if we trade you to the Conscriptors we can quit hiding and go home.'

"'There is no sense in harming us,' said Lieutenant Wright. 'We share a common dilemma.'

'We're your dilemma,' said Steve. 'Don't get too chumlike.'

"'We're both hunted,' said Owen Wright. 'We both have to feed ourselves. We're both in mortal danger,' he said directly to young Henry Berry. 'Let us work together.'"

"'Shut him up, Harry,' said Steve. 'He's just talking himself untied to get hold of a gun and shoot their way out.'"

"'What good are you to us?' Henry Berry asked Lieutenant Wright."

"'You hear me, Harry?' shouted Steve. Henry Berry gestured him quiet."

"Owen Wright went on. 'There are enough of us to bring considerable affliction upon your Conscriptors.'"

"'I don't like the smell of his talk,' said Steve. 'Can't understand half.'"

"'It's Yankee,' said Thom."

"'Being Yankee don't mean they can't learn talking,' said Steve."

"'Let him be heard,' said Henry Berry. "Maybe he'll say something. More'n you two are doing.'"

"Steven resorted to the primal threat of all elder brothers: 'Pa goin to whap your butt if you start consorting with the enemy.'"

"'Young man,' said Lieutenant Owen Wright, 'we are not the enemy. We fight this War to free people like you. With your knowledge of the area and with our numbers, we can steal everything that moves from every White in the county.'"

"'What do we do with it all?' asked Henry Berry."

"'Hear him out,' said Steve, who liked this part."

"'Eat what's to be eaten,' Owen Wright answered Henry Berry. 'Give some to your family, and burn everything else just to gnash White teeth.'"

"'Oughtn't do that to White folk,' said Thom."

"'Hush, Thomas,' said Steven."

"'President Lincoln's doing it all over the South,' said Owen Wright."

"'They'll get him,' said Thom. 'They'll get us.'"

"'Hush you, Thomas!' said Steven."

"'They won't get us if we work together,' said Owen Wright."

"'Maybe we don't want to be thieves,' said Thom."

"'Thomas what-the-hell-your-middle-name Lorry,' yelled Steve. 'Maybe you want to be starved to death along with Momma and Poppa on account maybe you don't want to be thieves.'"

"'Thieving's wrong,' said Henry Berry."

"'Make up your mind!' yelled Steven."

"'Hush you, Steven,' said Thom. 'Henry Berry knows the Bible. If he says thieving's sin, then hush you or not, it's sin.'"

"'So are wars,' said Owen Wright, 'but sometimes there's no choice.'"

"'Stealing ain't easy,' said Henry Berry."

"Owen Wright pressed on: 'We escaped near-naked from the Rebel prison in South Carolina with not a stick to hold in our hands. We survived by nothing else but stealing.'"

"'Harry, you know what Momma do if we steal one thing?' demanded Thom."

"'How about what will she do if she got nothing to eat come winter?' said Steven. 'Anyway, how she goin to know we stealing?'"

I'm goin to tell," said Thom.

"You'll be stealing right along with us."

Thom let that sink in.

Steve, as elder brother, looked thoughtful. Thom and the Yankees watched him for a clue to how he would decide, the whole proposition seeming to ride upon his decision. "Good," said small Henry Berry.

"I ain't decided yet," said Steve.

"If you hadn't already decided yes," Henry Berry said, "you'd be yelling 'no no no.' So let's untie these fellers and get planning." Steve nodded.

Henry Berry, Thom, and Steve assumed responsibility for selecting which farm would be first. Owen Wright was responsible for logistics.

Capture was not the only fear. Young Henry Berry knew that merely being identified would bring retaliation against their parents. And if the Yankees were identified, it would bring Rebel troops. So they executed preliminary raids, puzzling farm wives by stealing wash-line clothes for disguises. Then Henry Berry, Steve, and a private named Smith prepared for a real raid near Shoe Heel, far from the wealthy sections of the county. Smith, knowing the Lowerys were Indians, kept his hat tight on his young head for fear of scalping.

Henry Berry and Steven blackened their faces and Smith browned his. Lieutenant Wright's maps of escape routes seemed needlessly elaborate for so tiny a raid, the intended booty being only a side of pig and barrel of flour that Thom had scouted on the premises. But logistics demanded the full trappings. Steven and Thom thought such detail and risk for a pork chop was appalling.

At the farm, Steven, Henry Berry, and Private Smith accosted the terrified planter, his family, and both slaves. "What you want to do? What you want to do?" hollered the wife.

"We gwine thieve every shanty in dis heah corner of de county," blacked Henry Berry. "One herebouts every night from now on, hear? And den we comes back and we does it again."

Black Steve said "Mmm, hmmm." Indian Smith nodded gravely. They loaded flour and the hog side onto the farmer's cart, and hitched up his mule.

The farmer begged, "Take what you want but not the mule, not the mule, and you don't want that cart, you'll get caught with it," making good sense.

"We brings dem back," promised Henry Berry, and the outlaws hauled off their first booty.

Back in the swamp his promise was debated. The Yankee position: returning the cart and mule was risky. But Steve, to maintain some position as senior brother, took Henry Berry's part. "Harry's right. A man's got to come after his mule. And he's shamed if he don't come after his cart."

Northern farmers being a different sort, the Yankees didn't agree. But Henry Berry said he would not keep a man's means of livelihood. If they did so, he said, "We're bad as them."

"That's what we're trying to be," said Owen Wright.

Henry Berry returned the mule and cart himself. The farmer was waiting in a tree with shotguns. Afterwards, Owen Wright said, "We warned you!"

Henry Berry said, "He shot, missed, hit his mule's behind, then missed me again but killed his mule. He had to haul his cart back to the barn his own dumb self. Probably run over his foot doing it."

"How'd it feel being shot at?" asked Thom, full of excitement.

"Bad."

The new outlaws stowed their forlorn haul: a chunk of rotten meat, and flour crawling with more animal matter than was on the meat bone.

Next night they raided four farms ten miles from Shoe Heel. News of last night's outrage had crossed the county by now. Henry Berry told the raiders, "Don't shoot no one, the men will be off guarding Shoe Heel." And indeed, the raiders encountered only women, children, and slaves. Just one farmer had left a gun, and the raiders stole it. Afterwards the raiders sorted what to keep from what to give to Mary Cuombo and Allen Lowery. There was more than could be used. "Sell it in town," said Thom.

"No," said Steve, but before he could say why not, a sack of flour he was pulling off a wagon hauled off and whaled him in the stomach. Steve dropped the sack. It kicked him again. "There's a person concealed in this particular sack," Steve announced when he regained his breath from the stomach kick. The sack writhed on the ground. The others gathered. Steve poked it with his toe and the sack jerked violently.

"It's a devil or some kind of thing," said Thom.

"Open it and we'll find out," said Owen Wright.

"Not if it's a devil," said Thom.

"Wait," said Henry Berry, and pulled his hat over his face. The others followed his example. A Yankee who believed in devils only a little inched towards the sack and was about to open it when a Pennsylvania soldier named Tannenbaum said, "It ain't a devil, it ain't nothing but a girl I took for us."

"You what?" said Owen Wright.

"I seen this girl and she was pretty and I thought we could have her."

"Are you simple, Isaac Tannenbaum? I ought to shoot your balls into that tree." A soldier from Boston (who was probably an editor) respectfully reminded Owen Wright that a female was present, within the sack, and that the Lieutenant might wish to consider his language. "She's in a darn canvas sack, how can she hear?" hissed Owen Wright, but he did not swear again. "Scoop her up and put her back where you got her, and don't lay one finger on her or I will travel personally to Pennsylvania and find your momma and your sisters and show them how we do in Maine."

"Don't talk on my Momma," said the abductor from Pennsylvania.

"You want me to write her what you have done?"

"No sir."

"We're trying to fight a war here, not send ourselves straight to hell the minute a Reb musketball gets us."

"I just done it for all of us, I thought it'd be nice." No

one said anything to support the boy, but the ripple of assent was unmistakable.

"Well surely it would be nice," said Owen Wright, softening, "but that's the kind of nice you think about at night, son, and to yourself."

But Lieutenant Wright had misinterpreted. This was not a licentious abduction. Thom suggested to me (perhaps having had similar feelings) that Tannenbaum, just fifteen, simply missed his mother.

Tannenbaum moved, as ordered, towards the sack.

"Wish it'd been a devil, I'd like to have seen one," mourned young Thom.

"We'll find you a devil some other time, boy," said Steven.

Tannenbaum hauled the sack towards a cart. A head popped out and Tannenbaum was looking into the face of a boy his own age. "You ain't no girl!" said Tannenbaum, young Yankee face to face with a young Southerner.

"I know I ain't."

"You was when I put you in there."

"I was not."

"Well you got a dress on."

"No I do not."

"You surely do."

"I am not wearing no dress."

"I seen it, that's why I thought you was a girl, it was dark and I didn't see your ugly damn lying face."

"I ain't wearing no dress." But he seemed less than eager to come out of the sack to prove it. Owen Wright thought it time to intervene.

"Why are you wearing a dress, boy?" he said.

"I ain't."

"It's all right if you are, just say why." The boy almost started to cry, but set his jaw and spoke: "I seen everybody with guns and all, and I thought no one'd shoot a dress."

"Smart as a Yankee dollar! Be proud you thought it up! And right in the middle of a raid!" Henry Berry listened carefully as Lieutenant Wright went on: "We need a smart man like you."

"For true?" said the boy in the sack.

"Come out so we can swear you in!"

Henry Berry took in every nuance of how Lieutenant Wright was proceeding. The boy slunk down in the sack, turtling out of sight, refusing to be seen in a dress. "Private Tannenbaum!" cried Wright.

"Sir!" snapped the Pennsylvania boy, deprived now of all dignity.

"Well done!" snapped Owen Wright, giving him his dignity right back. "We needed such a man, and you brought us one. Excellent."

"Sir?"

"Good job!"

"Thank you, sir!"

Henry Berry wondered if it really was this easy. Now the lesson turned complex:

"Private Tannenbaum, I won't forget this. Now. Your trousers."

"Sir?"

"Your pants, Private Tannenbaum, they're needed.

Don't blemish your day of achievement by failing us now."

"I'm – there's nothing beneath, sir."

"Yes, we will all take that into account, but our new recruit must present himself and we need you to make that possible."

Lieutenant Wright could have forced the pants off Tannenbaum at gunpoint, so young Henry Berry knew this was a sophisticated maneuver.

"Understand me, Tannenbaum?"

"Yes, sir," Tannenbaum said in misery.

Lieutenant Wright announced to his men, "Corporal Tannenbaum, who has served us well this day, will now pass his britches to the new recruit." Ex-Private Tannenbaum did it proudly.

That night, the young Henry Berry went off to think. He played Owen Wright's maneuvers over and over in his mind, like a new toy. And he had problems to solve: how to keep his mother, Mary Cuombo, from finding out, how to keep from getting caught, and how to give plunder to his family without making it obvious to the world who the thieves were. Life had become a complex of dilemmas. Yet from Wright he was learning to turn the dilemmas to advantage. Next day Henry Berry took his brothers into the swamp away from the Yankees. "There's something good here," he tried to explain, "if we can figure it out."

Steven never grasped the concept and Thom didn't care, but Henry Berry tried to explain the value of turning a bad situation to such great advantage that, in the long run, it was good that it occurred in the first place. As they were telling me about this, I told them what my mother said: "When it rains on your garden party," my mother used to say, "sell umbrellas." Thommy asked what a garden party was. Steven asked about umbrellas.

Not even New Yorkers of commerce and politics fathom the principle, yet in these swamps an unschooled Indian boy saw one example and mastered it. When he could not explain it to Steven or Thom, he came to understand that arguing and explaining serve no purpose. People follow if they wish and won't if they don't. Henry Berry led his brothers back to camp. The Yankees were burying the excess spoils. "Stop," said Henry Berry.

"Don't be tempted," said Owen Wright. "We have enough to eat and to feed your family. Don't covet the rest merely because it's there."

"We give it away," said young Henry Berry.

"To whom?"

"We're not poor of poor folk."

"That's the quickest way to get caught!" said Owen Wright, the teacher but not a master.

"We won't get caught if we got friends telling us who's coming and when and where," said Henry Berry. "And whoever we feed, they're our friends."

"Besides," crowed Thom, "if everyone gets stuff, not just Ma, then nobody will figure out it's us, especially not Ma." Henry Berry was already too smart a leader to say that was the whole point.

"Are you saying," asked Owen Wright, who with

those three words descended from leader to colleague, "to rob the rich and give to the poor?"

"No sense the other way round," said Steve. "The poor got nothing to steal and the rich don't need it." Young Henry Berry let Steve claim ownership of the notion, knowing there was no better way to make him agree with it.

Henry Berry had it now: the power of saying little. The less you say, the more others believe your ideas to be their own, so they accept and even fight for them. I always dealt with my Editor like that and it always worked (except with regard to my semi-colons; which now and then he incorrectly alters.)

This was the founding of the Lowery band. And petty thievery would have been the limit of their activities, but for a man named James P. Barnes.

EIGHT

BORDERING ALLEN LOWERY'S farm was the great Back Swamp, part of the Carolina swamplands' thousands of square miles. For a century, Indian planters had been draining the swamplands foot by foot by digging ditches leading to government-built channels that emptied into the Lumber River. Once the land was dry, it had to be cleared a tree at a time, a stump at a time, and it was slow. The swamp's cypress trees have moisture-proof armor shells so they can grow up through the water. Each shell takes a family months to chip and burn away, so clearing a few acres can take years. Whites, able to buy the more expensive and higher land that has no cypress, can drain and plant almost right away.

Allen Lowery's low fields lay between the Back Swamp and the higher fields of Mr. James P. Barnes, a White man who had been Allen's friend for decades. They hunted and fished together, and shared the labor of their fields and the care of their families. They would have become aging comrades, withering side by side into eternity, rocking on the porch of the one on Monday, the other on Tuesday, and so on down the years. But it was not to be.

The root cause was the young gang's decision to target all wealthy White property-owners, including Barnes. Steven and Thom objected to raiding their neighbor Barnes until Henry Berry warned that sparing their neighbor would bring suspicion upon them. Yet because Barnes had been a good White uncle to the boys, the Lowerys refused to participate personally in the raids against him – so they never knew what the Yankees took from him.

Among other things, the Yankees took two of Barnes's hogs. They hauled them back to the swamp to slaughter, salt, and store with carcasses from other farms. A month later, the brothers randomly piled carcasses onto requisitioned wagons to be left secretly at the Lowery home.

The next week Mary Cuombo invited neighbor Barnes to dinner so he could share in the bounty they had received, she knew not from whom. She also sent to the swamp to invite her boys.

Every other poor family in the county knew whom to thank for the gifts of food, clothing, and household necessities. They expressed their gratitude by not telling Allen and his wife who the thieves were and by keeping the gang informed of the movements of the Conscriptors. By this same network, the young outlaws were also informed of the activities of the Home Guard Militia, a pack of rich cowards who had their own way of supporting their beloved War: a White boy from a poor family would be hired to go into battle using the rich man's name. In this way the rich avoided their duty and stayed home to spout patriotism and rush around the neighborhood chasing a few Indian brothers stealing corn. Robeson's Blacks and Indians gladly informed against this Home Guard and anyone else who might harm the outlaws—because the outlaws were depriving the White aristocracy of its only useful quality: its wealth. So young Henry Berry, Steven, and Thom knew when the Home Guard was too drunk to be dangerous and when the Conscriptors were at the far end of the county. This allowed the gang to come safely out of the swamp to raid or, in this case, to attend their family's feast.

Adding to the holiday pleasure would be Allen's brother George and George's three sons: Jarman the youngest, Wesley, and Peter. They had managed to avoid Conscription without hiding in the swamps.

At my desk, Henry Berry said, "I liked Uncle George."

"We all did," said Thom.

Uncle George was not so industrious as his older brother Allen, so he had more energy to make himself a pleasure to others. Allen worked thirteen unbroken hours before every evening meal, earning the love and respect of his family—but Uncle George earned their smiles. He would pick the youngest children up one after the other, pretend to break wind by a trick of his mouth, and then drop the child as if it stunk, sending every other child into screams of laughter that drew disapproval from the sour adults called parents. Uncle George was the favorite guest at any gathering.

Mary Cuombo prepared a fine outdoor feast and had her boys together again. They provided music. Neighbor

James P. Barnes brought two precious bottles of corn liquor, clear and strong enough to burn in a heaven-blue flame if anyone were wasteful enough to ignite it. It slid down the throat like warm honey and milk.

Uncle George brought every new joke in the county. For the whole evening he had everyone at a continual roar, tears of laughter cascading down the cheeks of the children and even the adults. When George let too much time pass between jokes, Henry Berry's young sisters would reach up and pull on George's lower lip to re-prime the well of mirth. Allen warned them not to twiddle the lip of a guest. Uncle George responded by thrusting out his lip and offering a tug to anyone who wanted.

To sit at my desk these eight years later and hear these hardened, murderous outlaws talk about the pleasure they took in their Uncle George! It was like remembering a childhood Christmas.

Mary Cuombo served pie after pie, each better than the one before. Red-berry, molly-berry, apple, grape-apple, and honey-nut was the order. Between each serving she poured her own pale-berry wine, a weak concoction compared to Barnes' liquor, but its delicate palate was remembered by the outlaws all these years later. It rinsed the mouth for the next pie and made new nestling room in stuffed bellies.

After drinking heavily, Barnes left for the outhouse. On the way, disoriented by his liquor, he fell into the garbage pit. There he found himself face down in refuse, where he came eye to eye with the detached ear of a pig.

He recognized the ear because in life it had been cut in a distinctive way by a fence wire.

Mr. Barnes rejoined the Lowerys as they were singing and eating the last pie. Mary Cuombo had saved him an unfairly large piece. He spoke. "Allen Lowery, a day has come I never expected to see." He brandished the pig's ear. George thought Barnes was telling a joke, and laughed. Barnes spoke again: "Allen Lowery, I know you had no hand in this. It can only be your sons and nephews, and now they have divided us. Tonight in ignorance I dined upon my own meat at your table." Allen leaned across the table to see the pig's ear. As he drew close Mr. Barnes produced in his other hand a pistol. "I leave your land and your poisoned hospitality forever. We are enemies. As for you," he said, sweeping an arc that included Henry Berry, Thomas, Steven, and George Lowery's three sons, "the Conscriptor will learn where you are. The law will drag you to the deadly breastworks at Wilmington!"

He marched into the darkness.

"These things were true?" demanded Mary Cuombo of her sons. "Weren't it us raised you up?" They said nothing. "Y'all had no right."

"Old Devil Scratch never before got in my house," said Allen.

"It wasn't old Scratch, Daddy," said Steven. "Only us doing what we got to." Like a staff, Allen Lowery's arm knocked his largest son backwards off his stool. Steven, though a head taller and pounds more, had no impulse to strike back.

Allen towered over his fallen son. "I'm shamed

account of you. All you." He stepped towards Thom and Henry Berry, arm raised. They did not raise a hand to defend themselves. He looked them nose to nose, the glow of corn liquor now perilous, and which would have been murderous to anyone but his own dear sons.

"We doing what we got to," Steve said from the ground. But Henry Berry said nothing. He had learned that explanation—like argument, like complaint, like logic—accomplishes nothing.

"Busts my heart," said Allen. His anger had given way to sadness, which would hurt him longer. "Let me believe it was old Devil Scratch, Gawd damn y'all. Go leave me be, and your Ma, too." He led Mary Cuombo into the cabin, shutting the door behind. Thom started after but Henry Berry held his arm. Uncle George moved into the darkness, ashamed, and Henry Berry's sisters went to the back door of the cabin to go in.

"Better come with us," Steven said to his cousins Jarman, Peter and Wesley, George's sons.

"First I got to tell Daddy we wasn't stealing," Wesley said. He feared his father's disapproval more than Conscription.

"Y'all will be stealing if you come with us, there's no choice," Steve said. Wesley started to argue but Henry Berry gestured for silence.

"You: that way," Henry Berry told his three cousins, pointing after their father, George. "Us: yonder," gesturing back at the swamp. "Come when you come." The cousins hurried after George. Henry Berry and his brothers stood in front of the cabin. After many moments the door opened and Mary Cuombo emerged.

She raised her face to be kissed by each son, then went in. A moment later the candle on the hearth went out.

Thom, trying not to cry, and Steven followed Henry Berry back into the night. From the darkened cabin Allen watched them go. Henry Berry took the road to the farm of Mr. Barnes, who met them on his porch, shotgun on his arm. "They hunt us to die in the pits at Wilmington," Steven said to him. "So we got to be hiding. We can't work a living in the swamp, so there ain't nothing to do but what we done. We didn't mean to harm you."

"What do you want?" Barnes said.

"We only..." But the expression of truth and good intent is a paltry thing. A man's pig is a man's pig. Without disrespect, Henry Berry quietly said, "We're sorry, Mr. Barnes."

Five nights later the young brothers and the Yankees carried out seven simultaneous raids netting foodstuffs, four excellent rifles, and ammunition. They returned to the Yankee's camp to sort the plunder, and then the brothers left for the Devil's Den where their Union allies could not go. Halfway there they encountered a looming figure silhouetted on a hilltop against the starred sky. They scattered, weapons ready.

"Talk to me, boys, it's George." They came out to their beloved uncle, who said, "They took Peter and Wesley to Wilmington. They'll die there." Thommy started to say something but George went on, "Ain't much, them two, nor Jarman either, but you know me, boys. What else I got?" His wife had birthed seventeen before dying with the eighteenth. Only Wesley, Peter and Jarman survived her cradle. George and his wife, a tiny death every year of their marriage, had consoled themselves knowing that they had each other and that whatever sorrow the Lord saw fit to give them, they would accept. One night the Lord saw fit to take his wife. George told her empty body farewell and took relief in the knowledge that there would be no more deaths of babies.

One day Thomas took me to a dirt hill behind George's old homestead. He showed me a row of old flat stones marking the children and a larger one for the mother, no inscription. No one I ever asked could remember her name.

The night he came to the swamp to curse the outlaws, he said, "I lay it in your faces, I who done you only fine and good."

"I'll get them back," said Henry Berry.

"You idiot chile, no one can fight them, else I would myself."

"I'll get them back."

"And they'll take them again, and you too. Damn you all for breaking my family."

"They'll be home for good."

George spat and started away. "You want to see our hide-out?" Thom called, reluctant for George to leave, but George did not stop.

"How did you find us?" called Steven after him.

George shouted back, "There's people in the world besides you that knows things and has done things."

Next day in Lumberton they learned that Mr. Barnes had conferred with a Mr. James Brantley

Harris, a notorious Conscriptor who had used Barnes' information to capture Wesley and Peter. Now Harris was leading the Home Guard Militia after Henry Berry, Thomas, and Steven. Thom suggested sending the Union soldiers to get their cousins from Wilmington. But the Yankees could not reveal themselves on so dangerous a venture. Other strategy was necessary.

"Treating our cousins like poor dirt Blacks!" Steven said.

"Yes!" Henry Berry congratulated Steven for the solution.

"What?" said Steven. Henry Berry said his words suggested a strategy.

"Right," Thom said, as if he understood.

Henry Berry explained: rich Whites easily bought themselves out of military service. "But our cousins ain't rich," said Thom.

"We are," said Henry Berry.

"We are?" said Thom.

They arranged with the Yankees to steal cash instead of food and goods. The Yankees would keep half; the rest would buy back George's sons. The money raids would begin in two nights with the new moon. Meantime the outlaws only had to avoid Harris and his men.

James Brantley Harris, a swaggering, red-faced bully, was the terror of Scuffletown Indians, whom he violated and beat at will. He was as mean to Whites. Everyone I interviewed had hated him and remembered their hate all these years later. As Conscriptor he had abused his power whenever his squalid morality saw fit. He was grossly fat, putrefyingly scented, and had only one set of clothes which, like himself, he never washed, even in summer. He had thick features, tiny eyes, uncut whiskers of dirty red, and nasal congestion that impaired his breathing. His great weight smothered his vocal apparatus, causing him to speak high and softly—though all he ever said was mean.

Harris's mistreatment of people was limited only by what he could get away with. Harris would use any maneuver on anyone's wife or daughter, White, Indian or Negro. When his advances or money could not persuade a woman, he threatened to hurt her children. If there were no children he used his fists. Harris relied on shame and the threat of murder to prevent his victims from accusing him, so no husband or brother knew to pursue him for revenge. Harris especially chose females left behind by the very wretches he conscripted to Wilmington, carefully sending the men whose women had pleased his eye.

One frequent victim of Harris's violence, a comely Indian girl, was being courted in more traditional fashion by George Lowery's son Wesley.

As the outlaws were telling me the Barnes story, Shoe-Maker John, who had slowly warmed to speaking to me, enjoyed providing the nastiest details. "Harr's was mean," said Shoe-Maker John, a true gossip. "Harr's hump on one gal, then another. Wesley Lorrie's gal told Wesley what Harris done to her. Wesley got a knife and go prowling. So Marz Harr's got to do something. Harr's had a hunger for Wesley's gal and wanted more of that pie."

Neighbor Barnes knew that Conscriptor Harris wanted to get rid of Wesley Lowery, and that Harris wanted to ingratiate himself with rich Whites by conscripting the Lowery outlaws. But this was not Barnes's revenge. Instead, his revenge came the next night after the outdoor feast when Mary Cuombo went to Barnes's home, hoping that a private, friendly word in the sober light of God's day would restore her neighbor's affection. Thinking Barnes would be friendlier if she went alone, Mary Cuombo left Allen in the road and walked up the path. Barnes was waiting in his doorway, shotgun ready. He said, "You're a woman, Mrs. Lowery, and it's not right of me, but if you say one word in defense of your outlaw brood I will shoot you for trespass, so please leave my property, ma'am." She had never been spoken to in that way before. Hearing it now from the man who had been her friend and protector for twenty years, she stood dumbfounded. Barnes spoke again: "It's not your fault, but you have to leave." He swung the barrel towards her. She was not frail, but she had never had a rifle aimed at her. Shaking, she tried to go but fell, dizzy. She raised a hand to beg a moment's grace. Barnes took her gesture for defiance, and shot her arm. Overcome with terror, the woman who had never let herself lose her dignity even within her own walls scrambled away on her belly through the dirt. Allen Lowery wrapped her bleeding arm and brought her home.

She told her daughters she had burned her arm cooking. But Barnes had a slave, a field hand also named James, whose family had benefitted from the outlaws' generosity. Mary Cuombo had cared for his sick wife when Barnes would have let her die during a busy planting season. The slave knew about the distant, tantalizing prospect of freedom that hung on the outcome of the War. And on December 11, 1864, he saw his master shoot Mary Cuombo.

Though terrified of the swamps, the slave James ventured in after the Lowery boys. The Union soldier who found him was suspicious but unable to shoot so shaking and miserable a wretch, and sent for Henry Berry. James made his report, received an apology and reward from the Union soldier, and was sent home assured he had done the right thing.

On December 12, 1864, Mr. James P. Barnes was going to the Clay Valley Post Office, a distance of one mile, when he was shot dead. The gang never talked about it, though they described every other murder and crime attributed to them (including some they didn't do, such as when Kentucky banks were emptied by the Jesse James gang disguised as Indians and calling themselves Lowerys). Thus, I went to the County Recorder's office, where the journals of deeds and misdeeds came under the authority of one Mr. Groone, an unpleasant man but one who did his job with rare skill. I hitched Patrick Lowery's horse to the courthouse rail. People stared as I dismounted, so to demonstrate my command of the situation I made a show of affection by pattying his ears and saying, "Wait here." He looked as if he would bite me. I escaped down into Mr. Groone's catacombs, damp-walled offices with sawdust floors, beneath the Court House. The ceiling, lower than Mr.

Groone's full height, had given him a habitual stoop. Two oil lamps burned all day with no fresh air, coating documents, desks, shelves, and Mr. Groone himself with oil residue. The thin cigars he smoked seemed more to protect himself from the bad air than for pleasure. On his outside door hung a sign: "Prepare To State Your Business."

He sat at an ink-stained table, his thinness emphasized by an odd angle of light from the lamps. He was so tall that, seated, he looked me face to face though I was standing. Everything about him – even his voice – seemed sharpened, as if to better penetrate the atmosphere. "Yes?" he inquired. I was an intrusion.

"I seek information."

"Information is what I have," he said. I asked for the records on the matter of Mr. James P. Barnes, deceased. "Despicable man," said Mr. Groone, and looked as if he wished to spit. He didn't explain his opinion.

"I wish to read the records."

"You can't," said Mr. Groone.

"This is the Office of Public Record?"

"Aye," he answered.

"Then I may read whatever I have a mind to read," I said. "Despite the efforts that ended seven years ago, North Carolina remains in the Union; therefore a citizen may see what a citizen wishes to see."

"Aye." I saw a window he might have opened, but apparently he preferred his oil and smoke even in this hundred degrees of summer. "You are welcome to look at anything you wish to read, but it will do you no good."

"I will judge what will do me good and what won't."

He cast an expression I had seen recently, though I did not remember where until he disappeared into his shelves, when I recalled it was upon Patrick Lowery's horse. A moment later Mr. Groone came out of the gloom and placed a dusty volume before me. The sharp handwriting was obviously his, but could have been Chinese for all I could read. "I said it would do you no good and I believe you will agree." The penmanship could be read by no man – except, he said, by his nephew, whom he had taught, and was thus the only person who could succeed to this position when Mr. Groone passed on. "The carpenter bequeaths tools and craft to his son. Might not I do the same for a nephew?" It seemed right, but what good were records if only Mr. Groone and his nephew could read them? "I will tell you what they say," he said.

"But then I must rely upon the truth of your telling."

"No more than you must rely upon the truth of my writing," he said, sensibly enough. I asked him to tell me about Barnes. He turned up the lamp wick, read to himself, shut the book, and turned down the wick.

"Well?" I said.

"Dead," said Mr. Groone, and stopped.

"It takes no book from the shelf to tell me this," I said.

"He was despicable." He stopped again.

"Is something wrong?"

"I am embarrassed that I cannot be certain of the date. I hope it is not crucial to you."

"I have heard December 12, 1864," I said.

"What someone has *heard*," he said as if the word now had no stature, "is, in every case, gossip and common report. This," he angled a sharp finger at the book, "is record."

"Then why cannot you document the date?" I asked.

He showed me that the date was written down, but admitted that it was illegible even to him. "I was not careful. It may have been the date you say," he said, peering, "or earlier or later, but indeed December, and eighteen sixty some-year." He shrugged and launched into the story: "Traveling on Chicken Road was Jamey Barnes, a mean sort, going to work in Clay Valley where he was Postmaster. He was accosted by party or parties unknown, who came with ferocious look or looks, and utterances of unfriendliness. He…"

"I beg your pardon," I said, "But facial expressions? And utterances? How are these recorded if the parties are unknown?"

He heaved a great sigh, opened the book, read, shut it, and said, "…who came and shot him."

"Nothing about expression or utterance?" I asked.

"This is skeleton," he said, tapping the page, "but a man can add flesh and blood, no?"

Instantly recognizing our kinship, I encouraged him to proceed in his own way. He hurried on with relish: "Mr. Barnes greeted the shot with expressions of surprise, crying, 'O, and would ye shoot a man all unarmed?' Such ejaculation was answered with another shot, then another, then another—" He glanced at the page, "—and another." Mr. Groone stood and continued: "One of the grinning accosters looked down upon their bleeding prey, cried, 'Thus to you!' and pinned a note to the dying man's coat." At this, Mr. Groone galloped—yes, galloped—into the gloom and shelves, rummaged, and returned with a yellowed scrap of stained paper, upon which was scrawled: "LEAV US BE." He looked in his book and said, "That's all there is."

"But the murderers?"

"The neighbors who found him say his face was shot away and he spoke through a mouth full of blood. They thought or perhaps wished he said 'Henry Lowery' before he died, 'who deserves not to walk the green earth.'"

"Did Lowery do it?"

"How would I know? I record," he said sadly.

I thanked this vat of gloom for his help and said I hoped to seek his services again. I returned to the Devil's Den, still with no details of this murder. "Ask Miz Rhody," Shoe-Maker John suggested. Afraid to seem too eager, I said she would have little to say. "Good, you got me believing you don't want to see Miz Rhody, so now you can go see her without no worry." Skin so dark, smile so white, and no fool.

Next morning, Rhody answered my knock. She looked at me, then down and away for a moment, then back into my face. It was to accustom her cabin eyes to the bright sun but it made me breathe shallow. She expressed pleasure to see me, which I hoped was genuine but could not tell. We exchanged pleasantries, thrice mentioning weather. I inquired after her mother-in-law, Mary Cuombo. I finally brought up the subject of my visit.

While she responded, her older children listened, for children love tales, especially of their poppa. She sewed as she spoke. Her pretty voice and elegant words enchanted me: "Mister Barnes was walking in the road. Along come Harry: Mister Henry Berry Lowery, sixteen years old, and his brothers Thomas and Steven. Harry shoot Mister Barnes, didn't let his brothers. Mister Barnes fell, buckshot here and here." She touched her side and her breast. Sally Ann's eyes, like Henry Delaney's and mine, were wide. Infant Neelyann napped under her Momma's skirt. "Harry say something from the Bible of righteousness and vengeance and blood of the wicked. Mister Barnes said, 'Don't shoot again, I am a dying man.'"

Rhody's daughter Sally Ann, at six the oldest, cried out, "Whap off his head!" Henry Delaney screeched agreement.

"Hush that, Sally Ann. It ain't nice," chided Rhody, but to please the girl she repeated Barnes's plea: "'Don't shoot again, I am a dying man.'"

Sally Ann gleefully cried: "Whap his head." Henry Delaney squealed.

Rhody pointed a hush finger and continued: "Brother Thomas look down and said, 'You shot Momma.' Thom's wicked anytime he's riled, but thinking about Mr. Barnes shooting his Momma, he could hardly talk.

"Then Harry say, 'Wesley Lowery,' naming the cousin Mr. Barnes caused to be conscripted to

Wilmington, and Harry shoot into Mr. Barnes' leg from this far off." She indicated the distance between us, which was less than I had realized so I moved. "Brother Steven aimed, but Harry didn't want anyone a killer but his own self. Barnes got one wound more than he got hands to cover, and Harry holler down, 'Peter Lowery,' Harry's other cousin, and bang! Barnes's other leg. I don't got to say '*Mr.* Barnes' no more, ain't enough of him left.

"Then Harry aim his shotgun, and Barnes hollered, 'It is enough, it is enough.'" She spoke Barnes' words in a comic voice, and if the description had not been so frightening I would have laughed along with the children. Rhody continued, "Henry Berry shoot in his face and no cheek or tooth was left." Sally Ann imitated the face. Rhody said Barnes died right then. She took a three-stringed hollow stick off the wall, to the delight of her children, and strummed as she sang:

The horrifying story
How old Jamie Barne come dead
His cruel and bloody murder
On my husband's handsome head

His name ain't nothing special
Though you might of heard it told
Was Henry Berry Lowery
Killed Barnes so mean and cold

They met Barnes on the highway
Below the noonday sun
Harry shoot him with a pistol

Harry shoot him with a gun

Oh Barnes why did you it?
Ain't I always been your friend?
Harry shoot him one more time
Worse than man can mend.

Little Sally Ann joined, frail and lovely with her mother's hearty voice:

They dug them in the red dirt
They buried him right deep
Harry watched to see him lowered
"I'm glad you ain't asleep."

Let this be a warning
Don't do my Harry wrong
Or maybe I'll be singing
'bout you in my next song.

I never wanted wife or children. But with that gentle bloody duet, Neelyann the pretty babe asleep beneath her mother's skirt, boy-child Henry Delaney tugging Rhody's sleeve for another tune, and the warmth of this family in the snug cabin, a longing entered my head.

Back at the Devil's Den, Henry Berry would not verify Rhody's tale. He did not even tell me the Bible words he'd have said, had such a moment occurred.

NINE

WHETHER OR NOT young Henry Berry killed Barnes, the Outlaw's admirers and enemies chose to believe he did. To his admirers, it was his first avenging heroism; to his enemies, his first barbarism. To both, it was the dry tinder that ignited hotter flames in the Old North State than ever did the Civil War.

The death of Barnes avenged the shotgun wounding of Mary Cuombo and the conscription of George's sons. All that remained was to get George's sons back from Wilmington.

No one knew the bearded young minister in gray suit and collar who stepped from the train in Wilmington. Within an hour of arrival he presented his guileless face in the office of General Earl Marion Hogge. The General soon found his official coffers (or himself) wealthier by precisely one-half the amount recently stolen from certain White citizens of Robeson county.

"Whatever else I say of Harry, he did get my boys Wesley and Peter home like he promised," the elderly George Lowery told me years later. George's sons returned with furlough papers signed by General Hogge himself, praising their lengthy service for which the grateful Confederacy now granted them permanent release. "They were back and we were happy," George told me. "But just when we thought they were safe, come the worst. And then the Almighty's arrows was in me, the poison drink up my spirit, and God set Himself hard against me. I still ain't found out what I done wrong. Maybe I slept drunk one time in church. I don't know why it came out that way with my boys."

It came out that way because the county was poisoned.

Yet for a moment, a miracle brought his boys home. The bearded minister who had visited General Hogge in Wilmington now came to Robeson county to visit Conscriptor Harris. He gave Harris the General's written directive that for the good of the Confederacy, George Lowery's two sons were now returned to the care of their family where they—and their young brother—were to be left alone. As Harris was reading the instruction, the Minister excused himself. Having completed all his earthly business, he returned to his maker and Henry Berry returned to his swamp.

Harris had no financial regret over the Lowery brothers' return, having already been paid his Conscriptor's fees. But Harris continued using the girl beloved of Wesley, and the newly returned Wesley was making mortal threats. Harris heard rumors that Wesley had contracted Yellow Fever in Wilmington and was planning to come close some dark night to infect him. Harris also heard that Wesley had purposely infected one or another of the other women with whom Harris consorted. The gang assured me that Wesley never had Yellow Fever, nor would have infected an innocent girl just to get Harris. But Harris could judge only by what he himself would do in Wesley's place, so he lived in fear.

Harris examined his women for the tinge of jaundice and demanded to see their water (even those whom he took by force) for albumin secretion. Only after satisfying himself in this manner did he satisfy himself in the other.

According to his widow, he stopped sleeping. He lay sighing and terrified of the Yellow Fever, because even monumental wickedness does not make a man brave. He drank more than usual and took greater refuge in his other vices. Extreme circumstances don't change a man; they reinforce what he is. Thus, one night, drunk and scared, he beat his wife so badly she could not see. Then he went out to find Wesley. He watched George Lowery's house until falling drunk asleep. George found him at sunrise, poked him awake, and said, "Believe me, Mr. Harris, you don't scare me, because I have got nothing to lose except what I'll defend to my last blood. Before I let you hurt my boys I'll face you and the whole worst you can do."

Standing up to the most dangerous White man in Robeson county took extraordinary courage; Henry Berry was not the only remarkable Lowery. George was another. And Allen. Mary Cuombo once told me, "Some say I married for Allen Lorrie's money, or his good strong arm or his land. No. I met Allen one day when he was building. I see him and stop to watch. He take this piece of pine or what he had, cut it here, cut it there, and put it with another piece. It fit but not exact. So he cuts more here and more there, works an hour matching, until they look like they together back in the tree. Working too hard to notice a stupid girl looking. Pretty soon I got to go home, so I wiggle so he'll look but he's working the next piece. I turn around and walk and never plan to see him again. He got no time to look at this gal even though I wasn't as painful to see as some. So I go but my head gets away and turns back. And he's looking. Course as soon's I turn he looks back to his wood like he never saw me. So I come the next day, and Lord, what! After all that work making one piece fit another piece like I said, and making a whole wall like that, what did he do? He covered it all over. No need of matched pieces. He covered them up and you can't see them. And he ain't looking at me, like I wasn't there growing down feet roots all yesterday and today like a fool. And there's no one but him and me, no congregation fighting for his attention. So I guess I might talk to the fool and I say, 'Makes no sense, mister!' He looks right at me, and oh, he has him a look, fifty years ago that look, he looks and he says . . ."

She stopped, jaw tight. I should have looked away. She went on. "He smiles, being he was a nice man, always nice the whole time I had him. He smiles and say, 'Beg your pardon, ma'am, what do you say?'

"Starting right then, that man have my whole heart. I stood like a pine tree dropping needles and gawping, staring like a child at circus. Finally I say, 'Fool!'

"He says, 'Pardon, ma'am?' No one ever called me

ma'am before, and no one called me nothing but ma'am ever since.

"But I still say, 'What kind of fool does all that work and then covers it so nobody sees? Makes no sense.' I always got to have my say. Now mind, in my head I'm already cooking him suppers for fifty years, it didn't take one more thing. I was chopped down, chopped up, and burnt to ashes by then.

"And he says, 'You don't see inside, and I don't, and Mr. Locklear don't. But we ain't the only ones looking.'

"I say, 'Who then?'

"He says, 'Somebody else.'

"I said 'OOOO,' figuring it out."

She leaned close to me. "This man, he thinks the Lord got nothing to do all day but watch Allen Lorrie make a wall. But that wall is the best one anybody ever made. When I go by that house I know what's inside behind the outside, and that is the difference between a Lorrie and everyone else. General Sherman come and burnt everything, but when he saw what Allen built, he said, 'Leave it, boys, that's Mr. Lorrie's work, nothing like it from here to home!' The Yanks tipped their hats and walked by. If they'd asked for Mr. Lorrie, he was new in his grave that very day."

"And every Lorrie's special someways, like Allen. Even little Jarman, George's littlest. Like Allen with wood, Jarman with books. He'd work for White folk all day just to borrow a book at night. Even went down under the Court House for books. Jarman come see me every week, bring something, maybe nothing but a leaf he found or some other silly, but something. He'd no more come with empty hands than with eleven fingers."

"Jarman go down under the courthouse, read, listen to that poor man tell the stories in his books, and then he'd come back and tell me. Then I tell Miss Rhody and she makes them into her damn lalala singing, but that ain't poor Jarman's fault. And now Jarman's in them books himself. The man who killed Jarman, devils scratch the skin off his fat hide every night, and if I knew how, I'd send salt for Satan to pour on him. Because the Lorries are special, mister. Allen, Jarman, George. And my boys. Who hurts a Lorrie knows not what they bring down on theirselves, good Lord willing or no."

Mr. Groone remembered Jarman Lowery. "Aye, he'd come, sit, read. All the law books and county acts and then wanted to read what I write in the record. He could make no more of my handwriting than you, so I told him what it said and he remembered every word. Lord in Heaven, I thought, record this: if the North wins and makes Blacks into lawyers, this injun mulatto stands ahead of the line.

"One day I was home sick. Jarman knocked. Nobody ever comes so I fetched my gun. He'd come visiting, and brought me a fistful of colored pebbles. I asked what he thought I wanted with such foolishness, protesting they were pretty but I have no place for nice things. I asked if he wanted a glass of water. Aye he did, and he set a while, and I lay down too sick to tell him any stories from the records, so he told me one. Then he asked,

'Who takes care of you when you're sick, who makes your food?' I said that full-grown-up people take care of themselves."

Mr. Groone walked in slow circles through the gloom of his office. "I am a private man. But he wanted to bring food that night. Well, being a gentleman alone, it is true I had nothing to eat. But I said I never allow anyone in when I am sick. He said I needed food and he would get it. Going, he offered to take the pebbles but I said please leave them for me, thank you."

Mr. Groone stopped speaking and sat. After a while he said I must go. He turned down the desk lamp, leaving himself silhouetted. I offered to walk him home to hear the story's conclusion en route; he said I was welcome to return during office hours. "I don't mind walking with you, Mr. Groone," I said.

"Tomorrow, sir," he responded politely. "Please."

I excused myself and left. Next day I returned. "It was ungenerous of me to make you repeat your trip," he said. I said something about having to return for other reasons. This is southern etiquette, a mutually accepted lie. He re-established his official atmosphere by sitting erect and turning up the lamp. As if talking about a stranger, he said that Jarman told his father, George Lowery, that Mr. Groone needed supper. His father thought it was too late to go out again. Jarman gathered some baked meat from the fireplace and set out, his father calling after to stay in the shadows and be vigilant.

Mr. Groone read to me from the book: "According to the deposition of his father, at or about 9:55 p.m.,

Jarman was proceeding westerly along the old State Drain, wearing woolen shirt and cotton pants. Someone approached in the darkness and called 'Who's that?' George Lowery says his son knew to answer such a question by saying 'Lowery, sir.'

"The person then cursed, saying 'Damn you, Wesley Lowery,' Wesley being the name of his brother, and fired three times, hitting Jarman twice. The dying boy recognized his murderer. The murderer cursed Jarman for being the wrong Lowery and left, thinking him dead." Mr. Groone closed the book and said, "Jarman lived long enough to go to a cabin and tell what happened. But the killer he named had twenty witnesses he was elsewhere. In several places, in fact."

Realizing Mr. Groone wanted to be alone, I rose to go. As my hand was on the door, he spoke quietly: "Sir." I turned. Standing, he held a small sack. He emptied it, scattering in the lamp's light a dozen common swamp pebbles of various colors.

"They are pretty," I said, inadequately.

"Stone. Pieces of stone," said Mr. Groone. He had no more to say and I left. I was to return many times, but we never spoke of this visit.

During my many visits, Mr. Groone expressed enormous malice for every villain of every bad act he had recorded. He used such words as hateful, abhorrent, despicatory, loathsome, bestial, odious, monstrous, atrocious, heinous, and a compendium of others. In Alaska, Eskimos need forty-one different words to distinguish among their many varieties of snow. In

Robeson county, Mr. Groone needed twice that number for the varieties of evil he had to record. Yet for the murderer of Jarman Lowery, he used none, and did not speak the slayer's name.

TEN

I USED THE TOPIC of George Lowery's misfortunes as a reason to visit Rhody. We sat in the doorway while her children played at the edge of the swamp. My most pleasant moments with her were always these first few. She hummed softly. "A pretty melody," I said. "Is it your own?" She shrugged. "Are there words?"

"Maybe," she said. She tried a phrase and stopped. "Maybe not." She tried again and quit again. "Can't recall," she said, frustrated. "Yowl." She began humming again, leaving me to my thoughts. I thought what a time I would have bringing her to Brooklyn, to church, and then home for Sunday dinner, after which Rhody would ask my father for a cigar.

A man may circle the world, but unless bold he goes home only with knick-knacks.

Eventually I told Rhody I was here to learn the history of Jarman's murder. She said it was the most important matter I had asked about. She complained that newspapers were flawed and hoped my writing would not be, especially on this topic. I asked what flaw she meant. She plucked at her blouse and asked, "If I was murdered while I was wearing this, what would you write about the last thing I ever wore?"

"I don't know," I admitted.

"That's what I mean. Listen, Mr. Writer. If somebody's murdered, the newspaper just says someone shot someone, or whatever. That's all. But not what it was like, what it looked like, what was there. Newspapers only say who done it and what they done. See?" I said I did not. "Tell me about this," she said, and plucked again at her blouse.

"Yellow," I said, looking away.

"And?"

"Bright yellow and buttons. Brown buttons."

"What's it made of?"

"I'm afraid I . . ."

"Wood?"

"Cloth."

"Cotton," she said. "What kind of cotton?"

"I don't . . ."

"Well, yowl, look at the thing, why don't you do it?"

"This is not the sort of . . ."

She put an edge of her blouse in my hand. "Loose wove cotton," she said, "and you got to write that, or else everyone in the newspaper wears the same thing and every room's the same as every other and that broom's the same as this shoe!" All the adults in the South think they are editors. When my Editor retires he should come here. "What about that tree?" she said, pointing at a lolly.

"Tall."

"It orange?"

"It's kind of . . ."

"Green. Ain't it green?"

"Yes'm."

"So you got to say, 'the green tree, the big green ole tree with bark like an ole lady's knuckles and needles like teeth, the green tree!'"

"That's poetry, ma'am, not journalism," I said.

"Nothing wrong saying how something looks. How you write about people? 'The man in the road has two legs?'"

"I just write what happened. Or my Editor chops it out."

"Send him up here, I'll tell him chopping or not chopping. See, wait." She went inside and returned with a wooden bowl. "My Momma's. Got it from her Momma. What is it?"

"A bowl."

"Not 'a bowl.' My Momma was an entire person, so her bowl's different from some other bowl. If she killed a man with it, you got to say what kind of bowl, not 'just a bowl.' You got to say: a bowl of ash wood carved with a knife, see the scrapes? Look here, they stop where Grampa stopped scraping, then they start back here again. And over here it's wore down where Gramma, and then Momma, and then me held it fixing bread, don't look at *me*, Mr. Writer, look at *it*. Worn so smooth it slips, so Gramma tells Grampa make another one, but maybe he's too busy whittling sticks so she up and whomps his head some black night. And you dare write my Gramma killed Grampa with just a bowl? Yowl, Mister Writer, if I sung songs about *just* a killing and *just* a hanging, you'd think everyone in them was nekked and there's nothing to touch, the whole world's empty. That's newspaper writing."

Then she sang about Jarman's death:

Harris, oh Harris, put a boy in the groun',
For meanness, for meanness he took him on down.
He shot him one time, he shot him another,
Poor boy, oh poor boy, to die with no mother.

Though she'd given me no new information, I went back to the swamp to write more of Jarman.

The night after killing Jarman, Conscriptor James Harris surrounded George Lowery's cabin with twenty Home Guardsmen and kicked down the door. Inside were George and his two remaining sons, unarmed, as Indians by law had to be. Peter held a mule whip and Wesley brandished a shovel of embers from the fireplace, pathetic against twenty shotguns. Peter's mule whip was a stubbed twist of dark leather a foot and a half in length, thongs shredded and worn thin with use, the handle smoothed and blackened in the sweat of plowing. The charred shovel in which Wesley held embers was made of hardwood, the length of the mule whip, and dried splintery by the fireplace.

The night air blew cool through the doorway across which George Lowery and James Harris faced one another. Harris wore an old gray wool hat. "Evenin', Mr. Laury," came Harris's high, soft voice. "Say evenin' to Mr. Laury, gentlemen." The men in the doorway nodded. "What you want?" said George.

"You mad with me, Mr. Laury?" asked Harris. George said nothing. "I'm here to help you, Mr. Laury.

See, your boys is breaking the law, and I'm here to help before they get themselves in trouble."

"They're furloughed."

"George Laury, you angered at me? What I done to you?"

"You know what you done."

"No I don't, Mr. Laury, I just now walked in. Why you mad so quick?"

"You know," said George Lowery.

"You got no proof, Mr. Laury."

"Jarman said it was you." said George.

"Didn't say it to me. Didn't say it to nobody."

"People heard."

"Don't listen to a dying nigger."

"What do you want in my house?"

Harris smiled apologetically. "I have a requisition for these two."

"Furloughed. Show your papers, Wesley."

"Canceled," said Harris. "Orders come today."

"Let's see."

"By messenger."

"Where is he?"

"Back to Wilmington." One of Harris's men laughed, and Peter and Wesley were marched at gunpoint out of the cabin. Harris called to Wesley, "Injun boy, got a how-do for you." Wesley turned. "She say have a good time in Wilmington."

Wesley charged back into the cabin, head down. The guards raised their weapons but Harris waved them off. He stepped aside to let Wesley's momentum carry past him and towards the timbered mantel, then flung his own 300 pounds against the boy's back and crashed the boy's head into the wood. Wesley crumpled, his broken face a sheet of blood. "George Laury, I got to teach your boy how to treat a guest," said Harris, and dragged Wesley outside. His men kept George and Peter inside at gunpoint as they listened to the beating. Finally Harris came back in. He took George's church shirt from the wall and carefully wiped Wesley's blood off his knuckles, in case it carried Yellow Fever. "He didn't put up no fight. No wonder they won't make injuns into soldiers, we'd might as well give up." He threw the shirt into the fire. Wesley's blood sizzled. Harris motioned his men to remove Peter, who dropped the mule whip and walked out on his own. "This here's a military action, don't y'know," said Harris to George, "so I order you to stay inside. For your convenience, I'm leaving two guards to remind you. They will have to shoot if you go out."

"This ain't right, Mr. Harris," said George.

"Who promised right?" said Harris.

Then everyone was out and the door was slammed. George Lowery stood alone in the cabin that had seen years of his children die, and where, when his wife had given out, he had come back alone. Often he had sat next to her when they returned from putting down one of the tiny bodies. Now the oil lamp provided no more comfort than it had on those occasions. The lamp was a cut of glass said to be from England. It illuminated the clay dishes on the mantel, glinted against the charred fireplace and iron cook pots, reflected off the pans the boys had hammered out of copper bought from a drummer, and silhouetted the timber bedstead that had held the wasted marriage. George smashed the glass lamp into the wall.

A long-bristled broom hung in a corner. It was of swamp sedge, its decorative air hiding the drudging years that had worn away half its length. Nearby hung an iron poker brought by George's wife as part of her dowry. He had used it to bang coffin lids down over her babies, then, finally, over her. He had thought its next use would be over himself, wielded by one of his three strong sons. But they, like those before, were beyond saving. His failure was complete. And he knew the men outside hoped he would emerge so they could shoot him and be done guarding.

George looked around the cabin that had brought his family only death. He thought it was his fault; he must have missed something he ought to have known. He sat by the eating board and quietly sang the hymn his wife had sung while burying each child:

Sweet Jesus in adversity
Do not abandon, stay by me,
Sweet Jesus in my every breath
Guide us in life, take us in death.

George set the poker down on the table by the mule whip.

Our love for Thee we will employ;
When life is more than we can bear
We'll hold Thee lest we be destroyed,
And follow ere we're in despair.

After each tiny funeral his wife had returned to this room to shed tears she would not allow in public. Now came his own tears, shed not only for her or her last child lost, but for every child who had come to this cabin through her Heaven's gate only to return, for this place was not fit.

George opened the door. The guards raised their rifles. He wanted to step out and let them shoot but he had not the nerve. A man does not fight the swamp his whole life to end predisposed to self-destruction. He closed the door, then the shutters, leaving no light but the red hearth coals glowing like a message from the underworld. His last sons had been taken to die and again he remained alive within this room, again powerless to save.

In his hand was the mule whip, which he did not know he had picked up. He curled it and brought it down on his knuckles, crying out at the surprising pain. He recalled the smacks he had given his gentle mules over the years and wondered now that they had not brayed in agony. Again he brought the whip down, then again. His hand bled raw but if there was pain, he no longer knew. He continued, striking his legs, his arms, his back, his face, his groin.

Now in his hand was the poker coming down against his raw knuckles. He brought it down upon the stool, smashing it to fragments. Piece by piece he worked the shadowed cabin room round, meticulously reversing the craft that had attracted the girl Mary Cuombo to her carpenter-love Allen. George was as skillful now, leaving nothing unsplintered, nothing hidden.

Finally he flung coals from the fire against the walls, where they heated the logs to ignition. Surrounded by his smashed possessions, he sang the hymn. The logs smoked and sputtered as the moisture in them boiled. Hungry flames hunted along the grain. He fed the sedge broom and the splintered furniture to the flames, prodding with the iron poker like a famished man at a cook-fire. The cabin he had built with his brother Allen and inhabited for three decades, and in which he alone now survived, began to give up. In wild jets the moisture steaming from the cracks convinced him he was blasting out a thing of living evil, like burning out the obstructing stump of an ancient giant cypress. Finally George knew this thing of evil, that it was alive, that it had nourished itself by consuming his wife, his babies, his sons. This thing of evil, dying now too late, all along had hidden in the walls. It swirled and cursed as it roared out of the swamp-logs that constituted the cabin. George roared back the hymn, roared the hate and grief of a score of deaths. With his iron poker staff of vengeance and purgation he attacked the spewing flames. His rod cracked new splinters from the solid wood, splinters that ignited to burn out instantly upon their creation the same way all but three of his children had done in this place of doom.

"It was Death herself screaming in that place," George told me eight years later. "Lying up silent she was, doing her business in there my whole growed life. Now I had her where she'd always had everyone I ever had. She did not like it."

The room was an oven scorching George's mouth

and lungs. The guards outside tried to pull open the door but George had barred it. One guard rode off to tell Harris while the other continued to guard he knew not what. "I killed Death that day," George told me. "That made her ill with me so now she won't come and get me. I got to wait forever, just thinking—unless I can find her to make it up with her."

The roof ignited to a heaven of flame. The back wall caved with a shriek of wood, a shriek that George knew was Death in rage that he was playing her at her own game. Air flooded in and fed the flames into an orb like the sun, so hot and abrupt that the guard out front ran fifty yards. The inrushing air was cold on George's lungs after the smoke, and he used that cold air to curse God that he was still alive to breathe it. Hair smoldering and clothes charring, George let his body take over and escape through the back wall and into the swamp. The guard never thought to look around back of the cabin and its wall of concealing smoke. "I didn't mean to make Death mad, I just lost my head," old George told me.

From the edge of the swamp he looked back at the fireball. "I seen Death riding up the smoke and never seen her since though I'm looking every day."

James Harris and the Home Guard were a mile from the depot with their re-conscriptees when Harris said, "I'll take them from here; you all go home." One pointed out that Wesley, badly beaten, needed carrying. "I'm no cripple," responded Harris. "Tie them together and I will handle it." The Lowery boys were bound and left with him. He later told his wife (though she begged him not to) what he did. "Hey Wessie Laury, watch," he ordered.

Wesley was barely conscious, so Harris slapped him and turned him towards his brother. "Looking, Wessie?" Harris fired his pistol into Peter's head. The dead boy fell by the roadside, the ropes dragging Wesley along. "He shouldn't have tried escaping."

It was late and the night's activity had filled Harris with other hungers, so with no more delay he fired into Wesley's face. He stopped at an Indian cabin to report that two conscriptees had attacked him, attempted escape, and now lay dead for their efforts. He demanded dinner, told the family to take care of the bodies, and went on his way. The men who found the bodies were curious that anyone so tied would have attempted escape, and that one was shot from the front, a peculiar angle from which to fire upon an escaping man.

Robeson's woods are green, its air warm, and its sky a blue never seen in the North. Birds see only green leaves and green fields below. Down in the swamps the waters are often still, and when a flock of waterfowl settles, blotting out the lake, the sense given is of the richness of life that the county supports. All things grow here, vegetation rich and thick, and wildlife of every size and kind. Even the air, always filled with feathered beings, is never at rest, never empty of life, its dazzling variety celebrating the flush of creation that God granted this happy place.

On a road far beneath the birds, unnoticed by them except for those who eat by noticing such things, lay the ruins of George Lowery's last two children, bound together and sprawled bloody. A few miles away lay their brother Jarman, killed so recently that the county had not yet heard.

But the county would hear. And Death, whom George Lowery thought he had killed when he burned her out of the timbers of his cabin, was not killed but unleashed to thrive like the county's green lushness. Neither the great War nor General Sherman had introduced carnage and horror here, but now James Brantley Harris had. Before going home, Harris stopped off to force himself on the girl over whom he had quarreled with Wesley. Though he lay with her less than a mile from the two corpses he had left for buzzards, he no longer thought about any of that. And later, as he rolled off her, he thought not of the affliction he had loosed upon the county, but only of his breakfast.

The girl turned away. "What's wrong?" he demanded. Hunched and shaking in the corner of the barn where he had trapped her, she said nothing. "You miss your Indian?" asked Harris. "He won't bother you no more." He relieved himself against the wall, hitched his suspenders, and left.

What she thought we cannot know, but several Indian women I talked to seemed to know what she prayed: "May God damn James Harris and everything about him." Her earlier prayers had gone unanswered, but this time she was heeded. Robeson county was now damned, for the time, in its entirety.

The guard who had stayed at George's blazing cabin was still there, afraid to leave and afraid not to. James Harris was notified of the fire and sent an order for the Militia to sift the ashes for bones. The warm embers had attracted two striped, angle-eyed snakes; the burning provided the chilly serpents a pleasant morning. But when one of the Home Guard stepped heedlessly and was bitten, his mates killed the basking serpents with shovel tips. Death had not entirely abandoned the hulk of the cabin; of the reptilians and Guardsmen, three perished.

The survivors found none of George Lowery's bones, so reported that the hellish inferno had incinerated him to ash, bones and teeth and all.

Word of the deaths, including George's, came to Mary Cuombo and Allen Lowery. With their two daughters they descended deep into mourning. Long past the following midnight, they were all asleep except Mary Cuombo. She often lay awake while others slept, to have time alone without having to give care or concern to anyone. She prayed in these moments, or hummed, or contemplated the cabin's dark recesses, with her strong old man breathing beside her. On this night she had been praying for the departed souls of George Lowery and his boys when she heard a noise from the front room. Yet both daughters were asleep in their customary places, and Allen lay beside her. The dogs had not barked as they would have at the approach of any stranger. Mary Cuombo listened. Soon she heard the back and forth motion of the rocker her husband had built, a sound intimate in its familiarity but now full of terror. She woke Allen by covering his mouth in their long-prearranged way of signaling danger in the home, without revealing wakefulness to a possible intruder. Allen listened, then with his long knife made his way past his sleeping daughters to the front room. There a figure, lit by moonlight from the open door, rocked before the cold fireplace with his back to Allen.

"Be you a ghost, George?" said old Allen Lowery after a silence. There was no answer. Allen felt the hairs rise upon the back of his neck, and he said, "I surely hope you mean no harm, George, for we always treated you kindly and have great sadness you're taken from us."

"A man died and went to heaven," said George without turning, and speaking in the voice he used to tell jokes, "'Saint Peter, Saint Peter, please let me in!' said the man.

"Saint Peter looks up from his book and saith in his deep voice, 'Oh, Mister Dead Man, first thing, tell us your name.'"

Mary Cuombo joined her husband in the doorway behind. The girls woke, recognized Uncle George's voice, and peered out between their parents. Not turning to his audience, George continued: "Well, the dead man he don't answer, he just says, 'Let me in, let me in.'

"Saint Peter he saith in that deep voice, 'If you don't tell me your name, I can't look in the Good Book to see what was what with your life.'

"'Well, I got to say the truth, Mr. Peter,' says the dead man, 'I must have left my name behind, for I am certain I do not remember one word of it.'" George turned to his relatives. His face was that of the dead, though he was breathing and talking as surely as all four were looking.

"Finish the joke," said one of the daughters.

"No joke," said George. "It happened. Heaven sent me back. And now I ain't dead and it's the middle of the night and I got no place to go. I ain't got one thing or one person left in this whole loathing world, what's a man to do?"

"A man's to pray, George Lorry," said Mary Cuombo. "A man saved from death is to fall down on his knees and thank the merciful Lord God for the gift of life."

"No gift," said George. "My living heart's going to feel like it does now for evermore minute I am alive."

Mary Cuombo said, "Time makes better, George. We all mourn everybody, unless they got to mourn us."

"Preacher said that once and I near took a smack at his smiley face."

"Want a smack at me, George?"

"No, Mary Cuombo, but I'm obliged for the offer."

Allen came to his brother, but didn't know whether to extend a touch. Mary Cuombo nodded him to. George said, "I know about mourning, Mary Lorry, I done it every year. But this ain't mourning, it's just ole moaning, just wishing the whole world would die and me in it. Y'all go back to sleep, now. I'll go in the barn." Allen's strong hand held him back. "Don't worry about your barn," George said, "I won't kill your ox or nothing."

"Why they burn your place?" asked Mary Cuombo.

"They didn't."

"We hear they did."

"I did."

"Why a man burn his own?"

"Wasn't mine. Don't know whose but it wasn't mine." He pulled away from Allen and started out.

"Stay here, George," Allen said. "Ain't safe out there for Lorries."

Allen and Mary Cuombo put George in their bed, Allen in the middle surrounded by brother and wife. The girls sat beside. George said, "If anything could bring a man back to life, this would, but I'm a dead man and you got me here lying in your bed with you."

"Lot of talking for a dead man," said Mary Cuombo.

"Hush," said Allen Lowery.

"A man was a-laying in bed with his brother and his brother's wife . . ."

"Hush," Mary Cuombo insisted.

"—and . . ."

"Shh."

Mary Cuombo awoke often through the night. George was looking at the ceiling as if to make it answer. The girls stayed awake watching him. Near morning the younger girl pulled the cover up under George's chin. He took her hand and held it, and Mary Cuombo thought that tears would finally come, the prerequisite to healing. But he just held the girl's hand as if it were a rope and he was drowning. He must have held tight, for the poor girl finally whispered, as mildly as she might, "Ow."

Instantly George let go and said, "Honey, I am sorry."

But she gave George back her hand, Mary Cuombo told me, proud to be able to say what her daughter had done.

ELEVEN

NEWS OF THE DEATHS of George's sons had not yet reached the swamp, where the flush of triumph over young Henry Berry's success as the bearded minister lingered. Henry Berry had defeated potent adversity and, they still thought, saved his cousins from Conscription. Henry Berry's brothers were proud to be led by such a man.

The brothers had swelled their number by the addition of Andrew and Boss Strong, whose family had benefitted from the gang's activities. And Shoe-Maker John, an escaped slave, showed up out of nowhere and told Henry Berry they needed each other. With this manpower, Henry Berry was making plans for new campaigns. The planning was suspended when Lieutenant Wright brought the news of the deaths of Jarman, Peter, Wesley, and (as it was thought) George Lowery; and that the killer was leading the Home Guard to capture Henry Berry and the gang.

In the presence of Mr. Groone, High Sheriff Reuben King questioned Conscription Officer James Harris. Harris claimed self-defense in killing Wesley and Peter. The murder of Jarman was not discussed, because Harris had witnesses that he was elsewhere at the time.

Sheriff King initiated no action for any of the murders. Except for Mr. Groone, the Whites in the county held Sheriff King in esteem, and were outraged when King was later murdered. I asked Henry Berry how it happened.

"Accident," Henry Berry told me.

"Sometimes we just doing our business on a raid," explained Thom, "meaning no harm, and someone in a house does something stupid."

"Being in the house be stupid," said Shoe-Maker John. "People sees us coming, they should go away. No sense staying home. We ain't their aunts."

"Sheriff King was rich," said Thom, "so we thought there'd be money."

"And Harry wanted to raid the Sheriff in his own house," said Steven. "Seemed like a good idea."

"It was," said Henry Berry.

"Not for the Sheriff," said Shoe-Maker John. "Heh heh." He didn't laugh, but said, exactly, "Heh heh."

The gang had taken extra care blackening their faces for the raid on Sheriff King's home. Face-blackening puzzled me. Why not a mask? And besides, I said, "Everyone knows it's you. And you're already wanted for enough crimes to hang you all, so why disguise yourselves?"

"Tell him," said Henry Berry to Andrew, but Andrew looked blank.

Henry Berry looked at Shoe-Maker John, who said, "I ain't telling him nothing or he'll find out I knows everything. Then I gets no peace till he go back where he come from."

"You volunteer every lewd detail you happen to know," I pointed out.

"Well yassuh, ain't no one got the low-down on the low-down but me, so I got to do that. But I don't got to tell you why they blacks their faces."

Henry Berry looked sternly at Shoe-Maker John, who replied, "Is that look a direct command from the Chief of the Outlaws, the King of the Swamp, *de Terror o de Souf land*?" Henry Berry's mouth made a shape like a smile, but nothing else in his face changed.

"You sound like you've been reading newspapers," I said.

"Well, yes I has," said Shoe-Maker John. "I'm looking if I be in them yet." He fixed me with an accusatory stare. "And I ain't!"

"You're Black, you can't read no newspaper nor nothing else beside," said Thom.

"I ain't seen you with no Wild Injun News," said Shoe-Maker John. "And maybe I can't read but I knows what my name looks like wrote out and I never seen it yet in a newspaper."

"Last year Shoe-Maker got ten Wilmington newspapers, and he looked all through every one of them," said Steven. "Every page."

"And I wasn't in none, either," said Shoe-Maker John. He glared at me. "You newspapers don't like Black peoples."

"He done it, too," said Thom. "I seen him, he looked at the whole stack of newspapers."

"I admire the diligence," I said.

"All the same paper from the same day," said Thom. "A stupid man."

Shoe-Maker John lowered his head and glowered up at Thom, his eyes blazing in anger. "You take that back," Shoe-Maker John threatened.

"I take it back, I take it back, lemme alone."

"Don't take it back, boy, I want to knock your head off for saying it."

"How about I give you my pinkie ring instead, we be even?"

"Let's see."

Shoe-Maker John looked to see if the ring was good enough to compensate for the insult. I had noticed the ring before, but on Shoe-Maker John's hand, not Thom's. Apparently it changed hands whenever the two tiffed. "Stole it from a rich lady," said Steve. "Keeps these two from killing each other."

Shoe-Maker John slid the ring onto his pinkie and flashed its red jewel for us to see.

"That's an old lady's ring," said Andrew, full of scorn.

"Yeah," said Thom.

"Now," said Shoe-Maker John to me, "I tells why they blacks their faces. Ready?" I nodded. "Good. Then there you are, see, sleeping in your bed, peaceful like you're dead and gone to White Heaven." He lay down to illustrate. "Like this, but White." I nodded. "So you sleeping there, and there your ole woman, a-snorin and a-wuffin, both you." He illustrated. "Then you hears something, you opens one eye." He opened one eye, rolled it around, then leaped up to play the bandit's part and shouted, "Wake you up White man, wake you up and get you scared, this here a RAID and you in big trouble if you gets in the way, so stay where you is and shut your eyes like you sleeping."

"Why not just leave him to sleep in the first place?" I asked.

"Because that's how we does, Writer," he responded. "We the experts. Anybody do it better?" I said no. "Of course not. Nobody does. We does. So we do and you write, can I kindly get a yes?" I nodded. "We don't ask why you write how you write, and you don't ask why we does how we do, what you think?" I thought it clear and wise. "Then we agreeable." He resumed his bandit role hollering down at his victim: "Now don't move, here we come in the house to take everything you got!" He turned to me and asked, "So if you the White man, what you do?"

"Nothing at all. Objects may be replaced, but life cannot."

"That's what you say on account you got plenty objects. But that boy in the bed, we taking all his objects in the world. He ain't goin' lie still while we finds the jewels, and by now his ole lady up squeaking, 'Stop them, James—' they always named James or Eureal or something, '—get up and tell him get out!' And she whomp him in the blubber. Now he knows us thiefs ain't goin' be nice and take that mean ole lady off with us, she goin' be right there with him until Jesus come back. And every time she get mad from now on, she goin' haul off on him account he didn't get out of bed and go save her hats. So he got to rise up and stop us. But if he do, then we got to kill the poor little fella with who we got no upset, and besides if shooting go on, maybe we get hurt. So we got to keep White boy in bed. So we stick some black faces right up in his face and we says [*and here I beg the reader's pardon*] 'Keep your pretty white pecker under the quilt where it belong, or it be swinging on a dead man!'"

"Mmm-hmm," blacked Andrew Strong.

"But it ain't scary if it ain't said by a Black man," Shoe-Maker John continued. "Thomas, show."

Thom, pleased to be included, put his nose to mine and said, "Keep your pretty white peenie, where is it? . . . or . . ." He stopped.

". . . *pecker* . . ." prompted Shoe-Maker John.

Thom's face came back at me and said in his most vicious and Negro voice, "Keep your white pecker pretty!"

"'Under the sheet where it belong,'" whispered Shoe-Maker John.

"You said blanket," Thom whispered back.

"Who cares, just say it."

"Keep your wee-wee under the blanket where it go or it's a dead man!" It was terrifying despite Thom's difficulty with the lines and his light skin. But then Shoe-Maker John brought his VERY BLACK NOSE to my own, teeth and eyes shining white in the devil's darkness around them, and showed the difference: "Keep your pale little dickie in the bed where it be, or it de-cease right after you, heh heh."

"Mmm-hmmm," blacked Andrew. "Amen."

I felt a shrivel of fear that had not happened with Thom.

"You changed it," Thom complained.

"So they blacks their faces on account their injian skin's too friendly."

Faces black, the gang closed in on the house of Sheriff Reuben King. At that time the gang was twice as large, so they well-circled the house and crashed in through doors and shutters on every side. Sheriff King was dozing over a Baptist pamphlet. A neighbor, Mr. Edwin Ward, had come to spend the night and was reading a book. "Some day I tells you what Ward was really doing there," said Shoe-Maker John in such a way that I did not want to know. The gang's black faces appeared throughout the room, the oil lamps were blown out, and a commanding voice—Henry Berry's—cried, "SURRENDA!"

Neighbor Ward sat as if paralyzed. Sheriff King woke to Henry Berry's rifle on his chin. By a fatal, instinctive movement King rose his bulk up, seized the firearm, and bent it to the floor. Henry Berry forced it up again, and in the struggle it fired through the roof. At the same instant a pistol was shot from close quarters into the Sheriff's head from behind, and he fell in agony. Another shot was fired at Ward as he reached for a pistol on the wall, and he was felled with a wound that bled for months.

The females of the family rushed in and stood horrified. The outlaws shared the horror, having intended no violence. "Water," gasped the Sheriff. "I am burning up."

"Damn you," Thom cried in anger, "why did you fight?" The High Sheriff of Robeson County fought for breath.

It was a bloody scene of groaning victims, screaming women, and the blackened faces of shaken outlaws trying to look vicious enough to discourage further resistance. Henry Berry filled a cup with water and dribbled it down Sheriff King's throat. "Sorry you're killed," said Henry Berry as he slaked the dying Sheriff's thirst. "But we're even." This was the Sheriff who had done nothing to James Harris four years earlier for killing George's sons.

The Sheriff grew quiet. Boss (killed before my arrival), and another gang-member of the time named Dial, took the women out and locked them in the salt-house. Also in the gang at that time were Pop and Henderson Oxendine, and others.

Sheriff King died some weeks later. The Oxendines were captured almost immediately, and so were Steven and Shoe-Maker John. They were sentenced to hang for killing the Sheriff and for other crimes, but dug their way out of jail, except for Henderson Oxendine. Terrified to crawl into the long, dark tunnel, he ended up the only one to pay for killing Sheriff King. He remained in the cell, only three feet from the mouth of the tunnel leading to freedom, and ignored the pleas of his brother, Pop, to forget his fear and come with them.

"He could have walked out with the rest of us," said Shoe-Maker John, "but he didn't. And I was right there and escaped with everybody else, but my name still wasn't in the paper like theirs." He put his black nose against mine, dropped his hand over my eyes, and said, "Maybe the hand that shot the Sheriff was this black one here, what you think?"

"I think it possible. More than possible. In fact definite, if you say so."

"Good, then I waits to see it wrote that way."

A circle of Sheriff King's own making had closed itself with Sheriff King's death. The circle began when King would not arrest Conscriptor Harris for killing George Lowery's sons Peter, Wesley, and Jarman. So the gang revenged on Harris themselves. Matters would have stopped if the gang had been pardoned by the Federal Act of Oblivion – but Conscriptor Harris had been a government officer, so the Act of Oblivion did not apply. Unpardoned, the gang had to continue their outlaw ways to survive. It was in the course of them continuing their outlaw ways that they raided the home of Sheriff King and killed him. In this way, the High Sheriff caused his own death by failing to prosecute Conscriptor Harris.

Four years earlier, when the gang learned that Harris had killed Peter, Wesley, and Jarman, young Thom said, "We got to hang Harris off a tree like we the Ku Klux. They can't treat us like this."

"They can. They is," said Shoe-Maker John. "They goin' to keep on."

"Then we catch him and blow his head off. Now. Well?" Tom cried, angry that they weren't already on their way.

"Momma," said Henry Berry. "Poppa."

Thom said, "We kilt Barnes already. Momma be no madder if we kill two than one."

"You can't face your Momma if you go 'round being a full-growed murderer every Tuesday," said Steven.

Thom's eyes teared. "I liked my cousin Jarman, Gawd damn, and I liked my cousin Peter and Wesley too, and even if I didn't, Harris got no right. And next they get Momma and Poppa if we don't twist some guns up Harris's fat ugly pooper and shoot up his head, and right now."

"Thomas Lowery," lectured Steve, "we are the Lorrie gang. We don't run off like little chiles. We ponder." Steven had long ago yielded the gang's leadership to Henry Berry and had now taken on the role of mature elder statesman in service to his young leader. Particularly with Henry Berry's growing reluctance to talk, Steven served as persuader and explainer. Now he told Thom, "If folks start thinking we Lorries ain't in control, they'll be laughing at us. We got to be responsible."

"I'll be responsible to blow his head off," said Thom.

"Yes," said Henry Berry, and directed that it be fast, seemingly impulsive, and savage enough to make people think that Robeson county was dealing with madmen who would strike wildly and instantly whenever harmed or threatened. "Cottonmouth up and strike," said Henry Berry.

"Yeah, we rattling," said Thom, grin breaking through tears.

"No, we striking," said Shoe-Maker John. "The thing about a rattler . . ."

"So?" interrupted Andrew Strong, who accepted the existence of snakes but saw no reason to talk about them.

Shoe-Maker John continued: "Rattlers warn you they's coming. They has spoke, now watch out."

"That's us," said Thom.

"It ain't us, we cotttonmouth, we don't warn. First thing Harris hears be his own howling. Rattlesnake fool. Cottonmouth's the King." Andrew wandered away into the dark. "And the venom goin' spread."

Andrew wandered back, happier where he could at least see a snake if there was one.

Conscriptor James Brantley Harris woke with the strong, delicious feeling of a pre-dawn piss coming on, warm reminder of his last drink before passing out the night before. He stumbled across the dark cabin and lunged outside for a good place to relieve himself, which usually meant anyplace not his own bed.

He did not return. There is no record of anyone's regret.

Upon finishing his piss, he mounted his buggy for Scuffletown to see what he might find to amuse him. He stopped behind a familiar shack, tapped the wall, and waited for the obedient appearance of a girl in nightdress who climbed into his buggy out of fear. He drove towards the hills.

From the brush the gang watched Harris's buggy pass into the hills and his morning's rutting. The outlaws quickly built a pair of blinds on opposite sides of the roadway, each within fifteen feet of the condemned. Andrew marked the closest spot the buggy could get so they could shoot without cross-firing at each other.

Thom wanted to disable their prey with a single shot, then club him to death. The others reluctantly discarded the suggestion, not for humane reasons but in order to show the population that the gang was taking revenge, not indulging themselves. Thom wished to indulge.

Soon the buggy returned. The girl was huddled in the carry box to hide her shredded garment and bruised face. When the buggy reached Andrew's mark, Thom—who had demanded the privilege—put a shot into Harris's left foot, then Boss into the right.

The girl leaped out and ran. She knew not to look back.

The gang's full volley turned Harris into a blubbery mass of split flesh, smashed organs, and splintered bones. He screamed and cursed as long as he had life. He reached his gun but managed only to fire into his knee. The mare bolted and hauled the buggy off. Hanging over the side, head bashing on rock after rock, Harris spurted enough blood to trail red in the dirt for hundreds of yards before the terrified mare plunged into a swamp pond.

"Maybe he ain't dead," said Thom, hoping he could kill Harris again. Shoe-Maker John pointed at a lump in the dust. "What's that?" asked Thom.

"Inside of his head."

Andrew waded into the water to calm the thrashing mare and release her from the overturned buggy. The water was foaming red with what was left of Harris's blood, but the mare emerged unscathed, wild-eyed, and ready to run off in any direction, which they let her do. Andrew left the pond quickly when he saw what sorts of creatures were busy at Harris.

Dead men, even when universally despised, must be buried. Harris's widow washed his meager remains, but not as carefully as she washed her hands afterwards, and leisurely dried them in the sun. The pallbearers were paid, for there were no friends. Moreover, the weight of the load was considerable, despite the appetites of certain swamp creatures.

The resting place was marked by a board. It was stoned and pissed on that night and many since by an assemblage of White, Indian and Negro women. In that way the response to Harris's death crossed racial lines. He had terrified and outraged Non-Whites and White women, and White men had found themselves sickened or at least embarrassed by his methods.

From his death would come violence and suffering no one would be able to stop. But to blame Harris is to simplify, for there will always be James Harris. The fault is not that there are bad men, but that we license them to run berserk. Society had licensed Harris.

Henry Berry wanted the execution of Harris to show Whites that the gang was a dangerous force. He thought this intimidation would protect all non-Whites. But the result was the opposite. Though the killing of Harris was widely approved, Whites feared it would inspire other violent revenges for generations of provocation. White lives were suddenly at the whim of a wild, deadly gang and anyone else with a grievance. There was no choice but to declare war on the gang. This was how Harris's evil infected every citizen. The infection took first hold with the killing of old Allen Lowery and his innocent son William.

Perhaps if Sheriff King had known he had only four years to live, he would have spent his precious time on something else. Sadly, no man sees ahead so King began to gather manpower and arms to wipe out the outlaws. But General Sherman was marching. Scavengers, or "Bummers," strayed ahead of his ranks to loot and pillage before the General arrived to burn, and they were already in Robeson County. The Bummers had no political, social, military, or ethical concerns, but they found eager assistance. They were secretly directed to the richest White homes and they were told all about their defenses. The informers were Robeson's long-oppressed Indians and Negroes eager for the kind of revenge they had only heard about, enviously, in the slaughter of Harris.

This traitorous insolence humiliated the Whites, the worst thing to do to a class that fancies itself as ruling. But they could not stop collaborative whispers from unseen informants, or crude maps of indefinite origin, or hurried warnings about dogs and weapons. No two treasons came from the same person or at similar time or place. They were too tiny to counter. So not only the property and safety, but the very dignity of White life was under attack: Indians infecting the county from within. Slaves nourish in White homes and bosoms recoiling upon their masters. The child-races were betraying the Whites who had lavished such care on them. It cried out for measures.

TWELVE

I SAT WITH Mr. Benjamin Colin Stopes, about 60 years of age, on his sprawling veranda. Despite the warm day he wore formal coat and high neckware. Mr. Stopes apologized for leaving me in order to fetch the refreshment, and went in just as his wife emerged, a fine southern lady supporting herself on a maple cane nubbed by the gold head of an African. Mrs. Stopes' flowing pale dress of delicate lace reflected a South that ended with the War. A ribbon seemed frivolously youthful upon her frail head. She asked me to stay seated as she approached and apologized that we could not be waited upon, explaining that they had let their slaves go just before the arrival of General Sherman because the poor Negroes were terrified of being killed by the Yankee fiend. The Stopes had since fended for themselves.

I said I was interested in how the arrival of General Sherman might have touched upon the career of Henry Berry, upon members of the Stopes family, and upon whatever hostile feelings might have existed been the White and subordinate races at that time. She smiled with warmth and pleasantness, saying, "Feelings?"

"Yes, ma'am."

"Surely you are not of the impression there were feelings?"

"I am a journalist, Mrs. Stopes, and only ask questions."

"The house," she said, gesturing, "has been restored miraculously, though the barn is gone and with it our song-birds. They have not returned these eight years and never shall, not in any event while I remain upon my feet to see it. Or upon my foot," she said brightly, glancing down. She had only one leg.

"Some slaves helped the Yankees when Sherman approached," I said.

"Yes? Perhaps my husband will have a judgment upon that, he does on so much else."

"Did you have any women who worked for you that might have had thoughts about the end of the War?" She did not understand my question. "Or perhaps the children of your servants?"

"Yes?"

"There were children?"

"Oh, yes, three. Or four, I believe."

"And how old were they?"

"When?"

"At Sherman's approach."

"Oh, I wouldn't know, how would I connect the one with the other? You cannot think that the children were involved."

"I'm trying to learn how the situation affected you and your life here."

Her polite smile was certain to outlast any topic. Her husband came out with cool drinks, speaking as he came: "Sherman burned the house and burned the barn. He burned trees two hundred years old. He burned the back quarters. We were pleased to see him depart but he left little else to be pleased about."

"Did your slaves know he was coming?"

"We would not have discussed it, other than they were afraid."

"Was there a change in their behavior?"

"We had good people," he said.

"None in your service might have wished to assist Sherman?"

"Go in, Harriet," he said. With her free hand she removed the tray of refreshments to provide a graceful reason for her departure. "What do you want?" he said when she was gone. I said I wanted to understand what had happened here. "It's over," he said. "And if there is anything I can say to terminate your interest, tell me what it is and I will be eager to say it."

"But you may know so much of interest."

"Less than a decade ago," he said, "a considerable part of a War arrived under my trees. It did not happen in order to provide historical curiosity, sir; it is our own matter. It is a matter to be forgotten."

"Do you not agree that the study of history, conducted coolly and from an objective distance, might help us avoid such ill events in the future?"

He responded quietly but from an intensity of feeling that would have aroused a northerner to thunder. "There will be dozens, hundreds of volumes. They will be written for a hundred years, as if nothing else ever happened here that merits recording. Yet not one word that any of you objective fellows writes down will say what it was like."

"It is better to try, even if we come wide of the mark."

"It is?"

"I believe so, sir."

"I do not." We sat in silence for a few moments. He continued: "You saw my wife's affliction." I nodded reluctantly as if noticing had been impolite. "It is from the events you are coolly studying. I assure you, sir, that her leg, which pains her every day in such severity that her journey out here is all she will accomplish until tomorrow, is not coolly distant from her. And thus it is not from me. She was a woman with whom I was able to live as a man might wish to do." He rose. "We live now as best we can, with peace, with dignity no matter what the self-righteous saw reason to inflict. The sun rises and sets here as always. Nothing I might tell you will alter that, any more than what happened here will have anything to do with whether or how something like it happens in the next place at the next time."

I knew that his slaves had first led the Scavengers, and then Sherman's troops, to his home. I wanted him to tell me about it. I gently emphasized my interest in his slaves. "We had good people," he said. "Therefore I am glad to say I cannot help you." He nodded farewell and went in.

I was surprised to see his wife return, her features covering the pain of this second trip. She pressed my hand. "He's old, you understand." She almost smiled, then made her way back inside, leaving me on the veranda. It was polished wood with a gloss that enriched its dark grain. I left it, remounted Patrick Lowery's horse, who had been looking very fine tethered beneath the ancient tree that remained, and we rode down the winding path towards the gate.

I could learn no more on this topic. Whites had nothing to say. Indians and Negroes had little more.

Yet there had been collaboration, and it forced the authorities to take measures. White Robeson County had known that Sherman would bring the end of the Great Rebellion. There would be no escaping his toll. But larger concerns would not depart with him. Scuffletown had to be taught that the end of slavery was not the White man's defeat. The most immediate, emphatic, and necessary way for the White man to teach that lesson was to take action against the outlaws who killed Conscriptor Harris.

But with Sherman's approach, there was no way to gather a Home Guard Militia large enough to master the swamps and capture the gang. Necessity demanded a different course. Though Mary Cuombo had already told me of it, and though I did not want to mix so morbid a subject with my sentiments about Rhody Lowery, I had to hear all of what both women might have to say. I asked Thom to take me, as was our custom, to the thicket at the edge of the swamp, bower of Patrick Lowery's horse. The animal had grown more cooperative, perhaps because I was becoming a better rider. He had even taken to stepping around the rotted marsh pits that I found the least pleasant. This may have been due to his fear of quicksand that could lay hidden beneath, but I took it as a consideration for me.

Before mounting, I gave him a lump of sugar—a common enough northern practice. But this strange new substance was unwelcome. He drew his lips up over his gums and held the white lump in his yellowed enamels as if it were a bug. I was afraid his reluctance had to do with me. Might not the lunatic who pattied the poor beast in public and said "stay here" when he was already tethered also feed him something wrong? In any event, he held the sugar in his teeth. Thom watched but said nothing. For a cold-blooded killer he was civil.

I thought the horse might not realize the sugar was to eat. To show him, I made smacking noises with my mouth. It opened its mouth and dropped the sugar to the ground. Thom did not know where to look. I saddled and left for Mary Cuombo's. The ride was gentler today, so I believed progress had been made. There would be setbacks, for not all things gallop apace.

I left the horse in Mary Cuombo's barn. As I started away, it lowered its great head to butt me. Not understanding the gesture I continued away. It emitted a small, plaintive whinny. "I won't be long," I said. He nipped my trousers. I stepped back and looked at the beast, perplexed. He dragoned his neck at me, blew hard and nipped again at my trousers until I understood he was concerned not with my departure but with the contents of my pocket. The sugar he had rejected must have left a grain upon his teeth. Now having had the chance to taste it, he wanted more. I gave him another lump. He took it readily, smacked it against his tongue, and the better to savor it, turned away.

Sweet progress.

Inside, I told Mary Cuombo the subject of this visit's inquiry. Normally she wanted her full say before sending me off for Rhody's "lalala" version, as she put it. Mary Cuombo had once said, "Harry stays in the swamps because he can't stand her tunes, always singing of this here, singing of that there, like varmints in the roof chattering all night when you're trying to sleep."

"I like her songs," I had said.

"I blame that on the pale color of your hide. You're the kind that weeds the swamp and sweeps it for mud and dust. Anyway, what do you know about songs?" I did not confess to her that I had made my own sedge-plant broom for dusting around my desk. But I deny weeding the swamp.

This time Mary Cuombo sent for Rhody right away, refusing to discuss this topic alone. She filled the time reciting recipes, which sounded delicious.

> BREAD: four sweet potatoes boiled, spoon butter, spoon salt, chicken egg. Pint corn-flour. Three gills milk. Hot coals on top, fifteen minutes. Sugar-wine-butter sauce.

> TURTLE-OYSTER SOUP: turtle, fifty oysters, four quarts water, bacon slice, spoon butter, twenty cloves, thirty allspice, spoon salt, pepper red, pepper black, pint cream, mace, nutmeg, boil four hours, throw wine.

I asked if there were oysters around here. She didn't know.

> HOG HEAD CHEESE: boil hog faces, peel skin; add tongue, brains, chop fine. Spoon salt, two black pepper, three spoon allspice, tie in dumpling, press three days.

I didn't know why she was reciting so intensely.

> Two beat eggs. Spoon butter. Teacup milk. Big spoon yeast. Pint wheat flour. Tomatoes. Salt. Sugar. Bake an hour.

"What is it?" I asked.

"Don't recall," she said. She looked down and shyly said, "Want to hear corn marsh biscuit'n tolerable greens?" Her voice was odd. "Favorite thing Allen ate." I was supposed to say yes, so I nodded, not having noticed that her eyes were shut. She reached over and gripped my hand in both of hers, and said, "Do you?"

"I would be pleased, ma'am," I said. "Pleased and honored."

"Would you really?" Mary Cuombo said as if she were shy eleven-year-old.

"Yes, Miz Lorry," I said. She looked like Rhody getting ready to sing.

"But you can't write it down for no one else, understand?"

"Why not?"

"Because I said. Yes?" I agreed, and she told me her husband's favorite dish. I have prepared it twice. It's the best thing anyone ever tasted. It takes ten minutes to make. I wish I could tell you.

After Allen's favorite recipe, it was hard to begin asking questions about the cruelest night in her life. Rhody finally arrived. She looked at our hands on the table, still clasped.

"You two goin' kiss?" Rhody said.

"Can't a body hold on a person's hand?" said Mary Cuombo. "Any kissing, you do it, Miss Rhody fancy gal." I became acutely embarrassed, which amused both women. Rhody asked why she had been sent for and Mary Cuombo told her.

"But we'll talk later," I said, the time still not being right.

"You get me rushing over and 'maybe later''?" Rhody said.

"Hush and be nice," Mary Cuombo said.

"Best have a good supper over here," said Rhody, "having fetched me quick for nothing."

"It ain't cooked nor am I cooking it," said Mary Cuombo. "Tonight different from any other night?" Rhody said she would cook. Mary Cuombo rolled her eyes and said, "I am goin for a spell of walking," and left.

I was in the cabin of the Outlaw's mother alone with the Outlaw's wife and my mind was not on my work. "What you looking at?" Rhody said.

"I beg your pardon, I did not have the intention of . . ."

"Of what?"

"Of discomfiting you."

"Dis-com-fit," she said back, imitating my Northern vowels.

"You could be a Yankee," I said, "the way you said it."

"Why I want to be a dolted thing like that? I'd talk like you: 'New York City up there.'" She had my sound perfectly; the woman could have been Mrs. Astor instead of Mrs. Lowery.

She knew Mary Cuombo's kitchen, and worked one side to the other. I enjoyed watching but I wanted a New York beefsteak, not boiled hamfats. Soon she had a big pot bubbling away. She opened the shutters to the swamp. The sun was lowering in its Carolina way to darkness in just a few moments. Mary Cuombo was not back.

"She'll be back when she's ready, and of course supper will be ruint and she'll say her piece about 'No wonder her man's in the swamp, the way you cook and how you sing.' Chaw, mister Writer?" I declined, and she went ahead, talking as she chewed and spat. "I never met Allen Lowery, Harry's Poppa, except when I was little, and I don't remember. But I remember the night I met Harry. Once I got him talking he went on the whole time how they killed his Poppa."

"Curious topic to discuss with someone newly met."

"He said he loved me when he first seen me, and he loved his Poppa, so we went together." Outside in the dark, Mary Cuombo was singing. Her voice was not so sweet as Rhody's, but it served:

It is hard to work for God

To rise and take His part
Upon this battlefield of earth
And not sometimes lose heart.

"That's mine," said Rhody, surprised.

"Ma'am?" I said.

"That's my night bird song, I made that tune for my song!"

"I think it's an old hymn," I said.

"No, sir!" She sang her words along with Mary Cuombo's from outside:

He hides himself so wondrously
The night bird she's a pretty bird
As though there were no God
She sings the whole night long
He is least seen when all the powers
The prettiest sound you ever heard
Of ill are most abroad.
As pretty as my song.

"See?" said Rhody.

Or he deserts us in the hour
She sings so him and me can dance
The fight is all but lost
And roll me in his arms
And seems to leave us to ourselves
And never do he lose the chance
Just when we need him most
Of keeping me from harm.

Rhody hummed her next stanza, swaying before the window, as lonely for her man as was Mary Cuombo outside at her husband's grave.

> It is not so, but so it looks
> And we lose courage then
> And doubts will come if God hath kept
> His promises to men.
>
> But right is right, since God is God
> The darkest nights he dances in
> And right the day must win
> Once that the moon's arose
> To doubt would be disloyalty
> He holds me like it's still a sin
> To falter would be sin.
> And when he's done he goes.

Mary Cuombo hummed without words. Rhody, I think, made up her next verse as she sang it:

> Night dancin' in the black of night
> He picks me off the floor
> He spins me when the moon is bright
> And then he's here no more.
>
> The night bird she's a pretty bird
> She sings the whole night long
> The prettiest sound you ever heard
> As pretty as my song.

Rhody danced as she sang, trembling before

the swamp, like a child trying to make something happen by wishing hard enough. She could not have remembered my presence. When she turned back she saw me as if I were a chair or stool, said good night, and lay down on a mat her own small length from me. I watched her sleep. I looked down into her face close and warm by the fire over which she had prepared the meal we never ate. She might have dreamed of Henry Berry as I watched her from the infinite, objective distance of the waking world.

There was no normal life for these people. Pain, loneliness, and death are our species' first fears, and all three were here in abundant supply. Yet these people had what I did not. I, the objective recorder, would never know another night without thinking of young Rhody swaying empty at the dark window for her husband, and of an old wife singing hymns over her murdered husband's grave. I thought of poor Mr. Groone, condemned to his lonely world, recording the passionate lives and deaths of others. Watching Rhody's breathing and hearing Mary Cuombo humming hymns while the moon crossed the sky, I saw no difference between Mr. Groone and myself. We feared neither pain nor death; of our species' three terrors we were plagued by loneliness alone.

Some days back, Rhody had touched my arm as I had come into her cabin, and earlier this very evening Mary Cuombo had taken my hand. Few other times in all my grown life had I felt the stark touch of another person. Why had I needed this troubled land to make me note this?

That night in Mary Cuombo's chair I dreamed of old Allen Lowery dying on this spot the night Robeson County matured to its destiny. Each time I half woke I thought I heard shots, a mass of men muttering outside, screams of women, and the dull thud of grown men's bodies under the impact of close shooting.

In the morning the two women told me the details: One of the leaders had been a Presbyterian preacher named Cobil or Cobhill, an old religious ranter. Another was Murdoch MacLaine, six years later shot out of his buggy by Henry Berry Lowery. These and twenty or a hundred more dragged out Allen along with his wife Mary Cuombo, his daughters, and his son Sinclear. The eldest Lowery son, William, was brought from his cabin in his own ox-cart. In Allen Lowery's barn they claimed to have found stolen goods, though Mary Cuombo swore that the vigilantes had brought with them every such article.

Cobil or Cobhill, whom Mary Cuombo called the Devil's own priest, shouted a prayer for the execution. To seem holy he pleaded for the life of Sinclear Lowery. Allen and his son William were forced to dig their own graves. Digging, Allen cut his hand on the shovel and Mary Cuombo was told to cleanse and bind the wound, giving her false hope of a happy outcome. But the men were ordered to pray. William attempted to escape and they caught him.

Then they stood Allen Lowery, 75 years of age, beside his son William, both enduring the ordeal with the "stoicism of their race," according to Mr. Groone. Allen and William grasped hands. In blazing torchlight, father and son died by duck shot and ball. By stray shot or intentional afterthought, the ox that had drawn William's cart was also shot dead.

Cobil or Cobhill tried to make Mary Cuombo confess to anything that could provide the killers with justification. They pointed their guns at her, blindfolded her, and fired over her head until she was paralyzed with fear.

After the War, the killings were looked into with no conclusion. Mr. Groone read me the deposition of the slave named Emmanuel Boner who had driven the ox cart that brought William to this spot:

> FREEDMEN'S AGENT EUREAH BIRNEY: State the names of the men who appeared to be in control.
>
> EMMANUEL BONER: Greggors, McKensey, McRae.
>
> AGENT BIRNEY: How many others?
>
> BONER: Twenty I see and more outside the torch-lights.
>
> AGENT BIRNEY: Do you remember names?
>
> BONER: Yes. Coble, McCrimmon, McCrimmon, McGreggors, Sampson, Brown, McAuliffe, Cummings, Monroe, Jacobs, Leech, Hunt, Jacobs, Morgan, Scott, Scott, Wilkerson,

Scott, Murphy, Jacobs, Scott, MacKay, MacKay, McLean, McLean, Taylor, McMillan, Taylor, Inman, Baker, McCollum, McCollum, Floyd.

AGENT BIRNEY: That is more than twenty.

BONER: That is who I saw. There were more.

AGENT BIRNEY: How can you remember them all?

BONER: I had nothing to do but look.

AGENT BIRNEY: Did you know Allen Lowery or William?

BONER: Yes.

AGENT BIRNEY: Did you see anything else?

BONER: Yes, sir.

AGENT BIRNEY: What did you see?

BONER: Wilkerson killed my ox.

AGENT BIRNEY: Why?

BONER: I do not know, sir.

AGENT BIRNEY: Did you see anything else?

BONER: No, sir.

AGENT BIRNEY: Did you hear anything else?

BONER: Drums.

AGENT BIRNEY: Those of anyone you have named?

BONER: No, sir.

AGENT BIRNEY: Do you know whose?

BONER: Yes, sir.

AGENT BIRNEY: Whose?

BONER: General Sherman, sir. They were coming. They crossed near the grave the day after.

AGENT BIRNEY: Did the arrival of the General have connection with these events?

BONER: I think so.

AGENT BIRNEY: What was that?

BONER: If they had come before, the White people would not have shot Mr. Lowery and his boy. And if they had not come at all, then I do not know what the White people would have done next.

AGENT BIRNEY: Do you mean they would have hurt someone else?

BONER: Yes.

THE DEATH OF ALLEN LOWERY AND HIS SON

by Rhody Strong Lowery

The number a hundred they came
For two, at the point of a gun.
Four shots – and two men of one name
Put under the ground and were gone.

Come tears without number
Fill up River Lumber,
Till all of them hundred
Is nothing but none.

Mary Cuombo did not call this song "Lalala." When Rhody stopped singing, Mary Cuombo told me the end of the story: "We took them out of the grave and brought them inside. We lay them by each other. Others bring water and rags and I lock myself in. Outside the hammering starts, but not like Allen Lorrie's hammering. When Allen Lorrie hammered it wasn't just banging. I strip my boy William naked and clean him. I was lucky with young ones and didn't lose as many as some, so it may be I owed one. He was a good boy, somewhat a temper, and a mouth you'd want to slap for what it said. But every time you'd put up a hand to do it he'd smile and you'd stop. Now that was a trick he figured out with that smile.

"It was dark when they shot him and I couldn't see his face good. Maybe he didn't smile at them but it looked to me like he did. He tried to run away but they shot his leg and then they held him up next to his Daddy and shot them both. That kind of smile only works on your Momma. Maybe on the Lord, too, so when I was done cleaning William I made his mouth do it and put him in his Daddy's old church clothes.

"Then I lay out Allen's new church clothes and start on him." She stood in her window looking out at the graves.

"You don't have to tell me this," I said.

"How do you know?" she said. "Besides, nothing to tell, I done it the regular way, and sat a long time. Until the hammering stopped.

"Now Mister Writer, I made a fool of Mary Cuombo on the first day I seen Allen Lorrie and I done it on the last day, too. No one else goin' to tell you what I done, because they are scared of angering me. Here is what I done: when the hammering stopped I went outside. Patrick's work was done. Now Patrick knows what he's doing, his daddy taught him, and he done it fair. But the lid didn't set just perfect. Maybe no one else would have seen that. But I did. Shouldn't make a difference, its intention being to lay in the ground till the dead rise and walk away and they won't look back to see how neat was the woodwork. But this was for Allen Lorrie, not just someone, and I get mad, I start smashing. Patrick tries to stop me, saying 'Momma, momma, what you do, what you do?' and I whap poor Patrick. He runs off safe to watch and I give him plenty to watch. Time I'm done, there's only splinters.

"Poor Patrick thought the Devil got hold of his Momma, and maybe so. I take Patrick's hand and say, 'Wasn't your fault, darlin'.'

"But he's scared and runs farther off and yells back, 'What weren't, Momma? What did you do it for?'

"So I told him, 'It's Allen Lorrie we are putting down, son, not just you or me. Allen Lorrie.'

"'Well, now we got nothing to put him down in, Momma,' he said.

"'We never did, boy. When Allen Lorrie put two pieces of wood together they come into one piece, not two stuck together. Now do it right. I don't care if it takes you all night and all next week. If you do another one like you done you'll be the one laying in it. Build me a box your daddy will be proud to lie in.' And Patrick did it. So we put them in the ground, William, then Allen. I did all the dirt my own self and my face was dry but I decided I better let myself cry in case Allen was watching. His feelings might be hurt if I didn't and he never done one thing to hurt mine."

From his place of hiding in the swamp brush, unarmed and helpless, young Henry Berry had watched the Home Guard Militia kill his father and eldest brother. It turned him from a boy saving himself and his family into a man who declared war on an entire county. By the time I arrived, fourteen Whites had paid their part of the penalty.

THIRTEEN

AFTER ALLEN LOWERY was killed, a possibility of peace yet remained. It began when Henry Berry first met Miss Rhody Strong at a churchyard picnic a month after the departure of General Sherman. Rhody stood under a tree and sang:

Injun hunter in the west
Took his arrows, took his bow
Goin' do what he do best
Hunter's name Geronimo

White men come from all around
Stop him hunting buffalo,
Get you off the White man's ground
Said it to Geronimo

Henry Berry, just full grown, moved off where he could watch her without his brothers teasing him.

Great White Father tells you no
Like he told to you before
Take your people up and go
No room for Geronimo

Injun warrior in the west
Told his chiles he got to go
Killing's what he does the best
Warrior's name Geronimo

Henry Berry had never before noticed Rhody Strong. But he did now. Her black hair flowed like snakes around her tiny body and her voice floated on the sunset.

Geronimo, Geronimo
Told the white man, this I know,
You cannot make my people go
People of Geronimo.

"Who's Geronimo?" Henry Berry asked.

"An injian," she said, sarcastic that this lowly boy didn't know.

"Mean from the first," Henry Berry told me. No shortage of words on this topic. "Like I crawled out of the swamp, and I ain't good enough to ask about her damn Geronimy. That kind of woman makes you gummy. I oughta walked away and talked to old ladies. But how she looked. Not like no turkey buzzard even though she is one. Worse than Momma. We should send them both after the Ku Klux, they'd pee their sheets and run for Jesus.

"One night I was coming home and she's singing – but not like usual. She was singing me away."

Go from my window
Go from my door

You come near my bed tonight
You won't come round no more

"So I look around and I see men hiding. They would have got me except her singing was too smart for them. But she can twist a man till ain't nothing left but red and holler. Momma told me the first day, 'A gal looks like that, walk off!' But I never listen to Momma about Rhody. They're the same varmint.

"One night Rhody's cooking my supper. Grabs a pot, burns herself. On purpose, all down her hand. I stick it in water and she's crying but she's talking about different stuff, not the burn: 'Lonely here,' she says. I can't help it if I ain't there much, and what's it got to do with burning her hand? 'Woman gets lonely with her man gone, horrible, horrible lonely,' she keeps saying. I tell her the swamp's no fun either, and she always comes in my head out here. Leaves me so sore I can't walk or piss. That happen when you think about them New York girls?" Not that I had noticed. "She tells me, 'Some ladies find out how not to be lonely.' Now I see what she's up to. So I tell her, 'I'll shoot myself and then him and then you.' That made her laugh but she didn't take nothing back. So I said, 'I'll shoot myself in the finger, him in the peter, and you . . . between the eyes, girl.'

"She says, 'Henry Berry, get every Injian together and fix things once and for all.'

"'I ain't no Geronimy. And why burn yourself?'

"'Because I gone swampy. I'm goin to hurt myself more, too. Or do something bad with someone. If you can't come home when you want, what good's being King of the county?'

"'I'll shoot anyone you mess with.'

"'I'll mess if you ain't around, and if you ain't around you can't shoot no one.'

"'Honey, a man got to hit a woman talk like that.'

"'Then we're both dead on the floor before one of us gets out the door.' I kiss her face and say she made me proud and I'd never hit her but I got to go and she got to understand. She says, 'I'm goin hitch up a cart, and me and Sally Ann go find Geronimo. He'll be glad of someone like me.'

"'Why, they got no poison ivy out there?'

"'I ain't fooling, I'll go find him.'

"'Then I'll shoot Geronimy too. Shoot off his Apache peter and get me a White man reward!' She laughed, but then she says not *every* man she knows is scared of Henry Berry. We holler a while, then I got to go. She takes out her damn church dress and I say 'It ain't Sunday!'

"'They's other reasons for a nice dress,' she says, and takes off her shirt and holds up her dress. Now I been on her the whole night and shouldn't care about no shirt coming off, but I did.

"I say, 'Honey, don't do it with no one, it ain't goin to be this way a long time."

"'See some ending in sight, Mr. Loorie?' and starts crying again, and though we had done all night we done again, her still crying and being a devil.

"Then I had to go. I shouldn't have looked back but I know she's in the doorway and that's the prettiest thing, so I look and she's there. I said, 'I am sorry, honey, but I still got to go.'

"'And I still got this dress,' she said, and Gawd how she looked.

"I left and I come back out here and fussed so bad that nobody said nothing, not even Thommy. I'm thinking, sure as the sun's shining Rhody won't do it. But a man's head's like the swamp, in the daytime something can look right but at night it rips you." I looked around us at the swamp. He pointed. "That way. I watched all night, thinking, *what's she doing*? And then, *what's she doing now*? What's she doing in that direction and what's she doing right now? I had bad nights but not like that one. I been shot, throwed under mules, bit by every kind of snake and whooped an hour by Momma but nothing like that night. I would have shot myself but then I'd never know what she done.

"Morning, I go back. She's sleeping, an innocent angel set down by God with baby Jesus pissing holy flowers. She opens her eyes. 'Why Henry Berry,' she says in a high squeak voice like she's surprised, 'You back? Come lie beside.' She's smiling and humming a tune.

"'WHAT YOU DONE, WOMAN?' I holler. 'I know what you done, what you done?' She starts crying and says she went and done it and she's goin do it again and she don't deserve me and I say right you don't, so I am goin kill you.

"'Hit me all you want,' she says.

"'No, I goin kill you, except you got to take care of Sally Ann,' I tell her. I am yelling and banging the wall. Poppa always said if I get a woman like his, build strong walls because I'll bang 'em, and I was. She puts breakfast out so I eat half and throw the plate. I throwed it to miss but she ducked right into it so she's full of beans and yelling. I wash her off and pull her down on me. I forgive her but next time I'll kill her.

"Right while we're doin' it, she says, 'Make all the trouble end.' I said 'I can't, honey, they want to kill us.' She says she's glad she still got the dress and that's when we done it like we was trying to kill each other. Was the making of Henry Delaney. She throwed stuff and hit and claw. We done it like that all night till I couldn't no more, know what I mean?" No. "Next morning she smacks me with a pot till I'm awake. I get out, yelling 'Goodbye, the swamp ain't this bad!' But I don't go in the swamp. I hide in the bush. I watch all day and all night, and two days more. Nobody come and she didn't go no place.

"So I go to the door and she's sewing, Sally Ann's playing, everything's usual except her dress is laying there ripped down the front. 'You ripped your dress,' I said. She grabbed it and put it away, trying to look guilty. I act like I'm mad, and I say, 'Now I know you done it and I goin shoot what you done it with, you cussed Jezzybelle!'

"'Shoot me dead, Henry Berry, I don't deserve to live. Look how he ripped my dress that you like.'

"I say, 'Ha ha, you didn't do nothing.' She looked at me, and Sally Ann looked at her. I look at both them dirty liars.

"'Maybe,' Rhody say, and 'maybe not.'

"'Ha ha,' I say.

"Rhody says, 'I done it the first time, anyways.'

"'Ha ha,' I say, but I ain't sure.

"Then she starts in about Geronimy again! No day but torture about Geronimy. 'Geronimy, Geronimy,' she says.

"'Then go marry Geronimy, Rhody Woodbrain Loorie, and don't tell me his name no more, what the hell kind of name Geronimy anyway? Too bad you are stuck with poor Harry.'

"'You goin to hear his name, Henry Squish Berry, cause you are stuck with Rhody Strong Lorrie and I don't shut up about nothing.'

"'Yes ma'am, that's right.' Then she sang lalala sumbitch Geronimy all night till I'm both ears gummy."

The Outlaw talked this much only on the topic of Rhody. I didn't like hearing it. I remembered when a neighbor child in Brooklyn got a pony. I cried every night in envy. One day walking home from school he began to talk about his pony. Three of us socked him. And lo! 25 years later I have a horse: Patrick Lowery's. If I socked Henry Berry would I get Rhody in 25 years?

Next day I had Thom take me to my horse. I said I was going to town. But as soon as Thom was gone, I let the horse wander the swamp however it wanted. Perhaps he would carry me to monsters to be consumed and I would no more have to think about Henry Berry or Rhody or myself. I gave the horse a lump of sugar.

I contemplated a mystery: if Rhody's pretended adultery hurt Henry Berry more than all the other substantial horrors of his life, why would he have entered such a union, or being in it, remain? Mr. Groone might be lonely, and I too, but in agony like Henry Berry? And Mary Cuombo, who grieves every day over Allen Lowery: had she not been tolerably happy before she met him?

In a more trivial way: my friendship with Patrick Lowery's horse was certain to end sooner or later. As I thought this melancholy thought I pattied his neck. He turned and nipped my leg. Better never to have met at all. Sorrow is the sole conclusion of ties. Burst them! Loose the reins! Go alone, ungrappled, loose, like the easy swaying of Patrick Lowery's horse beneath me. Drowsing in the heat, I wallowed in my thoughts.

I was tossed from my gloom high into the air. Patrick Lowery's horse had reared straight up, launching me backward. He had been startled by two great snakes, one of which he had trampled, the other poised to strike, protecting its wounded mate. I landed in the muck near the trampled snake and it whipped against me in its death throes. As instructed by Patrick Lowery, I moved slowly, no longer musing on human inter-connectedness.

As I moved I found myself dragged down. The more I struggled the deeper I was pulled. Like running in a nightmare. I thought of this strange dilemma like being in quicksand, a tired simile my Editor would not have allowed. But this was not the simile quicksand but quicksand itself.

I called the horse but he backed off; the snake was still thrashing. Did he not know that human life is more precious than horseflesh? Ought he not sacrifice himself? I waved the horse to walk around the snake, but the concept of around was beyond his compass. I tried to stretch my neck to call to him again but the tepid black swamp that had been after me all along closed over my mouth, then my nose and eyes.

Possibly the thrashing snake had died and its widow gone off, I didn't know, but the horse's soft nose butted the top of my head. I did not rise up from my sucking doom. He butted again, pushing me deeper. I clutched at air – and felt a hanging rein! I grabbed and pulled for him to giddap, but in a lethal burst of loyalty he stopped and tried again to butt me out of the muck. I was going down, only an arm aloft and it was going fast.

With me out of sight, the horse forgot I ever existed, and backed away. Or maybe he knew what his move would do. I clung to the rein with sudden hope. The lummox, feeling the tug and thinking he was tethered, stopped. But its few steps had pulled enough to free my mouth, let me draw air, and yell giddap, which he did, bless the brilliant bright brown thing. It required all his strength, for the mire held me tight. But at last I squirted free. I leaped onto my friend's back and kissed his neck. He snorted and shook his neck. He headed back to his thicket while I removed – from him before myself – a glistening horde of leeches. For a few moments I thought there might be something more to inter-connectedness than I had supposed.

But when I dismounted in the clearing, he revealed the purpose of his heroics by nosing my sugar pocket. Friendship? Nay! Like all else in the swamp, it was survival. My survival meant the survival of his sugar supply.

Henry Berry treated the county in the same way. He made sure the Whites he robbed survived. He left them their carts and horses so they could continue to make a living – so they would have something to steal on another day.

In their first raids the gang stole weapons. But when their Yankee allies left with Sherman, and with the growing post-War ferocity of the Home Guard Militia, the gang needed a substantial supply of ammunition. No farmer or shop had much to steal. The only possibility was the Court House armory. It housed a collection of decrepit weapons General Sherman had left behind for useless. But the Yankee marauders had missed a huge stock of first quality shot and powder. So one moonless night after the War, the outlaws hauled off fourteen wagons of ammunition. By sunrise fourteen empty wagons and all the horses had been returned, watered, fed, and hitched neatly at the Court House rail. But first Henry Berry had given his gang a strange order. The outlaws did what he told them to, but without understanding why.

Next day, all Lumberton understood. Not only had Henry Berry returned the carts to allow for the continuing productivity of their owners. He had also invented advertising. The fourteen wagons belonged to Lumberton's busiest merchants, mills, and stables. They went to and fro throughout the county all day long, so were regularly seen by most of the population. By ordering his gang to paint the wagons red, Henry Berry provided the population a vivid and continuous reminder of the ammunition the gang had stolen. No one could ever find themselves far from these scarlet reminders, and it made everyone nervous about confronting the gang.

To paint the wagons, the outlaws had stolen all the red paint in town, and poured out all the other colors. It would be months before a new supply would arrive to paint the wagons their original colors, and by then no one bothered.

With that simple stroke of red paint, Henry Berry added insult to triumph, cheered Negroes and Indians, delivered a fearful warning that unnerved the county, and introduced mercantile principles into the southern economy that the White tradesmen never figured out for themselves but will use forever.

The Tuesday after his red wagon triumph, young Henry Berry went to the Strongs' home. Rhody's brothers Boss and Andrew were butchering a stolen hog in the yard, and were covered in blood and flies. Rhody had eaten two buckets of unripe berries and now lay feverish and ill in the cabin, dividing her time between bed and outhouse. Her skin was dead white. Her hair was stuck to her face and to her stained frock. Running to the outhouse she splattered her legs with pig's blood, so she possessed to her person an olfactorian insinuation of butchering enmisced with the gaseous effluvia of her intestinal crisis (i.e., she stunk bad). Her fever dizzied her vision as if looking down into a revolving tunnel. Sound reverberated into broken echoes from deep, eerie places.

Henry Berry came from behind the cabin, self-conscious in his Sunday suit. He'd come a-courting to ask Rhody's hand in marriage. Not seeing her in the yard he looked in the window and saw her moments after she had wrenched herself into a knot on her bed, her innards cramped and swollen. Her father was standing over her and asking, "Child, why do you think berries don't stay green?"

"Not now, Poppa," she pleaded. She covered her head with the quilt to block the sound but came right out again, desperate for clear air. Her father went on: "The good Lord wants green berries to turn red, child, that's why they don't stay green." Rhody would have preferred this lesson at another time but her father was not one to miss a teaching opportunity. "Now tell me, child, why does the good Lord want green berries to turn red?"

"Answer your father," said her mother. A rising mound of green stuff in Rhody's throat prevented her.

"Berries," said her father, "molly-berries like you et and snatch-berries and red-berries too, turn red *to tell you when to eat them*."

Rhody prayed silently to Jesus to take her father away.

Her father, who loved his daughter and did not wish to see her in such pain again, said, "The ones you et were green."

"That's right," said the mother Rhody had loved until that moment. "Green as fuzz on a pond. Greeeen as fuzzz on a ..." The words spun in Rhody's fevered head. Mr. Strong held out a handful of green berries. "Look," he said and like a fool she did. She rose roaring like an ocean storm, careless of her dress flaps thus enabling Henry Berry looking in the window to see more of

Rhody than he'd often seen of any woman since he was young enough to nurse. Rhody lunged out of Henry Berry's field of view, so he couldn't tell she was after a bucket. Realizing he was in for a wait unless he could get Rhody out of the house, he went to ask Andrew or Boss to fetch her.

But Rhody got there first and rushed past her brothers to the outhouse. They asked if she needed assistance but she was gone and they returned to work. "Ooooh," cried Rhody from inside the outhouse. "Jesus, Jesus, Jesus," followed by sounds that can't be written down and words that must not be.

Another suitor would have fallen back to return another time. But Henry Berry Lowery was not one to consider retreat. He got to the outhouse, crouched low, and spoke through a crack at the bottom of the back wall. "Rhody, that you?" Her groans drowned him out. When her pain let up for an instant, she heard "RHODY STRONG TALK TO ME," from beneath. Her fever echoed the words, hollow and unearthly: "RHODY, RHODY STRONG! I come to get you." She screamed, tore out of the shack, flew back through her brothers' pieces of pig, burst into the house yelling to her parents, "DEVIL IN THE PRIVY, DEVIL IN THE PRIVY," and scrambled under her quilt, air or no air.

Father and mother left to investigate the outhouse. Henry Berry decided to take advantage of their departure to get Rhody's attention. Perhaps, he thought, he ought to have known better than to talk to a female in an outhouse, an easy mistake for a deep-swamp dweller. He climbed in through the cabin window. He saw Rhody grab a bucket and dive beneath the sheet, but not before he had a tender glimpse of the caked hair of his beloved, as well as her wet face and eyes as red as, well, berries.

She had not seen him. Under the quilt she wished for death just as Henry Berry sat and placed his hand upon the mound that was the head of his cherished. "Rhody Strong I come for you," he said. Normally she was neither superstitious nor excessively religious, but she had deep spiritual concerns about this unearthly voice following her, not to mention the hand of Death or Devil clutching her head. Yet she was no coward; be this Death or Satan, she would not falter. In a fearless tone she demanded, "Who is it?"

"Me," said Henry Berry, "Henry Berry, and I—"

Rhody heard the second of the Outlaw's two given names: Berry. She would have preferred her visitor to have been Satan come from the burbling intestines of hell to nabble her down. The result of hearing "Berry" was a gastric eruption heard outside the quilt, outside the cabin, perhaps outside the county.

Only a man truly intent on marrying would have continued pursuit at this time. But Henry B. Lowery would not be put off. He waited until her spasms paused. "Are you ill, Rhody Strong?"

"Right as rain, don't you worry about me mister, what you want?" It was her longest consecutive string of words this day.

"I come for you to marry with me," he said softly.

"Sir?" It was hard to hear beneath the quilt.

"Come out from under," he said.

"Not now."

"Come out."

"What for, Henry Lowery?"

"For to marry." As if on cue, the last of the berries erupted and again she made audible use of the bucket under the quilt. Henry Berry held his ground, waited, and then tried again, suspecting that a woman can mean yes no matter how viscerally she says no. Soon he was rewarded for his persistence: Rhody stuck her head out.

"You look nice," he said.

"You got your Sunday suit," she said.

He told her he was going to marry her. He told me, "I thought she was goin' say no and I'd have to haul her into the swamp. But she said 'What about a ring?' so I gave her six from raids. She said she don't wear stole jewels. I told her I stole jewels and everything else, too, if she marry a thief she gets what's thieved. You take it or leave it? She still say she won't wear stole jewels but she looks at them and changes her mind. 'Now you got six rings on one finger, does that mean you'll marry me?' She say she got to consider. I went home and told Momma I was marrying.

"'Ain't none to have you,' said Momma. I told her who and she started in: 'Mean, that Missy Strong. Let me find you a nice one.'

"'Mean like you, Momma. Now hush and be an ole lady for one time and get me up a party.'

"'No, she's mean,' said Momma.

"'Momma, do what I say or I won't marry her.'

"'That's right,' said Momma. 'She's mean.'

"'Fix a party or her and me will live in harlotry under your nose like mule flies.'" Mary Cuombo was persuaded.

Word spread across the county. Both families looked forward to the wedding. Preparing the celebration would be a healing activity for the recently widowed Mary Cuombo. She and Rhody met to plan. Both came unarmed, so both survived.

Rhody's brother Andrew entered the planning. He lacked Henry Berry's leadership abilities but was blessed as a thinker – though a slow one, who could answer nothing quickly except his name. He invented a scheme that could set to rest the deaths of Barnes, Harris, George's three sons, and Allen and William Lowery. Andrew's scheme was the flowering of the seed planted when Henry Berry first met Rhody.

One chilly autumn evening, Andrew's family gathered over a thick stew that had simmered all day. Andrew and Boss were in from the swamp. Along with Rhody, their parents, and the three younger children, they ate with appreciation. Andrew chose this time of warmth and plenty to propose his idea. "It is good to be together as one," he said, bringing the others (except brother Boss, who knew not to get involved, and the baby) to a mid-swallow halt. Eyes, not heads, turned towards the son who seemed to be having a spell. The impression was confirmed when he quoted Hebrews XIII: "*Be not forgetful to entertain strangers, for thereby some have entertained angels unawares.*" He had never gone willingly to church nor stayed awake there half an hour, but he knew the Bible's persuasive weight in this cabin. He continued, "*If thine enemy be hungry, give him bread to eat; and if he be thirsty, give him water to drink.*"

Andrew's parents, no strangers to crisis, exchanged a look to reassure each other that they'd survive this too, whatever it was. To draw out the demon that had possession of Andrew, his mother used her own knowledge of Proverbs, and delivered XXV:22: "*For thou shalt heap coals of fire upon thine enemy's head, and the Lord shall reward thee.*"

Outdone, Andrew left the Bible and simply said, "Invite the White people to the wedding." There was silence in the cabin about the space of half a minute.

"Sir?" said his father.

"Eat your supper, Andrew," said Boss.

Andrew said, "If the White people come we'll be friends." Another half minute passed.

"This may be," said his father. Andrew's mother howled with scorn at her husband's ridiculousness and her son's demonic possession. Her husband shouted back Proverbs XXV:24, his favorite: "*It is better to dwell on the roof than inside with a brawling woman.*"

She knew God had written Proverbs XXVI:3 for wives to have something to throw in their husband's faces: "*A whip for the horse, a bridle for the ass, and a rod for the fool's back.*" She had reminded her husband of this verse every few days all the years they had been married, so he went back to eating his stew, popping a great soft piece of potato into his mouth and swallowing it whole. But, relentless with Proverbs, she said, "*And the fool returneth to his folly as a dog to his vomit,*" which putrid thought brought his potato back up. Rhody had not recovered enough from her green-berry malady to ignore a potato popping out of her father's mouth and splashing back into the stew pot. She excused herself and ran to the privy, which she still did not entirely trust. That was the end of supper. But Andrew's suggestion – to make the wedding feast a healing celebration—was debated in the gang and both families. No one wanted White enemies at the wedding but everyone understood the benefit. Shoe-Maker John was against it, saying, "They won't come and if they do I'm leaving." But Andrew's plan won out and the gang began stealing food enough for the feast.

Meantime, Henry Berry fawned upon Rhody, his sweet swamp-flower. She teased but kept him at arm's length waiting for marriage, a White custom Henry Berry had never heard of. Now its victim, he thought it might be the source of the White race's problem.

Rhody's coyness was not virtue; it was fun.

"Good," said her father.

"Ain't goin' let him, either."

"Good," said her father.

"Why not?" asked her brother Boss. He wanted to know, because the upcoming marriage had aroused in him the same feelings—for some as-yet unknown female—that had brought Henry Berry to Rhody.

"It ain't right," Rhody said.

"It's wrong." Her father nodded.

"Ain't right in just what way, exactly?" asked Boss.

"Bible," said Rhody, providing no help. But her mother nodded.

"Makes no sense, then, the Bible," Boss said, earning a cross-table slap from his mother, who continued chewing her tomato. "Well, it don't," he said, wary for another blow from his mother so never saw it arriving from his father.

"You best talk with a preacher," said his father.

"Henry Berry's brother's a preacher!" said Rhody, proud to be marrying someone related to God. She was referring to Patrick Lowery, the owner of my horse. Among other occupations, Patrick was a tobacco auctioneer and a preacher, a common pairing because they used the same talents. But despite Patrick Lowery or any other preacher, Boss never changed his view that the Bible, like his grandmother, did nothing but prohibit everything he wanted to do. So he respected the Bible as he respected his grandmother and stayed away from both.

Patrick Lowery would not have been pleased to be consulted by Rhody's brother, because Patrick had not been asked to perform the marriage. Instead, in hopes that the Militia would not intrude on a White minister's service, a Scottish chaplain was enlisted, the Reverend Hector J. McLain. He had once demonstrated his sympathy for the inferior races by pleading for the life of a condemned Negro thief. When Rhody told him that Whites were being invited to the wedding, he was eager to participate. He carefully wrote a special sermon in which he praised unity of the races:

"We are here assembled today, children of God together with children of God, to celebrate with joy and love in the light of Christ Jesus who loves all folks the same, aye. That we are brothers and sisters with those we are like, and brothers and sisters with those we are not like, aye, is a blessing and sacrament on our community as it is a blessing and sacrament on the two young people joining together today, aye, joining with each other as the seed joins the earth, aye. Of separation cometh darkness and death, dragging us back whence we came, aye. Of conjoinment cometh the light of new life, say Amen.

Together we beseech, Almighty Father, that our separation may sink back under the swamps to drown and rot and die and putrefy. Say Amen. We ask the Almighty Father to DRAIN our hate like the planter drains the bog before he sows, and CLEAR the darkness of our hate, aye, as the farmer clears the cypress that blocks the sun from his field, and to FIRE OUT the roots of ensnaring hate, as the farmer fires out the stump that would break his plow. Say Amen.

As yonder Britches Bridge joins the side we're on to yonder side our neighbor is on, so God's love joins this man with this woman. So God's love joins us all. Say Amen.

Lord shine your countenance upon this union of you, Henry, and you, Rhoda. We pray that what we plant today will sprout. Abandon not the ones who love you. Dona nobis pacem, all of us. Amen."

The Reverend's hopeful sermon presupposed White guests. Two hundred and ten were invited. None arrived. "I tole you," said Shoe-Maker John. The wedding took place before two hundred Indians and Negroes.

Reverend McLain did not give his planned sermon, but did warn that no man must divide the couple, for God is strong. But so was the amassed force of the Home Guard Militia that suddenly surrounded the assemblage. A local newspaper reported:

> Captain Jeremiah McNair led his soldiers to arrest the outlaw leader. Respectfully delaying until the ceremony ended, they surrounded the wedding party of several hundred Indians and Negroes. Captain McNair civilly requested Henry Berry to be his prisoner for the murder of James Harris, whose death contributed to the defeat of Confederate hopes, as well as for the murder of James Barnes, killed with no cause. For the safety of the guests, Lieutenant MacPherson requested the outlaw to cross his hands to be tied. Refusing to obey this courtesy of civil procedure, the outlaw called for help from the guests. To maintain peace, Captain McNair told his men to stand ready to shoot. At this the onlookers became angered. The Captain ordered a volley of shots carefully intended to threaten, and resulting in injury to only one old Negro. At this, half the cowardly assemblage stampeded through the soldiery, who stepped aside and allowed these women and children to pass.
>
> Reverend McLain interfered, insisting that Captain McNair produce a warrant. When

told that as a Justice of the Peace the Captain required no warrant, or rather was his own warrant, the Reverend led a hundred guests in pursuit of the troops taking Lowery away. At Britches Bridge the troops turned to hold the followers at bay. The Reverend McLain dared the soldiers to take him into custody, which they did. The Christian character of Captain McNair led him to release the minister shortly. The outlaw remains in custody.

FOURTEEN

AFTER THE CIVIL WAR, the North forgave the South's bloody rebellion. Hoping the South would be as forgiving, Robeson's Indians had now invited the Whites to come and forget the past. Instead of wedding gifts the Whites brought rifles and soldiers. This successful attack on an unarmed wedding made some Whites feel better for their failure to win a real War against armed soldiers.

Sherman had burned Lumberton's jail, so McNair put Henry Berry in a hotel, shackled and guarded by sixty-five brave men. Next day the groom was transferred 50 miles to the Columbus County jailer, Sheriff Franklin Schenk, Jr. No one had ever escaped from his solid stone prison in Whiteville.

And the bride? Alone, ripped from her new husband's arms, seeing him jailed for killing two men, "I was a flower untouched," she told me. "Now Christmas was coming, and I was to be alone my first holy married Jesus Noël."

The authorities moved quickly. There was a hearing. Mr. Groone had the court records:

H. Lowery refused to respond to questions nor would he ask questions of the Prosecution's witnesses, which was his right. The Hearing Officer warned him of the seriousness of the charges and advised him to take advantage of all his legal rights, including cross-examination of Witnesses. The Prisoner said he would.

DEFENDANT H. LOWERY: What is your name?

WITNESS LEWIS GAINES: I have already said.

PROSECUTOR McEVANS: The Witness has already said his name, Your Honor.

HEARING OFFICER: I remind the Defendant that the Witness has already said his name.

WITNESS LEWIS GAINES: I am willing to say it again.

HEARING OFFICER: It is not necessary if Mr. McEvans objects.

PROSECUTOR McEVANS: I don't object.

HEARING OFFICER: The Witness may say his name.

WITNESS LEWIS GAINES: Lewis Gaines.

DEFENDANT H. LOWERY: Sir?

WITNESS LEWIS GAINES: Lewis Gaines.

DEFENDANT H. LOWERY: Are you married?

WITNESS LEWIS GAINES: Yes.

DEFENDANT H. LOWERY: More than one day?

WITNESS LEWIS GATES: Sir? Yes.

HEARING OFFICER: Does the Defendant have more questions?

HERE THE DEFENDANT NODDED.

HEARING OFFICER: It will be necessary for the Witness to respond aloud so the Recorder can write it.

DEFENDANT H. LOWERY: Write that I nodded.

HEARING OFFICER: Are there more questions?

HERE THE DEFENDANT NODS

DEFENDANT H. LOWERY: Write that I nodded again.

HEARING OFFICER: Will you be pleased to ask them?

DEFENDANT H. LOWRY: Sir?

HEARING OFFICER: Ask your questions.

DEFENDANT H. LOWERY: How are you?

WITNESS LEWIS GAINES: What is the question?

DEFENDANT H. LOWERY: How are you?

PROSECUTOR McEVANS: Is this a question?

HEARING OFFICER: Mr. Lowery, is this a question?

HERE THE DEFENDANT GESTURES

HEARING OFFICER: Please answer aloud, sir. Is this a material question?

DEFENDANT H. LOWERY: I don't know.

HEARING OFFICER: Then why do you ask it?

WITNESS LEWIS GAINES: I can answer.

DEFENDANT H. LOWERY: Maybe he don't feel good enough to be a witness.

HEARING OFFICER: How he feels is not material.

DEFENDANT H. LOWERY: Tell him, don't tell me.

WITNESS LEWIS GAINES: Shall I answer?

PROSECUTOR McEVANS: No, sir.

HEARING OFFICER: No, sir. Does the Defendant have further questions of this Witness?

DEFENDANT H. LOWERY: Yes.

HEARING OFFICER: Will you ask them, sir?

DEFENDANT H. LOWERY: How do you think I am?

WITNESS LEWIS GAINES: Sir?

DEFENDANT H. LOWERY: Sir, how do you think I am?

WITNESS LEWIS GAINES: I don't know, sir.

PROSECUTOR McEVANS: The Prisoner is frivolous, Your Honor.

DEFENDANT H. LOWERY: I feel pretty good.

HEARING OFFICER: Does the Defendant have further questions?

HERE THE DEFENDANT SHAKES HIS HEAD

HEARING OFFICER: Are you saying "No," sir?

HERE THE DEFENDANT NODDED.

HEARING OFFICER: The Defendant designates yes.

The prisoner was returned to Whiteville Jail.

Whiteville jail, Whiteville Jail,
Holds you tight if you got no bail
Dark as night in Whiteville Jail
Better stay out of Whiteville jail.

Bars of iron, walls of stone
Man inside ain't goin home
Walls don't fail in Whiteville jail,
Don't let them get you in Whiteville jail.

Mrs. Henry Berry Lowery—Rhody—journeyed by boat with her brothers Boss and Andrew to investigate the situation. She was fifteen.

Got no windows got no door
No one gets out of here no more
Whiteville jail, Whiteville jail

Sun don't shine in Whiteville jail.

All you killers, all you thieves,
None of you will ever leave
Whiteville jail, Whiteville jail
You can't get out of Whiteville jail.

Rhody, Boss, and Andrew arrived north of Whiteville, North Carolina. Boss and Andrew camped by the river. Rhody went into town. Her heart froze when she saw the jail, a squat, two-story structure, barred windows, walls a foot thick. Not knowing Henry Berry was shackled, she hoped he would look out a window. When he did not, she went into a nearby inn. The proprietress became suspicious of the beautiful girl here alone. Rhody said she was waiting to meet her aunt and uncle from the country tomorrow or soon after. The proprietress would not let Rhody take up space sitting that long in the busy inn, explaining that the situation was especially difficult because the proprietress's brother, who usually waited on customers and carried meals to the jail, had been jailed for drunkenness. So not only was the inn crowded but there was no one to help run it.

"I can," offered Rhody in a little voice.

"I can't pay much," said the proprietress.

"Just let me stay, and feed my brothers camping south of town."

"How many brothers?"

"Two."

The Proprietress knew a good offer when she heard

it, and Rhody had a job. Early that evening Rhody knocked on the door to the jail. Jail-keeper Sheriff Schenk knew the notoriety of his prisoner and was armed and alert for any sort of rescue attempt. But there seemed no danger from this barefoot young beauty who looked down at the ground, waited a moment, and then looked back up into his face. "Yes ma'am?" he said gently.

"I'm to ask how many for feeding," said Rhody, very small.

He knew how many guests he housed that evening but wanted to prolong her presence. "Come in, miss, and sit while I see to my records." She did, selecting a spot in good window light. Sheriff Schenk sat at his desk and took a long time to count all the prisoners listed to be fed, and did it twice over to be careful. Then he came to his lovely visitor, sat by her, presented what she told me were sheepy eyes, and said, "Seven."

Rhody returned his sheepy gaze. "With or without—" and she stopped.

"Ma'am?"

"—you," she finished, her tone chastising him for leaving himself out. The Sheriff sat speechless and charmed. Rhody filled the silence with whatever pleasantries she could think of: she complimented the jail's bars and walls but didn't know how else to entertain a jailer. She left and later returned with eight meals, by which time Sheriff Schenk had found and put on his other shirt. She gave him a plate. "This is for you. I did it myself. The one without onions is for my employer's brother, she says onions give him bottom gas." Rhody spoke like a refined young White lady.

Sheriff Schenk asked Rhody to sit with him as he ate, and said he would share with her. She called it an honor, because he was famous and admired even in the next county, Cumberland, from where she had come to meet her aunt and uncle. Sheriff Schenk got up to go feed the inmates. He invited Rhody to sit comfortably while he was gone, which she did right after she had explored his office and the next room. As he returned she watched how he worked the door lock with a key, something she had never seen before.

Each time Rhody brought meals to the prison, she sat longer with the Sheriff. By the fourth night he was beginning to believe she liked him. On the fifth night the girl broke into tears. "What is the matter? What is the matter?" asked the Sheriff.

"I learned today that my aunt and my uncle are dead and will not come. I am alone with two young brothers and helpless." She said she had no more job or place to stay at the inn, because he had let the innkeeper's brother out of jail. Sheriff Schenk offered to go and arrest the fellow again. Rhody said she would not profit by another's distress even though "I'm alone in the world with no pillow for my head." He was afraid that the obvious suggestion would scare away this fragile bird, so he said nothing. So Rhody fluttered, "If only there was a place somewhere." He said there might be such a place, which Rhody knew was the cot she had scouted in the next room. She also knew he cared for her, because he had been telling her all about himself, his work, his background, and everything else a man finds to fill the silence when he likes a beautiful girl and she has convinced him that she's interested in whatever he says. She asked what it was like to be a man alone and if he would ever marry. He said he didn't know who would have him. She looked down, waited, then up into his eyes.

He left to gather the prisoners' empty plates. When he returned she was asleep in the chair. He took the plates to the inn, which he could do without leaving sight of his office door. When he came back he roused her gently, saying that the place he had earlier mentioned was available in the next room. "I could not ask it of you," she said, and fell asleep again in the chair.

He carried her through the doorway and placed her gently on the cot. He sat across the room and watched her like a poor man guarding newfound gold. She opened her eyes. "Please," she said, and spread her arms to him. He came to the cot. She said he could not sleep fully dressed, and, a garment at a time, talked his clothes from him. He hesitated to remove his shirt, its length serving the modest purpose of a gown. Rhody got him to do it by taking off her shawl. It was enough. In an instant his shirt lay on the floor with his other clothes.

With her fingers on the first button of her blouse, she begged him to turn around so she could continue to undress. He turned away, for which gentle consideration he spent the night unconscious on the floor where he had fallen when she smacked his head with the pipe she had hidden beneath his cot while he was gathering the dinner plates.

Rhody took the keys from his trousers. She noticed how muscular and handsome his unclothed body was, and hoped her new husband's would be the same, not having seen it yet. Working the keys as she had seen the Sheriff do, she found Henry Berry, unlocked his irons, and led him out through the Sheriff's quarters. He saw the naked Sheriff on the floor and asked for an explanation. Rhody never gave him one, she told me, revealing a female trait I had not known about.

Rhody showed Henry Berry where the Sheriff kept his weapons. The Outlaw, still in wedding garb, took three pistols, two rifles, and enough ammunition to battle every foot of the way back to the swamp. Rhody asked if they should free the other prisoners.

"No! Bad men. This ain't a hotel."

They opened the street door, stepped outside, and faded into the Whiteville night. In wedding clothes, with his tiny wife, and armed, Rhody's handsome groom was a quintessence of escape.

Andrew and Boss stared straight ahead as they rowed the moonlit river from Whiteville. Behind them on the floor of the boat the wedding couple executed the delayed nuptial night, then lay back looking at the sky. She could not tell if he was asleep, nor distinguish the rise and fall of his breathing from the rocking of the boat. She pulled her discarded dress over him against the morning chill, preferring the cold against her own skin. Possibly neither Andrew nor Boss snuck a look at the pair behind them. But each brother, without consulting the other, decided to seek out a wife.

Rhody was content to have her husband back but she saw no way for the future to be safe and secure. She fantasized things turning out right all by themselves. A silly fantasy, but she was not yet sixteen, even if she had just broken her husband out of jail. At that age, daughters of my colleagues in New York are barely capable of choosing a hat, though they make the attempt almost daily.

In the moonlight Rhody wondered whether it would be good or bad if she were now pregnant. Would the Outlaw's child be an outlaw? Or would the mother die by gunfire before the birth? Could she still undo everything and go marry one of the neighbor farm boys? Could she want any of them after knowing Henry Berry, her own Geronimo? The future flooded over her as her brothers rowed home against the twisting Wacamaw River, then down the forbidding Lumber, also called Drowning Creek.

When they docked, Henry Berry stood in the boat with his wife's dress wrapped around his waist. He held a pistol lest anyone sight his return, and stepped ashore. Andrew and Boss tied the boat and stepped back onto the county that had rejected their last desperate offer of peace.

And Rhody was indeed with child as she stepped off the boat. Sally Ann Lowery was born in the cabin Henry Berry built over three-quarters of a year of nights. Mary Cuombo assisted the birth, disapproving of everything about the way in which Rhody was managing the business. But the old woman's hands were gentle during the surprising rips of pain for which no one had prepared young Rhody. And Mary Cuombo melted entirely as she looked at Sally Ann and saw her husband Allen Lowery's eyes looking back.

Mary Cuombo placed the newest Lowery at Rhody's breast and a wet rag upon her brow and said, "You done well, Mrs. Lorrie. Now you are family, and whether this chile lives or she's taken back, you made her and I am proud to have been here by you." Rhody smiled. Mary Cuombo continued, "Just don't do no lalala songs about the babe."

Rhody had kept the impending birth secret until pain drove her, at Mary Cuombo's insistence, to see the doctor. He announced the pain was not serious, and then announced her imminence to the Militia. The soldiers who had arrested Henry Berry at his wedding came again to arrest him at the birth of his child.

In the cabin, Mary Cuombo doused the lamp twice to signal Henry Berry that all was well with the birth, then once more to say it was a daughter. Instantly the soldiers knew he was there and searched the yard. But they were afraid to go past the clearing into the swamp at night, and in any case Henry Berry was gone with the second signal from his mother. Over the next weeks he dug a tunnel between the swamp and the cabin so he could come and go unseen.

With Sally Ann's birth, Henry Berry acquired the great obsession of every decent parent. It is not enough just to ensure a child's survival. He was driven to rid her future of everything hurtful and dangerous that had plagued him. He swore that someday Sally Ann would need no tunnel to get home.

Thus, the goal of each raid became more than just taking things. Each raid became a single piece of a greater mission, like the mosaic chips in his mirror-cup combined their pale slivers of light into an intense beam. For example, the gang stole every weapon they saw, not merely to use them but to drain the enemy. Ku Kluxers and Home Guard Militiamen woke up mornings to discover that night visitors (or squirrels, for all they could tell) had carried off their guns along with a hamside or two. Eventually, Robeson County had little with which to shoot and, often, not much for breakfast.

Events began to carry off a man's goods in his own cart. No one slept at night for fear of who was outside and what it was that rattled in the corner of the bedroom. No one went to bed without taking what he feared might be a last look at wife or child. Robeson County slept no more, because Henry Berry kept them awake to weaken them. As the insomniac weakens over time, so did the county.

At first, the county turned to the Home Guard, the same warriors who had both lost the War and shirked duty in it. These heroes managed only to march around terrifying everyone but the outlaws. Given their failure, the county and state governments offered the largest bounties in the Nation's history. When neither bounties nor Home Guard had produced results, Whites looked for other ways. Some tried to supplant Henry Berry by offering the inferior races a different kind of hope, and built a schoolhouse in Scuffletown equipped with a northerner to teach the young and guide their families.

Over the years before the teacher's arrival, the county had been lulled by the regularity of the gang's raids. The front pages ran only the most spectacular stories, such as the killing of Sheriff King. One paper printed a weekly humor column chronicling the comic regularity of the Home Guard's failures.

During those years, Henry Delaney was born and his father was at the birth. Rhody had demanded the presence of Mary Cuombo, which Henry Berry found surprising. But Rhody insisted. Mary Cuombo was eager, the birthing difficult, and the county had a second Henry Lowery.

Henry Berry Senior hoped that the gang's weapons and reputation would convince the Whites to let them come out of the swamp and live in peace, in return for discontinuing the raids. But the raids had left permanent wounds and a hunger for revenge. The customary southern show of cordiality made it seem as if everything would work out in the long run, but no one had any idea how.

In still seeking peaceful resolution, Henry Berry's greatest dilemma was his oath to avenge the murders of his father and brother. The Freedmen's Bureau offered a possible solution. The Bureau had been created after the War to protect the rights of Negroes and Indians. If Henry Berry could turn the case of his father's murder over to the Bureau, and if the Bureau achieved redress, the Furies goading him to private revenge would be satisfied. In the summer of 1867 Henry Berry found citizens to testify to the Bureau's officer, Mr. Birnie, who then issued a warrant for murderers:

> WARRANT.
>
> The jurors affirm that Rhodney McMillern, Robert McKenzie, Reverend John Cobil, Reverend Luthra McCrimmon, Angus Baker, Murdoch McRae, Brown McCalum, John K McLean, John Taylor, Henry Alfrod, Murdoch McLean, Robert Gilbert, Robert McNare, Sellars McKay, John Pratt Walker, John Smith, Edward Wilkersen, John Charles Southerland, Duncan Monroe, John Patterson, Angus Leith, Robert Fields, Archibald Watson, Rory McNare, Archibald McRimmen, Daniel McQueen, and John McLaughlin (hereinafter THE DEFENDANTS) were MOVED AND SEDUCED BY THE INSTIGATION OF THE DEVIL on the third day of March in the Year of our Lord One Thousand Eighteen Hundred [sic] and Sixty-Five in the county of Robeson in the State of North Carolina, and in the peace of God and the State they did feloniously willfully and of their malice aforethought make an assault and that the said Rhodney McMillern loaded a musket with ONE DOZEN LEADEN BULLETS and did shoot the musket to produce ONE MORTAL WOUND of which Allen Lawoury and also his son William DIED

> The said DEFENDANTS aided and abetted the said Rhodney McMillern to murder and so the jurors upon their oath do say that all the said DEFENDANTS did kill and murder Allen Lawoury and William AGAINST THE PEACE AND DIGNITY OF THE STATE."

Indians, Negroes, and many Whites united in hoping the Law would succeed. Prosecution by the State would affirm the status of Indians as legally protected citizens and so justify the gang's activities as self-defense. Pardons would issue, the raids would end, Henry Berry would return to Rhody and his babies, and the county would be at peace. The pollution of blood would be washed away. Plans were spoken of that would have been taken for granted anyplace else but seemed miraculous to Robeson adults and like fairytales to their children who had no such memories: to exchange a gift without fear it would be stolen, to store food without fear that thieves would take all but a few days' supply, that the roads would be comforting pathways linking one home with another instead of avenues for the approach of new dangers. People might even leave their homes in the evening to visit friends.

Mr. Birnie of the Freedman's Bureau carried the warrant to Raleigh and returned home to report its warm reception by the State Prosecutor. The community waited to hear from the State Prosecutor.

The response arrived, a single phrase scrawled across each name in a dead tongue: "NOLLE PROSEQUI":

unwilling to prosecute. Again the door to justice slammed shut.

Ancient Greece taught that civilization's first task is to take public charge of private revenge. Murder must be a crime against the state as well as the victim. But like a willful child, North Carolina turned a deaf ear to that ancient lesson. With *Nolle Prosequi*, North Carolina ceased being a civilization, as if the swamp had taken back the open fields cleared by generations of planters.

If the state had followed its own laws, there would have been peace. Instead it left Henry Berry Lowery to seek justice on his own: his fierce raids across the county stole the security of every front yard, every home, every warm bed.

Henry Berry was not a greedy man like Jesse James nor an impulsive killer like John Wesley Hardin. He was not after power or adventure. He was more dangerous: a man who wanted to be left alone. He punished so that the next brute would leave him be. Each raid left another whip-mark on the county's back. Henry Berry Lowery hoped that one or another lash would teach the lesson – or that taken all together, they would finally kill the pupil who refused to learn.

FIFTEEN

THE NEW YORK HERALD publishes its opinions and some opposed to them. This is because truth emerges only when viewed from several points. In a raid are two points of view: the raider's and the victim's. When intruders drag you from bed at gunpoint, destroy your home, mistreat your family, and carry off your necessary possessions, you don't care about the raiders' justifications.

The victim's point of view was ably expressed by the Widow Mary Norment, whose husband the gang killed. I needed several visits to gain her trust and cooperation. Her fine home was nestled among the poorer ones of the ex-slaves who still farmed her lands. She was about 35 years of age, refined though of Scottish stock, and with firm jaw, forthright features, and direct gaze. Her hair was dark but not long, eyes brown, skin bloodless but not cool. She wore pale dresses with black lace collars to remind her and her visitors that she would carry her husband's name, and his alone, to the grave, believing Name would be as important Hereafter as here. Once I almost said, "You would better honor your husband's memory by living a happy life." But she cherished the sad mission of widowhood.

After several visits she finally agreed to help me. One day she gave me the first of a series of envelopes scented by dried flowers from her husband's grave, and containing pages in her trim hand.

BY THE HAND OF MRS. NORMENT, this is how it was in Robeson County. Our men were off at the War fighting for our homes. Our unprotected families were attacked by mulatto robbers who were hiding in the swamps to avoid duty at the Wilmington forts.

The citizens of Robeson formed a Home Guard to defend us. Quickly and bravely they captured and killed the outlaw leader, William Lowery, and his wily old father, Allen Lowery, whose house was the headquarters containing stolen property. In revenge, the younger Lowery sons reorganized to plunder and spread terror.

At the end, our soldiers came home disheartened by the War's unexpected outcome and the condition of their families. The robbers had gone undisturbed. Because these living fiends had gone unmolested, every family was devastated by criminal visits and depredations. Our county was without justice, and the raids continued.

THE JOHN McNAIR RAIDS. 1864 - 71. Mister McNair had a large farm. When all the skilled White men had gone to War, he had to hire the Lowerys as carpenters, by which means they learned the premises. Mr. McNair was known for his kindness to Indians, though their treatment of him showed no gratitude.

The first raid was in April, 1864. They took a featherbed.

In June, 1864, they took a quilt, later found in Allen Lowery's house. In December they burned Mr. McNair's gin-house containing fourteen bales of cotton. In January, 1865, they took a large quantity of pork. Except for visits to the poultry yard, Mr. McNair was undisturbed until June, 1867, when they took another bed, pillows, blankets, sheets, combs, clothing, crockery, knives, silver forks, two rifles, and a linen napkin.

On 23 January, 1868, the band hid in the house before the doors were locked for the night. After the family was asleep, the band boldly entered the bedroom, took the candle from the nightstand, and used it to search the house. They stole $125, guns, and a gold watch. They broke open a trunk and took Mrs. McNair's summer clothing. Another time they shot a yard-dog.

In February, 1871, Mr. McNair, going to Red Banks in a wagon, met the outlaws. Mr. Steve Lowery caught his bridle. H.B. Lowery and Mr. Boss Strong asked if he had a pistol; he said no and pushed Mr. Boss Strong away from him. Mr. Boss Strong struck his head. Mr. Steve Lowery called, "Boys, I told you not to hurt him." H.B. Lowery took his pocket-book, but it contained only $1 and he gave it back. They told Mr. McNair to go, but say nothing about meeting them. A young lady with him was frightened.

On 14 July, 1871, the robbers approached the house and wanted to eat. They brought their own silverware, having before stolen Mrs. McNair's, but this was not it. They told Mr. McNair to take a letter to Lumberton ordering the release of their wives who had been arrested. After breakfast they left, leaving Mrs. McNair the silverware.

From the hand of Mrs. Norment.

At the Devil's Den, I asked the outlaws why they raided the same places over and over. Shoe-Maker John told me, "When you rob a rich man's stuff he buys more stuff. So we go back."

"They'll be expecting you!" I said.

"They all expecting us, and besides there's only so many rich houses."

Andrew had had time to think. "If they think we ain't coming to rob their house again, then they go help someone else guard against us."

Shoe-Maker John went on: "It keeps White mens home instead of out humping on Black girls. We keeping the Black people and the White people untangled, how come the Ku Klux don't say thank you?"

One night I ignored my fear and asked to go on a raid. "It was on a raid you got this," said Andrew about my desk.

"I mean a real, actual raid."

"This wasn't from no giftie party!" said Andrew, banging my desk. I waved him away with both my hands.

Shoe-Maker John understood. "He wants to see a face."

"You been shooting?" asked Steve. Yes, I told him. He picked up a chunk of bark. "Shoot this." He threw it up and I watched it fall. "Didn't do it," Steve chided.

"My gun's inside."

"If you was ready for a raid you'd been in and out and shot it before it started back down."

"Where's your gun?" I asked Steven.

"Inside," he said.

I threw a piece of wood into the air. He ran inside, emerged with his pistol, tripped, somersaulted, rolled onto his back, cocked the pistol, got aim and fired impressively as the wood was almost down. But missed.

Thom watched a nearby pine tree growing, and Henry Berry took interest in a bird. Shoe-Maker John was grinning at the ground. Andrew was trying to figure out what Steve had shot at and why everyone else was looking every place but at Steve.

I looked at Steve. Like my Editor announcing I had misspelled, I hissed, "You missed."

"You throwed wrong." He tossed me his gun and threw up another piece of wood. I cocked the pistol, forced myself to stay slow and calm, there was time, there was time, and I fired. I missed. I fired again. I missed. It started back down. I breathed out, whispered bang, and shot the wood to bits.

"Missed *twice*," said Steve.

The gang said I could go on a raid disguised as a Negro, though Shoe- Maker John doubted I could be credible. "You never knowed one," he said.

"You," I countered.

"Too refined, high class," he said, at which Thom insulted him in a manner that my Editor will replace with the words "that we cannot verbatim render here." Shoe-Maker John said something just as vulgar, though more insulting and funnier. More followed. The red pinkie ring changed hands twice.

Steven asked if I participated in every news article I write. I told him this was not merely an article but a whole book, and moreover it was the first time I had worked on a story in which I had taken up residence. Did he think I was a dilettante seeking adventure without danger? He said yes and asked what a dilettante was. I admitted I wasn't eager for danger but would do whatever I had to do in order to write a good story, so wanted to go on just one real raid. I explained 'dilettante,' emphasizing that I was not one. He asked if he would be one if he wanted to write just one real newspaper story.

A week later, gang and dilettante came out of the swamp heading for the home of David Townsend, Esq.

I'd earlier asked the Widow Mary Norment what she knew of the gang's past raids upon Mr. Townsend. She wrote it down:

> **DAVID TOWNSEND, ESQ., RAIDS.** February, 1865. The band entered the Townsend house after the family retired. They took valuable papers, coins, confederate money, a hat, a coat, guns, and a blanket.
>
> They came several more times. Once they took his buggy-apron and harness, his carpenter-tools, a bale of cotton, and tools from his blacksmith shop. In July, 1870 they went for provisions. By then the household was expecting them every night and Mr. Townsend slept with his gun at his side. He heard a noise and looked out. The robbers were trying to get into his smokehouse. He fired out the window. They returned the fire from all sides, leaving seven hundred shot-holes. No one in the house was injured except Mrs. Alfred Rowland, a daughter of Mrs. Townsend on a visit. When she heard the shooting she rolled off the bed and a spent ball struck her breast and buried itself in the flesh; she picked it out with her fingers.
>
> Mr. Townsend went outside and they fired. The ball missed his head, crashed through a window and lodged in the wall. He fired again. One told him to go on shooting, that they liked such

music. Mr. Townsend fired and hit, sending the speaker to listen to music less congenial.

Later the marauders threatened his life for having displayed violence against them. They went to his house several times for this purpose, but he removed to Lumberton for safety. Mr. Townsend has trained his people for the next arrival of the brigands and still sleeps his nights in town.

From the hand of Mrs. Norment.

We arrived at Patrick Lowery's horse. I gave him sugar. Chewing, he looked at me, his eyes huge in the dark. I was painted black as Shoe-Maker John, full member of the gang, Henry Berry himself at my side. If my Editor knew, he would have condemned my participation. My mother would faint. I questioned my ethics. And I was so frightened that I had forgotten my pencil.

Here come the bad guys moving down the line
Here come the bad guys looking bad-guy fine
Here come the bad guys to take your gold and pants,
Here come the bad guys doing the bad guy dance

Here come the bad guys, don't get in their way
They take away your women and they take away your pay

Here come the bad guys as mean as they can be
Here come the bad guys and one of them is me

Here come the bad guys they mean to do you harm
Here come the bad guys, go lock up the farm
Here come the bad guys with guns and shiny knives
Here come the bad guys to get your dogs and wives

Rhody wrote that lalala for me when she heard the gang was planning to take me on a raid. I hummed it continually to calm myself as we rode though a moonless night to the home of David Townsend, Esq., who had carefully trained servants to apply violence if we showed up.

Here come the bad guys, one he holds his breath,
Here come the bad guys, one he's scared to death.

I made up that part, en route, my heart in my mouth and my mouth in a straight line of fear. When the Townsend's lights came in view a poke from Thom told me it was time to look frightening. "Here come the bad guys, here come the bad guys . . ." and now I was climbing off Patrick Lowery's horse, now the gang and I were running across the field, and now my whole life is running before my eyes. Now I'm close enough to draw my gun and approach the front door, for this would be a raid of confrontation, not stealth. Andrew, Shoe-Maker

John, Steven and Thom hide as I cross the front porch side by side with Henry Berry Lowery. I yank my second pistol and point both at the heavy wooden door. We stand in silence. I listen for sounds within. We wait, fingers over triggers, muscles primed, all ears, all eyes.

Henry Berry, masked, hat over flashing eyes, looks at me. I return the look. He nods at the door. Off to the side Andrew emerges, quizzical. Steven, too, sticks his head out.

Henry Berry raises his hand and makes a knocking gesture, then points to the door. I understand this direction from my leader. Andrew and Steven withdraw. My hands being full with pistols, I give one to Henry Berry so I can knock. He puts it in my holster and directs me to return the other to its place under my belt. I breathe and knock. No answer. No one home, we should leave. Henry Berry nods to knock louder. I do. After a moment we hear movement within, and the door is opened by an ancient Negress with candle. She looks at my black face. "Yowz?" she said.

"Excu—" I start, but Henry Berry, having anticipated, kicks my ankle. Deepening my voice I continue, "This a raid, ma'am, we be comin' insides." I push past her and stride manly into the front room, a foyer with polished wood window seat, oaken-doored cloak closet, brass rack holding a variety of headwear, plants on a glass shelf along two windows, and paintings of the family or its ancestors, one of which I take.

There had also been a shotgun next to the front door. I see it as I turn to the old Black woman who now aims it at me. It is impossible to say which of us was more frightened. She was baffled at how to point a shotgun at both Henry Berry and myself simultaneously, because she was standing between us. She resolved her dilemma by turning her back to Henry Berry and expending all her attention upon myself. Clearly the moment required words, my words, some dexterously-crafted, exquisite verbalization, original and brilliant, to control the moment's danger. "DON'T SHOOT!" I cried.

The woman responded, "But Marz say shoot next time you all comes, and if I don't, he whup me." From behind her, Henry Berry poked her back. She thought it was a gun. "I don't mean no harm, Marz Berry, but my Marz whups mean." She lowered the shotgun. "Well, Marz just goin have to whup me," she said mournfully.

Shoe-Maker John came in from the back of the house like a White host greeting guests. He heard her words and said, "Now gramma, just tell Marz we said we goin' cut off your head and make Miz Townsend eat it."

"Oh, don't do it, don't do it!" She started to cry.

"We ain't. You just goin' tell him we *said* we goin' cut it off."

"He ain't goin' believe if I talking with it still on."

"You goin' tell him we said we do it IF you didn't put down the gun."

"He whup me anyway, he's a mean Marz."

"Madame," I said, but Shoe-Maker John rolled his eyes at me, restoring my dialect, "we goin' steal de whip off with us along with everything else. Marz Townsend can't whup you if we got de whupper." She gazed upon me as if I were A. Lincoln, and handed me the shotgun.

"Mmm-hmmm," said Shoe-Maker John.

Henry Berry shot me a look of admiration I shall cherish forever, then he nodded towards the back of the house. I recalled I was to do something back there, but could not recall what. Shoe-Maker John said, "Go wake them up. But be careful, Mr. White man." The old Negress looked at me. "We just calls him that," Shoe-Maker John told her.

I took the candle and went through the back kitchen towards a bedroom. In the kitchen a Black child, perhaps age ten, woke up under the cook-stove and stared. "You wasn't with 'em last time," she said.

"I was."

"Wasn't. Nope. You wasn't."

"Come with me," I said, prying her little fists from the stove. I dragged her to the front room. "Keep her here," I said to the old Negress.

"He wasn't with 'em last time," said the tot.

"Yes I was!" I hissed, and went back to work. The bedroom door was shut. I started to knock but remembered the plan and barged right in. I crossed the dark room to the bed, drew my pistol, leaned over and yelled, "Now do what I say, wake you up and keep your dickie in the bed under the blanket-quilt where it belong or that peter-pecker be hanging pretty off one deadman!"

Mrs. Townsend woke screaming. I backed away as she thrashed in terror. I put the candle on the bureau where it reflected in the mirror. I could see Mr. Townsend was not here, verifying the Widow's report that he was spending his nights safely in town. I relaxed and looked around. The room was impressive, its furniture of exotic woods, linens, and curtains embroidered in fragile patterns, and soft rugs upon the varnished floor. Poor abandoned Mrs. Townsend screamed louder. "Shh!" I told her. She obeyed. She obeyed. SHE OBEYED! In the enforced quiet, something changed in me. "Yeah!" I said, "Now get out that bed and come with me."

"You said stay under the quilt," she said, a skinny little woman.

"Now I saying elsewise," I said. "Come along."

"You'll have to turn your back, I am not dressed." Dignity is crucial to southern Scottish women, so I turned. But I am not as stupid as the reader has anticipated. I was an outlaw on a raid, a bad guy already obeyed. I was in control of all things. As I turned my back I watched her in the mirror, so I saw her reach under her pillow. I wheeled back, a pistol in each of my hands, and cried, "Don't you try it, don't you try it, don't you try it," each repetition higher than the previous. Somehow one of my pistols went off, smashing a plant. The explosion was deafening, so only by seeing her mouth straining did I understand she was screaming again. I lunged for the gun concealed under her pillow, but there was only a dressing-gown.

"Oh Madame, I am so exceedingly sorry, I thought you were . . . I implore you to accept my apology, I'll clean this up," I said, indicating the smashed plant. She stared as if she had never heard a Negro gibber White in her boudoir. "Please," I begged her, "I ain't goin' hurt you." She pulled the quilt over her to don her dressing gown. As I glanced away in shame of my error, two more explosions crashed through the air and then a third before I realized she was shooting from under the quilt. I dove to the floor amazed I was not dead, a splash of blood slicking the carpet because my left hand had been shot. With my right I fired in every direction until my gun was emptied. In the clicking silence I realized that either hers was empty too, or she was dead. I was shaking in great heaves and my left hand had a chunk of skin ripped from it.

No movement under the quilt. "Are you well, Mrs. Townsend?" I said into the darkness, a bullet having doused the candle. She moaned. I tried to remove the quilt but she clutched it. "I just wish to see if you are well," I said. "I won't hurt you." She sobbed like a child. Gently I yanked the quilt from her grip.

"Maybe she got another bullet," said Shoe-Maker John in the doorway behind. "Don't feel sorry for nobody till the next day." It was good advice. I threw myself to the floor. My pistol was empty, so I hollered, "Shoot her! Shoot her! Shoot her!" The wailing woman beneath the quilt had the presence of mind to throw her pistol out onto the floor. I scuttled to it. "Empty," I announced, so it was safe to get up and I did.

"Who care if it's empty if she ain't got it no more?" asked Shoe-Maker John.

"Just for the record," I said.

"Just for the record maybe she got another pistol."

I threw myself to the floor again. "How do we find out?" I asked.

"Oh for Heaven's sake, I surrender," said Mrs. Townsend, a waver in her voice but with the extraordinary control that characterizes the great southern ladies. She threw back the quilt as if appearing boldly naked in a public place, but she had managed to put on a magnificently becoming robe. It hung upon her as if she'd spent an hour at a dressing glass. She stepped regally from bed, not five feet tall. She stood before us, the full experience of southern dignity-in-defeat upon her grand face. "What is it you want?" she commanded.

"Jewels," I said, remembering. "Where you keeps them?" My pathetic dialect could have fooled only a deaf Maine sheep farmer.

"You took every bauble last time," she said.

"This is my first—" but she meant the gang in general, not me personally. I looked at Shoe-Maker John. What now?

"The new jewels," he said.

"Oh," she said. "Yes. The new ones. Mr. Townsend keeps them in town."

I took over. "Miz what-yo-name, now we goin' look for new jewels. If we finds them, we cut off your fingers and you don't wear no jewels no more. 'Less you tells us first where they be."

"Mmm-hmmm!" said Shoe-Maker John.

"My husband won't like it," she said.

"He like it less when you got no fingers," I said.

I felt another surge of outlaw pride when she opened a bureau drawer, removed its contents, slid away a back panel, and gave me a box. I looked at Shoe-Maker John for his congratulations. To my surprise he had his pistol ready.

"Maybe she got another gun," he said.

I felt like a small boy doing badly on the first day of school, and who wasn't going to do much better in the years to come.

Henry Berry came in, having removed his mask. Poor Mrs. Townsend saw who he was and went to pieces. I pitied her. Her bedroom had been invaded by three terrifying brigands, one the most feared thief in the Nation's history. She tried to scream but could not breathe to do so. Shoe-Maker John shook his head at the weakness of White women and went off to steal things. Henry Berry motioned me to seat Mrs. Townsend on the bed. He then gestured for me to sit next to her, which was difficult because her thrashing was something terrible. The old Black woman appeared in the doorway, too frightened to come nearer. Henry Berry sat on Mrs. Townsend's other side and took her hand, daintily, politely, and pressed it in his own.

"I won't hurt you," he said. She tried to withdraw her hand, but he held it and said, "I will protect you." She leaned back against me, away from this madman. "Like my own." Her wracked body stilled. "No one will hurt you." She looked at me. "*No one*," continued Henry Berry. He held her hand like a young suitor. She started breathing. He smiled and said again, like the end of a lullaby, "No one." He put an arm around her and rocked her like a child. I went to the door, where the servant and I watched the Outlaw and the old lady. She shut her eyes, breathed, leaned against him.

We returned to the swamp with our plunder. Shoe-Maker John and Andrew argued how long to wait before the next Townsend raid. Rich people, the gang had observed, take two to four weeks to replace essentials such as eating utensils and featherbeds, &c. A year for jewelry.

My feeling about the raid? I missed doing it even as we were still returning! Better than anything I remember. When I was a child we would sneak to a hill to snow-slide. There were other hills, but this most dangerous and forbidden one was special. Once we'd tasted its forbidden slide we forever wanted more. And the longing for next time always started during the current one.

SIXTEEN

THE NIGHT AFTER the raid I lay awake at the Devil's Den, wounded hand throbbing. Around me, the swamp at last sounded natural and comforting, even the death-screams. I realized I'd never come to believe that I had taken my last forbidden Snow Hill slide. It was the same about raids.

Here come the bad guys
Doing the bad guy dance.

I lay thinking of pistols and Patrick Lowery's horse strong beneath me as we came out of the night to take another man's house. Revenge for the abuse of the colored races had nothing to do with it. God help me, I simply liked raids.

Worse, the Widow Norment realized why I had asked for information about the Townsend estate. Finding me a menace and disappointment, she would no longer see me. I returned her writings, but first copied them. A journalist's raid: like stealing jewels from old ladies or a desk from a bank.

I read the Widow's writings aloud to the outlaws gathered around my desk. My lost boys gained a retrospective view of themselves in a way few can, for few are so chronicled.

I read to the outlaws as my mother once read to me. On these swamp nights, in the hours after reading to my castaways, I could hear her voice. Her tales done for the night, her hand on my brow, she would sing a lullaby. I slept as if the night would last forever.

With no introduction except to explain that the outlaws so often stole bedclothes because poor families needed them, here begins:

THE CRIMES OF THE SWAMP GANG, 1863-72.

by Mrs. Mary Norment, Widow of Captain Owen Clinton "Black Owen" Norment, White Man Killed by the Gang.

THE FIRST RAID ON THE HOME OF MR. RICHARD MCKILLOP. 14 December, 1864. Her husband asleep beside her, Mrs. Mckillop looked up to see a boy she had never seen before. He had a knife.

"I forget who . . ." said Steve. No one spoke for a while.

"That was . . . I don't remember," said Shoe-Maker John, though he did remember.

"Boss," said Henry Berry.

"Oh," said Shoe-Maker John. "Boss."

"Boss," said his surviving brother, Andrew. No one spoke for a while. I started reading again:

The young intruder said he was hunting deserters and asked why her husband wasn't

> in the Army. Then he demanded powder and a gun. She said no, the boy was not hunting deserters; he was too young and just a robber. "Then give me a shirt and a gun," he said. She woke her husband to get a gun while she got a shirt, not much worn as she was afraid to anger the robber. He said thank you and disappeared.

This was the outlaws' first look at their own history. If a full-grown adult saw himself in a mirror for the first time, he would be similarly awed. The mention of Boss took them by surprise, as if their departed friend had reached from death to touch them and say, "*I did it, I am with you.*" From then on whenever I read to them, a shadow outlaw, Andrew, listened just beyond the circle of my lamp's glow.

THE FIRST RAID UPON THE HOME OF MR. JACKSON MCKILLOP. 3 January, 1865.

"How long ago 1865?" asked Thom.

"Count it yourself," said Steven. Thom counted it out, thoughtfully. He had never thought about their seven-year run, but the Widow's tales started him brooding.

"Who care how long?" said Shoe-Maker John. "Nothing but old age waiting out there."

"You got as much chance of getting old as I got of swimming to Floradie," said Steven.

"Where's that?" said Shoe-Maker John. I returned us to Robeson by reading again. Thommy did not immediately come along.

Mr. Jackson Mckillop, the brother of Richard, was away in the army. His wife saw a White man outside the window. He opened the window and she shut it. He opened it again and climbed in.

"One of the Yankees," said Steven.

Mrs. Mckillop saw five more men outside. The one inside said, "We have others in the road." He searched the house and took a gun.

I asked why they went to the danger of a raid just for one gun. "We needed it," said Shoe-Maker John.

"You can't run till you can walk," said Steven.

"Or walk either," said Thom, which seemed true enough once we figured out what he had said, if not why he had said it.

THE SECOND RAID UPON THE HOME OF MR. JACKSON MCKILLOP. 5 January, 1865. Two men forced their way into the house. One was a stranger, heavy man named Williamson from Columbus County, who had come to be a member of the robber clan.

"Never heard of him," said Shoe-Maker John. Nor had the others.

He was later killed by some unknown person back in Columbus County.

"Good," said Andrew, who did not like strangers.

His short accomplice asked for wine. Mrs. Mckillop said she kept some for sickness. She brought a straw-covered demijohn and a brown jug. They took the brown jug, saying she would not need both for sickness, and if she did they would get her more.

"Nope, nope, nope," said Andrew. "Nope."

"Wasn't us," said Shoe-Maker John.

"Nope."

"Some raids were the work of others?" I asked.

"You think we the only bad demons in the world?"

Thom said, "Williamson wasn't ever with us, and the other one's that little Walter that used to hang with him. How'd they get in our stories?"

THE THIRD RAID UPON THE HOME OF MR. JACKSON MCKILLOP. 8 January, 1865. They came back a few nights later and asked for the demijohn, took a drink, and gave it back empty.

"Yeah, now that's us," said Shoe-Maker John.

"Was me who asked," said Thom.

"But if it wasn't you the first time, how did you know about the demijohn?" I asked. Thom had no idea, nor did anyone else.

"Maybe it was us the first time," said Steven.

"Nope," said Andrew.

"Something's wrong," I said. "It was or it wasn't."

"Right," said Andrew.

As if inventing something new, Henry Berry said, "Read it again."

> They called a few nights afterwards and asked for the demijohn, took a drink, and gave it back empty.

"We didn't ask," said Henry Berry.

"Thom says he did," I said.

Thom looked frightened and shut his eyes, a trapped victim of literature. "I don't know," he said sadly. "I thought I did."

"She says you did," said Henry Berry, offering a kind of support.

"If he didn't, why'd she write it?" Andrew asked, the eternal literary mystery.

I suggested that Mrs. Mckillop might have mistakenly thought they were the same intruders as before, and gave them the wine without being asked. The Widow Norment guessed that they'd asked for it when in fact they had not—a common, if deplorable, journalistic carelessness.

Thom said, "If someone talks a mistake, you punch his nose. What do you do about writers?"

I tried to change this discomfiting subject by telling them about history's first writings: drawings on cave walls, which were the records of early men who drew bison, eagles, and snakes.

"Snake pictures?" said Andrew.

"Snakes or whatever it is," said Thom, "they better

get it right. What good's drawing a dog if it's really a snake or a turd?"

"And the Bible?" thundered Shoe-Maker John. "If the Bible writing's wrong, we in trouble."

"If it's right we're in trouble too," said Steven.

Thom had been thinking. "What if there's a mistake in the picture cave? So outside you see a bobcat and think it's a mule, and you try to ride. Whoo! Writing's a hazard, and look here, it's White men do it. It's some kind of mean code."

I said, "Then we're lucky you can correct any errors in the Widow's tales."

"We don't remember if it's errors or not," said Thom. "Read."

> One robber came out of the dining room wrapped in a blanket. Mrs. Mckillop said it was hers, but he claimed he had brought it. She then went through the rooms with him, watching his every move, but he carried off many articles she did not see him take.

"That's you, Harry, that's you, that's you!" said Thom. Henry Berry smiled like a man in new clothes looking in a mirror.

> The robbers said they wanted her horse and buggy, but the buggy was too small so they hurried off without it to do worse.

I asked if I should keep reading.

"Yes!"

THE SECOND RAID UPON THE HOME OF MR. RICHARD MCKILLOP. 8 January, 1865. This time the robbers took the buggy, carriage, and horses. They went on to Mr. Henry Bullock's, taking a Negro to drive the carriage. The next morning they sent him back with the carriage, very much jaded.

"What's jaded?" asked Thom.

"Tired," I said.

"Then why don't she say tired?"

"It's a synonym, a different word that means the same thing."

"What for?"

"Like 'Thomas'," I explained, "or 'Thom' or 'Thommy'." He looked away, not sure he liked this personal involvement. "Your mother might call you 'Thommy'. I might call you 'Thom'. A stranger ought to say 'Thomas'."

"Yeah?" said Thom, and resolved to make strangers do it.

I said, "Jaded means tired of something. Bored with it."

"Like what?"

"She doesn't say."

"Why she leave out the good part?" he asked resentfully. I agreed.

THE FOURTH RAID UPON THE HOME OF MR. JACKSON MCKILLOP. 14 April, 1865. The night was dark as if intended for evil.

> The robbers shot into the house and robbed the smokehouse of its bacon. Later when Mrs. Mckillop went into a back room she found a dark man under the bed.

"Heh, heh, heh," said Shoe-Maker John.

> She ran to tell her husband but the dark man escaped through the window. He took nothing.

"Took the pillow," said Shoe-Maker John. If Widow Norment had still been on speaking terms with me, I would have told her so she could correct her error.

> The next morning, tracks were seen in the garden, where they had stolen Mrs. Mckillop's onions.

I marveled that the highest-bountied men in the history of the nation would steal onions.

"People got to eat," said Steven.

"Can't eat nothing without onions," said Shoe-Maker John. "White folks eats onions. Us too. She had good onions, Miz Mckillop. So we took half."

"Why half?" I asked. Shoe-Maker John despaired over my stupidity.

Andrew said, "If she knows we take them all, she don't plant none next year. So nobody gets onions. If we take half, next year she plants twice as much as she needs and everybody's happy."

> They came again several times but did no damage except to kill the yard dog. Their purposes were often thwarted here, and they stopped coming.

"Except for her onions," added Shoe-Maker John.

"Why did you kill the yard dog?"

"Barking and biting," said Thom. "What do you think? Dancing?"

"But wouldn't the gunshot warn of your presence?"

"Didn't shoot him," Thom said.

"Sounds mean," I said.

"Less mean than White people when their dogs start barking."

I thought I'd read enough for the first night. They disagreed, but had plenty to think about as they fell asleep. Thom discovered that if he thought hard about a just-told raid, he could dream about it.

The dark of the moon eliminated the next few reading evenings, because the blackest nights were reserved for raids. But the literary conclave returned with the moon, each outlaw seated in his place like first grade. I resisted the impulse to start with "Once Upon a Time," though Thommy might have liked it.

> **THE FIRST RAID UPON THE HOME OF MR. JOSEPH THOMPSON.** 8 January, 1865. Eight White men burst into the house shouting, "Yankees coming, the Yankees are coming!" They took prisoner Mr. Thompson and three

> gentlemen. They behaved roughly, cursing loudly—

"That was you," said Steven to Andrew, who was quiet except on raids, when he was fearsome and rude and often taken for White.

> —cursing loudly [I repeated] and firing off their guns—

"That was YOU," yelled Andrew, looking around for someone to blame.

> —firing off their guns in the house. Elderly Mrs. Thompson insisted that they return her things, but they shot a pistol over her head. They were drunk, having stolen Mr. Bullock's brandy. They took many guns and bed-clothing.

I asked, "Isn't being drunk dangerous during a raid?"

"Being drunk and acting drunk ain't the same," said Steven.

"You pretend?"

"If they see a bunch of be-drunked thiefs running and howlering up and down their house, it keeps them quiet," said Steven. I marveled. If every gang in America were this smart, no home would be safe.

> They stole the guests' hats and sent everyone home bareheaded. In the yard the Lowerys

packed the stolen property, saucily wearing the hats.

Henry Berry tipped his.

THE SECOND RAID UPON THE HOME OF MR. JOSEPH THOMPSON. 1870. The gang came to Mr. Thompson's farm to kill his superintendent Mr. Perry, a Militiaman who had shot at them. Steven Lowery forced Mr. Thompson to let them into the house. When Mr. Perry escaped through the back, the robbers demanded tobacco and bacon. But there was none, so they left empty-handed.

The gang listened unhappily to the failed mission. Thom said to rip it up. Henry Berry said no. I wouldn't have anyway.

THE FIRST RAID UPON THE HOME OF MR. HENRY BULLOCK. 8 January, 1865. The robbers drove to Mr. Bullock's in buggies they took from Mr. Richard Mckillop's. Eight burst in. One fearsome robber wore a hat down over his face in a stupid attempt to disguise himself. It was Thomas Lowery.

"Told you it don't work," said Steven to Thom.

"Just cause she say it don't work don't mean it don't work," countered Thom. "She makes mistakes. They was scared, wasn't they?"

"Yeah, because they was looking at some cussing

wild looner with guns and wearing a hat on his nose. That makes folks worry."

> One robber commanded Mr. Bullock to light a fire. With courage and wit Mr. Bullock replied, "If you want a fire, light it yourself!" The robbers went off stealing from garret to cellar. They threw things out windows into the wagons.
>
> Mr. Bullock had made a little brandy for his own use, of which the robbers partook freely and then carried off ninety gallons. They told Mr. Bullock they would not hurt him. He replied, "The Devil you won't." They had referred to physical hurt, but he meant monetarily.

The outlaws were reflectively silent. "What is it?" I asked.

"Good brandy," said Thom dreamily. The others nodded. They had liked it so much that they went and stole all he had every few months. So he stopped making it and the world lost his fine nectar.

"That's why we don't steal all the onions," said Shoe-Maker John. "But we couldn't leave no drop of that brandy. It was so good it'd make the preacher's wife pop up dancing out the chimney."

> **THE SECOND RAID UPON THE HOME OF MR. HENRY BULLOCK.** 17 January, 1865. Only three broke in. They took the remaining brandy. The next night, a colored man passing the house of Allen Lowery (the outlaws' father)

> went in to chat. He found the robber gang, Yankees and all, drinking Bullock's brandy.

Steven flew into a rage. "You go tell that Widder Normen there wasn't never one drop of Bullock's nor nobody's brandy inside Daddy's house not then or never, not from the day Momma moved in till right now. Tell that Widow."

Thom said, "If you want to drink, you got to go back of the barn down to the woods and then you still better hide up a tree because Momma's real good at spotting that sneaking-out-for-a-swaller walk. And if it ain't a holiday she comes after with her what'd she call it, her brandy-pan and you don't want to meet up with Sheriff Brandy-Pan. So why Widder Normen say we drinking in there with Daddy when we never?"

"To make you look bad," I explained.

"How a man look bad having a swallow with his own daddy?"

> One took a drink and said, "This brandy of old Henry Bullock's is good," by which the colored visitor knew that they not only robbed Mr. Bullock, but had committed all the crimes in the neighborhood.

"See? She uses it as evidence against you."

Thom said, "What for? We robbed everybody, we never denied. We even tell them it's us. But we don't bring no brandy in Momma's house."

"This Widder your friend?" asked Steven.

"No," I said.

"Good," said Steven. "We goin' burn her out."

"You can't slay the messenger," I said. They looked country blank. I explained. "'Slay the messenger' means you can't hurt the person who reports it."

"Why not?" said Shoe-Maker John.

"Law of the Land. The First Amendment of the Constitution of the United States. Anyone may say anything they want and no one may stop them."

"*Kill the White folk, kill the White folk*! I likes that First Amendment," said Shoe-Maker John.

"What's it say about burning folks?" asked Steven.

"Nothing."

"Good, so we burn the Widder."

"No, no you won't!"

"Why not?"

"Because if you do," I said like a testy schoolmarm, "the reading stops. I will throw out everything I have written and there will be no book about Henry Berry and the Swamp Gang. I can't allow you to hurt her just because you hate what she wrote." They were baffled. "If she's in danger because of what she writes, then so am I, and so is every writer."

"Then just don't write no lying," said Thom.

"Every piece of writing is a lie to someone," I said. The next hour was lost to arguing the First Amendment until Shoe-Maker John was fed up.

"The devil with no First Amendment. Read the damn story, we won't burn no Widder."

"Amendments are vital. You'd still be a slave if not for the Thirteenth."

"If not for an ax, you mean." He stood and leaned over my desk, just like I used to thrust myself at my Editor in response to his outrageous remarks about my writing. Shoe-Maker John put his nose on mine, but I knew this trick so I remained calm. "I ain't no slave," he shouted, "because I picked up an ax and made one less Master. Piss on your Thirteenth Amendment."

Quietly I said, "But your people needed the Thirteenth Amendment. It's even more important to them than the First."

"Thirteen just a higher number," he said. No one said anything.

"Well, ain't it?" said Thom.

"We goin' to hear the rest of that raid or what?" said Shoe-Maker John.

> The colored visitor watched as several times one or another of the escaped Yankee prisoners, who were in cahoots with the outlaws, patted the head of old man Lowery and said, "Ah, my friend, after this War you'll be a great general." In this way they took advantage of the dotard's gullibility, gained his confidence, and enlisted his aid, which finally caused this foolish old man's death.

"She can say that about Poppa?" demanded Steven. We had already talked the First Amendment to death so I read on:

> The colored visitor was frightened. He left without causing suspicion, which he avoided by

drinking several brandies. His honesty is beyond question, as he has served my family since he was a boy.

"White son of a bitch," said Shoe-Maker John.
"He's colored," I reminded him.
"Still a White son of a bitch."
"I'm White," I said.
"You a son of a bitch?" asked Steven.
"I don't think so," I said.
"Let us know when you're sure."

THE FIRST RAID UPON THE HOME OF MRS. MARTHA ASHLEY. 1 February, 1865. They called in a feminine voice, "Let us in, we want your money!" Mrs. Ashley told them they could not get it, she had it in her pocket. They tried doors and windows, but the cowards failed to get in.

"I saw her through the shutter," said Steven. "Pitiful ole lady, we decided to leave her be. Sometimes we got pity."
"But you went back," I said.
"Sometimes we got no pity."

THE SECOND RAID UPON THE HOME OF MRS. MARTHA ASHLEY. 6 February, 1865. The robbers knocked. Mrs. Ashley's farm hand Mr. Paul asked who it was. They said it was Needham Thompson a brother of Mrs. Ashley, and Council, a Negro of her father's. Mr. Paul opened and the gang rushed in, blackened and covered. They took bed-clothing and whatever else they could easily carry, for these lazy brigands take away such light articles as sheets but not anything heavy.

This was the first time that the entire band had come into a house at once. The news spread in a few hours.

"How was the poor woman to survive?" I asked.

Steven said, "She was rich until we robbed her six or seven times. Then we started leaving stuff for her so she'd have food and clothes."

"The Widow write anything about all that stuff we gave?" Thom asked.

She had not.

Steven said, "Some never get poor, no matter how many times we go back."

THE ROBBING OF DANIEL BAKER, McKAY SELLERS, WILLIAM A. SELLERS AND MRS. NEIL McNAIR. 28 February, 1865. There were four robberies on one night. The band was composed of thirty or forty Indians, Yankees, Black men and other things.

"Twenty-three," said Henry Berry.

They broke into the house of Daniel Baker to break open locks, trunks, drawers, &c. Not satisfied, they helped themselves to bacon in

> the smokehouse. Then they hitched Mr. Baker's horse to his buggy, loaded their plunder, and went to Mr. McKay Sellers. They demanded the bed-clothing Mrs. Sellers had concealed. They stole a buggy to haul plunder, and went up to Mr. William A. Sellers, brother of Mr. McKay Sellers. They took $800 in Confederate bonds—

"Two hundred," said Henry Berry.

> —and coins. They ordered a Negro to hitch mules to Mr. Sellers' carriage. Placing everything in the carriage they drove to the residence of Mrs. Dr. Neil NcNair at Argyle.

Mrs. Dr. Neil McNair was the most powerful woman in Robeson County. She once nearly whipped a Negro to death for failing to smile.

> With her husband's death, Mrs. McNair inherited the largest plantation in the county and ruled dozens of slaves. Her only son, Harley, gave his life for the Confederacy, and she remained loyal to it forever despite the Surrender. The gang took all this fine woman's valuables and were fired upon by an ailing Confederate soldier.

"Who was up in her bedroom," said Shoe-Maker John. "She liked them young soldiers, yes she did." The Widow Norment had not mentioned this.

The thieves marched away with as much as they could carry. Widow McNair said it was the worst thing she had ever seen.

The gang smiled.

THE RAIDS UPON THE HOME OF ROBERT McKENZIE, ESQ. February, 1865. The doors were locked. The robbers demanded entrance. Mr. McKenzie, at the fireside with his family, ignored them. They broke in and went from room to room cutting open mattresses, breaking open trunks, and behaving as they had learned from Sherman's raiders.

"Sherman's raiders learned from us," said Shoe-Maker John. "We was first."

Finding no money, two ruffians put a noose on Mr. McKenzie to hang him if he did not give up his money. He said he had none. They talked with his servants outside, and came back in. They told Mrs. McKenzie they'd hang him no better than a Negro, and started out with him. She begged for his life. They asked her where the money was hidden, crying, "Give it to us, give it to us!" She said they had none, pleading as only a wife can do for the life of her beloved husband. Her agonizing appeals touched their fiendish hearts. Despite their race and their crimes, they were influenced by home affection, and released Mr. McKenzie. They took his gold watch, dishes,

> knives, forks, clothing, and bedclothing. They took all but sixteen spoons, which were no good left behind because the thieves carried off the rest of the pattern.

> Allen Lowery lived only one mile from poor Mr. McKenzie, and often robbed his smokehouse and pantry. Old Lowery maliciously cut down Mr. McKenzie's fruit trees, and caused his cow to die.

"How come she got to lie about Daddy?" said Thom

"She's probably reporting what she was told," I explained.

"Then let's find out who told her."

> When the raids would not stop, Mr. McKenzie finally moved to South Carolina. His brother took over the plantation but it did no good. One night the robbers fired at him, wounding him in the leg. He moved away and left the place with Mr. Phipkin in charge, who frequently saw the robbers but they left him alone.

> One time, Mr. H.B. Lowery hung his brandy canteen on the fence and went off, forgetting it. He returned at night and found it where he had left it, but knowing he deserved death he was afraid it might have been poisoned. Mr. H.B. Lowery banged on the door and ordered Mr. Phipkin to take a drink. Mr. Phipkin told him it was not poisoned, unless he (Mr. H.B. Lowery)

had done it himself. Mr. Phipkin drank half the canteen, setting the fears of the robber at rest. The robber drank the rest. They talked until sunup and parted amicably.

THE RAIDS UPON THE HOMES OF MESSRS. DOUGLAS McCALLUM, JOHN McCALLUM, AND ROBERT GRAHAM. February, 1865. Mr. McCallum's family was startled by armed men in their home. They demanded supper, which was set out in the dining room. They ate yellow potatoes, field bread, and boiled meat. After dining they robbed the ladies' clothing. Mr. McCallum's sons were off in the army. He, a gray-headed citizen, was the sole protector of his wife and two daughters. The thieves took his clothing, guns, and seven hundred dollars in Confederate money—

"Eighteen hundred," said Henry Berry.

—which was soon to be valueless. They also took bedclothing and silver. They then went to the houses of Mr. John McCallum and Mr. Robert Graham. At the McCallum home, Mr. McCallum and his niece were the only White people. They noticed the marauders when a pistol shot was heard and the yard-dog stopped barking.

"Dumb Yankee," said Thom. The dog had barked,

so a Yankee soldier shot it. "Might as well yell 'here we are.'"

> More than thirty of them barged in, masked. They were profane and had no respect for age or sex. They left no change of apparel or bedclothing. Cursing, they demanded brandy. In his cottonhouse they made him dig in the cotton where they thought money and brandy were hidden, and lit a candle to look. He begged them not to burn anything. They found nothing. They left taking a Negro and a horse and buggy. When the boy returned, he was too intoxicated to talk.
>
> At four o'clock in the morning they reached Mr. Graham's, posting sentinels so no one could pass. They pounded on the front door. Mr. Graham was alone with his daughter and asked what they wanted. They said open the door or they would set fire. Inside they demanded guns and ammunition and plundered every room. They took a purse of silver, a silver watch which Mr. Graham prized having worn it from boyhood, and the rings from Miss Graham's fingers. They ordered them to prepare tomato-baked pork, stewed onion corn, and fruit. Mr. Henry Berry Lowery told the daughter to play piano and sing.

"She played awful! We should have busted the piano to give that family some peace," said Thom. "And she sang worse." Shoe-Maker John remarked upon the singing of White folks in general.

> After asking Mr. Graham about his sons in the army, they said he and his daughter must come with them as prisoners of war. He refused, and they threatened to take them by force. They put a noose on Miss Graham for this purpose, but Henry Berry ordered that no violence should be used, and said, "Boys, we have done enough here, let us go." They said they'd be back for bacon and corn.

> Bidding good night, Henry Berry gave the daughter a small gun, saying "Keep this. Times are getting worse."

It was late. Thom had drifted to sleep like the child who never quite hears the end of the fairytale. The other outlaws went inside, leaving Thom where he was. This quiet period was always my best time to write. Hours later I looked up. Thom was watching, I could not tell for how long. "You fellows do your work at this hour," I said, "and so do I."

"I can write my name," said Thom, "and Henry Berry's. I can write my Daddy's name." He came to the desk and stood waiting. I handed him a pencil and he wrote ALEN LORIE. I wrote ALLEN LOWERY beneath. He put it in his pocket.

"How long does it take to learn to write like you?" he asked.

"I'll teach you," I said.

He nodded, as if he would think about it but not very much, and drowsed into the cabin.

The next night the literati re-gathered, and the most extraordinary thing: Thom and Andrew arrived in costume: all armed, as if on a raid, like boys wearing soldier hats while grandpa talked of the Great 1812 War.

> **THE CRUEL SHOOTING OF DANIEL BAKER.** Monday, 18 November, 1866. The bandits arrived and Mr. Daniel Baker ordered them away. A bandit fired at him, shattering his leg so that amputation was needed to save his life. A more industrious, hardworking, and kindhearted man could not be found. He would have given the bandits anything they wanted. Yet the Lowerys made him a cripple and shortened his life, for he suffered horribly until death released him.

Andrew pulled his hat down over his face.

> **THE RAID UPON THE HOUSE OF MR. MALLOY McPHAUL.** 1868. A Black stranger came to the house of Malloy McPhaul and said he had been sent from Whiteville in Columbia County where Mr. McPhaul's brother lived, who was at the point of death and wanted him to come immediately if he wished to see him alive.

"Heh, heh, heh," said Shoe-Maker John.

Mr. McPhaul took the first train. Arriving at his brother's, what was his surprise to find him in excellent health. He had been fooled.

"Heh, heh."

Filled with dread foreboding and distracted fear, not knowing what indignities his poor family had suffered, Mr. McPhaul hastened back home where he found that a party of three men had taken everything.

"Heh."

"And we made him happy, because his brother wasn't dead," said Thom.

THE MURDER OF SHERIFF REUBEN KING. 23 January, 1869. Quiet Lumberton was thrown into consternation by the news that Sheriff King had been shot. He was sitting at his fireside when the robbers came in and Mr. Henry Berry demanded money. If the Sheriff had complied he would have been safe, but he grabbed for the robber's rifle.

Running for re-election, Sheriff King had offered his own money as a bounty upon the gang.

"We wanted to get it first," said Shoe-Maker John.

> In the struggle between the robber chieftain and the Sheriff, the gun fired into the roof. Shoe John hastened to –

"Who?" said Shoe-Maker John.

"Shoe John," I said, smiling.

"I finally gets in my name and she writes 'Shoe John'?"

"We call it a 'typographer's error'."

"What?"

"Typographer."

"Then I shoots me a typographer."

"These errors creep in now and then."

"If you shoots them typographers when they creeps in, then they creeps out." I promised to share this wisdom with my Editor.

> Shoe John rushed to—

"She done it again!" cried Shoe-Maker John.

"No, sir, I just went back a line," I said. Re-reading was still not a familiar concept to the gang.

> Shoe John rushed—

"Quit!" he cried.

> —to help his comrade by firing a revolver through the Sheriff's right shoulder and into the left lung. Mr. Ward, a visitor, raised his arm and a robber shot him, a painful wound. In the confusion and fright, the robbers escaped.

Physicians were called, who pronounced Mr. Ward's case favorable, but not so Sheriff King's. The shot had entered a vital part. The Sheriff lingered seven weeks and died such a death! in the midst of his family, and at his own hearth. If there is greater divine punishment upon one man than another, it will be on those midnight assassins who committed crimes of the blackest dye.

"Was that a curse?" asked Thom.

"More like a wish," I comforted.

THE RAID UPON THE HOUSE OF MR. HENRY BULLOCK, SR. May, 1869. Mr. Bullock was surprised by the arrival of men disguised as Negroes out where he was superintending his farm hands. He was a veteran of the 1812 War, and ninety-five years of age but able to attend to his farm. Two robbers jerked him around despite his age and feebleness, and ordered him to the house.

"I just poked him which way to go," said Thom.

"I socked him," admitted Andrew.

"Why?" I said.

"Called me niga."

"Should a shook his hand," said Shoe-Maker John. "Should of called me, give him blackie lippin's all on his old face."

In the house they took $30 in coin that old Mrs. Bullock had saved. They took clothing, bed-clothing, and provisions. They found a jug of brandy and forced the old lady to drink some first, fearing it was poisoned. This was the character of the gang. Age and decrepitude could claim no mercy. The robbers cared for nothing but plunder. They were here today, ten miles away tomorrow, casting a shadow, throwing gloom around many a hearthstone.

"We're bad stuff," said Thom, pleased.

"Shadow and gloom!" said Shoe-Maker John.

Thom spun a pistol on his fingers. It went off and shot the brim of his hat. We all looked as if other things were occupying us.

THE RAID UPON THE HOME OF MR. DAVID McKELLAR. May, 1869. They took $350 and a shirt.

"No shirt," said Steven.

"Yes," said Andrew, holding out a shred of the one he was wearing.

THE RAID UPON THE HOME OF MR. M.K. GRIFFIN. May, 1869. They cursed Mr. and Mrs. Griffin with abusive language and demanded their money. They took everything and said they would be back. Mrs. Griffin was so badly frightened that she never recovered.

> **THE RAID UPON THE HOME OF MR. GEORGE WILLIAMS.** 1869. They broke a door down and fired at Mr. Williams' oldest son, Edgar. But due to their lack of skill they did not hit him.

The gang shouted me down, protesting that they shoot to scare, not injure. Andrew explained that most wounds they inflicted were accidental, because they generally missed on purpose. Scared Whites are more obedient and helpful than wounded or dead ones. Only a victim's display of bravery ever led to injury.

> The gang left, taking nothing. Their firing at Edgar seemed to have been recompense for some old grudge.

"Grudge that sumbitch walking of the earth," said Shoe-Maker John.

> **THE RAIDS UPON THE HOUSE OF MR. WILLIAM C. McNEILL.** 1869-present. Few have been harassed as much as Mr. W.C. McNeill, one of Robeson's most quiet, inoffensive, and law-abiding citizens. He is a small gentleman with twinkling eyes and homespun clothes.

"That son a bitch and every son a bitch kin to that son a bitch is a son a bitch," stated Andrew.

In 1869 they robbed his pantry and dining room, removing articles and eatables. Early 1870 they again stripped his dining room, now refurnished. In October, 1871, Mr. McNeill treed a coon when he heard human footsteps nearby. Next morning H.B. Lowery knocked, armed like a pirate but calm. He had a dead coon on his shoulder. With him was his brother-in-law Boss Strong, as armed as Mr. Berry. "Mr. McNeill," said Mr. Strong, "since your dog treed this coon, we thought to bring it to you. Harry wishes you would lend him that dog."

Mr. McNeill was no coward. He said. "I won't spare that dog, but I have another one I might lend you."

"Oh, never mind," replied Strong. The outlaws walked off as demurely as honest neighbors, leaving one to wonder why Mr. McNeill did not take the opportunity to shoot them from behind.

"Because Boss walked backwards around White folks," said Thom.

One night in 1872 Mr. McNeill saw a man at the barn and demanded, "Who is that?"

"What in h–l is that your business?" he heard.

The old man's Scottish blood mounted. "You better go away this instant."

The intruder answered, "Know who you are talking to?"

Mr. McNeill went in for his gun. His wife and daughter begged him not to go out again but he did not listen. They followed him to the doorway. Outside he called "Who are you?

He heard, "Lowery's band, G-d D–n you!" Mr. McNeill ran back inside, when they put sixteen buckshot at a distance the size of his hat from where he had stood, and wounding his accomplished wife in the thigh, riddling her dress, and wounding his beautiful daughter in the breast.

The day following, Mr. Henry Berry Lowery went to Mr. McNeill to deny the shooting and express rage at whoever it was. Mr. McNeill refused to see or to have anything to do with him. On the next day—

"Can I ask something?" spoke Andrew. I nodded yes. "If he never saw Harry how's the Widow know he was goin to deny it?" This kind of question was normally asked by my Editor. I said I didn't know but that it was good evidence the Widow was making it up.

"Nope," said Steven. "Harry was goin' to deny

it because it wasn't us." Henry Berry agreed. Still, Andrew's question was a good one.

> The raids on the McNeill family did not stop. "I should be given some sympathy," Mr. McNeill said. "I have been robbed time and again, my wife and daughter have been shot, my son-in-law and his family have had to come to me to feed them, and my sons are banished on penalty of death. These robbers have defeated me utterly."

The outlaws cheered, and we concluded the evening's reading. They hauled out their musical instruments for an hour's songs.

SEVENTEEN

WE WERE KEPT AWAKE all night by creatures battling out in the darkness. It sounded like a war of prehistoric beasts from when the whole world was swamp. Towards sunrise we heard a series of thunderous bellows that could have been Hell ripped open to the light of Heaven. Then the swamp hushed, its usual chatterers silent. We finally slept and as a consequence I did not get to Rhody's until afternoon.

She had gone to get Sally Ann from the new school in Scuffletown. I waited inside. There were flowers and patches of bright cloth here and there, and a delicate dried stem on Geronimo's picture, fragile against his Apache features. I dozed and dreamed of riding with Rhody on a northbound train.

Real life arrived in the form of a command from behind me to raise my hands or "I'll shoot your brains all over the fireplace and your balls up the chimney." I decided I had better obey, even though I had never heard a woman's voice speak in such a way. But neither had I ever fallen asleep uninvited in the home of Rhody Strong Lowery, who now circled in front of me pointing her pistol at the latter of the targets she had mentioned.

She smiled when she saw it was me. Even holding a

pistol, she had something about her that made me want to put my head in her lap.

"You can put your hands down, now," she said.

"And you the gun," I said. We both did.

"I'm glad I didn't shoot your brains all over the fireplace," she said. "Or your balls, either."

"Me too," I said, and my face went hot.

Sally Ann came in with a small rifle I thought was a toy, but when I asked if it was, she shot it out the door. Her mother told her she mustn't shoot her rifle in the house. "*You* were gonna," said Sally Ann.

"And if I do, then it's for real and you could do it too. Now put it away." Sally Ann wiped the stock and barrel, and hung it in its child-height rack.

The tot said she was happy it was me, though it would have been fun to have helped shoot my brains into the fireplace and the other thing too. I am distressed to report that she used the same language her Momma had used. I asked how she liked school and in an instant transformation from warrior to child she made a face. She said she was learning to read, which she confessed to like, and she even liked her teacher.

Young Henry Delaney carried in his baby sister and dropped her. He looked at me with miniature Henry Berry Lowery features and expression. Slightly cowed, I extended my hand and said, "How do you do, young man?"

Puzzled, he stared at my hand. "Shake the man's hand, Henry Delaney," his mother said. "Don't stand there like a duck." He wiggled my wrist so as to shake my hand. I taught him the usual method, though I liked his. Having conquered the mystery, he marched to his mother and extended his hand. "You don't shake hands with your Momma," she said.

"Whyn't?"

"Only men shake hands." He marched to Sally Ann, but she used the same excuse and pointed him at me. During the remainder of this brief visit I shook his hand a dozen times, and did the same on every visit after that.

I asked Rhody if she had any songs about the raids. "No," she said without interest. "Let 'em hum their own damn stuff." Did she want Henry Berry to stop the raids? "He knows what I think." Would she tell me? She pointed at Geronimo. "He don't do raids. He got an army. He got a war. Not raids. Raids just make folks so mad that Harry can't show his face the rest of his life unless we fight a proper war." I asked why not leave? "I'd be out of here before Henry Delaney's next pee, but Harry says we got to stay where his Daddy's buried. Hell damn, I say, scoop the old man up and carry him, but Harry says it ain't funny. I said I ain't funnin', we got to go or he got to get every Injian and some flags and start him a damn war. So don't ask for no songs about no raids. Sally Ann, sing him your song.

In school Sally Ann had made up (and written down!) a song. Poor girl was not happy to be shown off and would not sing until she thought of doing it from behind her Momma's skirts. Then this child, who would have blown out my brains a few minutes earlier, sang in a little voice:

I like it when the Sun come up

I like it when the Sun go down
I like to drink milk in a cup
And looking at the moon

My momma cooks and makes my clothes
She makes my brother wipe his nose
She washes baby sister's toes
She helped me make this tune.

I have spent no finer moment in this life. Moved in a way I choose not to think about, I thanked her for her song. She came from behind Rhody and handed me a paper: the song in her own penmanship. She asked if I wanted it. I said yes.

I returned to the swamp, thinking how I might inject into the next night of reading some of Rhody's reservations about raids. But the Widow Norment's next report accomplished that task for me:

THE MURDER OF MR. O.C. NORMENT. 19 March, A.D. 1870. As described by his Widow.

At nine o'clock this night, Mr. Norment is murdered at his front door. He resided four miles from the hut of the man who ordered his murder, H.B. Lowery. Mr. Zach McLaughlin, a member of the robber band, was assigned to do the deed. He waited outside, having entered the yard by taking down fence palings. The family would have heard the intruder but the children were making noise frolicking with their father. With the laughter of innocent children in his

> ears, the outlaw waited. Mr. Norment took his children to their room for their bedtime story, never thinking that soon his home would be desolate and desecrated. Outside the demon listened to the merry prattle of the little ones, and to the gentle tales told lovingly–

"He was telling about talking animals," said Shoe-Maker John. "No kind of thing to be telling childrens. How they goin to get along in the woods if they stop and talk to a bear instead of running for their lives? He was talking about witches, too. Preacher says don't be saying nothing about witches or something bad will happen."

"Something bad did happen," said Andrew.

"Shh!" said Thom, eager to hear, though he already knew.

> Yet the demon did not give up his dark purpose. He had a heart of stone. After the children were slumbering, Mr. Norment sat near his wife by the fire. He remarked that he heard a noise. His wife said—

Andrew asked, "How come she say 'she' if she means her own self?"

"It comforts her," I said. "It makes her feel as if she's writing about someone else." Andrew thought about that. As did I.

> His wife said she had dropped a hairpin while preparing for him to brush her hair, his gentle evening habit. He said no, it was something else,

but expressed no uneasiness. He opened the door and stepped out, and said the night was pleasant and she should bring the brush. As she got up, she saw the flash of a gun and heard him groan. She sprang to the door. She did not hear the shot. As he fell she caught him and pulled him inside. He told her to lock the door and get his rifle in case they broke in. He instructed her to fire twice out the window to summon help and to frighten off the killers. She did as he said and kneeled to support him and rock him so he could use both hands to hold the gun.

Soon her father (Mr. J.D. Bridgers), with several members of his family, got there. They called her to unlock the door. Knowing her support was necessary to the comfort of her husband, she said she could not. They burst in to find her kneeling with her arms around the wounded man, and his blood on her dress.

Mr. Norment sent for Dr. John Dick, four miles away, and dispatched a Negro boy for Dr. R.M. Norment, a brother in Lumberton, fourteen miles. When they were expecting Dr. Dick, the family heard the report of a gun. They were afraid that the outlaws had shot the doctor, but he arrived with J.F. and T.C. Bridgers. They reported that three men had shot their wagon mule, that they jumped out, and in their haste left the medicine. A Negro volunteered to go for

> it if Mr. Bridgers lent him a gun, which he did. A short distance from the house the boy saw a man in women's clothes run into the bushes.

The gang had no idea who the boy was. And they denied shooting the mule.

> The Negro returned with the medicines, and at 4 o'clock in the morning Drs. R.F. Lewis and R.M. Norment arrived. They pronounced amputation necessary. At 8 o'clock the operation was completed, but Mr. Norment was dying. He revived for a few minutes given by his Maker to say farewell to his young children and then to his wife, who—

When I told the gang she'd stopped in mid-phrase, Thom and Andrew started to cry. I think we all did. The force of the written word! To bring tears for the wife of a dying enemy. How dare writers ever pick up a pen?

> After the shock, the loss of blood, and the chloroform, the patient died at nine in the morning. By trade he had been a mechanic. Those who knew him can testify to his usefulness. His death spread sadness in the community. Soldiers tried to find the killers, but without success.
>
> I here state the true reasons why—

"There," said Andrew. "She said 'I.'"

"Speaking as writer, not participant."

"What's the difference?"

I no longer knew.

> I here state the true reasons why the robbers shot Mr. Norment. After the War, he was made Captain of the Militia, and was ordered to capture the murderers. I myself, being his wife, warned him—

"Now she's telling it and she's in it too," said Andrew. "Can she do that?"

> I myself, being his wife, warned him of the danger, but he said he had to follow his orders.

Shoe-Maker John said, "She tell the story good, but it ain't so and she knows it, poor gal." The gang agreed.

Steven said, "She's glad he's dead."

"She loved him!" I pointed out.

"My black shit. He whup her every night."

"How could you know?" I asked.

"Looking in windows, Writer. I seen. If I was a writer I'd have plenty to write what I seen in windows in my life. One time I near bust in on that man to make him stop. He was whupping till she just laying there and he kept on. I thought he goin' kill that lady. Why you think we . . . ?"

"Meanest slave-owner in the county, too," said Steven to fill the pause. "Killed one."

"Killed two," said Shoe-Maker John.

"One," Thom said.

"For all you knows, three."

"Every time someone do bad to a Black you say it was twice," Thom said.

"It is," said Shoe-Maker John.

I asked, "If he beat her, why would she speak kindly of him now?"

"Ain't there no women in New York?" said Steven. How was that an answer?

So the outlaws had wept though knowing the Widow lied. As a journalist I honor true writing. But when words the reader knows to be false still affect him to tears, it is immoral writing. Irresponsible reading. *Fiction.*

> **THE RAID UPON THE HOME OF MR. JOHN PURNELL, AND OTHER RAIDS.** April, 1870. On the 21st of April, 1870, H.B. Lowery, Boss Strong, Andrew Strong, Shoe John—

"Doom drop down from de sky on her," said Shoe-Maker John, still waiting to hear his name right.

> —and another came to the home of Mr. John Purnell at sundown. Here they stole his gun—

"The one *you* use, Writer," said Steven.

The gun had come off the page and into my actual life, instead of the other way around! I went and got my storied pistol. Who knows what else might leap from a page while we sit in our chairs safely reading?

> Here they stole his gun and ordered Mrs. Purnell to cook supper. She made cooked greens and green corn pie, and they had the audacity to thank her. They took 200 pounds of pork for spite, more than so small a band of men could ever consume. Then they went over and stole 100 pounds from Mr. Duncan's smokehouse, and more from J.C. McMillan's, John McCallum's, and James H. McQueen's.

"All them folks," said Andrew. "All their stuff." He was being thoughtful, not arrogant. I told him that reading about yourself doesn't always match how you think about yourself.

"They goin' be mad," Thom said.

> **THE RAID UPON THE HOUSE OF MR. ZACH FULMORE.** May 1870, the third Sabbath. The robbers went to the house while the family was at church.

"We're goin' to hell," Andrew said. "For surely we are bad."

"Keep in your mind who we bad against," said Shoe-Maker John.

"They was in church!"

Shoe-Maker John pulled off his shirt and turned around. In the light of my lamp we saw the scars. "Whenever you think bad what we do, come looky here. Hear?"

> The Negro left in charge had fallen asleep and was awakened by four armed men. They ransacked. Mr. Chaffin and his wife were guests visiting Mr. Fulmore, but had also gone to church. The robbers took clothes, a watch, keys, and a penknife from their trunk by the bed. They also took the trunk and the bed.

Thom had given me a penknife, which I now examined. He assured me it was not the same one. Next day, Steven told me that Shoe-Maker John had been whipped near to death before the War. "For what?" I asked.

"What do you mean?" Steven said.

"Did he do something to deserve it?"

"When one of them deserves something, they hang him."

We had no readings for a few nights, to allow me time to write. The second hiatal night, Thom absently sat in his listening spot. I reminded him we weren't going to read for a few nights. "Just setting," he said. The night we began again he was early.

> **THE FIRST RAID UPON THE HOUSE OF MR. JAMES D. BRIDGERS.** 17 August, 1870. The outlaws came to shoot Mr. Bridgers' sons. They made noises in the dark to draw them outside. The Bridgers knowing themselves to be outnumbered by a dozen men waited inside for them to come closer. The gang knew their opponents were armed, so they satisfied their

murderous desires by shooting harmless cattle. They killed two cows and wounded others. This showed fiendish character.

I agreed, and demanded an explanation.

"Meanness," said Henry Berry.

I put down the pages and asked, "Why did you shoot cows for meanness?"

"They shot at us," Steven said.

"The cows did not!"

"The Bridgers boys," said Steven.

"Then shoot the Bridgers boys. Shooting cows is barbaric."

"So is shooting us," said Andrew.

Steven said, "If someone shoots at us we got to shoot back. But we got to miss on purpose or we can't rob them again next time because they're dead. But if we miss, then next time they shoot again. So we got to keep them from shooting in the first place. That's why we shoot their cows or windows or something. One time shot four hundred punkins. Most fun Thommy ever had. And them folk never shot at us again."

Intelligent thinking. Shooting cows still seemed barbaric.

THE SECOND RAID UPON THE HOUSE OF MR. JAMES D. BRIDGERS. 14 July, 1871. The robbers came at noon. They ate eggs, spoon bread, salt beef sausages, and lemon curd, thanked God and the cook, and conducted themselves quietly. They paid for the cows

destroyed the previous year. Steve Lowery played
his banjo. Everyone was in fine spirits, though
all agreed there was nothing entertaining about
his music.

Steve looked around, wounded. "What?" he said quietly.

"You play very well," I said.

"No one ever complained before," he said, more quietly. No one knew what to say. "Maybe no one likes it. And I'd never of known except this lady wrote it thinking I'd never find out because I can't read."

I said that the Widow hadn't been there, so she couldn't judge his music.

"Then why'd she say it?" demanded Steve.

"She don't like you," said Andrew.

"I hope so," Steve said, preferring to be disliked for himself than for his music. I am the same with my writing.

We stopped the stories to get right to the music. Each outlaw sang in turn while the rest accompanied, though Steve would not touch his banjo. Suddenly Thom pointed at me. I said I knew no songs, but then remembered. I took a paper from my pocket and said I wished to perform a piece composed and *written down* by the hand of Miss Sally Ann Lowery. Never has more attention been concentrated upon me.

I like it when the Sun come up
I like it when the Sun go down

I like to drink milk in a cup
And looking at the moon

My momma cooks and makes my clothes
She makes my brother wipe his nose
She washes baby sister's toes
She helped me make this tune.

Henry Berry got up, bid good evening, strapped on guns, and headed home. The others decided it was a good night to visit home, and followed. Steve took his banjo. I had the Devil's Den to myself.

EIGHTEEN

I GAZED AT the portrait of Townsend's ancestors on my tree, pretending they were mine and that I missed them. When I was a boy I had an imaginary friend; now I sat and wrote down a whole imaginary family. I read them over, then touched them to the lamp's flame. They flared.

The swamp was old. Owls hunted. One hooted, something chirrupped, something splashed. "Wak-wok," said a brush-frog. "Wak-wok," answered ten thousand relatives. "Wak-wok," they said over and over the whole night as they had for a million years. I found brandy in the store-box, sampled it, then drained the bottle. I tried to keep a grip on the distinction between the swamp without and within.

Sitting on the ground I drank more brandy. My next thought came late the next day: I wondered how I came to be under my desk, my arms twisted around the legs of my chair. The sun was setting, the gang was not back, and I was as drunk and alone as the night before.

I looked at the ground where I lay under the desk. I thought, "I cannot come out. I am not able." I had seen too much of these damned suffering people, too much of this damned swamp, too much of myself. I had been pretending to write substance but the emptiness of my words howled tonight and cackled aloft like an editor on a broomstick. I covered my head. I pressed my face into the cool dirt. "Alone, alone . . ." My maudlin tears puddled the earth into little swamps. "I cannot, there is no going on." A night breeze rolled a pen off the desk to land in the tiny swamps I had wept into existence. I don't remember climbing out from under the desk but must have, for now I was sitting at my desk, wiping mud from the fallen pen, and beginning anew. Back at my business.

Long later, the outlaws returned from their home visits. To the next night's reading, Henry Berry wore a new shirt Rhody had made. Thom's hair was combed and waxed down. Steven no longer lounged against a tree, but sat straight and unsupported, the better to show off his new hat. Andrew's beard was trimmed; not shaved but trimmed. Shoe-Maker John was fatter. They waited. I started reading to them. All was right again with the world.

THE RAID UPON THE HOME OF MR. E.H. PAUL.

Thursday 4 August, 1870. The day bright, nature in her glory smiled. It was the day to decide the great political contest. The candidates had spoken, the field was quiet. At last, true citizens would go to elect men who would uphold the law, bring the murderers to justice, and restore peace.

While they were away voting, a crime shocked the community: the robbers broke into the turpentine distillery of Mr. E.H. Paul. Violating a home is outrage sufficient, but to discourage initiative by attacking a business is a crime against the state and Nation, damaging the very foundation of civilization. It is even worse on election day.

"I hope you are all ashamed," I said.

"My head hanging to my feets," said Shoe-Maker John. "But I don't see no heads down here with me. Keep a-reading and shame them, Reverend Writer, shame these lection-day robbing bad boys down to the ground."

THE RAID UPON THE HOME OF MRS. WILLIAM McKAY. 3 October, 1870. The robbers, together with four other men, all disguised black—

"I wasn't disguised," said Shoe-Maker John.

—appeared at the home of Mrs. William McKay looking for Mr. John Taylor, her brother, who was not there. Six robbers stayed outside and five rushed in, shooting a dog which was a pet. They captured the family, and the family's Negroes ran off.

"They was running for good seats for to watch," offered Shoe-Maker John.

> The bandits took jewelry, bedclothes and apparel. They ordered Miss Pattie McKay, a stepdaughter, to play pianoforte, which she unwillingly did to keep them in good humor.

"She loved it. It sounded like a pig come in to die in the house, but we were polite and smiled and she loved doing it," Thom said.

"That was the other one, this one cried the whole time," said Andrew.

> After she played, H.B. Lowery demanded her gold ring. She tossed her ring to him, calling him cruel. With a charm making it tragic that he chose no higher calling, the Chief Outlaw replaced the ring onto her finger, asking instead for the flower from her hair, which she put in his beard. Touching his cheek, she asked why he was a robber. He said they needed all they took, and told her other pretexts to pardon himself.

"Henry Berry, now tell the truth, next night didn't you go back to that girl?" asked Thom. Henry Berry said nothing. "Didn't he, Shoe-Maker John?"

"No suh, Marz Thom. He went to church. Heh, heh, heh."

> **THE RAID UPON THE BRANDY STILL; THE OLD FIELD FIGHT; THE KILLING OF STEPHEN ANGUS; THE WOUNDING OF ANGUS McLEAN.** 4 October, 1870. This outrage came to be known as "The Brandy

> Raid." The robbers took all the brandy Mr. Leach had distilled after purchasing the raw materials from his fruit-growing neighbors. The robbers filled every available keg, pitcher and pot. Unwilling to rob without causing pain, they struck old Mr. Leach with a gun stock, disabling him, and they slit a Negroes' ear.

"Why?" I asked.

"Denied!" said Shoe-Maker John. "We wouldn't do that."

Thom said, "He tried to cut Andrew so you slit his nose."

"Oh yeah, well I admits the nose. Why the lying ole bitch say ear?"

"To make us look bad," said Thom, now familiar with writing.

I asked, "Don't you look just as bad slitting ears as noses?" Thom had an answer and I did not wish to hear it. I returned to reading:

> They ignited the liquor that they could not carry away. The blaze consumed not only the brandy but all the buildings. When the news reached Lumberton, Captain McLean knew the stolen brandy would hurt the robbers' ability to defend themselves, so he went in pursuit with eight men. They took the drunken outlaws by surprise. Captain McLean cornered them where John Shoe—

"That does it, give me them!" He reached for my

papers. I yanked them away. "'John Shoe?' She do it on purpose! Give me them papers else I throws you in the swamp." I sat on the papers. "You won't?" I shook my head. "Then I go burns her house. Right now. Who's with me?"

No one. They wanted to hear this tale and others, no matter what Shoe-Maker John was called. Literature wins and damn the cost. "You is all a disappointment to the congregation," he said.

"Sit," said Henry Berry. "Sit, John Shoe."

It was a moment that sends observers diving for cover. Neither Shoe-Maker John nor Henry Berry was armed but they were the sort to bite each other to death. Shoe-Maker John thought a long time and finally said, "I'll sit, Loory Berry," and sat down.

"John Shoe, John Shoe, John Shoe," chanted Thom. Shoe-Maker John threw himself onto Thom and the two tried to kill each other until Henry Berry signaled Andrew and Steven to pull them apart.

"Apologize," said Henry Berry to Thom.

"If he's sorry he jumped me."

"I am," said Shoe-Maker John. "Here." He held up his hand to give the ring to Thom, but Thom was already wearing it. There was a confused moment until Thom took off the ring and handed it on the sly to Shoe-Maker John, who put it on, showed off its red jewel, and then presented it to Thom.

"I am sorry for calling you John Shoe," said Thom, but he laughed as he said the name and they began to kill each other again. Steven sat on Thom. Henry Berry and Andrew sat on Shoe-Maker John. I read again.

> Captain McLean cornered them where John Shoe lived—

> Shoe-Maker John lurched.

> —and all the drunken robbers were at his house. Capt. McLean was joined by fifty armed farmers, angry because the outlaws had burned down the distillery that bought the fruit they grew. The cowardly outlaws ran into an old pine field to hide behind stumps. Firing began. Stephen Davis, a fine young hero of the late War, bravely rushed at them, firing and making the outlaws fall back.

"He was drunk," said Shoe-Maker John from beneath Henry Berry and Andrew. "Didn't know what he was doing."

"What made him come forward?" I asked.

"The Devil," said Shoe-Maker John.

Steven said, "We pretended to be out of ammunition so they'd charge us. Then we were going to shoot at their feet so they'd run and we could go back to the swamp. It always worked before and no one ever got hurt, but now this drunk Davis had to be a hero." Somewhat more in the Rebel South than elsewhere, military strategy is often built on whiskey and glory.

> While the brave youth's pistols were spouting death to the villains, Henry Berry took cruel and deliberate aim and without feeling or justification, shot poor Davis in the head.

"No," said Henry Berry.

"Well you should have," said Thom. "What was he doing? He run right on us and there he was, what was he doing? So close he could have poked us and shooting every which way he was too drunk to hit us. I never figured out what he was doing."

> Mortally wounded, Mr. Davis reeled and staggered into the swamp. The next morning he was found face down in the mud. Steven Davis, who had stood the storm of shot and shell in many a battle now lay dead at the hands of robbers. Robeson County had lost a noble youth.

Steve said, "Nobody shot him. He drowned. Tripped on his gun and fell in the mud. Drunk."

"I went to pull him out," said Andrew. "They shot at me and I had to go back. He drowned."

> Carrying their cruelty further, one robber tried to follow him into the swamp where he lay dying, but Mr. Davis's brave comrades let fly a fusillade of shots he could not penetrate and the coward fell back. Captain McLean stationed 300 men in a cordon around the perimeter so the gang's only possible escape was to high ground where they would be vulnerable. The Captain sent for the artillery brigade. News spread quickly and the county began to celebrate the defeat of the Lowerys. Within hours the artillery brigade, led by Sheriff McMillan, was cheered through Lumberton by joyous citizens following

> behind to witness the attack. Just before nightfall the artillery arrived at the cordon and fired at the concealed outlaws.

"Heh heh," said Shoe-Maker John.

"What?" I asked. Steven explained that by the time the artillery began firing, the gang was back in Lumberton. They marched into Sheriff McMillan's unguarded office and freed an Indian and two Negroes who promised a return favor: to report that they had been freed by Henry Berry Lowery himself, and the exact time, and that the Lowerys could never be caught because they had dug tunnels under the whole swamp.

The Sheriff never believed this ludicrous claim, for there are thousands of miles of swamp. But many citizens believed it because it meant they would never have to pursue the outlaws again, since a network of tunnels would doom any attempt to failure. I did not believe there were tunnels, but the gang would not say how they escaped the cordon. "How?" I demanded.

"Me and Boss followed the others," said Andrew.

"Snuck out tippy-toe," was Thom's contribution.

"I forget," said Shoe-Maker John. "Ask Marz Steven."

Steven said, "Harry's the only one who can explain."

I turned to Henry Berry. "I followed Andrew and Boss," he said.

I read on for Widow Norment's explanation, but:

> Unfortunately they escaped, evil spirits guided by the Devil.

Shoe-Maker John said, "Yes, ma'am."

NINETEEN

THE MURDER OF MR. J.R. TAYLOR. 8 October, 1870. On this morning the dead body of Malcolm Sanderson, called "Malc," was found near Mr. William C. McNeill's sawmill. The gang had killed one of their own.

"NO," SAID Steven, looking at the ground.

"Then who?"

"John Taylor," said Andrew. "A bunch. Tom Russell. John Patterson, the Pursells, them two McNeills. I was with him. They told us, 'You'll never see morning again you damned nigas.'"

"You ain't nigas," said Shoe-Maker John, wriggling out from beneath Andrew and Henry Berry.

"So?" said Andrew.

"Nothing, Injian, just you ain't, is all."

Coroner Chaffin examined Sanderson's body and reported "Death by gunshots."

"Why did they kill him?" I asked.

"Go on to the next story," said Andrew.

They couldn't catch us," said Shoe-Maker John.

"So they made up that Sanderson was in the gang and shot him."

"The Widow Norment tells it differently," I said.

"That's why she's a widder."

> Mr. John Taylor had been persecuted by the robbers because he would not rest quiet in the face of their crimes.

"And he was a son of a bitch," said Steven.

> The gang killed Sanderson and fixed Mr. Sanderson's murder on Mr. Taylor to get rid of him. A Radical judge jailed poor Mr. Taylor. Mr. Taylor's many friends were indignant at this outrage, and got him free on a writ of habeus corpus. Three days later Mr. Taylor was killed by H.B. Lowery, Stephen Lowery and Boss Strong, who—

"Now she leaving me out! This woman—" began Shoe-Maker John, but I used an immoral device: I added in his name myself.

> Henry Berry Lowery, Stephen Lowery, and Boss Strong, who *along with Shoe John*—

"Damn," said Shoe-Maker John at the form of his name, which I had used for plausibility.

> —fired on him, all three of their shots passing through his—

"Four," said Henry Berry, to include Shoe-Maker John's shot.

> —passing through his head, the first through his temples, taking part of the skull and scattering his brains across the mill dam where they floated down the bank with the current.

I thought I heard an animal, but the sound was from Andrew.

> Mr. H.B. Lowery seized the quivering body and robbed $20 from it.

"Forty," came the correction.

> Mr. McNeill thought he would be killed next. But the savages wanted a witness to Mr. Taylor's death. The outlaw Chief gave Mr. McNeill half the $20 from the body (which money Mr. McNeill later gave in full to the victim's family), and sent him on his way.

Shoe-Maker John put his hands on Andrew's shoulders and said, "Say something, boy, or that's how it's goin' be in his book." Andrew looked at Henry Berry, who nodded.

Andrew spoke: "Malc was my best friend. He never done nothing wrong. They wouldn't have even come after him except he was with me, but they got us and tied his arms to mine." He held out his wrists to show rope scars. "They took us to Mr. Inman's and his damn son Giles was there, and a bunch of others. I kept telling them let Malc go, he done nothing, but they just hit me. They took us to Mr. Taylor's, then over to Mr. McNeill's. Mr. Taylor come out and spit in my face. He spit in Malc's face too. Malc start to cry, saying 'Mr. Taylor, save my life! Save my life!'"

"Did you say anything?" I asked.

Andrew didn't answer. Shoe-Maker John said, "It's no shame, boy, to try to save your life." Andrew said, quietly, "I cried too, and said the same thing as Malc."

"Good," said Henry Berry. The word dropped gently.

Andrew continued, now quietly. "Mr. Taylor kicked us and said, 'If all the mulatto life-blood in the county was in you two, and with one kick I could kick it out, I would kick you to hell.' They took us to the dam and said we was goin' to die. They wouldn't none of them look at us so I knew they was goin' do it. Taylor blindfolded us. I asked if we could pray and them sons of bitches talked a long time before they say, 'Certainly you may pray, but quiet.' I never heard a prayer like Malc's, he said 'Thank you for everything,' and 'Thank you for letting it be that . . ." Andrew stopped and moved out of the lamplight.

I looked to see if anyone else would continue, but no one knew this part. "You don't have to go on," I said.

"Yes, you do," said Henry Berry.

Andrew's thin voice floated back on the darkness. "Malc praying, he said, 'Thank you for letting it be that I get to die with my friend Andrew Strong. There's nobody I'd rather.' He was goin' pray more, but someone hit his face with a gun." I asked Andrew how he could tell, if he was blindfolded. "The sound," he answered. I was sorry I had asked. "They said, 'Shut up, damn niga, we are tired waiting to shoot off your head.' Someone else said, 'Don't pray so loud anyhow, God got good ears.' Malc stopped, and I didn't pray. Someone said, 'Amen, now let us do what we come to do.'

"Malc asked them to take his penknife out of his pocket and give it to his wife. Someone said yes and they did. I said, 'Please Mr. Taylor, don't kill Malc, he ain't in the gang, he never done nothing bad, you will kill an innocent boy if you kill him.' Taylor knew it was true because he said it to his own men when they caught us, but he tells me shut up. Then everyone moves off and I can't hear what they saying. But I keep working on the ropes and pretty soon I got us loose except our hands. I tell Malc, 'Nothing to lose, turn around and run!' I thought he knew which way and I ran but he wasn't with me. By the time I got my blindfold off I turned and seen him run right into them, he still hadn't got his blindfold off, and they got him again. They shoot after me but it's dark and I was gone. I stopped a ways off, thinking how to get him loose, but I hear three shots and then one more and then a bunch. So I come home."

Mr. Groone had the records of the hearing following Taylor's arrest:

> **THE STATE OF NORTH CAROLINA VERSUS JOHN TAYLOR. ROBESON COUNTY DISTRICT COURT. 1870 OCTOBER.** John Taylor accused of Accessory before the Fact to the murder of Malcolm

Sanderson, the night of Friday 7 October, inst. Defendant present. Witness Andrew Strong called by State and sworn, testifies.

QUESTION: Were you taken into custody lately?

ANDREW STRONG: Yes.

QUESTION: Were you held with anyone else?

ANDREW STRONG: Yes, sir. Malc Sanderson.

QUESTION: Does he have another name?

ANDREW STRONG: Yes, sir. Andrew.

QUESTION: That is your name, sir. Did he have the same name?

ANDREW STRONG: No, sir. His name was Malcolm.

QUESTION: The witness is uneasy, Your Honor.

ANDREW STRONG: I'm sorry.

QUESTION: Did they take you and Malcolm Sanderson away?

ANDREW STRONG: Yes, sir.

QUESTION: Where?

ANDREW STRONG: To Mr. Inman's.

QUESTION: Please look at the table. Please state what you see and if you have seen it before.

ANDREW STRONG: Rope.

QUESTION: Have you seen it before?

ANDREW STRONG: On Mr. Inman's saddle, and they tied me to Malc with it.

QUESTION: How do you know this is the same rope?

ANDREW STRONG: You said before.

QUESTION: Are there distinguishing characteristics by which you can ascertain it to be the same rope?

ANDREW STRONG: Sir?

QUESTION: How do you know it's the same rope?

ANDREW STRONG: Blood from our arms, sir.

QUESTION: Please hold your wrists for the Court to see.

HERE WITNESS raises his arms.

QUESTION: Please pull back your sleeves.

HERE WITNESS pushes his cuffs.

QUESTION: How did you get those cuts on your wrists?

ANDREW STRONG: They tied us.

QUESTION: Did they take you anyplace else?

ANDREW STRONG: Yes, sir.

QUESTION: Please say where.

ANDREW STRONG: Mr. Taylor's.

QUESTION: Did anyone go into Mr. Taylor's house?

ANDREW STRONG: Yes, sir. Then they came out to say Mr. Taylor was not at home but at Mr. McNeill's.

OBJECTION, overruled.

QUESTION: Where did they tie you?

ANDREW STRONG: At Mr. Taylor's.

QUESTION: How many of you were tied?

ANDREW STRONG: Two, sir.

QUESTION: How were you tied?

ANDREW STRONG: With rope, sir.

QUESTION: But how?

ANDREW STRONG: I see. Two men held us and someone tied.

QUESTION: I mean to ask in what way was it that the rope held you?

ANDREW STRONG: I see. Our elbows were tied behind us and then we were tied to one another.

QUESTION: Did they take you anywhere else?

ANDREW STRONG: Yes, sir.

QUESTION: Where?

ANDREW STRONG: Mr. McNeill's.

QUESTION: What time was it?

ANDREW STRONG: Dark.

QUESTION: Did any of the party go up to Mr. McNeill's house?

ANDREW STRONG: Yes, sir.

QUESTION: How much time passed before they returned?

ANDREW STRONG: Right long, sir.

QUESTION: Did anyone return with them?

ANDREW STRONG: Mr. McNeill, sir.

QUESTION: Please state his first name.

ANDREW STRONG: William, sir.

QUESTION: What was said upon the arrival of Mr. William McNeill?

OBJECTION, overruled.

ANDREW STRONG: Someone says did he know any of the men there and he said no. Then I said can I have some water.

QUESTION: Was it given to you?

ANDREW STRONG: Yes, sir.

QUESTION: Could you see inside the house?

ANDREW STRONG: No, sir.

QUESTION: When did you first see Mr. Taylor?

ANDREW STRONG: I always knew him.

QUESTION: When did you first see him this time?

ANDREW STRONG: He came out of the house. I called Good evening, Mr. Taylor" but he went back. He came out again and talked to a man I didn't know, and I could not hear. I called to him, saying could I speak to him. He said to speak. I asked him to save my life. He walked away.

QUESTION: What caused you to think you were to be killed?

ANDREW STRONG: The men asked if we liked the moon because we would never see the sun rise.

QUESTION: Did Mr. Taylor accuse you of anything?

ANDREW STRONG: Yes, sir.

QUESTION: What did he say?

ANDREW STRONG: I robbed his store and I spied. And other things.

QUESTION: Do you remember what other things?

ANDREW STRONG: No, sir.

QUESTION: Do you know why you do not remember?

WITNESS INAUDIBLE.

COURT: Why not?

QUESTION: Please repeat why you do not remember.

ANDREW STRONG: It was hard to listen because I thought I was to have to die, sir.

QUESTION: Did Mr. Taylor say anything to the men who arrested you?

ANDREW STRONG: He said that mulattos had burnt him down and stole from him. Another said I would never burn anything else but I'll burn where I was going.

QUESTION: Were you told again you would die?

ANDREW STRONG: They said I would not be alive in the morning and make my peace with God.

QUESTION: Where was Malcom Sanderson during this time?

ANDREW STRONG: Tied to me.

QUESTION: Did he plead with anyone to save his life?

ANDREW STRONG: Yes, sir.

QUESTION: To whom did he plead?

COURT: Does the Witness hear the question?

QUESTION: To whom did he plead?

COURT: Is the Witness well?

QUESTION: Whom did Mr. Sanderson ask to spare his life?

ANDREW STRONG: Everyone, sir.

QUESTION: Please state the places where Mr. Sanderson begged for his life.

ANDREW STRONG: He said that before they arrested me they told him—

OBJECTION, overruled.

ANDREW STRONG: He asked them not to kill him and he asked them again when we were going to Mr. Taylor's, and to Mr. McNeill's, and when they took us to the dam, and he was crying because he did not want them to kill him.

QUESTION: Mr. Sanderson was crying as part of his plea to be saved?

OBJECTION, sustained.

QUESTION: What happened after they took you to the dam?

ANDREW STRONG: Mr. Taylor said if you have anything to say, now is the time because soon you will not talk any more. Malc said, "Please give me a trial, everyone knows I am a hard-working man." Mr. Taylor said everyone knows he worked hard to shoot White people and rob them. Malc said, "Ask Mr. Wessel in Lumberton because I worked for him all year driving his team." Mr. Taylor said, "Boys, do what you are going to do." The rest is what I said. They took us to the edge of the water. When they were talking I got us loose and told Malc to run. He said, "Oh Lord" when he ran into them, and they shot after me.

Mr. Groon's records showed that two days later a Negro found Malc Sanderson's body behind the mill, shot at such close quarters that his hair was burned.

"They let Taylor go," said Steven. "So Harry said, 'We got to kill him ourselves. It's the only law we got.'"

"But I'm the one who killed him," said Andrew, coming back into the light. "Blowed his head down the pond."

Mr. Groone told me what the records said: "Mr. Taylor came across the dam with Mr. McNeil. The outlaws were concealed beneath the swamp moss in the water where Sanderson was killed. When Mr. Taylor was within ten feet they rose up shouting his name. One shot the brains out of Mr. Taylor. The rest shot the body."

Andrew looked into my face from a foot away. "That's how they do to us, Writer. And there's nothing to do back but kill them till there ain't one left. Because they shot Malc like that."

> **THE RAIDS UPON THE HOUSE OF ALEXANDER McMILLAN, ESQ.** Sunday, 12 September, 1870 (and following). The McMillans were building a coffin for a neighbor's child. Five robbers came disguised as Negroes.
>
> "She found me out," said Shoe-Maker John.
>
> They marched into the kitchen. Breakfast for the family was on the table, yellow turnip roots, spiced rice, red corn cake, eggs and ham—
>
> "Pretty good rice," said Thom.
>
> —to which one helped himself. The others robbed bedclothing, apparel, guns, pistols, and one dollar.

"One dollar?" demanded Henry Berry, disgusted. "Thomas?"

"Not me. Was Luther." There had been many gang

members over the years, but I had not yet heard of Luther.

"Who's Luther?" Thom told me that "Luther did it" meant the blunder was the speaker's own. Luther was the imaginary outlaw who made all the mistakes.

I found my own use for Luther. I often cooked for the gang, a practice I had started on evenings the gang was resting before raids. I cook badly but they tolerated it well. One evening I cooked worse than usual. The crust of my varmint pie turned green and the filling congealed so solidly that we could not cut it into portions, not even with an ax. The gang got hungrier and hungrier because my horror smelled good. But when it could not be cut, they kindly blamed Luther. They licked the stuff and politely said it was worth licking. From then on, any unsuccessful dish was called "Luther's Stew"—as was any situation so tangled that nothing could fix it. The swamp itself was Luther's Stew, and the situation beyond.

The Luther's Stew I cooked was left out for the buzzards but they couldn't pull it apart. Even the rats despaired. The stuff petrified for weeks until one day it was gone. I never cared to consider what kind of beast had been so able.

THE UNJUST PUNISHMENT OF CLEARANCE TOMS, EX-SLAVE. Spring, 1871. This old ex-slave had angered the outlaws by voting with whites and supporting conservative principles.

"Tried to get us killed, too, why don't she say?" demanded Thom.

"Why don't who say?" said Andrew.

"The lady who wrote it," said Thom.

"Oh, I forgot," said Andrew, for which the others made him feel foolish.

> One night the robbers came to Clearance's house and claimed it was the headquarters of the colored soldiers of the Home Guard Militia and Ku Klux Klan. Clearance said they spent only one night there and he could not order them out because the house belonged to Mr. McKenzie. The robbers said, "You vote with white men." He replied, "I can vote as I please." They accused him of lying about them. Old Clearance became badly frightened. They said they would not kill him but intended him for a good whipping. A voice in the dark said, "No, don't whip that old man."

Thom had been reluctant to see the old man whipped.

> Mr. Boss Strong said, "Yes, and we will take his clothes off to do it." Mr. H.B. Lowery ordered him whipped with his clothes on, which Boss did severely. The poor old Black boy recognized Steve and H.B. Lowery and the two Strongs; the other three he did not know.

"He knew me. He goes, 'Shoe-Maker! Shoe-Maker,

stop them.' Why don't she tell that? How he yelled my name if he don't recognize me?"

> Clearance had an enemy, a Negro named Ben Bethea. Bethea was in the robber gang and had sent the outlaws to whip Clearance. This was the usual way Bethea revenged anyone who slighted him. He had the insolence to call himself a preacher, though his sermons were exhortations to vote Radical. This abuse of his religious calling made him the most dangerous Negro in the county.

"What am I, the maid?" said Shoe-Maker John.

> After the whipping of Clearence Toms, Bethea was dragged out of his house and deservedly shot.

I interviewed Mrs. Bethea, who told me that her husband had been at after-supper prayers when a White man called, "We want you to comc out."

Ben Bethea said to his wife, "Ole woman, they goin' kill me."

"Go get your hat," a man ordered. Bethea was later found whipped and shot. The party was led by Mr. Robert Chaffin, County Coroner, and included the Ku Klux and others. According to Mr. Groone, Chaffin withdrew when it became a killing party, leaving Malcolm McNeill in charge.

A radical judge signed a warrant for the murderers, so the killers had to leave the county. McNeill became a poor clerk in Baltimore and the others had no success at all. Yet this was poor compensation to a county of Negroes who had loved old Ben Bethea in life and now revered him in death.

"Ben was all right," said Thom.

"Yes, he was," said Steven.

Thom said, "I can almost see him, preaching, singing."

"I seen him last night," said Steven.

"Yeah, I dream of him too," said Thom.

"I *seen* him."

"Who?" said Andrew. The gang looked at Steven. They didn't like ghosts, because so many had cause to haunt them. Andrew was particularly disinterested in haunts, but Steven went on: "Ben comes round when we sleeping to stand over us and preach."

"He does not," said Andrew.

"Says we're goin' to Hell if we ever stop what we're doing."

"He mention me by name?" said Shoe-Maker John.

"Leaned over you once like he was goin to shake you awake, say hello."

"No, he did not," said Andrew. "Did not."

"You telling true, Marz Steven?" demanded Shoe-Maker John. I believe Steven had made it up, but seeing how seriously Shoe-Maker John responded, was forced to proceed. Or maybe Ben Bethea, the singing preacher, was indeed haunting his old companions not to give it up.

"I wouldn't lie about this," Steven assured Shoe-Maker John.

"How'd you know it was Ben?" demanded Andrew.

"I know Ben when I see him, don't I?"

Ben Bethea, a full-blooded Negro, had been a hymn-singing, praying, preaching politician. His flock had never been told by their old owners that they could vote, or which way to vote to benefit themselves. When Bethea told them, the White mob killed him. But his songs and sermons were repeated more and louder after his death than before. His name inspired resistance against the Confederates whose disgrace had been to have to haul down the Stars and Bars but who had not buried them. If "Luther Stew" meant mistake, then "Ben Bethea" meant the immortality of struggle.

I wondered what "Henry Berry Lowery" would come to mean.

Except for Andrew, the gang spent the night singing ghost songs. The clouds made an ideal darkness for such spirits as Ben's to walk and stop for a spell to share in a tune, heh, heh, heh.

TWENTY

THE NEXT NIGHT we continued with Widow Norment's tales.

> **AN AGREEMENT OF ELEVEN BRAVE YOUNG MEN IN ROBESON COUNTY.** March, 1871. A plan for ridding Robeson County of the robbers was entered into by F.M. Wishart, Murdoch A. McLean, George L. and Frank and John A. McKay, W.H. and Archie D. McCallum, Archie J. Mcfadyen, Mengus McNeill, and Greeley and Faulk J. Floyd. Armed with revolvers and rifles, they went to hunt the outlaws, determined to kill or be killed.
>
> "Heh, heh, heh," said Shoe-Maker John.
>
> Few know what these heroic men attempted. Few would have chosen the dangers they faced. Often they suffered hunger, thirst, weary limbs, aching heads, wet clothes, cold, frost, and heat. Yet on and on they went, tramp, tramp, through the impenetrable bays and swamps, encountering the sullen anger of the Indian, the

cowardly hiss of the Negro, the arch scowls of Whites with Black hearts. They were ridiculed, slurred, and censured. They braved it all.

A week later they met again at Plainview. Owing to sickness and other causes, only five reported. They were determined, despite their shrunken number, to find the notorious outlaw, Shoe John.

Shoe-Maker John raised his eyes to Heaven.

They saw Shoe John near his residence. W.H. McCallum fired from twenty paces, striking the outlaw in the neck. Rather than accepting his fate, the outlaw arrogantly returned the fire.

"Oh, I begs your forgiveness."

F. McKay fired, striking his back. George L. McKay and J. Douglas McCallum also fired. The villain reeled and fell towards the swamp. Fearing the gang was near, the heroes picked up his ragged old hat and left the blood-stained place.

"Ragged ole hat? I had just stole it."

Returning next day with the Sheriff, they saw no corpse. Diligently, they followed a trail of blood into the swamp. They pushed through the worst tortures of nature, spending much of the day. Finally the trail circled back where they had begun. The Sheriff became angry at these outlaws, who could not act with gravity even when one of them was killed.

"Heh."

Two coon children in Shoe John's shack told the Sheriff "he were shot twice but caught dem bullets in his teeth."

Shoe-Maker John stood and proudly announced, "What they also said, but the Widder's too fine to mention, was that I swallowed them bullets and be-pooped them out the next day."

He was not killed after all, but seriously wounded. When he could travel, he left the county. He was caught and thrown in the Whiteville jail but acquitted under the "Amnesty Act," with the shocking condition that he go back to Robeson County and never leave it again! Thus the gallows was cheated and Radical law sent him back to stain his hand with more blood of Robeson's good people.

"I got killed one or two other times, too," said Shoe-Maker John. "Some day I goin' be surprised to find myself dead."

The hunt for outlaws went on. The heroes were fatigued but the county drafted ten men from each town to serve by one-week turns under F.M. Wishart, who pursued the outlaws relentlessly.

"Them brave White boys only just did what they could to stay alive one week until ten more came and they could go home," said Shoe-Maker John.

On the 10th of July the authorities arrested the outlaws' wives and children. The outlaws did not like this lawful act, and waited like panthers. They fired on the arresting party while the children and wives were being led to prison. Archibald A. McMillan was instantly killed and Archibald Brown and Hector McNeill died the next morning. Two more were wounded in head and foot, respectively. James Lowery, an Indian youth who had risen above his station to serve nobly against the outlaws despite being a Lowery himself, was also wounded. The remaining soldiers bravely returned fire until the outlaws fled. The prisoners were carried in triumph to Col. Wishart.

She omitted Henry Berry's threat to retaliate by carrying White women off to the swamps, which resulted in the immediate release of the outlaw's families.

THE RAID UPON THE HOUSE OF MR. ANGUS S. BAKER. 1 November, 1871. The robbers took beds and bedclothes, clothing, and a caged bird.

"Bird?" said Thomas. The outlaws looked at each other. No one remembered any bird. "A bird would of been nice."

> **THE MURDER OF COL. FRANCIS MARION WISHART. 16 May,** 1872. Colonel F.M. Wishart was a decorated officer who had sworn to stop the outlaws or die. One morning one of the outlaws called on the Colonel and asked him to come to a friendly conference. Wishart said he would. The outlaw gave him the time and place.
>
> The rest of this sad story is too well known. The next Thursday someone brought a message to Col. Wishart. True to his word, the Colonel saddled his mule. He rode alone, honorably unarmed, to the spot named.
>
> That night a citizen found his body. The treacherous, cowardly fiends had concealed themselves. The first hint that Wishart had of their presence was the shot that sent his unsuspecting soul into eternity.

I did not need the gang to challenge this entry. I already knew, and suddenly understood what the outlaws had already discovered: the outrage of reading what one knows about themselves to be false. The pen may not be mightier than the sword but can equally infuriate him.

THE KILLING OF GILES INMAN AND RODERICK THOMPSON. 21 April, 1871. Sheriff McMillan, along with F.M. Wishart, A. McCallum, J. McCallum, F. McKay, G. McKay, A. Mcfadyen, Mengus McNeill, and a large troop of others surrounded H.B. Lowery's cabin—

"Every son a bitch in the world always trying to get us," said Thom. "All them names she got in there all the time. They hate us."

"That's why we're in the swamp," said Andrew.

"I never knew how many they was. What if they get us?"

"They ain't yet, Thommy," said Steven.

"They're so many."

Steven fetched a rifle from the cabin. He stood over us looking mean, a dark, frightening sight. Gentle Andrew got his rifle and stood there too, looking meaner than Steven and ready to chew up a rattlesnake.

"How they goin' get us, Thommy?" said Steven. "And you're meaner than us both together."

"They so many."

"Maybe you want us to give up and die?" said Steve.

"Maybe we make every damn Injian and Black help us," said Thom.

Henry Berry's words came so quietly I could hardly hear: "I have trodden the wine-press alone and of the people there was none with me: for I will tread them in mine anger, and trample them in my fury; and their blood shall be sprinkled upon my garments, and I will stain all my raiment."

"Amen," said Steven.

"Yeah, amen," said Shoe-Maker John.

"I don't get about the wine," said Andrew.

"It's religion," said Shoe-Maker John.

"Harry, Rhody says we oughta—" Thom didn't stop when Henry Berry held up his hand, "—get everybody together like an army, and—"

"I know," said Henry Berry.

"So there'd be enough of us if they come at us all at once." Thom's thought was not new. "They killed Boss, didn't they?"

No one spoke so I read:

> —surrounded H.B. Lowery's cabin, when to their surprise they discovered he was inside with his whole gang and his wife and children. Sensing opportunity, the Sheriff went for more recruits. Somehow the outlaws made a coward's exit. Not content at their undeserved escape, they attacked from behind. They wounded Mr. McKay and killed young Giles Inman, age 18, who had done no greater wrong than wish to cleanse the county. Boss Strong killed Roderick Thompson, a resolute youth. More than 100 had come, but the gang disappeared like ghosts into the swamp to hover and strike terror some other night.

"We the ghosts of the swamp," said Shoe-Maker John. Andrew didn't like ghost talk, but Shoe-Maker John went on: "Writer, you know why the Ku Klux wears sheets?" I did not. "So they look like ghosts of drunks killed in the War. They come hang a Black boy, they want him to think it's ghosts."

"I don't believe you," said Thommy.

"You would if they came for you." He sat by Thom. "Boy, listen. They the ghosts of the drunk Rebs, but we the ghosts of the swamp. We just got to scare them worse than they scare us."

"Harry," said Thom, "shoot me for saying it, but Rhody ain't goin' to sit quiet forever. I talked to her. Andrew, give him the gun so he can shoot me." Andrew had no notion whether Thom was joking. He looked at me, of all present, for guidance; I waved him to sit down. "Harry, just think on what I'm saying," said Thomas.

"Thank you," said Henry Berry, chilling in tone.

Quietly, I began to read:

> **THE APPEARANCE OF MR. JAMES McQUEEN, ALIAS DONAHUE.** Autumn, 1870. Now at last did hope appear. Mr. James McQueen, or Donahue as he is called, obtained a Henry rifle, took three days' provisions, and went to the dreary swamps. He arrived at the house of Andrew Strong.

Henry Berry moved towards me. "Should I skip this one?" I asked.

"No," he answered, close to me, face to face, where he stayed as I read.

> Mr. McQueen approached the cabin. Inside were outlaws and females. He peered through a cat hole, saw an outlaw lying upon the floor, inserted his rifle, and shot off the top of Boss Strong's head, killing him instantly. He deserved to die more slowly.

Henry Berry's gaze flickered but held.

> Boss Strong was the youngest outlaw, a child in any decent society. He was Henry Berry's closest companion. Boss was nearly white, with dark hair of reddish tinge that curled in a civilized way. He had thick down on his lips but otherwise was beardless.
>
> Mr. McQueen still hunts for the cowardly outlaws. They dread him, and well they might, for he moves as noiselessly as a cat.

Henry Berry sat. No one looked. On him and the others something heavy was beginning to weigh. Not only grieving for Boss. Something else had been settling upon them since we had begun the Widow's tales. It had to do with the dark sight of themselves as the Widow portrayed them. A good man who is outlaw must live without thinking, without caring how others see him, without caring how he sees himself. Whether it is wise for any man to look in a mirror depends on who he is.

TWENTY-ONE

I THOUGHT THE EVENING had seen sufficient Widow Norment, but the next tale, I saw, would alter the mood, so I continued:

> **THE RAID UPON THE SHERIFF'S OFFICE AND THE STORE OF MESSRS. POPE & McLEOD.** 19 February, 1872.

The morose gang came to and greeted the title with applause.

> The peaceful Lumberton morning was disturbed when Robeson county's iron safe was found in the street fifty yards from the Court House. Alarm was raised, citizens aroused, and they hurried from every direction to see. The next thing missing was a horse and red cart from the stables of Mr. A.W. Fuller. The door of Mr. McLeod's store was open. On further examination he learned that his own safe was missing.

The gang was smiling like boys who'd run off with a cherry pie.

> Mr. McLeod's safe had contained money belonging to the firm and to others deposited for safekeeping. Valuable books and papers were also in the safe. The outlaws also took dry goods, clothing, boots, shoes, guns, &c., and books. They took the books to throw off suspicion.
>
> Squads of citizens went out to search and found Mr. McLeod's safe a mile away empty but for a crude leaving of the gang.
>
> Thommy laughed.
>
> The loss was twenty-seven thousand dollars. In Mr. McLeod's measured reactions, we see southern breeding: "The thieves robbed my business, took three thousand dollars from my home, and forced me to feed them at my table. When my wife told Henry Lowery he had impoverished us, he said, 'I know where to come when I want anything.' He looked in my pocket-book and said, 'Sixteen dollars, is that your whole pile? Well, I won't take it,' and he returned it with five more of his own."
>
> "Seven," said Henry Berry.

"I don't want vengeance," said Mr. McLeod. "Just let them leave the county, for they will never give us peace."

I cannot be so mild. The venom will not cleanse itself. It comes from the time of slavery in Scuffletown's free Negro settlement. The Lowerys, shiftless and predatory, a family of impure blood, waited for the chance to strike. The opportunity came when Freedom fell with tropical heat upon Scuffletown, warming to life these Lowery vipers. Now they have turned the heads of the colored people, who always need someone to show them which way to go. The only solution now is Lynch law and extermination.

Thommy shivered. Until he heard:

RUMORS SPREAD THE LOWERY BAND BEYOND NORTH CAROLINA. April, 1872. Our shame has extended beyond our borders. One afternoon in Columbia in the distant State of Kentucky, seven men rode down Buckston Street to the Bank. Four went in and began a robbery. The cashier created a ruckus and was wounded. When the three robbers outside heard the shots, they began riding back and forth shooting at everyone they saw, crying "We are the Lowerys of North Carolina!" The Lowery infamy was so widespread that even this far

> away the name scared everyone away, including the Sheriff.
>
> The robbers disappeared into the hills. They were not the Lowerys, but only Jesse James and F. James; R. Cole; H., D., and L. Dalton; and one who shot the teller from behind.
>
> Thus does our poor county endure everything, from these national humiliations to local disgraces such as the Moody affair. The name of Robeson County is ruined.

"The Moody affair?" I asked.

Shoemaker John smiled in a way that told me it was a sordid tale. "I knows who done what to who and who done it back." I smiled. "Oh," he said. "I see you be interested."

"What makes you think so?"

"You don't get that look on your poor pale face except when it come to Miss Rhody." By watching Henry Berry, I had learned to cover up any revealing reactions I might have, and I did it now. So did Henry Berry.

"Now," said Shoe-Maker John. "Here's about Albert Moody, who married the ugly daughter o' Sheriff King."

He pushed me off my reading chair and sat in it.

"Now all the Sheriff's daughters was ugly, but Marz Moody married the most ugliest of 'em, the most fattest, and the most awful like her daddy. Marz Moody done it because Sheriff King was rich."

"Is this a true story?" I asked.

"I beg your White pardon?" Shoe-Maker John said. I

withdrew my question but he said, "If I say it, don't that make it true?"

"Yes, sir," I answered.

"Nothing comes out these lips but the SAD AND HORRIBLE FACTS of the swear-to-Jesus truth."

"Of course," I said.

"But since you don't believe me, you can just go ask elsewheres about the Moody disgrace."

"I didn't mean to doubt you."

"Too late. You pissed in the well."

"I'm abjectly sorry," I said.

"Might as well abject the well."

"I did not mean to offend you. I would like to know the story of the Moody Disgrace. If you decide not to tell me I will regret not hearing it, but even more will I regret having offended you, a man of whom I am most fond and for whom I have abiding respect."

"Well now," he said, pleased. "Marz Moody ugly wife, who is also the Sheriff ugly daughter, she looked like a pig nose on top and worser and worser on down to her feets. So nobody can blame Marz' Moody for what happened once the joy of the blessed Jesus wedding faded after a couple minutes. Now, they lived over here, see, and he worked over there, see, so he got to go from over here to over there. And that's where the trouble come in, because from over here to over there the road passes the house of the Widder McDaniel. Now the Widder McDaniel, she got three chillun. The girl chile name of Katie Ann was as pretty as Miz Moody ugly. So Marz Moody lay in bed every night alongside his she-ox and he thinks about that Katie Sue chile, and . . ."

"Katie Ann," I corrected. "And how do you know what he was thinking?"

He stood. He walked across the clearing, turned, and looked back at me. He shook his head. He thought for awhile, then decided to ignore my question and go on with the tale. He said that one night Mr. Moody was wandering around Lumberton sipping brandy. By chance he bumped into a young man named John Brown, whose skin color and features were just what Mr. Moody needed to turn his fantasy into action. He shared his brandy until John Brown agreed to play-act the role of Johnny Lowery, who would supposedly be Henry Berry's brother. Mr. Moody gave John Brown a pistol and they went to Mrs. McDaniel's house. They shot the yard-dog the way they thought the Lowerys would have done. This poor old pet, mostly blind, died for the lust of a man with a homely wife.

Mrs. McDaniel verified the story, and told me, "They were cussing and banging, and cried, 'We hear you in there.' We became frightened. I put my boys Ralph and Justin in the bed. Katharine Earline my daughter opened the door. Mr. Moody comes in. Looking back over his shoulder he says, 'Step in, Mr. Lowery.' I thought all would be well for we had helped the Lowery gang whenever we could. I was honored they were here."

Mr. Moody, pretending to be afraid of John Brown, said to Mrs. McDaniel, "This gentleman has me prisoner at point of gun. It is Johnny Wesley Lowery, the worst Lowery. Look at his expensive clothing stolen this very night from a man afterwards shot down in a pool of blood! Now we're his prisoners!" Brown performed to the best of his abilities, running around, shouting, and shooting. He cried, "I'm hungry and you had better do something about it!"

"I have only a chicken, but I don't wish to kill it," said Mrs. McDaniel.

"Do what he says," warned Mr. Moody, "for he is blood-crazy and needs no excuse to slaughter us all."

"I don't want chicken, I want honey!" shouted Brown.

"I have no honey."

"I know you have honey! Give it to me, give it to me!" Brown called, pointing the pistol about.

"He'll kill us where we stand," said Mr. Moody.

"For the love of God, I have no honey," cried Mrs. McDaniel.

"Truly there is none," said Katharine Earline.

"You had better hand it over."

"Let alone about the honey," Mr. Moody whispered to Brown, for Mr. Moody was not going to this trouble for John Brown to dribble honey down his throat.

"In that case," said Brown to Mrs. McDaniel, "you had better cut the chicken's throat or I will cut yours, for you know how we Lowerys are." Mrs. McDaniel knew the Lowerys were not like this.

Katharine Earline started to help cook, but Brown ordered her to go into the other room along with Mr. Moody. Mrs. McDaniel said no.

"When this Lorry say do, you better do!" Brown shot the pistol at the wall. Mrs. McDaniel sent Katharine Earline to sit beside Mr. Moody in the other room. John Brown stayed in the kitchen to watch his chicken cook.

Katharine Earline reported to me, "Mr. Moody told me what the outlaw ordered us to do, but I'm ashamed to say what it was."

"If we don't do it," Mr. Moody had warned her, "he'll shoot us."

"Perhaps we can say we did it, and deceive him," she suggested.

"Alas, I am a man of religion who cannot lie. But I will, if necessary, die with you rather than force you to do what he ordered us."

"Why does he order this?" pleaded the poor girl.

"We decent people can never understand. We can question only on peril of our lives. You see his frenzy! We have no choice." He approached the crying child, but John Brown yelled in, "Get in here, supper is ready."

"I was never so glad of supper," she told me.

John Brown was enjoying his role too much and had now interfered with Mr. Moody's plan. Brown ran around shouting orders that made no sense, and pointed the pistol even at the cat.

While Mrs. McDaniel and her daughter were washing the pots, Mr. Moody whispered an order to Brown. Brown brought the yard tub in and filled it. "Now give that girl a bath," Brown ordered Mrs. McDaniel.

Once convinced she had heard correctly, Mrs. McDaniel protested that her daughter, fifteen years old, could take a bath on her own without being given it, and second, it would shame the girl in front of two men. Brown poured a bucket of water onto the fireplace and doused the lamps. The cabin was pitch dark. "Now into the bath," Brown ordered in a frightening cry.

"She can't see," said Mrs. McDaniel, but her daughter interrupted her, glad that it was dark. "But why a bath?" Mrs. McDaniel asked.

"Because I said so and I am a Lorry! Johnny Wesley Lorry" He fired the pistol. The flash briefly illuminated the raging outlaw, a drunken Mr. Moody squinting to see the girl in the darkness, a terrified mother, and poor Katharine Earline clutching her clothes. Everyone dove for cover. There was no telling whether Brown would fire again, or where. Then it was quiet again. "Is the bathing begun?" demanded Brown.

"Mother, must I?"

"It's dark and no one will see," said Mrs. McDaniel. "There will be no harm." The men sat listening to the sounds of garments dropping and of splashing. In the dark, Mrs. McDaniel silently laid her hands on her the cleaver with which she had cut apart so many creatures before but never with such need. With a great cry she brought it down at John Brown where he sat. It came to rest instead deep in her wooden table, because Brown had moved closer to the girl in the tub. Mrs. McDaniel struggled to pull the blade out. Brown, unaware of the cleaver, pushed her away from the table and said if he heard her moving again he would shoot her. Mrs. McDaniel told me that she still jerks awake at night, dreaming of her empty lunge. And she still can't look at a knife without her arm twitching.

"When you're done with your bath, go and lie where you sleep," ordered John Brown. "He'll go with you."

Soon the girl said, "I am ready," and went to her pallet next to her young brothers'.

Mr. Moody followed her through the dark cabin to the other room. He reached for her but clutched instead her young brothers. They had been alarmed by the evening's events. Having an uncle of behavior, they knew where to kick Mr. Moody, even in the dark. In the other room, John Brown took Mr. Moody's cries of pain for pleasure, and told Mrs. McDaniel, "You had better not go in there."

Mrs. McDaniel took advantage of the commotion and darkness to go for another knife that resided under her own pillow. But Mr. Moody, free of her mule-kicking sons and again seeking the bed of his intended, stumbled upon Mrs. McDaniel. He either thought she was Katharine Earline or no longer cared to be selective. He said, "I don't want to do this but he will kill us," which would have made sense to Katharine Earline but not to Mrs. McDaniel. Moody groped her dress. The boys, hearing their mother's distress, landed on him with furniture, and Mrs. McDaniel resisted him with noise, fists, and teeth.

In the darkness of the other room, Katharine Earline took a log from the hearth and said softly, "Are you there, Mr. Johnny Wesley Lowery?" John Brown said yes and she slammed the log into his jaw. Discouraged, he found his way outside and fell face first into the dead dog, quitting the adventure. Katharine Earline joined her family and used the log generously on Mr. Moody.

On this occasion, justice did not fail. Mr. Moody was forced to take his wife and flee to South Carolina.

They would have a long and happy life together because Katharine Earline's log had made Mr. Moody as ugly as Mrs. Moody and left him just one eye to see her with. John Brown was arrested but no one knew how to charge him. So he ate Mrs. Moody's chicken without cost. "Except we had to teach him about playing at being in the gang," said Shoe-Maker John, as if warning me.

"What did you do?" I asked.

"Too terrible to tell."

TWENTY-TWO

THAT NIGHT WHILE the gang slept I sat at the edge of the clearing to watch the season's first glow-bugs. The pulsing little fliers swarmed across the lake. A slice of moon lit the swamp like a cathedral.

I heard in my ear, "Long time ago was this niga, see? Mean niga, bad niga, A NIGA OF EVIL of the FIRST DEGREE."

I looked to the swamp, its violence and putrefaction silvered over, its shadows dotted by glow-bugs. Behind me, Shoe-Maker John continued: "A niga of evil disposition that wouldn't listen to nobody, not to no Black man nor no White man nor no Injian. He was ill of nature and wicked as they come. He was UNREDEEM! So when Marz Death come for him, the Evil Niga say, 'I ain't goin, don't ask, I ain't going no place.' So Marz Death leap to Heaven and tell the sweet Lord. So the Lord send down His Only Begotten Second Cousin. The Evil Niga say, 'Go away, Marz Second Cousin, I ain't goin, I ain't goin no place.' So the Only Begotten Second Cousin leap back up to Heaven and tell the Lord. And the Lord say, 'In that case I washes my Hands of the Evil Niga. He is UNREDEEM and staying that way.' Which is like I told you. So the Only Begotten

Second Cousin holler down to Marz Death, he say, 'We got no more to do with that Evil Niga up here.'

"So Marz Death jump down to hell-fire and finds Marz Debbil and tells him, 'Begging your pardon, Marz Debbil, but Marz Lord God on High got no more to do with that Evil Niga, so it's up to you, hear me?'

"'I accepts,' answer Marz Debbil in his low scary voice. 'So go snatch you some other soul and leave this perplexion to me'."

Shoe-Maker John stopped. A cloud moved towards the moon, blotting out the stars but not the glow-bugs. I shivered. Shoe-Maker John said in my ear: "I can stop, chile, if my tale ain't to your interest."

"I hope you will continue," I said.

"I thought maybe you say that."

But he did not go on. I looked around. He was watching the moon, which was reflected in cold white dots in his eyes. "Well?" I said.

"Bye and bye," he said, and bye and bye he went on: "Well now, Marz Debbil pick the weeniest one of the Hundred Misbegotten Sons of the Debbil and send him. The weeniest one sashay up to that Evil Niga and he say, 'Bad niga, now you come and go with me.' But the Evil Niga bump that weeniest one's head till the poor little weeny would of been killed if he wa'nt already dead. He jump back to Marz Debbil, crying 'Daddy, Daddy, that niga bump me wicked and I ain't goin back NO NO NO.'

"Well now, Marz Debbil he grow angry. His face turn red and his tippy tail. He summon Field-Massuh McFestus, the biggest debbil in the place, along with Boss-Driver Beezle-Bob, the second biggest, and tell them 'Go you get that Evil Niga and take this SWORD O' DARKNESS in case he give you sass.' So up they goes to that Evil Niga. But that Evil Niga, he curse Field-Massuh McFestus and Boss-Driver Beezle-Bob and he grab that Sword o' Darkness and whup them with it till they flap back where they come from, holding their forky tails. And they wake up Marz Debbil and tell him, 'If that Evil Worsest Niga in the world come down here, we quit. Looky here my busted horn and I got no tail left, he took it and the Sword o' Darkness, too.'

"So now what to do? Evil Niga won't go up to Marz God and won't go down to Marz Debbil, but he was goin die like is given under all things. So what to do with him, what to do? Well, Marz Debbil didn't get to be top devil by not knowing what to do. He say, 'Now Marz Lord God don't want the Evil Niga, so that's that. And I don't want the Evil Niga, so that's that. So only thing left, start him his own hell."

Shoe-Maker John stopped. "Coming to the scary part now," he said. I said I would survive. "I hopes." He watched a cloud moving towards the moon. Not until they were almost touching did he begin again: "Then Marz Debbil pick out the HOTTEST COAL IN HELL and send it up to the Evil Niga, along with word what the situation goin be. But that Evil Niga, he un-interested. He resting. He say go away. He get mad. He take the Sword of Darkness and smash that hottest coal of hell in fiery pieces. He hit so hard it smash every one of them fiery pieces into more littler ones, and the littler ones into more, and all them go flying. And Marz Debbil he say the Evil Niga's new hell is goin to be every place them fiery pieces go flying. And God looketh down and smile on account of He don't have to go down there and he say, 'Yea, verily, that'll teach him.' Then God give that new hell a new name, so that it don't get confusions with the hell that already is. And the name God calls that new Hell be . . . you know it, Writer?"

"Yes," I whispered, watching the swarming glow-bugs fill the world.

"That's right," said Shoe-Maker John. "And we in it. And the fiery pieces are them glow-bugs right there, and Hell's every place you ever see one."

I turned to look up at him, but at that instant the clouds closed over the moon and I saw only glow-bugs reflected in his eyes.

He blinked, and went back towards the cabin. He moved into the circle of dim lamp light at my desk. He bent, and as the clouds had done to the curtain of stars, and as he had done to my thirst for tales, he quenched the lamp, blotting out all the world except the glow-bugs and his deep, rich laugh.

TWENTY-THREE

SUCH SILLY TALES affected me too much, and I knew why. I visited the one man I thought might help. "I will consider it an honor," I said to him, "if you would accompany me for a sip and supper this evening at 6:15."

"I like supper as well as does the next man," said County Recorder Groone.

We began with a sip. He was too polite to ask why I had invited him. Nor could I tell him that because I was unhappy I had come to the unhappiest man I knew to help me. But I told him that my glut of accumulated information was making me question too deeply, and that I wondered if this recorder of evils, altercations, and sufferings had the same difficulty.

"You can become too full of your subject," he said.

"Which can interfere with one's ability to write it down," I said.

"If you don't write it down, no one will care," he said, an unexpected sentiment from a man who spends his days writing things down. "Do you know about the nature of obsession?" he asked quietly, as if frightened to say the word.

"I believe I do," I said.

"The inability to stop. Not by choice." He sipped

his wine. "Henry Berry Lowery causes men to become obsessed. Aye. Colonel Wishart, for example. He had a full life, did he not? Yet he quit it to pursue Lowery. Some men are obsessed with seeking gold they'll never spend even if they get it. Others with power, or love — or Henry Berry Lowery. Yes? Yes. Naught to do with choice."

I said, "I came to North Carolina only to report a news story." Mr. Groone smiled and signaled Mr. Lear to fill our mugs.

"I am sure that is why you came," he said. "Things change. Colonel Wishart's career is apropos, and my records, as always, are open to you."

We ate Mrs. Lear's fine dinner. She came from the kitchen with dessert to accept our appreciation. And though I had not intended to ask Mr. Groone anything else, the good berry wine led me to it. "What," I asked, "is the cause?"

"Of what?"

"All . . . this," I said with a wave of my hand.

"The Inn?" he said.

"The trouble."

"I see no trouble," he said, looking nervously about.

"This county," I said. "This damnable, damned, damning county! When people in it have difficulty with other people in it, why don't they simply strike each other on the nose and go about their business, as we do in New York, instead of carrying on these incessant feuds?"

"Aye, that trouble," he said.

"Yes," I said. "Why is it?"

"We're cursed," he said.

Cursed by obsession? By inability to stop? Utterly without choice? "What makes you say the county is cursed, Mr. Groone?"

"What other explanation can there be? Consider Colonel Wishart."

TWENTY-FOUR

THE TRUE EVENTS of the SHORT LIFE and SURPRISE DEATH of COLONEL FRANCIS (Frank) MARION WISHART

NAMED FOR the Swamp Fox of the Revolutionary War, Francis Marion Wishart fought in the Civil War and came home vowing never to touch another weapon. He married and became a shopkeeper whose customers were mostly poor Indians. He treated them fairly, although his father and brothers were known for their activities against Negroes and Indians. His father commanded the county Militia, which did everything it could against the lesser races. When the father died, the State appointed his son Francis in his place. Francis's wife, Lydia, opposed his accepting the post, because she had married him only on his vow never to fight again. Nonetheless, Captain Wishart of the Confederacy became Colonel Wishart of the North Carolina Militia, with orders to stop the Lowerys.

But the White populace had given up hope that Henry Berry could be captured, so Wishart's Militia was an apathetic variety of temporary draftees. He had to drag them out of barn lofts and from beneath beds.

"The Colonel spent his time searching for his men," his widow told me. "Once he found them, he could not make them stop drinking long enough to sit on a horse without falling off and getting trampled." These were the soused heroes who never ceased waggling their Rebel Stars and Bars.

Wishart wanted Whites to do the same thing that Rhody wanted Indians to do: arm for war. All of them. Batter the enemy. Undo them entirely. Rhody believed nothing less could succeed; Wishart believed the same. Henry Berry remained unconvinced and Wishart's warriors kept going home to drink.

One morning Wishart was surprised to find that he had a full complement of a hundred men instead of the usual 15 or 20. But his hundred would be useless if they left or got drunk before the enemy could be found. So he arrested Rhody, her children, and the families of the rest of the gang, reasoning that the gang would fly to the rescue and make itself easy prey. But Henry Berry threatened to haul White women into the swamp, an offer that sent the county elders into hysterical conference. At the same time, Wishart's troops assembled at the jail where the women and children were held, certain that the gang would obligingly strike in that very place, on the assumption that "If you take a man's woman, he's coming to get her back." This assumption was Wishart's second-worst blunder over the whole of his command, because for the plan to work, the outlaw gang would have to cooperate. The gang would have to arrive at the jail rapidly, before the loyal militiamen drifted home. The gang would have to start a battle despite the possibility of hurting the very women and children they came to save. And the gang would have to throw down their guns and stand motionlessly out in the open, preferably atop low buildings against a clear sky – because Wishart's marksmen were dangerous mainly to targets that were unmoving, unarmed, and eager to die.

Hundreds of Whites, sniffing safe victory and wanting to be seen among the brave, came to join. One group of 23 was rushing to do battle when they stopped for a drink and a nap. While they slept by the river, their sentry noticed the approach of a canoe manned by Henry Berry himself. The sentry should have alerted his comrades but this was his glorious chance. He crouched in cover and prayed no one would wake before Henry Berry came into range. Finally, he fired twice from a few dozen feet. The Outlaw's body slammed into the water and the canoe capsized. The sentry fired four more shots. The shots woke the sentry's comrades and the sentry cried, "I killed him, he's mine!" They saw the canoe floating by. They reasoned that the Outlaw was clinging to the far side, so the current was carrying off thousands of dollars worth of bounty. Shouting and shooting, they crashed through the brush to the river bank. The canoe slowed as if snagged. When it began moving back upstream they stared like a bewildered herd until shots killed three of them.

The Captain, Bobby McRae, ordered his colliding men back to the battle front. The two who obeyed fired at the canoe. The Outlaw remained shielded behind, so the rest came and fired, too. Soon the troops were out of ammunition, but the Outlaw was not. Eight more men were wounded, two mortally, and none could flee without being exposed.

They thought they would wait the half hour until dark, and escape. But the first two who tried it were shot dead in pitch blackness. Morning found the rest still pinned in place. The inverted canoe hovered ominously, like a Yankee monitor ship confronting the Wilmington forts. By late afternoon they understood that the canoe was long abandoned.

Nonetheless, Colonel Wishart still had the gang's women and children in jail. He had Lowery where he wanted him—so long as the county government did not cave to the Outlaw's threat of kidnapping White women into the swamp. "We do not listen!" cried Wishart in response to the threat. But the county's elders did. "All things taken into consideration," they decided, "it is only humane to release the wives."

Some months later Wishart went to see Rhody, his former prisoner, in her cabin. Rhody was nursing the baby when she turned to see a man in the doorway. "My name is Francis Marion Wishart. I am the Colonel of the Militia charged with bringing in your husband."

"I know you," she said.

"I can help Mr. Lowery."

"Quit trying to kill him, that'd help him."

"May I come in?" She nodded at the chair. He sat, leaving his rifle in the doorway. "If you persuade your husband to surrender, I can arrange a brief sentence after which he will be a free man." Rhody said nothing. "The state of North Carolina has promised me artillery.

He could be killed." Rhody still knew to say nothing so that Wishart would say everything. "Are you not afraid, all alone at night? Do you not miss him? You have three small children, Mrs. Lowery. You need your husband to come in from the swamp. If you lose him, who will defend you?" Rhody nodded toward the door. Wishart turned to see Sally Ann, who had silently tipped his rifle onto the stoop and aimed it in his direction. Her finger was on the trigger. "You will hurt yourself," he said in a calm voice.

"Go away," she said.

"It's all right, Sally Ann," said Rhody. "Go play." Sally Ann started away, hauling the rifle. "Leave the man's rifle, honey," said Rhody. "Take the baby." Sally Ann took Neelyann from Rhody's arms and went outside but did not relinquish the rifle.

Wishart began again: "If he gives up, there will be some punishment, but the State has ways to punish men it doesn't want to punish. Soon he'll be back and it will be over." She said nothing. "Do you think he'll be willing?" said Wishart.

"I don't know if I am willing," said Rhody. He asked her to consider and said he'd return for her answer. He left. Rhody thought about what he had said, and then thought to look outside. At the end of the path Sally Ann had rested the muzzle of Wishart's rifle on a stump, and was holding the Colonel at bay. "Chile, I told you let the man have his rifle." Sally Ann did as she was told, but first amazed the Colonel by removing the shells and tossing them into the swamp.

"Thank you," he said as she handed him the gun.

She did not reply, a trick she had learned from her mother. Wishart called to Rhody, "I hope you will help me, Mrs. Lowery."

"I just did, Colonel Wishart."

A few nights later Henry Berry was home. The children were asleep. Husband and wife sat before the fire. "Henry Berry," she said, and he knew the subject by her tone. "Henry Berry. Henry Berry."

"Ma'am?"

"Get you a horse and a buggy and go find him."

"Who?" he said, though he knew. She pointed at the picture of Geronimo.

"We got three choices," she said. This got his attention, for usually she nagged of only two. "One," she said, "we leave. Two, go see Geronimo and learn about making an army." She stopped.

"Three?" he said. She told of Wishart's offer. "I can't sit in jail," Henry Berry said. But Wishart had implied better. Maybe he could arrange a pardon after a short sentence. "And if he don't?"

"Seen a jail we can't get out?" asked Rhody.

Wishart returned a week later and Rhody said Henry Berry was willing. At the Devil's Den, Henry Berry revealed what he was going to do, strapped on his weapons, and walked away. Thom called after, "What in hell we do now, Gawd damn you?" Henry Berry kept going.

"He'll be back," Shoe-Maker John told Thom.

Next morning, Colonel Francis Wishart put Henry Berry into a jail cell. Wishart asked, "What will you do when this is over?" Henry Berry didn't know. But Rhody did. He would farm their land, be a carpenter, and raise up their young ones, which instead of three would be ten or fifteen.

By afternoon, Thom, Boss, Andrew, and Steven had left the swamp to take up life at home. Shoe-Maker John cursed their stupidity and stayed. They told him and themselves that they only wanted to do the normal things of living. "What things is that?" demanded Shoe-Maker John, knowing that outlaws have no answers.

That evening, Steven and Boss visited jail. "What you goin' to do?" Henry Berry asked.

"Farm," said Steven, but spoke as if saying "piss." They knew they had been fighting for the chance to live and farm in peace. But the act of fighting for it had ended their desire to do it. They were brigands now, not dirt farmers.

That night, a turnkey, paid by the Ku Klux Klan, thrust a pistol into the dark cell and fired four shots. Henry Berry was twisting the turnkey's wrist by the third shot. The fourth shot went through the turnkey's eye.

At dawn Henry Berry returned to Shoe-Maker John in the swamp, who said, "I knew you'd be back. Never gave it a thought."

"Then how come you're awake?" asked Henry Berry. Shoe-Maker John smiled and went to sleep.

Next morning Wishart came to Rhody's cabin. Sally Ann ran him off.

Henry Berry's escape started a new wave of White violence, which included the killing of Boss Strong. The gang struck back in a renewed surge of raids and attacks, relentless for months. But Colonel Wishart was not through. His near-success drove him on, the way a gambler's near-win drives him to bet again no matter the odds. Wishart sent Henry Berry a request: "Let us meet to talk, alone and unarmed. I give you my word and I want yours."

"Let him talk to his own self," said Shoe-Maker John.

"Take someone secretly, in case it's a trap," I said.

"No," said Henry Berry. If he agreed to go alone, he'd keep his word. He trusted Wishart, having seen him at close range. He knew Rhody trusted him, too. She had said, "He never stopped being kind to Sally Ann, even when she stuck his rifle at him," and that marked him as trustworthy. Sally Ann had other feelings.

Andrew questioned the Indians who had shopped at Wishart's store. They all considered Wishart's word as trustworthy as Henry Berry's. Andrew and Steven went and told Wishart that he would be contacted.

Henry Berry sent me to tell Wishart where and when to meet. Steven and Thom instructed me how to confront Wishart, and to speak without humor or fear. Shoe-Maker John told me to keep my eyes on Wishart's, and Andrew tucked my pistol close within my coat. I rode to the Wishart home and was admitted. Trembling, I told Wishart the name of the road where the meeting would take place and the time of day. "And what day will that be?" Wishart asked.

"This one," I responded.

Wishart thanked me and smiled. I said good

day and left as if I had noticed nothing. But I am a journalist. I know one smile from another. I know a smile of thanks when I see one, and Wishart's had not been one. In a news interview, such a smile would have prompted me to track down the rat I had sniffed. This was no interview, but there was a rat. I returned to Patrick Lowery's horse, who never smiled at all, and I went to find Henry Berry.

He had already gone to meet Wishart.

Later that day, Henry Berry waited in the open by a deserted road. Despite the gang's objections he had come alone. His weapons were piled fifty feet away and in full view. He had removed his shirt, hat, and boots to show he was unarmed. At the appointed hour, Wishart approached on his mule. He dismounted and walked past the Outlaw's weapons towards Henry Berry. Henry Berry held out his hands to show himself unarmed. Wishart removed his own shirt and boots for the same purpose. "We alone?" he asked.

Henry Berry nodded. Wishart continued towards Henry Berry.

To Mr. Groone, Wishart's sad story illustrated the power of obsession. As a warning to me, Mr. Groone told me how obsession had given Wishart no choice but to expose himself to terrible danger. But Mr. Groone did not know that obsession had driven Wishart in a different direction: the good Colonel abandoned his beliefs and most cherished moral standards. Obsession had not yet done that to me, but long ago had done it to the county.

Ten feet from Henry Berry, Wishart removed his

hat as if to discard it, and said, "You are a dead man, Henry." When Wishart dropped his hat and revealed his pistol, Henry Berry's expression did not alter. A strong man looks the same winning or losing. And having gambled on the word of an obsessed man, he had lost.

But in the brush lurked a timid Yankee who had come south to report a few events passing in the county of Robeson. I held my breath. I drew my gun. I fired twice. I missed.

Harry lunged for Wishart's gun, but Wishart stepped back. Wishart looked towards me, then told Harry something I couldn't hear. Wishart raised his gun to shoot Harry's chest, and I breathed out, as Steven had taught. I whispered bang. My shot drilled Wishart's head. He collided into Harry before dropping to the dirt. If I hadn't been afraid to hit Harry I would have shot my pistol empty at the corpse. Wishart had been within a finger's press of bringing down Henry Berry Lowery. Instead, for smiling at a newspaperman, Wishart was dead.

I was still hidden, but Harry thanked me by name. "How did you know it was me?" I asked.

"You missed twice," he said. In fact I had missed thrice, for I had been aiming at Wishart's chest. I saw no need to mention it.

"I might have been Sally Ann," I said.

"And missed twice?" We stood over the body. "Obliged," he said. I waved off his thanks, but I remember it.

I had killed to protect an outlaw from the authority of the State of North Carolina. I was sunken as far into this swamp as a man could go. But write down this: I would do it again. Write it down. From the moment Wishart had smiled at me, I never thought about choice. Choice never came into it. Harry told me that the last thing Wishart said, which I hadn't heard, was a complaint that the Outlaw had lied and not come alone.

That night Harry made me tell the gang my tale. Shoe-Maker John asked, "Whyn't you just tell him to stop?"

I was stunned. It had never occurred to me. I should have said, "Colonel Wishart, I have you in my gunsight. I will shoot if you do not throw down your weapon." That would have been a civilized man's first idea, yet I thought of it no more than any reader would have done. How civilized are we, after all?

Steven said I was too scared to act normally, but that would pass once I had killed another dozen men.

"You goin' to be famous," said Thom. But Steven pointed out that I would be wanted for the murder of a State Militia officer, a hanging offense. So I decided to abjure fame and leave the community guessing—the very opposite of what a newspaperman is supposed to do.

Come listen to my story
Of a man we should know well,
The man he was a hero
His tale I'm proud to tell

The man he should be famous
The same as Jesse Jame,

I can sing his praises
But I cannot say his name

Sally Ann wrote the rest, with only a little help from her mother:

Bad man try to shoot my daddy
Try to shoot him dead
My friend he shot the bad man
Right up in his head

Oh he who'd shoot our daddy
Must be the very worst
So thank the man with no name
Who shot the bad man first

He shoot old Wishart in the head
Sent him falling down to hell
So now I'm here to thank you
Though your name I cannot tell.

Rhody said, "If it wasn't for you I'd be a widow." I hadn't thought of that.

TWENTY-FIVE

THEN SOMETHING HAPPENED I have to include but couldn't make myself write down. So remembering that the Widow Norment had considered writing a book of her own, I hoped she'd have what I needed. So late one night I fed her dogs to quiet them and snuck into her yard as her husband's killers had done. She was awake, as I could tell by an upstairs light.

I climbed up over the kitchen, crossed the lower roof, and peered through a second-floor lace curtain. Inside, the Widow Norment was doing what I had hoped: writing. The night was warm and she was lightly dressed, so my mind drifted from my mission. I had from time to time thought about the companionship of a wife and family but not closely considered all it might mean. Now I saw.

I once covered a Peeping Tom who spied until he was caught, to his shame, and jailed. I wrote that his spying was senseless and sordid, but here I was doing it. I continued doing it until the Widow put her pages in a desk drawer and blew out her candle.

With no moon, the Carolina night is tar black. I waited outside the window, giving her time to fall asleep. But abruptly the window swung outward and I had to duck to dodge a knocking. Her pale shape, gowned in gossamer, swayed over me as she breathed the night air and gazed at the heavens. Over me, her scent filled the night. When I die, if St. Peter says I must forsake that memory to get into Heaven, I might not. It felt almost permissible to reach up and touch her. I almost did.

I had read that the Lover loves everything about the Beloved, pleasant or not. A colleague once claimed to adore the nose-wart on his editor's sister, because he loved her. He who loves is doomed. In the dark, as I was enveloped in the Widow's scent and close enough to feel the warmth of her body, she cleared her throat and spat into the night air. A veil of residue sprayed down upon my face like the cooling rains of Heaven. I know the reader must be disgusted and shocked, but I closed my eyes and mouthed silent endearments that I had been waiting my whole life to say. I opened my eyes and she was back inside. I had mouthed my adoration into thin air.

She went into her bedroom. I heard a fall of material as she took off her gown on this sweltering night. I could not imagine this happening so close to me. When I was certain she was asleep, I came in like a mild breeze, felt my way to her desk, and took her writings. I peered into her bedroom. The darkness was prudishly impenetrable. I had never seen an unclothed woman, so my mind's eye pictured the only thing it knew: a white marble Grecian figure, armless on a pedestal, with a carved title-plate: the Widow.

I hurried out the window, across the roof, down the kitchen wall. I sprinted the mile to Patrick Lowery's horse where I had left Henry Berry's invention: the magic flame box, by which I copied the Widow's writing.

How could a timid man like me so brazenly find himself with two such loves as Rhody and the Widow Norment? I wondered how a married man with a mistress endures the constant terror of discovery, when I was in terror that either woman might find out about herself!

There were other terrors. Wishart's death brought bad times. He had been a danger, but had kept the Ku Klux at bay and held the bounty hunters in check, allowing none of them to interfere with his military actions. But with Wishart gone, bounties were raised so high that one quick shot could profit a poor Negro or Indian enough to support everyone he knew forever. We could trust no one. Even I was in peril, though not by name: there were four separate rewards for me.

Everywhere but the swamp was dangerous for us, so when any of us ventured out together, our shared peril made us closer. I now knew why such men take risks for each other: facing mortal hazards together, the distinction between "me" and "you" disappears. That is why I could not bring myself to record some of the events that occurred at around this time, and needed the Widow Norment's assistance. She had written, and I had copied:

> After the Lowerys decoyed and slaughtered the noble and patriotic Colonel Francis M. Wishart, the outlaws sent a message to his two brothers, A.S. Wishart and Robert E. Wishart,

to leave the county or they too would be killed. But the brothers were from a military lineage, and armed themselves. They took Mr. James McKay and Mr. James Campbell with them, and a bounty-hunter who had been a Yankee lieutenant and was now returned to pursue the rewards offered for the gang. They set out for the swamps after the outlaws.

They paid for information and learned that one of the outlaws, Thom Lowery, often visited the house of one Furney Prevatt. The Wishart brothers and their comrades hid there. Soon Thom Lowery came out with a woman. They heard him say he would take her to a meeting next morning at Union Chapel. The Wishart company waited at the main road in suspense and anxiety until 8 a.m., when the couple were seen in the distance. Coming where the Wishart company had crossed, Thom examined the footprints. Furney Prevatt said, "What is the matter?" Thom said he was worried about these footprints, but he didn't care and "would go to Union Chapel or die." Then the Yankee stepped into Thom's sight. Thom called his name and stepped towards him, and the Yankee fired. Thom turned to run, and Mr. A.S. Wishart fired a ball through his body. The outlaw ran fifty yards. They thought he would escape but he fell with a heavy sigh. They rushed towards him but stopped when he raised a rifle in one hand,

> pistol in the other. Happily he was too far gone to shoot, and fell back a corpse. He clutched his rifle so firmly that they had to cut his fingers to get it from his grip.

I stopped copying, thinking what might have gone through Thommy's mind in that fifty yards. "I can do 'er, I can do this, all I got to do is get to that brush, I can do that, I told Harry this would happen, damn look how close that brush is, I'm goin to make 'er!" Poor Thommy.

Rest you in peace, Thomas what-the-hell-your-middle name Lowery.

> Thom Lowery had been a thieving sneak, capable of murdering or anything else mean. He had a nasty look.

He always looked like he was looking at Forbidden Snow Hill.

It was dangerous for the gang to venture out to the funeral, but I went. I expected weeping, wailing, and loud singing. Thommy would have wanted hair yanked, garments torn, and mourners leaping into the grave. But it was a silent funeral. I helped carry the coffin.

I wanted to have to strain under his load, but it was like carrying the featherweight of a child. As we walked, Thommy's body shifted slightly in the coffin, as a sleeper might do. In my hands I felt the palpable movement of his weight. Then we lowered him down. Mary Cuombo sprinkled earth and the Minister said what ministers say. Rhody sang over his grave:

Drop him down, drop him down,
Another man dropped down
In the ground, in the ground
Another man dropping down

Bend your head, drop it down,
Tears is shed, dropping down
On the ground, on the ground
Another tear dropping down

Voices down, voices down
In the burying ground
Another man he is gone
Down down down

Back at the Devil's Den I asked Harry if I should write it all into the book. He said the less about funerals the better, and went into the swamp. Steven went inside and polished Thommy's other boots. Shoe-Maker John made me tell him about the funeral, thanked me kindly, and shook my hand as if I had been the Minister. He went to the edge of the water to pray, or maybe talk to Thommy. He flung something high and far directly at the setting sun. Its red jewel glimmered in the sun. As if materializing out of thin air, a black-feathered bird swooped down, caught the ring in her beak, and disappeared as instantly as she had come.

Shoe-Maker John came back, leaned over my desk, and said, "He was a good boy." I nodded. "Make sure that's what you write, Writer. And you never know if I'll learn to read and find out if you write something else. Hear?"

"Yes, sir."

"Good, because I was talking to Thommy just now and he said 'watch that my grave's clean.' I said, 'Thommy, I can't go to your grave, they'll get me,' and he says 'Oh yeah, then watch what he writes.' So I am. Then we talked about this and about that. Then he says he got to go now, he sees them waitin' on him. I say, if he sees ole Ben Bethea, tell him hello. And Thommy says, 'Anything for you, Marz John.'"

TWENTY-SIX

ENCOURAGED BY THOM'S death, the Wishart Brothers spread the word and attracted fifty fearfully armed bounty hunters. Among the last to arrive and join the company were two from undetermined places, the most violent men the State had ever seen. One was a gaunt Negro, black as any African, muscular and heavy bearded, and he rapidly learned the swamp.

His companion was never seen close enough for anyone to describe, for he always lurked in shadow. He wore his hat over his eyes and his collars high because, he explained, he was a wanted man. This grotesque duo wished only to capture the Lowerys, take the rewards, and move on. The county was desperate enough to welcome such desperadoes. The two reported several near-successes and became the Wishart Brothers' greatest resource.

One morning at Henry Berry's request, Steven and Shoe-Maker John stole bushels of peaches, wagons-full more than we could ever give to poor families, and in any case the stuff was already rotten. We carried it, along with twenty barrels of stolen molasses, to a far corner of swamp miles away, and dumped it there.

Henry Berry would not say why. Then he directed us to add rotting meat and carcasses.

A week later the bearded Negro bounty-hunter and his high-collared cohort announced, to thirty of the Wishart's most dangerous men, the discovery of the Devil's Den. So that none of them could go capture the gang alone and claim the rewards, they would all go right then, without delay, and with no contact with anyone else lest there be an information exchange. They crossed the swamps and came to the very thicket where we had earlier dumped the peaches, molasses, and meat.

"Y'all goes in this way," said the bearded Black, "and make no noise. You," he said to a young sheriff from Georgia, "stay here in case we need you. When the rest of you hears me shoot, run in them brushes shooting and hollering. And when the gang runs out the other side, me and Luther be waitin right there to pick 'em off."

"Mmm-hmm," said the high-collared man on Patrick Lowery's horse.

Blacked Henry Berry and I went to our position. Harry shot in the air and led me off at great speed. We heard the bounty-hunters shoot as they charged into the thicket. I had never seen Harry run so desperately. When the Nation's most dangerous outlaw runs that fast, it's good policy to persuade your horse to do the same.

We went half a mile and stopped. Henry Berry stroked Patrick Lowery's horse to quiet him as much as the panting animal could quiet, and we listened. Far back were shots, howls of anguish, and an unwordly thunder of buzzing. "What have we done now?" I asked.

"Fed the wasps," said Henry Berry. The reek of sun-soaked rotting stuff had attracted every wasp in the swamp.

Next day, Steven and Andrew guided the young Georgia sheriff back to the Wisharts. He could barely move and his eyes were swollen shut. He reported that the desperate victims had tried to shoot the swarming insects, and failing that, shot themselves or were stung to death.

After that, bounty-hunters avoided the swamp. For the same reason, it became more dangerous for us to come out.

But we did come out, and our tactics were not exhausted. On the Court House door we posted the names of everyone associated with the Wisharts. We offered $300 for each one killed; $500 for multiple or disfiguring wounds or anything interfering with sight or walking; $100 for any detached part of the individual such as a hand, and $1,500 for a recognizable head. The bounties were triple if claimed by anyone else on the same list.

By nightfall, the entire list was gone from the county. The Wisharts quickly hired salaried professionals to replace them—not random amateurs in search of a reward, but experienced mercenaries with discipline and terrible abilities.

Yet these men did not cause our next loss, for which I had to return to the Widow Norment for yet another story I could not make myself write. I got what I wanted and returned to read it to the gang.

> Mr. William Wilson, a native of Guilford county, incurred the anger of Steve Lowery and Andrew Strong. They went into Mr. John Humphrey's store in Scuffletown where Mr. Wilson was a clerk, and accused him of talking about them. Andrew Strong told Mr. Wilson "that he would give him until the next day to leave the county, or he would kill him," and then left. In fear, Mr. Wilson loaded a shotgun. At 4 o'clock p.m. Andrew Strong was seen outside leaning against a post with his back towards the door. Mr. Wilson shot him dead, and delivered the body to the Sheriff.
>
> Thus perished Andrew Strong, elder brother of Boss, six feet high, slim, nearly white, and with dark red hair. He could wear a look of meekness. His voice soft and treacherous. Great soft eyes that seemed ready to shed gentle tears, but he had no soft feelings. He was a cowardly sneak—

Harry grabbed my pen and struck out the last two words.

"What was Andrew DOING?" demanded Harry. I did not understand the question.

Steven explained, "You don't threaten a man, then come back in an hour and stand there backwards."

"Tired out," said Shoe-Maker John.

Drop him down, drop him down,
Another man dropped down
In the ground, in the ground
Another man dropping down.

For the first time, I asked outright: why not get out of Carolina? I knew Henry Berry knew nothing about anyplace else and that his Daddy was buried here. I knew that the Indian part of his blood had been here thousands of years. But these same reasons had been abandoned by all those Europeans, including his own ancestors, who had turned their backs on their native countries and come to the unknown land of America. They left generations of daddies in graves. When things get bad enough, people go elsewhere without their dead daddies. I demanded to know why the gang didn't just up and out. I even said where: "Westerly! Westerly lies opportunity, safety, freedom. Let's go." I nagged like a mother.

Steven said, "It ain't the worst idea you ever had, but we can't go."

"It has been done, you know, to dig up the deceased. We can go." I had an answer for every objection, or I would make one up. I did surprise myself by saying "we" instead of "you."

"It ain't the deceased," said Steven.

"Then what? We'll find land like this, call it New Scuffletown, why do you think New York is New York? There was old York, and people . . ."

"Bounties," said Steven.

"Bounties here, bounties elsewhere, but no one knows us elsewhere."

"Bounties double outside the state. And no swamp to hide in."

"Bounties double?" This made no sense. Why? The outlaws did not know.

Mr. Groone did. He provided three reasons for double bounties: first, so no state is victimized by another's outlaws; second, so felons take no benefit in fleeing; and third, to entice hunters into the trouble and danger of pursuit. So much for the gang leaving, I thought.

As I had done to Thommy's funeral, I went without the gang to Andrew's. funeral. A kindly looking stout White gentleman was speaking with mourners and holding Sally Ann's hand.

"Who is he?" I asked Rhody.

"The schoolteacher. He wants to see Henry Berry."

"Oh yeah?" I thought. I was a full-fledged, grizzled outlaw. He was little and fat, and though he smiled broadly he was gratifyingly nervous at seeing a grizzled outlaw like me drawing near. Sally Ann ran to me in a surprising way, her arms out for a hug, and got one.

Rhody told Sally Ann to introduce us but the child could not remember my name or her teacher's, and in the excitement had probably forgotten her own. Rhody helped her. It was clear by the way Rhody spoke his name—Ephraim X. Saunders, Jr.—that she liked him. He had come from Boston, though he was Canadian, so he hadn't fought for the Union despite having wanted to. Now he was teaching Indian children—including Sally

Ann and, soon, Henry Delaney—to read and write. I was pleased to meet him, and said so.

"I'm sorry for your loss," Schoolteacher Ephraim X. Saunders said, pressing my hand. He took my arm and led me away from everyone else. "You know Henry Lowery?" Could he not see I'm one of the grizzled outlaws? "Can you arrange an audience?" I sized him up. I scrutinized him. I took his measure. I was not impressed, but if Rhody wanted him to see Henry Berry, I would arrange it. If Rhody wanted someone to fly to the moon, I would arrange it.

"For what purpose?" I asked him.

"To help him," he said.

"Schoolteacher, eh?" said the grizzled outlaw, but I did not spit.

"Yes, and I know the situation," he said. I promised to set up a meeting.

Later, I thought of the possibility of a second teacher, one for Negro children, since State law did not allow mixing races in school. I wrote to my Editor for the first time since I had been here, though he probably thought I was dead or maybe even resigned. I described Mr. Saunders and his background, and asked if the Herald's tradition of charity (especially regarding newsworthy matters like this) might support a teacher for Negroes. If the Herald would sponsor one teacher, other sponsors might be found. The project could spread all over the South, and education would repair what White morality had demolished.

Mr. Saunders and Henry Berry met at Rhody's cabin. Saunders wanted to speak with Henry Berry alone. I didn't like being cut out. But since there was no place for Rhody and me to go except to wander the countryside together, my desire to participate in the meeting gave way.

O my promiscuous, cheating heart! In my mind, the Widow Norment waited for me in her window. Yet now I was with Rhody. I took Henry Delaney's hand, he being age four and a fine walker. Sally Ann carried Neely Ann, the baby. I wanted to hold Rhody's hand. I had never held one. I did not even know if grown Indians held hands. Eventually Henry Delaney thrust his free hand into his Mother's, and with me holding Rhody's through relay of Henry Berry's son, we five, a temporary family, walked the meadow at a tot's pace.

Not trusting schoolteachers, I was afraid we would return to find Henry Berry murdered. Still, we dallied longer than the Outlaw and the schoolteacher talked, and we returned to find them waiting. The schoolteacher had something to tell us. I was grateful not to be dismissed outside to play shoot-the-donkey with the children.

"It is necessary," Saunders said, in that teacher's drone every boy hates, "that Henry, his brother, his friends, his mother, his wife and children, and the families of those who are his associates, leave the county."

Rhody started to speak: "Harry will never—" but the schoolteacher went on. They always do.

"The men who brought me here are not friends to the Indians. They only want to provide the smallest amount of assistance that will keep you quiet." Obvious stuff. "By teaching well, I have been doing my poor best to help. If the children read and write, there are grounds for hope."

Yes, of course, though his schoolish nasality made it sound undesirable. And I begrudged him Rhody's obvious respect, gratitude, and affection.

"Now, Mrs. Lowery," Saunders said, his tone making me desperate for recess, "you will remember when you and your children were arrested. This time, and forgive me for saying it, the plan is to murder you and your little ones, as well as the families of others in the band."

"Why?" I demanded. Such a plan would never bring Henry Berry into captivity. It would only make him a worse danger.

But Saunders answered, "To stop those who give the gang support and information, without which the gang will be captured."

"How do you know about this plan?" I asked.

Saunders said, "I arrived early for a meeting. Waiting outside, I overheard. I am no church goer but that Sunday I went to give thanks for the fortune of having overheard. I am afraid," he added in a voice that revealed fear beneath his brave exterior, "that they plan to include me in their massacre."

"But why?" asked Rhody.

The poor man's voice shook as he answered, "As an example. I am too much a friend of the Indian." I didn't have to ask who these killers were: legitimate government officers who were also Ku Klux. If they would hang helpless old men dragged from their homes, they would exterminate schoolteachers, women, and babies. "I was hired to teach the children, but I also help with nourishment and health, and wherever else I can make a difference." He was trying to speak coolly but his voice trembled. Most men marked for death would take the next train back to the world. Rhody went to his side, kneeled where he sat, and took his hand.

"We'll protect you," she promised. Harry nodded. So did I.

The poor schoolteacher wept. He said he had lived with this terrible information for days, afraid to tell us. He said our departure must take place within a week or ten days. To reduce the chance of discovery and interception, the families should be gathered up at the last minute without warning. "Where will we go?" I asked.

Saunders answered: "A great distance or you'll never be safe. I'm a scholar, and by study I have located a site in the State of Wisconsin—a cold climate, but for that very reason none will think you have gone there. The people of Wisconsin, largely good German, are hospitable to other races and regard Indians as the true owners of the nation. They don't go so far as to give land back, but they sell at a fair price. Even now they await you to settle and prosper."

"A problem remains," I said.

"I believe Henry and I have addressed every question."

"Bounties," I said.

"Of course I know that, sir."

"And do you know they double outside the state?"

"That is why I selected Wisconsin," he said. "Bounty

there is outlawed. A bounty-seeker who comes is subject to arrest, and if he captures his quarry, the bounty goes into the public treasury. Who will undertake the risk with no chance of reward?"

"Why would they have such a law?"

"They found that bounty hunters are often worse than the quarry."

I began to think the exodus could take place. "What about danger en route?"

"Leave secretly by dead of night. The families need not know where, which way, or even exactly when until after departure. Travel by secret routes. It is worked out." It sounded like the greatest adventure in the world, as good as Forbidden Snow Hill.

"How long to get to Wisconsin?" I asked.

"Not as long as we'll lie dead in the earth if they kill us," said Rhody. If there were to have been any debate, that ended it. We began to plan. Saunders would travel with us through several states and then return to Boston. None of us would ever see Robeson County again.

"What will we do in Wisconsin?" I asked.

"Live," said Rhody. "Plant potatoes. Eat 'em. Have babies. Spank children. Grow old. Have children read. Sit in a privy without worrying some White man going to shoot through the wall. Who knows what we will do, Writer? Tell us what they do in New York and when we get to Wisconsin we will do it. What you think?"

I thought it was the finest declaration of independence I ever heard in my life.

TWENTY-SEVEN

SIX MORNINGS LATER I met with the schoolteacher to discuss final arrangements. His isolated cabin revealed simple needs and good sense. My competitive feelings disappeared at the sight of his pathetic desk: a rough plank on stools with farm crates for drawers. I concluded our meeting with a firm handshake. The grizzled outlaw had accepted Saunders. We left together. He went off to school and I watched him go. We were heroes in this strange world, each in our own strange way.

My next errand was to the train depot. Waiting for the westbound, a small part of me considered boarding the next eastbound for New York. In only two nights I could be sleeping in my own New York bed. But the larger part of me is a victim of *wanderlust novelias*, a delightful illness common in Americans. It increases the hunger for travel to new places, and has side symptoms of dislike for returning over old tracks. Our upcoming trip to Wisconsin's lakes, and its snow as high as your eyelid, stirred me. There would surely be a Forbidden Snow Hill to show Sally Ann.

I contemplated that our trip of weeks or months would be at the rate people are meant to travel. Railway velocity is excessive: two days to New York, two more back—which was why I was waiting. Newspapers are efficient and I was expecting a response letter to my request for a new teacher. I would urge them to send the teacher to Wisconsin, where our settlement would be a model for the oppressed from all over the South. It would be a fine undertaking for the New York Herald.

Northerners move quickly and their railroads run late; southerners are the opposite. The Wilmington train arrived promptly and I asked if there was something for me. There was, bless the iron horse and the Herald.

In all things, there are turning points. They arrive unexpectedly. My Editor (now Associate Publisher, God help the Herald,) wrote that he was happy to learn I was not yet dead. "As to your proposal for a second teacher: I am pleased to say that the idea is well-received. You are requested to be patient for a time, and we will soon have a response for you. Yours Very Truly, &c."

But that was not the turning point. A post-script held it: "P.S. You are, by the way, mistaken about your Mr. Ephraim X. Saunders, Jr., whose background we looked into this afternoon to provide information to the gentlemen who will study your proposal. No schoolteacher, but he is a writer familiar to several here in the office. He is well enough known in Boston, where he has written several books. Could yours be a different chap with the same name? Not likely, I imagine. Please let us know, for it will guide the selection of the individual we will send to join him, should our decision be positive, which I may say on the sly it almost certainly will be."

The dog Saunders! A WRITER IN THE MANGER! And he was here! In guise of a schoolteacher. What then was he doing here, if not writing a book? *My* book! This outsider thought to make himself the hero, the inside spy, by playing Moses leading us to the promised land of Wisconsin! And then writing about it! My own part would be scrawled in some footnote, if at all. I would be lucky ever to find my book in print, much less noticed by anyone while they were all busy poring over Saunders' scribbling. It is one thing to save people; it is quite another to tell their story. He can have the former; the latter is mine.

The New York Herald does not employ reporters who get scooped. I will drink hot blood, I will eat a porcupine, but I will not see my story pre-empted. The Herald has the best editors living, even including my own, and hire the best reporters. No Herald reporter worth the name is ever scooped!

I stormed to the schoolhouse. The magpie was teaching, as was his little place to do. I considered ending his lesson with my rifle, but 1) children were present, 2) it was not an accepted professional practice, 3) we needed Saunders to execute arrangements in Wisconsin, and 4) I did not absolutely know he was writing a book.

Saunders saw me through the school window. I commanded cheer into my face and a keep-up-the-good-work smile that any decent writer would have seen through. I went back to his pretentious cabin and looked through the dung boxes the wretch used for file drawers. And by thunder and lightning, I found it! Lying beneath a reading primer was A MANUSCRIPT, face down. I had only to turn it over to see the title and I would know. I hesitated. I had even less right to do this than I had to steal the writings of the Widow Norment. After all, the schoolteacher was a fellow writer in the same exile as myself. But by now I was a raider through and through.

When I turned over the manuscript and read it, my jealous fears were trivial compared to what I discovered that he had written.

I rushed to the Devil's Den to tell what I'd found. Henry Berry was understandably suspicious of my competitive feelings about Saunders. He wanted to hold Saunders' manuscript in his hands for himself and have Mary Cuombo verify that I was reading it right. I told him that school was over for the day so I could not get the manuscript without being discovered. I would go for it tomorrow morning.

Next morning during school hours, Shoe-Maker John and I went to Saunders' cabin. I took the manuscript, but Shoe-Maker John said, "Wait."

"Why?" I said. "Harry wants to see it."

"If we take the book, the teacher goin' know." He was right.

"Then you have to verify what it says for Henry Berry." I said.

"Me?" he said. "How?"

Never was there such cause to curse illiteracy. We were stymied. We needed someone else who could read. Rhody and Mary Cuombo were too far away. By the time we brought them back, school would be out and the schoolteacher would have come home. "Come on," said Shoe-Maker John. He led me back to school and pointed to Sally Ann. I went to the door. Saunders was inaccurately explaining synonyms. He invited me in. I apologized for interrupting and asked for a word in private. He came outside.

"I am dreadfully sorry," I said, "but Sally Ann is needed."

"Is everything all right?" he asked.

I reassured him, but "with the arrangements for departure, something of a personal nature has come up and her mother needs Sally Ann's assistance." Men are cowards regarding anything "of a personal nature" in women.

Soon Shoe-Maker John and I were walking down the road with Sally Ann, who was pleased to be released. We got to Saunders' cabin. I prayed she had been a good student. "Can you read this?" I said, putting the manuscript in her lap. She looked at Saunders' excessively neat writing, and nodded. "Would you, please?"

"Don't you know how to read?" she said.

"Certainly I know how, but . . ."

"Your Daddy wants to be sure you're learning," said Shoe-Maker John. Her Daddy was enough for Sally Ann, and she started. She stumbled on some words, but sounded them out. Shoe-Maker John listened first with envy of her ability, but then with horror. He would remember every word for Henry Berry:

HISTORY OF EVIL
THE BAD MEN OF THE SWAMP
MURDERERS AND THIEVES
IN NORTH CAROLINA

"Evil," "murderers," and "thieves" slowed Sally Ann but she managed well enough, and went on:

> Victory over the Outlaws, as told by the man who saved a county, Mr. Ephraim X. Saunders, Jr., author of seven books and a brave Spy Among Savages.

I picked out the most important sections. Sally Ann read as if her life depended on it, which it did. Chillingly, Saunders had written in the past tense, as if the story had already happened.

I feared the effect this would have upon little Sally Ann. But it was necessary, so together she and Shoe-Maker John learned of the following (I paraphrase, to shield the reader from Saunders' wretched rhetoric):

Saunders (Sally Ann read) spent months gaining the confidence of the naive Indians. Then he convinced the silly wife of the Savage Outlaw Chief to arrange a meeting with her husband, in which Saunders fabricated a plot regarding the destruction of the outlaws, their wives, and their children. The Outlaw Chief was easily convinced to form a wagon train bound for Wisconsin.

It was a death trip.

In the margin was an unflattering description of myself, and other recent notes to be worked into the text.

The manuscript went on to describe the massacre, which was in Virginia so the bounty would be triple. In addition, the booty included money that the outlaw refugees were carrying in vain hope of buying land in Wisconsin. The killing ground was a narrow mountain cleft that had been the site of a Confederate ambush during the War. It was ideal for the two hundred mercenaries and Ku Klux who swept down to exterminate the entire party: the unprepared outlaws, their wives, and, as Sally Ann read most quietly, "... the children, for the crusaders could not allow the spawn to return home and enrage Indians left behind by reporting what had happened, or to live to be adults and seek revenge, as is eternally the way with savages."

Sally Ann knew these were her teacher's words, and that she could read them only because he had taught her. Is there greater violation than that of a child by the very adult she trusts? Something dreadful was happening to her as she read, something darker than the tears she read through. Soon Shoe-Maker John had heard enough. To ease her crying, he drew up and looked terrifying for her. He said her father was even fiercer, so no one could hurt any of us because she had read to us perfectly. She asked how Shoe-Maker John knew it was perfect if he could not read.

"I knows what I knows," he said. "Don't I?" Sally Ann nodded and thrust her chin as if daring the world to knock it. We sent her around back to get Patrick Lowery's horse while we restored the manuscript to its original place and condition.

Putting things away, we found a map of the

mountain pass where the ambush would be. As we examined it, a shadow fell. We turned to see the doorway blocked by schoolteacher Saunders, pistol in hand. "I will shoot you unless you have a prize of an explanation." Shoe-Maker John tried to pull a pistol. Saunders shot him in the arm, and Shoe- Maker John's gun went flying. "You're both dead," said Saunders.

"You have nothing to gain by killing us," I said.

"I'll judge that," he said. "Come outside or I'll shoot you bit by bit right here." I helped Shoe-Maker John to his feet. Saunders, watching us closely, did not see the dark barrel of a rifle just behind him snaking up from a low angle and into the door frame, aiming at his head. Hearing something, he glanced to the right and slightly downward. He was looking directly into the barrel as it fired from five inches away.

Suddenly the schoolteacher had no head. An eruption of scarlet sprayed over me. What remained of Saunders spun, then toppled out the door beyond my line of sight. The rifle followed him down and in an emphasis of redundancy, roared again, lurching the corpse back into sight as if still alive.

Shoe-Maker John found his other pistol as I tried to get mine from beneath my belt, in case we were the next targets. But the rifle in the doorway fell to the ground, and into view stepped Sally Ann, blood-covered, nothing in her expression. I have never seen so terrifying a sight as that child with her quarry's blood dripping down her face and hands. It dripped onto my Spencer rifle that she had wrested from its strap on Patrick Lowery's horse. Her eyes were white on the dark background of her skin and Saunders' blood. I ran to her. She stepped back as I came too forcefully, and she tripped over the corpse but I caught her. She clung to my neck, her shaking body as stiff and tight as an iron post. I helped her and Shoe-Maker John onto Patrick Lowery's horse, and we went to Rhody's.

I wrote to my Editor, asking him to find out about the status of Indians in Wisconsin. He responded by asking when I might get back to work, and told me that Wisconsinites have no use for Indians but to shoot them. Saunders had lied at every turn. If it hadn't been for my Editor's speedy reply to my first letter, and my frenzy that I might be scooped, Saunders would have succeeded. I'd have died alongside Harry, Sally Ann, Rhody and the rest. Hundreds. An editor's PS had changed history.

We got Sally Ann home. Rhody summoned Mary Cuombo. They bound Shoe-Maker John's wound, and bathed and held Sally Ann until she seemed something like a child again. I told everything we had discovered.

"Make a song about Sally Ann," I said to Rhody, who was holding the child deep in her lap.

"She'll make it herself," answered wise Rhody, "when she wishes and how she wants."

Shoe-Maker John went to tell Henry Berry about Saunders. Henry Berry did not want a school child to find the corpse so he sent an anonymous message to the Sheriff. Saunders' death was greeted with mystification by most, and with sorrow by Indians he had touched for the good. But the Ku Klux and others who had already left for the massacre site would understand well enough.

I went to ask Mr. Groone if any states were exempt from the double-bounty policy. He looked through his books and found none. I threw prudence to the pigs (an expression specific to Robeson County) and named the state in which I was interested: "Wisconsin is not an exception?" He consulted a different chapter.

"In fact," he found, "west of the Appalachians the bounty is triple. Beyond the Rockies and in the territories, the multiplier is four. Have you a quarry in mind?"

TWENTY-EIGHT

STILL RECOVERING from his wound, Shoe-Maker John had stayed one morning to tend Neelyann. Rhody went to bring old Mary Cuombo some medicine. Rhody returned to find Neelyann playing quietly and Shoe-Maker John gone. Soon the Sheriff announced that he had Shoe-Maker John in irons in the new Lumberton jail, heavily guarded by the local Militia and Federal troops.

I attended Shoe-Maker John's trial. Chained to the defendant's table, he confessed that he alone had done everything the gang was ever accused of, and more that he made up. He swore that no one else ever stole one thing or hurt one person, that only he had murdered, and that we had constantly tried to stop his evil ways.

"So get them bounties off their heads," he cried. "They just want to be left in peace and to leave y'all in the same peace." He pointed at his own breast and said softly, "This the Evil Niga right here, me and none other." Shoe-Maker John was sentenced to hang. The Government feared Henry Berry Lowery, so the Judge announced that the jail would be guarded by two hundred Federal soldiers and an emplacement of artillery.

I started to leave the courtroom to go report to Henry Berry and Steven, hoping we would have a plan. But the Judge asked the Condemned what he had to say, and I remained—without sitting—to listen. Shoe-Maker John rose beneath the weight of his shackles. We were the only two standing. "Your Honor, am I allowed to say what I want?" He spoke with greater refinement than his assigned White lawyer had done. The Judge responded that Shoe-Maker John could say, and the recorder would record, anything of reasonable length that was decent, threatened no one, and befitted the dignity of the Court. "Then I wish to say," he said directly to me, "that my friends must not interfere. These Whites want to hang me. Let them. My teeth caught the bullet too many times. I'm tired and don't want to do it no more. I won't live to see the walls come tumbling down, which they hell-fire goin' do." The Judge cautioned Shoe-Maker John about threats. "No threat, Judge Yo' Honor, it's the Bible. And for the information of the court, the Bible never been wrong one time what it predict. Didn't you Confederates lose your sorry War just like it said?

"And for them Injians bein' blamed for what I done, I'm sorry. Go on, now," he said to me, "tell Harry what I said. Then write what I done." He took a step towards me, shackles dragging the table behind. "And write my name in there, Writer. Write my name and get it right, else I'll haunts you to a fare-thee-well!" Then he said to the Judge, "I apologizes, Marz Yo' Honor de High Judge, I sneaked in that one threat, but he my frien', he understand, and now I done. That be that. Shoe-Maker John, he restin'."

Later, Harry made me repeat it over and over to see if there was something hidden. But there was nothing. "I know what he means," he said.

"Don't be tired, Harry," I said. "You can't."

"Why not?"

"Because your Sally Ann blew off a man's head with a rifle and she'll remember it until she dies. You have to help her know there was reason for it, that it wasn't just some other thing that happened."

"Maybe it was," he said.

"You go to that hanging, Writer," said Steven. "And write it good. Don't give us no Widow Norman shit. She writes like an old lady and sometimes you do, too." I promised.

"Take Sally Ann," said Harry. No, I said, she doesn't need to see another death. "Do it, Writer," he said.

"Why?" I demanded.

Steven answered, "She's got to remember more than just what she done. Like you said, she got to know why." Harry nodded.

"What if Rhody says no?" I asked Harry.

"Smack 'er." But she'd shoot my balls off, I said. He nodded.

I called for Sally Ann late that night. Rhody left the younger children with Mary Cuombo and the three of us went to the courthouse. We waited all night outside the cordon of soldiers. No one else was there except an old Negro woman who sat on the ground. None of us said a word all night.

Before dawn, others gathered. Later that day I

submitted a dispatch on the execution of Shoe-Maker John. It got his name onto the Herald's front page.

> **SHOE-MAKER JOHN ON THE GALLOWS**
>
> Old North State Hangs Black Brigand
>
> Convicted for the murder of County Sheriff Reuben King and other crimes, the feared and notorious Outlaw SHOE-MAKER JOHN was conveyed from the Lumberton, North Carolina jail in a red cart, and made to climb the gallows before sunrise today. His infamous swamp comrades had vowed that the State would never hang one of their number, and for eight years had not broken that vow. Atop the platform, the Condemned man peered through the morning gloom around him.

I thought he was looking for the gang. The soldiers had the same impression and stirred uneasily.

> The place of execution was guarded by a detachment of two hundred United States Army soldiers under the command of Colonel Roderick P. Bradley. The gallows were of rude construction, trap held with a rope tied to the upright joist, to be severed by ax. A Minister was in attendance to condole with SHOE-MAKER JOHN and guide the path he must take. SHOE-MAKER JOHN was a handsome Negro. He had piercing eyes with dark, barbaric lights in

them. Pride and stoicism were his expressions. He uttered his forgiveness of the hangman before it was requested. His executioner was a Northern rough named Marsden who resembled a boarding house sailor, of lower estate than the man he was here to hang. This Marsden asked SHOE-MAKER JOHN if he was ready. The Condemned looked out at the paths beyond the soldiers and the handful of onlookers as if to see his environs for a last time before being sent to new ones. Then he nodded readiness. The hangman placed the noose upon his neck, but the Condemned spoke in a deep voice. "I will not pray with rope around my neck, son, and ask that you remove it as the Lord Himself would wish. You may put it back when I am through." From below, the Sheriff signaled, and the hangman removed the noose. SHOE-MAKER JOHN bowed his head, but rather than pray he began to sing in a basso profundo that shook the gallows and the souls of those in hearing. He sang so slowly that each line took half a minute, but his voice was so stirring that the hangman alone of all showed any impatience. The well-known hymn is reproduced here, permission of the Southern Methodist Publishing House.

AMAZING GRACE! (how sweet the sound!)
THAT SAVED a wretch like me!
I ONCE was lost, but now I'm found,
WAS BLIND, but now I see.

Now the Condemned man fell to his knees, and the Minister saw fit to imitate him. They prayed together silently, eyes shut, for some minutes. The Commander of the soldiers grew nervous at the delay, and signaled his men to stand ready.

The singing reverberated throughout the sleeping town, and now, at first one or two, then by threes and fours, did Negroes appear, brought from their beds by his voice or by other Negroes who had heard it. After a few minutes SHOE-MAKER JOHN completed his silent prayer, and rose. The hangman started to him but SHOE-MAKER JOHN by expression of face, and the Minister by gesture, repelled him sternly back, as if commanding Death to be patient. Again SHOE-MAKER JOHN sang the same words, even more slowly than before. The soldiers became certain he was delaying for rescue, and cocked their rifles.

AMAZING GRACE! (how sweet the sound!)

Your reporter is at loss to describe the feelings that came over the assemblage when a woman who had waited there the entire night now rose and joined her voice to that of SHOE-MAKER JOHN:

THAT SAVED a wretch like me!
I ONCE was lost, but now I'm found

Every soul present joined, including your reporter and the soldiery, whose eyes never ceased surveilling the area.

WAS BLIND, but now I see.

Shoe-Maker John had not been waiting rescue, but for his people to come witness. They now arrived from every direction. He knelt again to pray. The Sheriff, certain that the prayer was a delay for rescue, signaled Marsden to proceed. But the ruffian was blocked from drawing near SHOE-MAKER JOHN by the bold Minister, who laid hands upon the hangman. He reminded the Sheriff that the law allowed the Condemned his prayers, and there was no danger for there were soldiers and artillery.

By now the street had filled with Negro men, women, and children, almost all in nightdress that was mostly of the rough pale cotton fabric they could afford. But some were in rich fabrics and colors that had once belonged to the wealthy.

I didn't report the source of these clothes. The gang rarely gave daytime dress to the poor, afraid the original owners would notice. We had not anticipated an occasion when nightdress would be worn in public.

Mothers held children high to see. Older children crowded against the soldiery but fell back when the Militiamen raised their weapons, not to shoot but to frighten them back a small space. SHOE-MAKER JOHN spoke to the Minister, who ripped open the Condemned's shirt and took it from his body. The Condemned then turned, showing deep and ancient scars upon his back that none would forget. As he turned, he sang:

THROUGH MANY dangers, toils, and snares

I HAVE already come;
'TIS GRACE has brought me safe thus far,
AND GRACE will lead me home.

Now the assembled Negroes knelt to pray, some quietly and others louder. The sound of their prayers, each different, filled the air. In the sun's first light, SHOE-MAKER JOHN sang out over the cacophony:

SHOULD EARTH against my soul engage
AND HELLISH darts be hurled,
THEN I can smile at Satan's rage,
AND FACE a fearful world.

Every Negro in town was awake and now joined singing, even the youngest who knew no words. The soldiers, this reporter, the hangman, and the Sheriff himself removed their hats, faced the Condemned, and sang, and Colonel Bradley did as well, saluting.

WHEN WE'VE been here ten thousand years
BRIGHT SHINING like the Sun,
WE'VE NO less days to sing His praise
THAN WHEN we first begun.

Now as if a Director of Choir had signaled all in attendance to hush, SHOE-MAKER JOHN and the old Negro woman sang alone, eyes on each other.

AMAZING GRACE! (how sweet the sound!)
THAT SAVED a wretch like me!
I ONCE was lost, but now I'm found . . .
WAS BLIND, but now I see.

SHOW-MAKER JOHN sang the last line again, by himself, slowly. There were no more.

SHOE-MAKER JOHN nodded the Minister, who took the blindfold from the hangman and covered the eyes of the Condemned, but he spoke again and the Minister removed the blindfold. The Minister took the noose from the hangman and placed it on the neck of SHOE-MAKER JOHN, which the Condemned seemed to wish to do for himself but his hands were bound. The Sheriff called to the hangman, who removed the noose from the neck of the Condemned and immediately put it back again, the law of the State requiring that the hangman and no one else place the noose. SHOE-MAKER JOHN again refused a blindfold, which was

> his right. He begged the hangman to release him from his pain, and the hangman tried to oblige him by swinging his ax at the rope affixed behind. He missed the first blow, and prepared for a more careful second attempt. On this attempt he succeeded to sever the rope, thereby opening the trap and closing forever the eyes of SHOE-MAKER JOHN to this world. Proud and brave died this Outlaw of the southern swamps, such that any observer would be glad to admit that he witnessed it and was better for it. The Negroes who witnessed did not leave the spot until sundown. And thus endeth the story, life, and career of SHOE-MAKER JOHN.

As the gallows trap opened, Sally Ann turned away but Rhody made her look. Going home, Sally Ann chattered of everything except what she had seen.

That night Henry Berry and Steven came to Rhody's cabin. The children were asleep, and Mary Cuombo had come despite being sick. "You could have saved him," Rhody said to Henry Berry.

"He told us not to," I said.

"Tell us something we don't know, Writer," she said. "You're schooled, you must have some new thing to say." I almost said there was no hope, but Sally Ann woke and came to stand behind her father.

"What is it you want?" I asked.

"Just to live," Henry Berry answered.

"Hurt 'em," said Mary Cuombo.

"Who?" I asked.

She answered with a sweep of her arm, a gesture leaving out no one in the world. But she dropped her arm in mid-sweep, meaning there was nothing left to do.

Henry Delaney came from under the quilt and stood bare-bottomed and sleepy by his older sister. He was holding baby Neelyann. He came over to shake hands, as I had taught him. Perhaps it was the sight of the two tots that made Mary Cuombo decide to talk. She rose. Sally Ann was quickly at her side to support the ailing woman, whose voice was faint: "William gone. And Thomas. Allen. George's Wesley. Peter. Jarman." She looked at Rhody. "Your Andrew, your Boss." She looked around the room. "John Shoemaker. Stevie next? How long? Then you, Henry Berry Lowery? How long?" She put out a hand to her grandson. "Henry Delaney here, how long?" The boy, too young to understand, smiled. Mary Cuombo looked at Henry Berry. "Henny, you think if you do the wrong thing, something bad will happen. It already happened. Nothing can get worse. So go do something, boy." She said to Sally Ann, "Set me." Sally Ann seated her grandmother. Their resemblance flashed in the dimness like a torch, two ages of the same woman.

Henry Berry said, "I don't know how to do more than I done."

In two distinct syllables dark as her eyes, Mary Cuombo intoned, "Hurt them." She rose on her own, snatched Geronimo's picture off the wall, and threw it at Henry Berry's feet. "Go ask him. He got no swamp. He must have some other way." She kneeled in front of Henry Berry. "I will try to be gentle with you, Henny, but I got to have my say about your swamp. It has done you bad. Without it, you'd of been like him." She pointed at Geronimo. "And wouldn't be no Thommy gone, and no Andrew gone, and no Boss gone." Henry Berry looked away. "We wouldn't be crying what to do. We would of done it. So God damn your swamp, Henny, God damn it and God damn you along with it unless you go ask the man in that picture what's to be done. And then come back and do it."

Going to find Geronimo seemed fine to me. Better than a new Forbidden Snow Hill in Wisconsin. "Geronimo knows what he's doing," added Rhody.

"How do you know?" I asked.

"Songs," she said. "Want to hear?"

"Jesu Lord of Hearing, please don't let her," said Mary Cuombo. That might have turned into a fight but Sally Ann laughed just right.

"I am not fooling with you, now, Henry Berry," said Rhody. "Listen to what your momma said. Geronimo ain't in all them songs for being a fool. I am throwing you out until you come back knowing what he knows."

A wise man knows when his woman is wiser, I imagine. Henry Berry looked from Rhody to his momma to Sally Ann, who asked, "Can I go?"

Little Henry Delaney, still holding the sleeping baby, came to sit in his Daddy's lap, where he fell asleep. Sally Ann took the baby. I wanted that Matthew Brady picture fellow here.

Steven took Mary Cuombo home and spent the night there. The rest of us stayed at Rhody's. Sally Ann put the little ones to bed. "Well girl," said Rhody to her daughter, "if your Daddy goes off, we be okay?"

"Who?"

"You, girl. Me. Your nekked brother there and that bundle you just put down to sleep."

"How long?"

"Nobody knows."

Sally Ann turned, sat in her Daddy's lap, wrapped her arms around his neck, and refused to move. If he had tried to get away he might have hung himself, so he slept the night in the chair holding his little girl. Rhody gave me the bed and slept on a mat.

In the morning, Sally Ann gave her father her permission to go. She said she had to stay to care for her mother, brother, and sister. She instructed him to come back as soon as he was able.

TWENTY-NINE

A WEEK LATER, Patrick Lowery's horse and Steven watched our train leave. Neither waved.

Mary Cuombo and Rhody had made Henry Berry a three-piece suit. He had shaved off his beard and cut his hair. On board he hid his face by pretending to read a newspaper the whole five hours to Wilmington. He left the newspaper behind when we changed north for Philadelphia, then west to Pittsburgh, where we strolled the city until our Chicago departure. Walking in public, Henry Berry missed his ninety pounds of weapons. He was used to people thinking he could happily slaughter everyone in sight, but now he looked like a distinguished member of some respectable profession.

He hated Pittsburgh's stench. "Chicago will be worse," I said.

"Then Gawd damn Chicago," he said.

With North Carolina behind us, he had started to talk. This was as novel as any of the sights along the way. At first he had been intimidated by conductors, because they were men in uniform whom he could not shoot. But now he chattered with them about any subject at all, and with other passengers as well.

In Chicago I bought a book about Geronimo. It was

badly written and amusing on that account alone. We reboarded for the southwest. Facing us sat an elderly lady with faded hair and her grown granddaughter whose golden hair had years to go before it faded, and many hearts to break. She read while her grandmother tried to untangle a Luther's Stew of knitting yarn.

Tired of reading, I said to Harry, "It's earlier here than home." He looked as if I had just set a trap for his leg. "Noon here is one in the afternoon at home."

"Good," he said, meaning he wanted no more of it.

"Farther west the difference is two hours. Then three, and so on." This new system of time zones had been a topic of great debate and misunderstanding a few years earlier in New York.

"Very good," he said.

"Imagine it! Noon in the swamp but morning out west."

He gave in and said "How come?" The grandmother was listening as well, though pretending not to.

"Where is the sun at noon?" I asked.

"In the sky," he answered.

"Where in the sky?"

"Up."

"Up where?" I asked.

"What are you talking about?"

"Point where the sun would be at noon," I ordered.

"No."

Grandmother, now curious, stopped untangling her wool and pointed straight up.

"Thank you," I said. "Now. Where will the sun be in

an hour?" She was confused. Henry Berry reached over and angled her arm. "Yes," I said.

"Good," said Henry Berry, taking my book and pretending he could read it.

"And what direction is that?" I demanded.

"Up."

"West," I said.

"Good."

"May I put my arm down?" asked the grandmother. Her granddaughter looked up from her book.

"Not yet," I said. "With the sun directly overhead, it is noon here." I raised grandmother's arm directly up. "And in an hour, the sun will be there." Grandmother was confused. Her granddaughter tilted grandmother's arm back to the west. "So now it's noon there and one o'clock here."

Harry turned a page. The wrong way.

"It is always noon directly under the sun!" I announced, as if I had invented the system. "The sun drags noon along with it and pulls the rest of the hours trailing behind." All at one instant, grandmother yanked down her arm and returned to her untangling, granddaughter returned to her book, and Harry looked out at the passing darkness where there was no sun.

"Covered wagons traveled only three miles a day," the granddaughter said. Harry's eyes rose into his forehead, anticipating another idiotic discussion. "I wonder what they talked about then," she snapped. Harry smiled. I gave in and napped.

A hundred miles later, a worried Henry Berry poked me awake. He asked, "So how do we get to Monday?"

"Sir?"

"Say it's Sunday. Rhody got me in church and Preacher talks till noon. We leave. Sun's up there." He nodded to the grandmother who recognized her cue and pointed straight up. Henry Berry continued, "Sun moves over there." She moved her arm. "I run and keep up with it."

"You couldn't," said the granddaughter, who read books and knew.

"On a horse," he said. She smiled the way girls do when they know you're wrong. "On a fast horse. And I get to Chicago right under the sun. Still noon."

"Right," I said. Grandmother put down her arm. Henry Berry put it back up.

"What day is it?" he asked.

"Thursday," said Grandmother.

"Not today," I said. "The day he left church and is now in Chicago."

"We left Chicago," she said. "That's where we were." I remembered the gang's early difficulties with the Widow's tales. Some representations of reality take getting used to, and Grandma had not yet made the journey. I explained Henry Berry's supposition, and she smiled at its simplicity. "Then, of course, it's Sunday in Chicago," she said. She put her arm down in a way that made clear she would not raise it again.

"Then what if I follow the sun to Californay?" said Henry Berry.

"Where's that?" I said.

Ignoring my question he said, "What time will it be?"

"When?"

"When I'm there and the sun is straight up," he said.

"Noon."

"What day?"

"Sunday," I said.

"The world's round?" I nodded. "Sooner or later I got to come round back to church?" I nodded. "Where's the sun?" I pointed up. "Time?"

"Noon."

"Day?" They all looked at me. I didn't know. "So what happened to Monday?" demanded the Outlaw.

I was sorry I'd brought it up. Harry smiled like noonday sun. Granddaughter retreated to her book. Harry began a chatter with Grandma, who revealed, in case we needed to know, that she had been in hospital for six months, suffering illnesses and intimate complaints that she disgorged in unfortunate detail. Then she told of her husband and his lingering illness, a year and a half wasting away, and he died; her brother, ailing twice that time, and he died; her older sister, who stopped eating, talking, and she died; and a pet I could not tell whether cat or bird, but which shed (either feathers or fur) in great dank clumps, and died. I retreated to my execrable book on Geronimo:

> Apache-Indians are blessed with good eye and acute hearing, and survive without what the White man requires. They battle occasional battles with neighboring tribes, harming

> other savages. Those killed in these traditional contests are not missed, for the Indian birth rate is even greater than the Negro's. Their skirmishes are not fought over substance, for they seek to own no land, store no goods, and no more of anything they can eat or carry. This may make the unwary think such battles merely satisfy primitive superstitious need. But no, the contrary! Indian manhood is measured in war, and determines which male savages will propagate with the best female savages.

By now Grandmother was describing the choking sores in the throat of her niece's dog (or perhaps son), and who was going to die.

> White settlements, making available scalps of new colors and in hitherto unimagined numbers, give young braves opportunity to demonstrate battle-worthiness. Thousands of young Indians demand to participate, even if they like the peaceful Whites. Thus the attacks multiply, and thus young braves, striving for predominant squaw-pick, remain a continuing menace to Whites. This unleashing of aboriginal male impulses disappoints all attempts to bring the savages into the civilized community.

The book was useless except for the mention of a government official named Mr. Franklin Clum who had a friendship with Geronimo, and was apparently his White guardian. We hoped Mr. Clum would gain us access to Geronimo, a simple favor but with weighty consequences. Advice from Geronimo might help Henry Berry free a county, and the influence could spread. The lesser races might join nation-wide to save themselves. The few Whites who cared about them would never have the will or power to do it for them.

The railroad left us within three day's overland to our destination, New Mexico's San Carlos Reservation. We hired a covered buggy drawn by two friendly burros. The renting agent warned me, "That's no country for White men," and that we should get through it as fast as possible, because "The desert does not like you, señor."

Our second morning in the desert, we were surrounded by armed, silent Indians waiting courteously for us to emerge before they scalped us. Western Indians not only practice scalping but had instructed Whites who now did it to each other as well as to their instructors. Henry Berry knew it was a blunder to teach anything to Whites. First they get it wrong and hurt themselves. Then they get it right and hurt the teacher.

I pulled on my hat. The leader asked Henry Berry, "Where do you go?"

"Geronimo," said Henry Berry. The leader removed his red arm band and gave it to Henry Berry. The band rode away.

At San Carlos we found Mr. Franklin Clum. He was an official of the U.S. Department of the Interior, so we didn't reveal that we wanted Geronimo's help creating an Indian army in North Carolina. We claimed to be from the New York Herald, here to report on Mr.

Franklin Clum's success bringing Geronimo to heel. Mr. Clum offered us a selection of cool drinks, saying, "It is gratifying to receive the Herald's leading reporter this distance."

"You flatter me," I said. "But yes, the Herald wants your story well told."

"I can understand that," said Mr. Clum. "We know the Indian, and have brought him to know and appreciate us." Then he asked who Henry Berry was. I said he was my assistant, helpful for protection, carrying baggage, arranging for lodgings, cleaning them when necessary, & etc. Henry Berry's face did not change.

Later, Harry said of Mr. Clum: "Woman's hands. White teeth. Fox eyes." It is true Mr. Clum neither faced the direction he looked nor looked in the direction he spoke.

When I asked to interview Geronimo, Clum said, "Every tribe of savages wants civilization, but there's always a renegade like Geronimo. He and I have a good relationship, but he'll give you bad information. He doesn't understand the situation. And he manipulates and maneuvers Whites, even myself whom he regards as kin. Anything he might have to say, I can tell you better and more accurately."

I said, "Journalism is best when it uses the words of each individual involved. I can best make your case if I hear him first, and then you correct his misleading statements." Harry's nod inspired me further: "We must see Geronimo alone, Mr. Clum, or your presence will remind him to avoid statements he knows you'll correct. And I'll tell him I'm here to write about him, not you."

"He's not that gullible," said Mr. Clum.

"Everyone is gullible when they think I'm writing about them. It never fails," I assured my gull. "Believe me, I know how to do this. I write for the New York Herald, not the Albuquerque Cactus."

"You're a wise man," Mr. Clum said. He warned me that Geronimo would pretend to still be at war. Indians need their dignity. "That's why simply shooting them doesn't work. They're more concerned with dignity than dying, so they don't care if they get killed. They mount suicidal attacks upon White soldiery or even on simple, unarmed settlers." I wondered but did not ask how they mounted suicidal attacks on unarmed settlers.

Mr. Clum agreed to let us interview Geronimo, but suggested an interpreter. "I'm told he speaks good English," I said.

Mr. Clum said, "The offer of an interpreter was my indirect way of providing protection for you."

"He's sufficient protection," I said, indicating Henry Berry.

"Is he?" said Mr. Clum.

"Yes, I think so," I said.

"You won't mind if my concern leads me to stay directly outside the door with my men-at-arms?"

I minded a lot, but I know when a line is drawn. "I'll be grateful," I said, and the wariness disappeared from his eye.

Next morning, Mr. Clum and four soldiers led us into a compound, threw open a door, and stepped aside. Henry Berry and I went on in, shutting the door behind. My eyes adjusted to the inside dimness. The Apache and Henry Berry had already locked eyes. The Apache stood straight. His face was as cragged as if he were 70, though he was 45. He wore ragged buck-skin trousers and a black headband. His feet were bare. For long minutes the two Indians looked at each other. Finally, as if something had passed to his satisfaction, Geronimo nodded Henry Berry to sit and said something in Apache. Henry Berry responded in made-up gibberish.

Geronimo turned to me and said, "This Chief, he does not speak English?"

I wondered what Geronimo had seen that told him Henry Berry was a 'Chief.' And Geronimo's voice took me by surprise. It was musical, warm. I told Geronimo that Henry Berry knew English, and Geronimo said to him, "This is not my tent but you are welcome."

"I also live where it is not my tent," said Henry Berry, as if there were any tents back in Robeson County. Geronimo nodded. His face was a deep color, though there wasn't enough light to see whether it was yellow or closer to red. Its lines crossed his brow at various angles, and dropped alongside his straight nose to frame his mouth. His eyes were not the piercing beacons in the picture on Rhody's wall or that I would have expected from the warrior who had inherited the place of Cochise. His tiny eyes were pale, aged. As if he had read my mind, Geronimo said, "You heard of Cochise?" Henry Berry nodded and Geronimo went on: "They gave him a valley so he lived there. They gave him food so he ate. They brought medicine to his children so they became well. He put down his guns and planted crop. Then they came and shot them all."

Henry Berry described Robeson County, and explained why we had come. Geronimo said he was not a chief but a medicine man. Henry Berry said he was no chief either, but a leader of outlaws. Geronimo said that every chief who is not your own chief is a leader of outlaws. He said bullets don't hit medicine men, so he would be a good outlaw. Henry Berry invited him to join the gang. Geronimo said time would tell. Henry Berry asked about Geronimo's army.

"The way is to find a different way," Geronimo said.

"We have no other way."

"An army is what they want you to do."

"I don't think—" I started to say, but got the sharpest look from Henry Berry I had ever seen.

"An army is what they want you to do," said Geronimo again, without looking at me and as if saying it for the first time. "They treat you bad so your women tell you to go make an army. So you decide to do it. And the day you decide to do it, that is the day they win."

"They tell of your success all over," said Henry Berry.

"The mouth that tells it is White."

"The songs."

"What we have to sing will not come out of the mouth."

"The White leader here says you are content."

"Franklin Clum comes to my tent, he eats my food. He says, 'My friend, you are my friend, I want my friend to fight no more. We have peace, friend. No longer does the White friend hunt his Apache friend.' Does a friend say 'friend?' Did you?" He looked at Henry Berry, then continued. "Listen to me. Once you have an army you think like the White man. Once you think like the White man he cannot lose. If you have a hundred they have two hundred. If you have a thousand they have ten thousand. There is no end of White warriors. If you have arrows they have rifles. If you have rifles they have cannon. They will do to you what they did to Cochise, to me. When your army hurts the White, they turn it 20 times back on you. Do not make an army. Hawk does not run on the ground to kill wolf. Hawk must fly."

He told us of Indian warriors, some famous, some not; some who survived, some who did not; some whose tribes still existed, and some whose did not. Some names were in English and others could not be made into English, but all had wanted only to be left alone. All met defeat the same way. Yes, their armies won occasional battles; even a General Custer might lose a skirmish or two. But even if he were ever annihilated, another White would come wipe out the victors. They kill you, your children, your women. "When the White soldiers are finished, then come soft White men like slugs." He nodded towards the door. "The White chiefs."

Henry Berry said nothing. "I will show why you must not make an army," the Apache said. He motioned Henry Berry not to interfere, and then handed me his headband. I thanked him. "You will earn it, so give it to someone you want to live forever," he said. Suddenly he turned me around. With one hand he pulled tight at my hair, and with the other he wrenched my arm up my back as if to break it. In pain and fear I yelled, expecting Harry to help me. He didn't. Soldiers burst in with Mr. Clum. Three held Geronimo while another beat him with fists, then a pistol. I demanded that they stop. Henry Berry started to interfere, but backed away at a look from Geronimo. The medicine man was beaten until his face looked like it could never heal; then he was thrown into a corner. Barely able, he looked up at Henry Berry. The Outlaw nodded.

Clum's men pulled us outside. "You're lucky we were here," said Clum. "He'd have killed you. I've seen him do it." Enraged, I told Clum he could expect to see his brutality spread across the newspapers as fast as wire would get it there. "I think not," he said. "The correspondent whose name you are using is on assignment in Carolina."

Damn Samuel Morse! Damn his telegraph. Henry Berry watched to see me in action. "Yes, it is true," I said. "I'm not from the New York Herald. But I am a writer. I hid my real name because I have already written about you and these Indians. I didn't want to be recognized while I was gathering information for my next book." I showed him the wretched volume I had purchased in Chicago and said I'd written it. "To disguise my identity I pretended to be angry at your measures to protect me from the savage." Clum looked skeptical, but I knew what I was doing. I said. "I'm commissioned to write a new book describing how you control the savages by wise administration, rather than by the continuous military force that peaceful Americans abhor and can't afford. It is the kind of wise administration that people hope for in governors' mansions—and higher."

As I continued, Geronimo appeared in the doorway. Clum didn't notice, being too busy looking off at the horizon where he saw his name embossed on a volume, and perhaps on the White House. With Geronimo bloody behind Clum, I longed for Mr. Matthew Brady.

Clum led us away, his mind on destiny. I looked back at Geronimo, wishing I could tell him I bore no grudge. Henry Berry later assured me that my pain didn't concern Geronimo, because the headband had paid for it.

Clum accompanied us across the desert with 50 soldiers. For three endless days he told me about himself, alternating between bragging and false modesty. Aside from himself, his chief topic was gossip. At the depot I was afraid he was going to board our train and talk about himself all the way back to North Carolina. But he hugged me to his bosom, called me friend, and reminded me that the way I represented him would shape the entire settlement of the West. If Mr. Clum has managed to read this far into a book that fails to mention him until so late, he will now learn that I represent him as a disgrace to himself, to his country, to the White race, and even to his Scottish forebears, though only a truly extraordinary villain could bring greater disgrace to the Scots than they had already done for themselves in Robeson County.

THIRTY

IN AMERICA, EASTWARD is the direction of the defeated. We came again to Pittsburgh. Between trains we bought Henry Berry his first store-purchased clothes. He wore them back to the depot. He didn't look out of place in this immigrant city. He was not an Indian all dressed up, but an American in a new suit. White people admired him for a White person.

Back on board we were too gloomy to talk. In Philadelphia we saw the Liberty Bell. I read Harry the inscription: "Proclaim liberty throughout the land unto all the inhabitants thereof." He touched its crack. We returned to the depot. Once on board for North Carolina, I slept.

The man in the new suit who had been staring at the Wilmington Star for five hours jostled me awake. Out the window I saw Patrick Lowery's horse tethered at the depot rail, who turned away from his noisy iron cousin steaming to a halt. We disembarked and I greeted him; he nuzzled my pocket but took no other notice. Henry Berry and I headed out of town and through the countryside, me on horseback. "Hello," said Steven suddenly behind us. We turned. He was with a hundred Indian men and boys who had silently fallen in to follow.

Indians in Robeson County don't travel, so they have no rituals for returns: no embrace, no hearty handshake. Henry Berry nodded to Steve as if they'd parted an hour ago. "What's this?" I asked, referring to the hundred men. Steven said they were some of the folks ready to join the new army once Henry Berry told them how to proceed. We trudged on silently.

That morning Rhody was in her new yellow dress. The delicate garment was not cut for chores, so it slowed her work. She was inside gathering blankets for a wash when the small hairs on the back of her neck told her to turn around. Henry Berry Lowery was in the doorway.

"What's that suit?" she said.

"What's that dress?" he said.

He stepped in and shut the door. Steven, the hundred men, and I waited outside. Sally Ann, Henry Delaney, and Neelyann appeared from the swamp. Henry Delaney shook my hand. We all stood in silence.

But there was no silence in the cabin, because Rhody did not know there were people in her yard. Most—not all—the men were embarrassed. The children were unconcerned, simply waiting for Poppa to emerge. Finally there was silence inside, then more screams, but not the kind we'd been hearing. They got louder: crashing, banging, finally a gunshot. Henry Berry burst out. He was not wearing his Pittsburgh suit. He was not wearing anything. He stood in his doorway, as is any man's right.

"Turn your head," I said to Sally Ann. But she ran to her Daddy, who scooped her into his arms. She clung to him as if nothing might ever force them apart.

Henry Delaney, dragging Neelyann, joined them. Again I wished for Mr. Brady and his camera, though this particular picture might have been too natural for my Editor.

The cabin door opened. Rhody came out in a blanket, took her family inside, and shut the door. The audience began to tire of this domestic drama and looked to me to assume leadership. "You're a writer, go in and talk to them," Steven said. Apparently my height on horseback made him think I could handle this. He might as well have asked the horse.

I went to the door and knocked, stern as a sheriff. Young Henry Delaney opened the door, looked at me, shook my hand, and shut the door. I heard Rhody's voice, and he opened it again. I went in.

Rhody still had the blanket around her. Her yellow dress was on the floor. "What did Geronimo say?" she asked me.

"Didn't Harry tell you?" I asked.

"I never yet called my husband a liar and I ain't now, but I want to hear you tell it." I did. "What you think, girl?" she said to Sally Ann.

Sally Ann opened the door. Outside all eyes turned to her. "Go home," she yelled to the men who had come to be in an army. She came back in.

"Well?" Rhody asked me, as if this were a story I was writing and I was supposed to know what came next.

"Ma'am?" I said.

"Now what, Writer?" I didn't know. She stormed at me from across the room. "What do we do?" Her eyes flowed, and God help me, I reached for her. I put my arms around her there in front of her husband and children and held her as she cried. Harry sat hanging his head, pillow in his naked lap. Sally Ann came to her weeping Momma. Henry Delaney followed, and the baby wriggled in among us. Rhody continued weeping, and my arms embraced Henry Berry's family. Rhody's tears finally quieted, and she looked at Henry Berry through the twine of bodies.

She broke away, ripped Geronimo's picture off the wall, and threw it into the fire. Harry and I were after it in an instant, knocking out the flames with our bare hands.

Rhody went outside. Steve was alone with Patrick Lowery's horse. Rhody went to the far end of the yard bordering the swamp, as if to plunge in and disappear. Harry went to the doorway, not with his pillow. "Gawd damn it, Rhody Damn Wood-Brain Strong!" he called to his wife half a hundred yards past Steven. "Gawd damn it. Gawd damn it."

"Don't you Gawd damn at me, Henry Squish Berry Lorry," she cried back.

"What you want me to do? What can I do?"

"I hate it," she called. "I hate this Gawd damn swamp. I hate everything. I hate Gawd damn Geronimo, and I hate you, Henry Gawd damn Berry damn Lowery. And I hate this Gawd damn writer."

"It ain't my fault," Henry Berry said. I wanted to say it was mine, just to make things better.

She yelled back at Henry Berry, "If you don't fix it then it is your fault, because there is no other man alive who can."

"Tell me what to do and I'll do it."

"Burn them, I don't care. Shoot them. Poison their wells, cut them so their wives can't have no more babies, I don't care what you do, I know you can't do nothing, just make them leave us alone. Throw their heads in the swamp. And put your pants on." She slammed her way into the privy and we all turned our backs.

"What you doing, honey?" Henry Berry said softly.

"What you think?" We waited. Finally Sally Ann came out of the house and knocked on the privy door. There was no response.

"Got to pee," she said.

She was admitted. In a few moments she led her momma out by the hand. "Henry Berry," said Rhody, "I'm sorry I am expecting you to know what to do, because if there's nothing, then that is how it is. Let's just be happy you are home, and maybe tomorrow or the day after we will think what to do. It ain't your fault you're scared."

"Shit," said Henry Berry and went into the cabin. Rhody followed.

I remembered our two souvenirs: the desert warrior's red arm band and Geronimo's black headband. I told Sally Ann where they came from, and put Geronimo's on her head. She said she would give the desert warrior's arm band to her Momma. "She won't want Geronimo's," she said.

Steve and I went back to the Devil's Den. I told him what Geronimo had said. To my surprise he seemed relieved. I was, too. There is respite in losing. "But when I think of all them sons of bitches . . ." Steve said, and that was the whole of the thought.

THIRTY-ONE

I SLEPT around the clock. When I woke, the autumn sun was low. Henry Berry was not back. Steven had set out my paper and pencils. I made us supper, lit my lamp, and settled to work. Though what I wrote was not comforting, it was good to hold a pencil again and I wrote until sunrise. Inside, Steven had gone to sleep in what had been Thommy's place, and I went to sleep again in my own. I woke mid-day to find myself alone, and busied myself like a housewife. I put the place in order. I made dinner, but no one returned to eat it. I ate my solitary meal, abandoned by gang, universe, and even the dogs. I wrote all night and spent two more days alone in the swamp and, for all I could tell, alone in the world. Eventually I stopped writing. I prayed to wake up where the gang was, risky or not. I dreamed of Thom, Andrew, a shadowy stranger I took to be Boss, and Shoe-Maker John. They were with Henry Berry and Steve, and none talked to me.

I woke in the darkness. Something had happened to the earth. The people, like the dinosauria, had disappeared all at once and for no known reason. Only the swamp creatures survived. At sunrise, throwing caution to the alligators, I set off to see whether Patrick

Lowery's horse was as extinct as the human race. Thinking I might never return, I stuffed my manuscript in my shirt. Hours later I stumbled into the thicket where Patrick Lowery's horse was wondering why I had come from the wrong direction.

I went to Rhody's cabin. No one there. I went to Lumberton where, as all lost men who must go somewhere, I went to the inn and for a long while sipped red berry wine. When I rose to go, Innkeeper Lear said he'd be open for another hour. I said I had things to do and places to be—nekked drunken lies. I returned to Patrick Lowery's horse who did not want to wake up. But we rode off. Without thought, I found myself at the Widow Norment's home. There was a moon, which makes raids dangerous. But brave with red berry wine, I crept across the roof to the Widow Norment's window. Inside she was reading. I wanted to invite her out on the roof:

"Mary, Mary, the night air is cool and refreshing, come out. Spit into the night to your heart's content."

"Oh good sir, I may not join you, for the servants will see."

"Hang the servants!" I'd say, an unfortunate image in these parts.

"Nay I cannot."

"Come dance with me in the moonlight, Widow. Let me lie by you until the dawn, and stay the days of my life until their evening."

Eventually she disappeared into her bedroom with the candle. I opened the window and entered to stand hidden among the curtains. I heard her preparing for bed and lay down. I found an angle from which I could watch her as she read. When she finally doused the candle and left the room, I went in and took her manuscript from the desk, thicker than before, and wondered what she could have been writing while Henry Berry and I had been out West. Steve had pursued no solitary raids, so the Widow would have had nothing to record. Perhaps she had stooped to fiction.

I stowed her manuscript under my shirt with mine and climbed out. But I carelessly let the window click shut. I froze, then inched across the roof and slid down. As my feet touched ground, a rifle barrel poked my back. The Widow. I threw up my hands and said, "It's not what it seems!" I don't know what I meant, but she didn't shoot.

"Who is it?" she said, unable to see me in the shadow of the house.

"No one," I said.

"Who are you and what do you want?"

"Nobody and I only want to leave you in peace." I started to move away, but she fired over my head. I heard shouts from the servants' quarters. Knowing I would soon be surrounded, I did what Henry Berry would do: I grabbed the rifle away from her and ran. The Widow, no coward, jumped onto my back. At full speed I tried to get her off as she clawed my face from behind and pounded at my skull. I pried her arms off and she fell backwards, her legs clutching around my waist as I ran. I finally managed to force those powerful legs apart and dove through the fence.

I ran towards Patrick Lowery's horse. Servants with torches were shouting and running from every direction. The Widow's damnable dogs came at me. I'm a city boy, unequipped to contend with hounds and Negroes chasing me. But I'm in the gang as well, and refused to be taken during a raid. The disgrace would hurt the sales of my book, I thought, and then wondered how I could think such a thing at such a time.

Torches everywhere! Did this damned Widow have a hundred servants after me? I flew onto Patrick Lowery's startled horse. Behind me the Widow shouted to her servants. I sped recklessly into the swamp, riding low on my steed's back so a branch would not sweep me off. We were 50 yards in when pursuers shouted that they saw us. There were shots, then a command not to shoot or they'd hit each other.

I urged the terrified horse onwards. Trusting me for the first time, he complied. He lowered his majestic head with me close alongside his great neck. We had all but escaped when, two hundred yards into the safety of the swamp, the poor horse stumbled— though not so much a stumble as a giving way. The unexpected movement threw me from the saddle and far into a bush, from which some startled night creature crossly raced. Behind me in moonlit silhouette the horse was down in full panic, reins snapping like whips and angry snakes, and only one foreleg free to move. I had never heard a horse's whinny rise to the level of scream, but it did. It was not only pitiful and terrifying to hear, but a beacon to the pursuers, who headed for the horse but away from me. My old friend would be my savior.

Patrick Lowery's horse was in quicksand, a piece of damned bad luck for there was hardly any of the stuff in this part of the swamp. The poor thrashing beast sank lower with each movement. I raced off into the swamp, my escape assured. But I heard the horse sucking for air, and like a fool I stopped. I knew he was only a dumb brute with no feeling or intellect, but my frail city self gave in to the worst pathetic sentimentality. After all, in the same straits he had not abandoned me.

I went back, though with no idea what to do. I thought I could pull him out if I only had the strength. I grabbed the reins. His thrashing stripped them out of my hands. I tried to calm him, speaking softly. He half listened, and slowed his thrashing, earth-bound leaps. Again I had the reins, and this time I held. I pulled but with no success.

My pursuers were just a few steps away. But I preferred capture to hearing those dying screams for the rest of my life. A dozen confused and frightened Negroes closed around me, and escape was out of the question. They had brought ropes to tie me. I assured them of my surrender and begged them first to help save the beast, who panicked again as more yelling Negroes with torches crashed towards us. As the quicksand sucked him lower, I threw myself through the air onto his back. One of the Negroes threw ropes. I slid two around and under the horse and called to the Negroes to pull. They did, but the quicksand held fast. I pleaded to pull harder. I talked quietly into the horse's ear lest he buck me away or snap the ropes. My voice quieted him, which made me proud even at so tumultuous a moment.

I kept my mouth in his ear, smelling his sweat of terror, and I murmured calm sounds, for he could be quieted only instant-by-instant, panicking each time he stopped hearing my voice.

More Negroes arrived. They shouted instructions, warnings, and encouragement to each other. I realized that this very shouting frightened the horse. I cupped my hands tight over his ears and shouted at the Negroes to quiet down. It took a while to make myself understood, but finally all were quiet, and we labored intensely and silently for long, long, moments.

One Negro took charge, noiselessly gesturing to his fellows what to do. I continued calming the horse. It all had the feeling of a nightmare. Nothing was actual; all was mute as if our ear drums had been stoppled. There seemed no promise of waking into a real world.

Finally, as if lifted by a hand of Heaven but actually the result of tugging and pulling by 20 frightened men, the horse stood on hard ground shaking in every limb. The men used the ropes that had freed him to bind me, but first I was allowed to assure myself that the trembling horse was intact. Once my hands were tied I pattied him with the side of my head. Then we watched each other as they led us in different directions.

They dragged me to the Widow Norment. I begged her to have the horse removed to Patrick Lowery, which she did.

I was resigned to being jailed. I could complete my manuscript there. I would be that much more notorious, and more copies would sell. I was bound over to the Sheriff, taken to Lumberton jail, and relieved of my possessions including my manuscript. I asked the Sheriff to give the Widow her manuscript, and asked when I might get mine back. He said he would look into it.

He looked into it by reading it. As a result I was no longer facing a brief jail sentence for having entered the Widow Norment's home, but now charged with the murder of Colonel Francis Marion Wishart. My trial would be in one week, my manuscript the chief evidence against me. I could blame the book, or fate, or my profession, but the fault was that damned horse.

My fourth day I had a visitor: Rhody, accompanied by two deputies who stayed. She said nothing. I humiliated myself by weeping. My hands were shackled to the wall and I could not wipe my face. I wanted her to say that everything would be fine, that we would walk again in sunlit meadows and then go home to New York and never again hear of North Carolina or any Lowerys. She hummed softly.

She wiped my tears with her sleeve. "Can I pray for him?" she asked. A deputy nodded. "Oh dear Lord ..." Her voice trailed to a whisper. I strained forward. She said holy words, then mouthed words to the hymn she had been humming. She left, still humming. The hymn was, "You Will Be Free."

THIRTY-TWO

"HOW DO you plead?"

"Guilty."

I wanted to live long enough to finish my book, for it seemed a fine idea to write of my own approaching doom. But they'd hung Shoe-Maker John the morning after his trial.

Thought the courtroom was nearly full, I knew no man in it but Mr. Groone, who was recording the proceedings. He would not look at me. There were two women: Lydia Wishart, whom I had made a widow. And Rhody, whom I had saved from being one.

The Judge warned that I was pleading guilty to a capital crime and asked if I understood the consequences. I said yes. He stated that in spite of my guilty plea, a bench trial was necessary in a capital case, and apologized that I had to go through the inconvenience. I said that I had no engagements. A series of legalities commenced. I passed the time by looking out the window. The day was cloudless. A delivery was in progress, sacks being unloaded from a faded red wagon. Passengers waited at the depot. People milled about the street exchanging gossip, and I must have been the topic. I could see the door to the Inn, a few customers coming and going. Every so often another faded red wagon passed. The morning train came in, stopping beyond my line of sight. In the courtroom the legal rigamarole seemed to be winding down. My lawyer, a Mr. McFea, was making a speech that had nothing to do with me until the Judge waved him to shut up. The Judge was making some notes when the back door of the courtroom banged opened and a gentleman unknown to me entered. He seemed like a New York person. My impression was confirmed when he was followed by a gentleman I knew well: my Editor! now Associate Publisher of the New York Herald. He marched in, in full Editorial bluster and rage that one of his journalists was being threatened.

Following him was a young man who opened a tablet of paper and began to draw everyone and everything in sight. It unnerved them all, from Judge down to spittoon-boy. My Editor sat himself in front, snapped open his own tablet, and began to write at a furious rate. The older gentleman turned out to be an attorney who worked for the New York Herald. He begged ("begged" is a legal term, not his tone) the Judge to accept his petition for recognition as counsel for the accused. He demolished the Prosecutor's objections, which came in hailstorm succession: first, that Mr. McFea, my dutifully present assigned counsel, had been awake during much of the proceeding; second, that a New York attorney cannot practice in North Carolina; third, that no one can enter a proceeding this late; and fourth, that the defendant had already entered a plea of guilty so there was no purpose to such carpet-bagging counsel. But my man had made himself a master of North Carolina rules and statutes. He sent Mr. McFea elsewhere to sleep, and sat unmovably at the defense table. He never glanced at me, apparently considering it irrelevant what I might look like or what I might have to say or think. He was a lawyer of the same cut that my Editor was an editor.

The young sketch-man drew the faces of everyone in the room. As he completed each one he rolled it with a flourish and placed it prominently on the seat beside him.

My new attorney argued that the only evidence was my manuscript. "And his plea of guilty," said the Judge.

"Obtained within the umbra of the illegal and shocking investigation of his manuscript! Where do you get your people? This case must be dismissed. There is nothing else for it!" He did not speak in genteel, southern tones. He barked. He demanded – harshly, rapidly, unyieldingly. Nothing mild or civil in it. He did not understand the Dixie mind, but I had no way of telling him.

And I had no way of knowing how he was here – until my glance fell upon the tall, crooked man trying desperately to record my attorney's torrent. A smile was straining Mr. Groone's thin face.

My attorney argued that my manuscript in my own hand, and illegally seized, must not be used as evidence, lest it be a case of self-incrimination which is forbidden by the United States Constitution, of which the Judge might have heard and perhaps would even concede to be the Supreme Law of the Land despite the recent unpleasantness and rout. Even if the Judge were to barbarously admit such evidence, surely His Honor recognized the difference between evidentiary fact and artistical *fiction*, which latter is made up by and for the entertainment of imbeciles and not for a truth-finding court of law. My man referred to the reputation of southern jurisprudence as a disgrace to the civilized world, and offered His Honor the opportunity to begin to alter that reputation.

My Editor sat silent and anonymous, as Editors always do when they're out in real life—and he wrote down all he heard and saw.

My lawyer placed a great dossier on the Judge's desk, and cried, "On Constitutional grounds and upon such precedents as I list herein which even include some from the State of North Carolina (which State, I was delighted to discover, keeps track of its legal proceedings more or less the same as the rest of the Nation), and are as follows . . . ." And he narrated the entire contents of the dossier, which took three hours. Having been provided a copy, Mr. Groone had no need to write, so was able to look around and enjoy what he had wrought. Finally my attorney finished and said, "There is no alternative but to dismiss this case and to apologize to my unjustly accused client for the unconscionable, cruel, and unusual manner of incarceration and punishment he has been forced to suffer for six days—"

"Seven!" I shouted.

"Seven," my attorney thundered, as if that made it one hundred times worse. "My God, seven!—and to restore his manuscript to its proper owner." The dog pointed to my Editor!—then gathered his papers and still without looking at me started out of the courtroom.

The Judge said, "I must take this under advisement, Counsel."

As if a bugle had blown "Charge!" my attorney charged back to the bench. He pointed at my Editor and commanded, "Write, sir, that this Judge—and insert whatever his name might be, Lee or Jackson or Mac-what-you-may-call-it—has taken the third part of the Fifth Amendment of the only Constitution of the United States of America under advisement; and YOU," he shouted at the young sketch-man, "draw this Judge's face well and fairly, and caption it, 'Judge Mac-What's-it takes self-incrimination under advisement'."

"You will not bully this court, sir!" cried the Judge.

"I did not come all this way to molly-cuddle it, sir; on that you may rely. I did not travel here for pleasure, for I don't like *railroading*, neither the pitiful sort you employ in these parts for transportation nor the sort you perpetrate upon my client. Nor do I bully; I have merely asked these famous journalists to report the factual news, which I reckon they will do; and none in the Nation do it better or in a manner more widespread."

My attorney knew the Dixie mind after all. Any White southerner would rather die howling than be humiliated. The judge found sufficient legal cause to dismiss the case right then, and at his bidding Mr. Groone returned my manuscript —to me, over my Editor's objections. I shook Mr. Groone's hand. He had saved my life and was giving me back my manuscript;

could I be in greater debt to anyone? "You will forgive me, I hope, for taking the liberty," he said.

"If you had not taken the liberty, I would have suffered the worst. I am indebted to you, sir."

"Oh no, not to me. Mrs. Lowery urged me to take the liberty of which you speak. What I mean is to beg your forgiveness for having taken the liberty of reading your manuscript." I tried to recall all that I had written about Mr. Groone. I started an apology, but he interrupted. "One must record what one sees," he said. "Which no one knows better than I myself."

"I'll miss you," I said, knowing I had to go home to New York.

"As I you," he said. "Perhaps in your book, you'll mention that Mr. Groone was unhappy when he said goodbye to you. For it would be true. Yet the joy of acquaintance outweighs the pain of parting. Farewell." He gathered his papers and left.

Rhody had already gone. I would have liked us to say goodbye.

THIRTY-THREE

WE YANKEES LOOKED out the hotel window. The crowd filling the street was angry at my release, angry at my Yankee lawyer, angry at it all, and bent on assuaging their anger by hanging me. Several of these fellows brandished ropes. Seeing them, my Editor threw open the window. "Draw!" he cried to the sketch-man in the other window. This silenced the crowd. "Draw!" he cried loudly enough to be heard all up and down the street. "Draw every scoundrel down there, draw every wart and wrinkle, what they're wearing, the scar on that man's brow, the sore on that one's neck. Draw the crooked teeth of that one, the bent shoulder of that, that little beard and this big nose. And draw the stench wafting up of the whole unGodly mob. Draw everything!" Never did so many look up at Michelangelo as now stared up like worried cattle at this Yankee doodler.

"Write 'K' for Klan on that one, on that one, and that one," I cried, pointing at those I knew to be Kluxers. One panicked, pointed out five I had missed, and ran off.

"My artist is quick," yelled my Editor. But the mob was quicker, and the street was soon empty. A Robeson

County mob will hang a man but won't gamble. By morning we'd be on a train and out of this terrible place.

I lived through the night, but did not sleep. I watched my editor read my manuscript. "No wonder they wanted to lynch you," he finally said, "you still can't do semi-colons. Yet some of the text is acceptable. But Sally Ann must not shoot her schoolteacher."

"Sir?"

"Little girls do not shoot their schoolteachers."

"This one did," I said. He shook his editorial head. "Why not?" I asked.

"There are limits."

"Am I to lie?" I said.

"You are to omit it."

"Omission is lying."

"We omit daily," he said. "When appropriate, it is our duty." He went to sleep. I sat awake, listening to my bowdlerizing Editor's smug snores. *Omit Sally's heroic shooting?* I fumed. I went to the window for air. Below, as if on cue, stood Sally Ann in moonlit silhouette on the far side of the bridge into the swamp. Patrick Lowery's horse stood asleep alongside, motionless as marble in the moonlight. Down in New York, pigeons would be sitting on him. Sally was here for me.

But I must write this: I could never be safe here. I belong in New York, where my book would be praised and I would not be ambushed. My North Carolina friends would become memories, which was all they should be. These were not my people nor this my world, in which I near lost my life for a horses sake that didn't like me. My place was New York, where I was atop the feeding chain. So I will never know why, with boots and manuscript, I tiptoed out of the room, down the stairs, through the hotel lobby, and outside. The dirt street was empty dust but for an old Negro woman coming towards me in the moonlight. She walked with me across the bridge to Sally Ann. Suddenly my Editor's voice rang out like God's from above. "What do you think you're doing, you idiot?" I kept walking. "Your book is good!"

"Thank you," I called without turning.

"Get up here. Your book is excellent!" I stopped. "I liked it," he said, not easily. I turned and looked expectant. "I enjoyed reading it!" came wrenching out of his mouth as if Satan had dragged it against the wishes of his flesh, soul, and the entire guild of editors. "Do you hear me, you God damned ingrate?"

"Yes sir, I do, thank you," I said. The old Negro woman waited.

"I won't delete your murderous damned lethal child, you hear?"

"Yes, sir."

"Then what do have you to say?"

"Thank you for praising my book, sir."

"We came all this way to save you and bring you back to New York, you worthless hack."

"I don't like New York."

"You do like New York, you vermin, now bring back that book." He repeated all the reasons I must leave this place. They were all true. Then he said, "When you left New York you were a good enough reporter. Now you'll be my lead man. Your book will make you famous and wealthy. There'll be no talking to you. You'll be in Heaven, able to flout your publisher and your editor."

I did not move, nor did I turn away.

My Editor went on: "You can do whatever you want with semi-colons. I know you are considering it; why else did you stop?"

"To hear you praise my book."

"At least leave me the book! I came all this way!"

"I'll send it when it's finished."

"And what if you're killed?"

"The swamp's a terrible gamble," I admitted. The old Negro woman nodded. She patted my rump to get me moving again towards Sally Ann, smiled a toothless good night, and limped away. With my editor keening in the window and the sleepy young artist drawing my withdrawal, I joined Sally Ann. Patrick Lowery's horse greeted me with alarm. I mounted and pulled Sally Ann up behind me.

We lit out.

When we got to Rhody's I thanked her for telling Mr. Groone to save my life, and said I was not returning to New York. Rhody said I was a fool. I asked her why she had sent Sally Ann after me if staying was foolish. She said maybe Sally Ann had come on her own, and I was a fool to stay no matter who wanted me. But I was no fool. Better to die that very night in a land with Rhody, Harry, Sally Ann, Mr. Groone, Steven, and even Patrick Lowery's horse. Better to live in this swamp with ghosts of the gang and in fear of my life than safe in my empty New York room, writing about people no more important to me than the scrap of paper on which I wrote. I had come all this way for just a few people I might call, a little, my own.

THIRTY-FOUR

AT THE DEVIL'S DEN I spent days reading my book aloud to Henry Berry, who tried to imagine how a stranger would take it in. When I came as far as I had written, he asked, "What's the end?"

"Not all stories have an end."

"Go to have an end," he said. Will I never be free of editors?

I said, "If you want an ending, we have to do something that can count as an ending."

"Just write 'drowned in the swamp'," said Steve. "They'll leave us alone. They happy, we happy."

"Write we went to Mexico," said Henry Berry. "Wherever that is."

"Say we dressed up like ole White ladies and went to Raleigh," said Steve. I said I would not poison my book with fiction, and went to sleep.

Morning, I woke alone. Due to recent events, no misfortune seemed too terrible to come true, and my sore mind had become a fictionalizer. I knew in my heart that Steven and Henry Berry had gone and got arrested, I knew in my heart that militia had killed them, knew in my heart a snake ate them, I knew they had left me here forever, and I knew in my heart they were returning to kill me. A bullet would get me any minute.

When I finally calmed down, a sharp report sent me diving for the bushes. I hid for hours until, knowing it to be my last move on earth, I ran to the cabin. Later that day, knowing it would be my last exit, I came out with two pistols. The privy door, normally open except when in use, was shut. Knowing someone inside was waiting to shoot me, I opened it. Empty. I slammed the door. It made the sound of the report I had heard. Yet my mind continued its anthology of worst possibilities. Why not good possibilities? The outlaws are pardoned, Rhody has a sister, Jesus comes down . . . but no. My brain, sealed up within its ghastly musings, had become the Edgar Allen Poe fictionalizer of my organs. "For the love of God," I cried to myself.

No one returned. Night, my macabre fictions progressed. Dawn, I cleaned pots and floors in a totemic attempt to make the outlaws return. I polished Thom's boots and buried them. I yanked weeds, as Mary Cuombo had predicted I would. But one was not a weed. Before I saw it move it struck my wrist and flashed away leaving two red puncture marks. Now indeed the essence of the swamp entered into me. Come, I thought, sit upon the ground to die, and I fell, dizzy. By afternoon, fevered. I swelled. Evening, my vision was in shifting mosaics, a magic picture puzzle. Without thinking, I lay down on Thommy's pallet. Something kept happening in the night but I don't remember what. Sunrise again, awake on Henry Berry's mat, thoughts muddy. Dizzy, to my desk. I looked down on myself from above and a voice described the scene—badly. I remembered the catastrophes that I knew in my heart must have overtaken Harry and Steve. I lowered my head to my desk, like a schoolboy seeking solitude in his own arms. The desk banged my forehead.

"You worry too gawd damn much, Writer," said Steven's voice behind me.

"You got to have faith in us," said Harry.

I turned. Dizziness sent me sprawling from my chair. I tried to rise on the shifting ground. No one there. I called, angry that they teased a sick man. "For the love of God," said my brain, "don't believe everything you hear."

"A man's got to believe something," said Harry.

Thommy said, "Not me, I don't believe nothing."

"That the whole trouble with you," said Shoe-Maker John. Andrew smiled at the promise of a fight between Shoe-Maker John and Thommy. A swooping bird dropped a red-jeweled ring at my feet.

"The only trouble with *me?*" retorted Thommy, but I put my hand to my mouth and there was silence.

I understood. I had become insane, an awful thought but at least it was an explanation. To test this hypothesis I took my hand from my mouth. "Maybe it's ghosts," blurted Thommy before I clapped my hand back. Later, Shoe-Maker John sang all the verses of "Amazing Grace." I know only the first verse from memory, so it was ghosts after all. That meant Henry Berry and Steven were dead now, for they chattered all night. Thommy asked me to read. The gang sat outside the lamp's periphery. I read about the hanging of Shoe-Maker John. Each time I came to his name he shouted it out himself. Then I started reading the death of Thommy. "Don't read that," Thommy said. I explained that his death had had the greatest impact of all upon the gang, so I had to read it. When I came to his funeral, he wept. "Not everyone gets to cry at their own funeral," I said.

"Don't be sure," Thommy said.

I read Boss's death and Andrew's. In the corner of my eye I saw Andrew, arms wrapped around himself, rocking. Thommy beside him. The shadow of Boss stood off alone.

I skipped to now, the present moment and read it aloud, though I couldn't recall writing it. "Implausible," said editor Thommy of these last few paragraphs. I wondered where he'd gotten such a word, until I remembered using it in describing his funeral.

"Implausible?" I growled. The gang agreed. "It's not enough that you were a pack of thieves and murderers and now you're ghouls or lunatic visions, but must you fall so low as to be, not just editors, but CRITICS as well? Well, let me tell you something: Yes, it is *implausible.* Every word, *implausible. Implausible* that I left Manhattan where, if there's trouble, you call a copper and that's the end of it; and where dead people come back only to shriek and go boo, not sit around like old ladies and listen to book readings. *Implausible?* Yes! Even this very moment lecturing a gang that ain't here, that's half dead or maybe all dead, and that dares to call my *exact report* of what *they themselves* have done *implausible!* Without *implausible* what have you got? Nothing!"

They disappeared. "Good!" I said. "Then good night."

I thrust myself back to sleep. I woke falling off Patrick Lowery's horse at Rhody's door. The cabin was deserted. So was Mary Cuombo's. I rode to the church. From dense cover I saw hundreds of people where I was afraid they'd be: in the graveyard. Implausibly, not only Indians, but Negroes and many Whites. Even the Widow Norment. When I saw Rhody, Mary Cuombo, and Sally Ann, I knew Henry Berry was dead.

"Easy, Writer," he said. I clapped my hands over my mouth. This was no time for ghosts or lunatic voices. Henry Berry's death was, for me, the end of the world. "No," said Henry Berry, pulling my hands from my lips. "It's the end of the book. The best part. So look," he ordered, "and write down what you see."

Having been a journalist I knew this principle, but said, "I don't want to see it."

"You do," he said.

"I can't. I can not."

"I chose you because you can. I CHOSE you."

"No," I said.

"Why not? It's plausible." And he was gone.

THIRTY-FIVE

THE MINISTER WAS done. The crowd stirred. A choir sang, twenty voices from this Indian church and another dozen from some Negro church or other. Mary Cuombo touched the coffin as she sang with the choir.

A slender red swamp reptile slid over my boot, trying to get to the interment. It lifted its head, looked out at the mixed congregation, changed its mind, and turned back. I drew my pistol but then remembered not to move. The serpent flicked its tongue. I did not move again, since such creatures don't strike anything still. A shot would reveal my presence and bring pursuit. But I held the pistol to threaten the creature. It rested its head on the pistol barrel and waited for my slightest twitch or blink. A deadly beast with bright, angled eyes, and the choir sang:

Thee we adore, eternal name,
And humbly own to thee
How feeble is our mortal frame
What dying worms we be.

Snakes are said to be deaf, yet this one swayed to the choir's rhythm.

The years roll round, they steal away
The breath that first they gave;
Whate'er we do, where'er we be,
We're trav'ling to the grave.

The coffin was lowered. In swamp country, coffins sink lower over the years and dissolve into the moisture, releasing the remains to become the swamp. With so eternal a thought I kicked at the snake. He had been watching my eyes so never saw it coming, heh, heh, heh, and I booted him a good distance. Planning another encounter on some future unsuspecting day, his slit eyes memorized my face as he arced out of sight.

Rhody and Sally Ann sprinkled soil. Mary Cuombo spoke to the coffin. Sally Ann sang alone, too faint for the wind to carry her words.

Two men shoveled over the coffin. Negroes and Indians murmured their prayers. At the back of the crowd, a pair of White hands began to clap a macabre applause. Others joined, the White hands of White people who would not let the Outlaw alone even in death. White wives reached for husbands' hands to silence them, looking at the ground in shame. Now what had seemed a meeting of the races became a living graph of the distance between them. The crowd drew apart by color, slowly, afraid that anything quick would bring violence. Every man's hand hovered by concealed knife or pistol; every wife nervously drew her man and children close, and then drew the family towards others they knew.

The Widow Norment stepped to the grave, drawing

the attention of everyone nearby and by relay the rest. I remembered the night she spat out her window. If she spat now it would result in violence. But she bent to kiss Sally Ann, then greeted Rhody, hand to her cheek. The women, my two women, stood that way for some moments. They put out the fuse.

I traveled back through the swamp to Rhody's cabin where I waited in the tunnel until I heard the family arrive overhead. I tapped. There was silence, and then the bolt was slid away and the trap door opened. Henry Delaney's little face looked down. He shook my hand and shut the trap again. I pushed it up myself and climbed into the midst of Rhody, Mary Cuombo, the Minister, Sally Ann, Henry Delaney, Steven, and Neelyann.

They thought I was ignorant of the situation. No one wanted to break the news. Rhody sat me between herself and Mary Cuombo. She sent Henry Delaney outside with the baby. There was something I was expected to do, but no one said what.

"I know he's dead," I said. "I want to know how it happened." I looked at Steve. He deferred to the women, who are always in charge at such times. Rhody gave way to the Outlaw's mother.

"Oh, they were waiting for someone Harry wanted to get, and—" Mary Cuombo stopped. She looked at me and said, "I'm saying what happened."

"Yes ma'am," I said quietly. "I'm listening."

"I see you're listening," she said.

"She's expecting you to write," said Rhody. I quickly had my pencil and was ready.

"They were waiting to get someone," Mary Cuombo said, making sure I wrote as she spoke. "Who?" She looked around.

"Kin to Giles Inman," answered Steven.

"Kin to Giles Inman," Mary Cuombo said, as if I'd not heard. "So they . . ." She stopped again and looked at my paper.

"What's the matter?" I asked.

"Where you write 'Giles'?"

"I didn't think . . ."

"Everything belongs, hear? I got no comfort but to tell it," she said. "You got none but writing it."

"Yes ma'am." I wrote the name.

"They made two blinds," she said. "One for Stevie, yes?" Steven nodded. "One for Harry, across the way. They set themselves in, and . . . "Again she stopped, though this time I had been writing every word. "Steven, boy, come sit. You tell it, you was there."

"Momma, it's for you to do."

"You, Stevie." He would not look at me. "Get what he says exact, Writer," continued Mary Cuombo. "Or Rhody will make up some lalala song and nobody will know nothing about Harry dying except it rhymed." Steven started to talk but Mary Cuombo went on. "This be in the paper?" I nodded. "The book?" I nodded. "Hear, Stevie? Go on."

Steven took a breath. The Minister lay a hand on his shoulder. Surrounded by women and religion, with every word, the surviving Outlaw controlled his voice: "I helped him make his blind, then went and finished mine. Then we got a wait, so I take it easy. Then I hear a shot. I can't tell if it's Harry or what, so I call out, 'Harry!' Harry say nothing. I don't know he's shooting or someone shot or what. I call again, 'Harry!' and nothing. I crawl over." He stopped.

"Stevie got where Henry Berry was," Rhody went on, her eyes lowered out of sight, "and there Henry Berry Lowery lying on his back, his own gun shot, and . . ." she took a breath.

Sally Ann finished: ". . . and his whole face blowed off!"

Well, a theater actor I interviewed years back said it can be hard not to laugh on stage. Now, like to an actor in a tragic scene controlling an errant giggle, I bit the inside of my cheek, breathed tight and deep, set my face grim in stone. Thommy had told me this same fable long ago at the New Bridge when they tested it on me. Steven started again, pretending to fight tears: "The ramrod was busted. Harry had been loading his rifle and it went off in his face."

The Minister being there, I nodded gravely, lips sealed, jaw fixed. The Minister spoke to the family, blessed us all, and left. When his buggy was out of sight I volcanoed into laughter. I grabbed a cup and opened the cabinet where Rhody kept brandy. It wasn't there. "Where is it?" I demanded.

"Here." I turned around. Henry Berry poured my cup full.

"How come you got to drink on every occasion?" complained Mary Cuombo. "Lucky you ain't in my house."

"To the resurrection!" I said, and sipped.

But my laughter gave way to resentment at having been left out of everything. "Where were you, damn you?" I exploded. "You left me in that Gawd damned swamp and I thought you were dead for sure!"

"I wanted you to," said Henry Berry.

"Gawd damn you, Henry Squish Berry Lowery!" I said. "Why?"

He said, "So you'd write it right. I forgot you heard it before."

"I'm not writing one thing."

"You got to. It's all we got left," said Harry, as close as I ever heard him to pleading.

"Then get you another writer." It was my resignation, signed, sealed, and flung in the boss's face. "I don't fiction. Not me! I cannot. No. Can not."

But oh, for the love of God, what Harry said next. "I chose you because you can. I CHOSE you."

I chilled inside top to bottom. He said that before when he was just a figment of my fevered brain.

With the deceased himself at my shoulder, I sat down and fabricated his obituary. Rhody wired my fiction from the depot. The Herald ran it, then the Wilmington Star and others. Henry Berry Lowery was journalistically, and therefore officially, dead. And that was that. Of course there would be rumors that he still lived, and there were even claims he was seen. But for all practical and official purposes, I had written him to death.

THIRTY-SIX

I MADE A LAST night visit to the Widow Norment. I wanted forgiveness. Getting into her room in my usual way, I appeared before her. "I won't hurt you," I said. She reached beneath her writing table, but I yanked it away, along with the pistol it concealed. "I only want to say that I regret whatever alarm and pain I have caused you." She nodded, a marvel of composure. I praised her behavior at Henry Berry's funeral, and said, "I have read your writing, madam. I admire your thorough reportage. I'm proud to call you colleague. And if I were to rob and steal for the rest of my days, there would be no victim so dear to me as you."

The awkward Yankee who came to Robeson County a thousand years ago could not have said such things aloud. She responded, "I deserve no such praise."

I said, "I hope that when you think of me, you will reflect upon more than my sins against you. I am not the fiend you think."

She said, "Your sins are all I know of you." She backed away through the doorway.

"Forgive them as you can." I pressed my hand to my lips, then turned to go. Stopping in the window without looking back I said, "I shall never forget you, madam, as long as I live." That was her wish too, for she fired a pistol at my back. The ball smashed into her desk, not me, splintering that fragile piece and scattering her manuscript.

TWO YEARS LATER I visited Mr. Groone at his home. For my visit he had purchased a supply of the Inn's red berry wine. "If we were more often together," I said as he poured the third glass, "we would become hopeless drunkards." I came to the point: "Tell me what you know about Henry Berry."

"Dead," said Mr. Groone.

"Yes, but surely you have heard some tale or two."

"Aye, in the way I hear that Abraham Lincoln still strolls Washington and that to a colored lady in Alfordsville the Nazarene's face appears regularly upon her husband's boils."

"You don't believe such things," I said.

"When anyone thinks they have seen Henry Berry, they report it to me. I record what they say." He said he would copy over a few of the reports for me. I asked for his own opinion on the matter.

"Dead. As you assured me."

"Your tone says you have other thoughts." I detected no such thing, but it's a useful device to say so.

My good friend said, "I'm impressed by your perception. I do have thoughts. Other knowledge, I might say."

"And what is that?" I asked.

"Well," he said, relishing the chance to try out his theory on me, "a new outlaw far in the west has been making a reputation. I have heard and have reason to believe that Henry Berry Lowery did not in fact die but in fact is that outlaw."

If Mr. Groone is right, then you who seek Henry Berry must go west.

I went to visit old George Lowery. He still prayed that Death would carry him to his wife and children. "So," he said, "how is Allen's son?"

"Which?"

"The trouble-maker, what is his name?" He said. I reminded him. "Yes, that one." I told him what the obituary said. "No," George said. "It ain't true, I made that story up, I told it to him when he was a boy. A hunter hidden in the blind, his own gun blowing off his head before he could shoot the yearling deer." I was outraged. Not only had Harry made me publish a fiction, but a plagiarized fiction!

"Henry Berry's as alive as me," George said. "And I know where."

"Where?" I asked.

George pointed down. "Tunnels. I seen them." He told me that the outlaws never come above ground any more. Their tunnels go out under the swamp and past, under the floorboards of every White home in the county. Listen close and at night you'll hear Lorreys singing down there. Put your ear, you'll hear talking, playing their fiddles. Henry Berry ain't in a churchyard. Folks who want him just got to look under their own house."

A year later I was summoned from the swamp by Mary Cuombo. Her health was better and she was more cheerful since the death of her son had been announced. Now a New York newspaperman was coming, and she wanted me there.

"Which paper?"

"The Clock, I think," she said. At noon a pup from the New York Times, along with his sketch-man and a third who served no more purpose than his newspaper, arrived. I let them in, identifying myself as the servant. The pup wrote down that in the new South, a mulatto Indian woman could have a White servant. "Not just any Indian woman," I said. "This is the mother of the deceased outlaw, Henry Berry Lowery,

THE KING OF THE OUTLAWS
THE SCOURGE OF A COUNTY
FRIEND TO THE POOR
FIEND OF THE NIGHT
GORE- HUNTING

The Herald had used these headlines years ago. This pup wouldn't know that, so he'd use them in the Times, heh heh, and be fired for plagiarizing.

Mary Cuombo had a great sense of occasion. Though in perfect health, she had retreated to bed, somehow drained all color from her cheek, and spoke in a whisper, forcing the reporter to lean so close she could have gummed his ear.

"How is it," asked the Times pup, "to be the Mother of the famous deceased outlaw?"

"Uh?" said her feeble voice.

"Mother of famous outlaw," I shouted. "Dead."

"I'm not dead," she gasped.

"Him! Not you," I corrected her.

"Him either," she said.

"Not the reporter," I said. "Your son the famous outlaw."

"He's not dead," she said.

"Yes," said the reporter. He showed her the Herald obituary.

"Aaarhhhg, the Herald," she said, and threw the clipping onto the floor. "My son Harry visits."

The reporter pulled me aside. "Can this be true? Or are these the rantings of a demented lady?"

"Oh," I said, "she's not seeing things, no." Now the Times reporter got very excited, for here was a story!

"Where is he?" he asked.

"My son?" said Mary Cuombo with a motherly smile.

"Yes!" he shouted.

"Got many sons," she rambled. "Used to have more. So many, so many. What were their names?"

"I speak of Henry Lowery!"

She turned her head to me, that head clear as a robin's eye, and asked me, "Lowery, Lowery, which one's Lowery?"

"Henry," I said.

"Henry, Henry . . ."

"Yes," I said, "the
SAVIOR OF HIS PEOPLE, the
BANDIT OF ROBESON."

"Ahhh," she said, "the BAD son." The reporter scribbled hysterically and she went on: "He tole me, 'Momma, O Momma, it's time for me to be good, Momma.' And I said, that's right, my boy. And he did it."

"In what form did he do it, Mrs. Lowery?"

"Missionary."

"Where? Where, where?"

"Southern Metho—" but stopped. "I'm not allowed to say."

The Times article stated that anyone who wanted to find Henry Berry would have to search every missionary outpost of the Southern Methodist Church; and as only the New York Times would, listed all six hundred of them.

As promised, Mr. Groone gave me a digest of H.B. Lowery sightings, in his angular, clear handwriting.

> **SUNDAY 25 DECEMBER, 1875.** Attending Christmas service in Ashpole Church, Eulah McCann, White person, bowed head to pray and noticed a figure outside the open window. She looked outside and saw Henry Berry Lowery, weeping and trying to read the prayer-book in her lap. He gestured to her book, so she gave it to him and he withdrew. After the service Miss McCann went outside and found nothing except her prayer-book lying closed on the ground under the window. A fifty-dollar bill and a

lock of dark hair in a page marked a prayer for remembrance of the dead.

FRIDAY 17 FEBRUARY, 1878. At three A.M. Elizabeth Stewart, unmarried White lady, was waked from sleep by movement in her kitchen. Seated at table was a man she could not identify. She asked who it was and what he wanted. He said never mind who, and he wanted breakfast. She woke her servant, Lucille, who boiled six eggs ten minutes, which she sliced and fricasseed with butter, salt, pepper, greens, and bread, and this was consumed. While he ate, Lucille whispered to Miss Stewart that it was H. Lowery, whom she had seen many times and recognized. Lucille said it must be his ghost, for the windows and doors were locked from within. No living person could have entered without breaking. Miss Stewart went and asked him outright if he were H. Lowery and he said yes, it was. She told him she did not think ghosts had appetites. The specter said she was mistaken, as she could see, and demanded another portion, which they provided and then waited in the next room. When they returned the specter had gone, every door and window still bolted within. The dish and cup were neatly by the bucket, a portion of egg unconsumed in spite of Lucille having taken the trouble.

SATURDAY 18 MARCH, 1878. Angus McKillop had his bag-horn practice interrupted when two figures approached. He recognized the Outlaw Henry Berry Lowery and a Negro, also deceased. When the two came near, the one in shape of Mr. Lowery pointed to the bag-horn and said, "'Tis an ill blare ye make, laddie!" The Negro one said, "Aye, and 'tis loud as well! Ye are disturbing of the swamp-land." Lowery then broke the bag-horn in half. After paying three dollars for the destruction of his instrument, the men left.

MONDAY 26 JUNE, 1878. Menzies Campbell, a Negro employed by Lear's Store, was sent to Eureka for plow-parts. Returning in the evening the cart-driver was hailed from the roadside by a figure he had not seen as he approached. Recognizing the man as Henry Berry Lowery, and frightened of ghosts, Mr. Campbell urged the mules onward, but the Phantom leaped straight up and sat beside him. "Menzies, take me to Rennet," said he, a dozen miles.

"Sir, I cannot, for I am expected back."

"Do as I say or you will never go back again," threatened the phantom. Mr. Campbell took the phantom and left him at Rennet at a burned church. Told that the ruins of the church had been leveled seven months ago, the brother of

Mr. Campbell went and found it to be the case. Menzies refused to go there again.

MONDAY 30 OCTOBER, 1878. In a thunderstorm with high wind, Mrs. Winnie McRae, White widow, and three of her servants, Negroes, went to secure the barn loft. Going in, they saw strange men. She thought they were travelers taking refuge against the rain and wind. She brought them in the house, where they were silent and polite. She gave hot tea and cakes to all, one politely declining. They sat in the front room until the end of the storm, while Mrs. McRae played the piano and some sang. One played on a banjo. They were seen by seven of Mrs. McRae's servants, all over forty years of age and churchgoing. Each swore the men were Henry Berry Lowery the Outlaw, Steven and Thomas his brothers, Shoe Man John, two brothers of the Strong family, William Lowery another brother of the chief Outlaw, an older man the father of the Outlaws; and a White man with moustache and beard, blue coat, blue wool shirt, black pants, brown boots, and note pad. All were well-armed."

After Henry Berry's funeral, Harry, Rhody, Steven and myself gathered. "Henry Berry," I said, "what will you do now that you are dead?"

"Go to Heaven."

"Some day, I hope. But for now?"

"Who cares?"

"It's a new time. You got to do something new," said Rhody.

"Maybe sheriff."

"Henry Squish Berry, High Sheriff of Robeson County," she joked.

"Why Robeson County?" I said.

Suddenly a joke became a possibility. Lawmen out West were hard to find. Few men wanted so dangerous a position far from civilization. I gave Henry Berry an example from the Wilmington Star: a young hoodlum was terrorizing the new state of Kansas. This man Willum Kidd had become a general menace and new settlers were passing on by to go live elsewhere.

"What did they do to him?" asked Henry Berry.

"To catch him?" I asked.

"To make him that way." I said I didn't know. "Where'd you say?"

"Kansas."

"Where's that?"

"West."

"So I go west to Kansas, shoot the little son of a bitch Willum, and I got me a job? What say, Steven?"

"We could."

"What say Rhody Lorry?"

"I ain't going. They hate Indians there worse than here. I won't bring up my young ones where it's worse and I don't know nobody."

"So I got to stay here," said Henry Berry.

"What for?" said Steven.

Henry Berry pointed at Rhody. "Ain't nobody that pretty no place."

"You ain't been every place, Mr. Lorry," Rhody said, pleased.

"He has," said Harry, meaning me. "He never saw no one as pretty either. Did you, Writer?" I expressed no opinion.

"Pretty woman's no reason to stay someplace," said Rhody.

Steven said, "How about Harry and me go catch that Mr. Kidd bothering them, the Writer writes it and we all get famous? Then we sneak back here and you look at Miss Pretty a while."

"Then you're back where you are now, figuring what to do next," said Rhody.

"Go to Kansas," I suggested. "Promise the kid you'll let him do anything he wants if he'll leave in six months. He leaves, you get credit for chasing him out and saving the county, then come home. The kid will go terrorize some new county, and its elders will want to hire whoever solved the problem before. The new position will be yours."

The plan appealed to everyone, though I warned Henry Berry that the young outlaw might not cooperate.

"Then I shoot him," said Harry. "There is no shortage of other outlaws."

Some who know things say Henry Berry invented a name, took a position in Kansas with Steven as deputy, and worked the plan several times in different places, the young outlaw cooperating fully. After the fourth six-month return to Robeson County, it is said, Henry Berry made his western journeys alone, though Sally Ann was growing eager to go.

Knowing he'd be the target of any new gunman looking to make a fast reputation, he used a different name for each new job. He made several of those names famous, and brought Sally Ann the sheriff's star from each.

Thus, Henry Berry's reputation(s) as sheriff can't be reported. But behind a series of badges, he made White settlement of the West safe from the worst elements of the Whites themselves.

> **THE LONESOME DEATH OF THE LAST ROBBER** by Mrs. Mary Norment, Widow. We come finally to the end of Robeson County's Outlawery. No pen can describe the relief in bosoms at the announcement that "the last outlaw is dead." Their haunts lie desolate. Their paths through swamp and woodland are grown over with briar and bramble. Their terror has ended. Steven Lowery, the last Outlaw, was playing his raucous Negro banjo by a farmhouse he had robbed the night before. When he threw back his head to sing, the farmer fired, ending the unwanted music and ending Steven Lowery's unwanted career on earth, sending the blood-stained wretch to answer before a great tribunal. With a deep groan, he fell lifeless.
>
> **From the Fayetteville *Eagle*, 26 February 1881**

> We take this opportunity, the KILLING OF THE LAST OUTLAW, to say that there is no more courageous, whole-souled people in the world than the White citizens of Robeson, who all through the Lowrie war, whether under command of a United States officer, or a State Militiaman, or the county Sheriff, conducted themselves with courage and a high sense of duty.

Rhody wrote no more songs of her husband. But she had something to say:

> TELL THEM, Writer, he don't die. He don't stop. Tell them, those people who stole our life, they don't know what will happen. No wagon wheel may break, nor cow go dry nor well go black nor crop fall short or fail, nor drought or storm may come nor White babe come sickly or dead, no bad thing will come on them or on their children or their children's children but Henry Berry made it come.
>
> TELL THEM, Writer, about Sally Ann.
>
> TELL THEM, Writer, if they want Henry Berry, don't look in no grave. Tell them look in the shadows.
>
> TELL THEM, Writer, that when we're all nothing but mud returned to swamp, and our children and their children too, still Harry

Lorrie goin' live. So tell them. Tell them he live forever.

TELL THEM, Writer. And tell his people too.

AND TELL THEM my Harry was the handsomest man I ever saw.

EPILOGUE

LEAVING RHODY'S CABIN, Sally Ann leads me through the tunnel into the swamp. Wearing Geronimo's now thread-worn black headband, she carries her full-size rifle across her back as naturally as she carries her black hair. Her sheriff- badge collection lines her rifle strap. Up out of the tunnel, she stands tall as me. The sun drops behind cypress and pine, and the swamp-land settles into its dead time between the cries of daylight creatures and those of the night. Greens sway against the sinking blood sun beyond.

I say goodbye until my next visit. "Want me to go with you, Writer, so you'll be safe? I worry about you."

I decline her offer for now, though she'd keep me safer. But I must be alone to tell the tales.

I kiss her brow. She walks back to the cabin, too proud for the tunnel. I walk a hundred yards into the swamp and lay a chunk of sugar on the tongue of Patrick Lowery's aging horse. He accepts. I mount, and ride the familiar path. Sunset deepening, to Mr. Matthew Brady or any other observer in the fading light, horse and rider fade, meld one into the other, and compound with swamp, impossible to distinguish from the rest within.

SAMPLING AND REFERENCE SOURCES:

"Pursuit of an organized band of Negro robbers and murderers: an encounter with the outlaws." New York

Times October 8, 1870, page 1.

Jenkins, Jay. "Lowry's daughter buried by Indians." Charlotte Observer 2 April 1962: Sec. B p. 1.

"The Lowrey outlaws: particulars of the murder of Col. F. M. Wishart in Robeson County, North Carolina — base and treacherous assassination." New York Times May 8, 1872, page 3.

Norment, Mary C. *Th e Lowrie History, As Acted in Part by Henry Berry Lowrie, the Great North Carolina Bandit. with Biographical Sketches of His Associates. Being a Complete History of the Modern Robber Band in the County of Robeson and State of North Carolina.* Wilmington: Daily Journal Printer, 1875. (Secretly written by the author of *Th e Swamp Outlaws: or, The North Carolina Bandits; Being a Complete History of the Modern Rob Roys and Robin Hoods.)* Compson,

Benjamin. *Refl ections on the Great Dismal Swamp.*"
Louisiana Inmate Collection. *circa* 1931. "Claims Henry Berry Lowry, leader of band of outlaws, alive at 92." Robesonian 5 April 1937: 1. Rpt. in News and Observer 9 May 1937: 1.

"Hero of Lowry Gang passes at age of 89 years." Robesonian 23 Feb. 1938: I.

Townsend, George Alfred. *Th e Swamp Outlaws: or, The North Carolina Bandits; Being a Complete History of the Modern Rob Roys and Robin Hoods.* New York, 1872.

Wishart, Francis Marion. "Diary of Col. Francis M. Wishart, commander of action against the Lowry outlaws of Robeson County, North Carolina, 1864 -1872, and comments by an unknown author." Private collection.

Criminal Papers on Henry Berry Lowry. NC State Archives, Raleigh.

"Robin Hood come again." New York Times 22 July 1871: P. col. 5.

"The North Carolina outlaws: Lowrey and gang — authorities defi ed — pursuit by soldiers." New York Times October 11, 1871, page 11.

"The North Carolina Bandits." Harper's Weekly 16 (30 March 1872): 249, 251-2.

U.S. Congressional Joint Select Comm. to Inquire into the Condition of Aff airs in the Late Insurrectionary States. Made to the Two Houses of Congress, 19 Feb. 1872. 42nd Cong.

"A new expedition: proposition to capture the Lowery Gang of Outlaws—singular enterprise of a fourth ward character." New York Times 18 March 1872: P. 5 col. 3.

"The Lowery Gang." New York Times 4 May 1874: P. 2 col. 3.

"Rhoda Lowrie: widow of the noted outlaw in jail for retailing liquor without license." Robesonian Nov. 1897: [3].

"Henry Berry Lowry is dead." Lumberton Argus 3 Nov. 1905: 3.

"Th e Lowrey outlaws: particulars of the murder of Col.F. M. Wishart in Robeson County, North Carolina–a base and treacherous assassination." New York Times May 8, 1872, page 3.

Bibson, J. Press, Sr. "What became of Henry Berry Lowrey, notorious Robeson bandit chief?" Robesonian 12 June 1922: 6.

"A notorious desperado killed in North Carolina:a company of soldiers aft er his confederates — a defaulting book-keeper in Chicago. New York Times December 18, 1870, page 1.

Henderson, David H. "Face to face with the Lumbee ghost?" Th e State 56.5 (Oct. 1988): 10-13.

MacTaiper, F. "Horses of the Swamplands." St. Nicholas Magazine November 10, 1873: 31- 40. "Last of Lowry Gang baptised at 83." Robesonian 16 May 1935: 1. McEachern, Stuart. "Eight years of terror." Th e State 20.26 (29 Nov. 1952): 6. Rockwell, Paul A. "Lumbees rebelled against proposed draft by South." Asheville Citizen-Times 2 Feb. 1958. [UNC-WL Clippings File] Lawrence, R. C. "Wishart and the Loweries." The State 26 Aug. 1939: 6-7. Rpt. in Robesonian 28 Aug. 1939: 8.

Evans, W. McKee. *To Die Game: the Story of the Lowry Band.* Baton Rouge, 1971.

Barton, Garry Lewis. The *Life and Times of Henry Berry Lowry.* Pembroke NC, 1979.

Knick, Stanley. Did Henry Berry Lowrie escape Robeson become the Modoc's Captain Jack?" Robesonian 25 Feb. 1993: 4A.

MAYN001. Maynor, Malinda. "Violence and the racial oundary: fact and fi ction in the swamps of Robeson County, 1831-1871." Honors thesis (History and literature), Harvard College, 1995.

"Rhoda Strong Lowry, 1849-1909." In: North Carolina women: making history. By Margaret Supplee Smith and Emily Herring Wilson. Chapel Hill; London: North Carolina UP.

Pugh, Eneida Sanderson. "Rhoda Strong Lowry: The Swamp Queen of Scuffl etown." American Indian Culture and Research Journal 26.1 (2002): 67-81. 42 notes.

CPSIA information can be obtained
at www.ICGtesting.com
Printed in the USA
LVHW030856160222
711207LV00001B/43

9 781665 512015